WEIRD TALES

WEIRD TALES

BEST OF THE EARLY YEARS: 1923–1925

EDITED BY

JONATHAN MABERRY AND JUSTIN CRIADO

Weird Tales Best of the Early Years: 1923–1925
Edited by Jonathan Maberry and Justin Criado

EBook ISBN: 978-1-68057-366-4

Trade Paperback ISBN: 978-1-68057-365-7

Hardcover ISBN: 978-1-68057-367-1

Cover design by Janet McDonald

Published by WordFire Press, LLC

PO Box 1840

Monument CO 80132

Kevin J. Anderson & Rebecca Moesta, Publishers

WordFire Press Edition 2022

Printed in the USA

Join our WordFire Press Readers Group for new projects, and giveaways. Sign up at wordfirepress.com.

WEIRD TALES

BEST OF THE EARLY YEARS: 1923–1925

EDITED BY

JONATHAN MABERRY AND JUSTIN CRIADO

Weird Tales Best of the Early Years: 1923–1925
Edited by Jonathan Maberry and Justin Criado

EBook ISBN: 978-1-68057-366-4

Trade Paperback ISBN: 978-1-68057-365-7

Hardcover ISBN: 978-1-68057-367-1

Cover design by Janet McDonald

Published by WordFire Press, LLC

PO Box 1840

Monument CO 80132

Kevin J. Anderson & Rebecca Moesta, Publishers

WordFire Press Edition 2022

Printed in the USA

Join our WordFire Press Readers Group for new projects, and giveaways. Sign up at wordfirepress.com.

Contents

FOREWORD:
CONFESSIONS OF A
WEIRD KID

JONATHAN MABERRY

The world is weird. Everyone knows that.

It's weird now and has been consistently weird for a long damn time.

And the weirder the world becomes—with wars, plagues, social unrest, a cranky climate, polluted oceans, political upheaval, religious extremism, terrorism, mass murders, doomsday cults, conspiracy theories, nuclear weapons, and too many other things to list—fiction gets weirder.

Fiction has always been used to reflect the world through various funhouse mirrors. We use fiction to tell stories, and even when our source material is something from the real world, writers love putting their own spin on it. After all, the *Epic of Gilgamesh*, *The Iliad*, *The Odyssey*, and similar landmark works are hardly objective reporting.

We like to take elements of the real world and use them as scaffolding, or as bones on which to construct something bigger, better, weirder. This is why movies like *Apocalypse Now* and books like *Slaughterhouse Five* often tell us more about the nature of wars like Vietnam and World War II than we might learn from history texts. Oh, sure, the history books are useful and necessary, but real stories don't always have a good third act or a satisfying conclusion. There's often a lack of closure, and they're frequently written in such broad strokes that it's hard to find a relatable proxy through which we can *feel* rather than merely *know*.

The 20th century, with all of its new publishing houses and innovations in mass production and distribution, saw all kinds of new fiction genres and subgenres spring into being. And a big part of that was due to the pulps.

In the off chance that you don't know what the pulps are (and what rock have you been living under?), they were originally a cost-effective way of mass-producing magazines for the general public. It started with *Argosy* magazine launched in 1896. Each issue had about 190 pages, give or take, and was printed to be read but not necessarily collected. The pulps were printed on rougher "pulp" paper, with the edges left untrimmed. Early pulps boasted no exciting cover art—that would come soon enough—and were printed by the ton with old steam-powered presses. The writers weren't paid very much, and the per issue cost to the public was small. Similar, in many ways, with the cheaply made dime novels, and often overlapping.

Argosy exploded from a cheap experiment with only a few thousand copies printed to a massive success that sold more than half a million copies per month. Other editors and publishers saw the benefits of producing low-cost, high-volume, and high-concept, magazines of the same kind, and within a few years the pulp era was born.

The pulps were everywhere, and that invited more people into the world of prose storytelling. This aligned with changes in education in the early 20th century. More kids went to school than in previous centuries, and those hungry minds—able to read—were ravenous.

During the Great Depression, the pulps really mattered, even though the cover price—now fifteen cents or more—was a challenge to the masses of economically shattered readers. And yet, the escapism available between the covers of pulp magazines was worth so much. A kid could sit down, open a pulp and read about Doc Savage, The Spider, The Shadow, G-8 and his Battle Aces, The Green Lama, Solomon Kane, John Carter of Mars, Tarzan, Conan, Buck Rogers, The Phantom Detective, Captain Future, Sheena, The Green Hornet and Kato, Zorro, the Avenger, and thousands of others. While tagging along—or, by imaginative proxy becoming—those heroes, that young reader could go anywhere, be anyone, experience everything. By reading those stories, they were able to *be* the heroes and, sometimes, the villain. Fu Manchu, John Sunlight, Dr. Satan, The Octopus, Doctor Death, Ming the Merciless, and others who were equally lurid, fantastical and fun. Many of the pulps served to expand upon established genres like westerns, detective stories, war stories, and adventure.

My introduction reading beyond the narrow confines of what was required in school came in two flavors. When I was seven in 1965, I began reading the Bantam Books reprints of the Doc Savage novels, originally printed in the 1930s and '40s. Doc was created by publisher Henry W. Ralston and editor John L. Nanovic, along with considerable additional material by Lester Dent, the writer who turned out most of the 181 potboilers under the house penname of Kenneth Robeson.

But the first novel I bought with my own money—I didn't get an allowance, so I collected bottles for recycling and helped old ladies carry their groceries at the Acme Market in Philadelphia—was *Conan the Wanderer*. Like the Doc Savage books, this volume of Conan stories was a reprint. Unlike Doc, the book was not a novel but a collection of four shorter works—one by L. Sprague de Camp and his buddy Lin Carter, and the others written by Robert E. Howard.

I devoured that book with as much delight as I had Doc Savage.

But there was something about the Conan stories that spoke to a different part of my mind. Or soul.

Despite the deaths and violence and big-ticket evil mastermind destruction of the Doc Savage novels, they were a bit more of a confection. You knew the good guys would win in the end. It was inevitable. And Doc himself was a spotless hero (or, at least after the first couple of pretty bloody novels he became a nonlethal hero).

Conan was not even a hero.

He was a thief, cutthroat, conqueror, and savage. He had no civilized virtues, was as far from spotless as a Jackson Pollack painting, and was the "hero" only because everyone else in the story was much worse. That antihero vibe would later inform the careers of fantasists like Michael Moorcock and his moody kin-slaughtering immortal Elric of Melniboné, and the late Karl Edward Wagner's actually-a-freaking-villain Kane.

Conan was first, though.

While collecting and reading all twelve volumes of Lancer Books' reprint series of Conan stories, and studying every detail of the forewords, I hungered for more. Turned out that Howard also wrote equally edgy stories about King Kull, Bran Mak Morn, Solomon Kane, and others. Morally questionable, frequently ill-tempered, politically incorrect to an incredible degree, and yet unbelievably compelling. All of these characters had been introduced in some old magazine I'd never heard of—*Weird Tales*. Long gone, belonging, I thought, to another age of the world. So, I focused on the reprints and read on.

Then something extraordinary happened in 1970.

The librarian in the middle school I attended in Philly recognized my fascination with strange fiction of all kinds. This was a school in an economically-depressed part of the city, and there was very little interest demonstrated by my classmates for that big room filled with books. I doubt half of my friends could even *find* the library, let alone tell you what was in it.

I hung out there all the time. You see, apart from being an avid reader, even as a kid I knew I wanted to be a writer. The librarian saw and understood this. As it turns out—and this is an example of really good *weird*—she was the secretary for two clubs of professional writers. One that met in Philly and the other, less frequently, in New York.

The New York crowd was really a loose collection of genre writers who met in a publisher's penthouse. There was no rhyme or reason to those meetings except that in the pre-internet era, big writers launched their books in New York because that's where publishing lived. At those meetings—and by "meetings" I mean cocktail parties with zero agenda—I got to meet people like Ray Bradbury, Richard Matheson, Avram Davidson, Harlan Ellison, Robert Block, Leigh Brackett, Manly Wade Wellman, and others. Yeah, I know. Holy smokes. Bradbury and Matheson actually spent time mentoring me every time my librarian brought me to one of the meetings.

And as for the Philadelphia writers group, well, that was definitely more structured. It was a group called the Hyborean Legion, and they all met at the home of George Scithers, a writer, editor, and legendary curmudgeon.

One of the most frequent attendees at those meetings was L. Sprague de Camp. Sometimes Lin Carter, too.

The entire group was built around a love bordering on mania for Conan.

Yes, sometimes the world is really just that weird and that cool.

De Camp and I became friends. First, he was a kindly mentor, but as I grew past my teens into my twenties, he became a good friend. I would visit his grand house in Villanova, outside of the city. I can still remember his writing room. A big desk, lots of useful clutter, all kinds of curios, and walls of books.

And it was in that room of literary wonders that I met another greatly important pulp character. Not a hero, or even an antihero. I met a god. Kind of. His name was Cthulhu and he attacked me.

I'll explain.

No, I wasn't wrapped in the coils of a tentacular monstrosity whose very appearance is too horrific to behold. It wasn't that kind of attack.

Cthulhu hit me in the head.

I'll explain.

I was at de Camp's place for a book release party for his work *The Fallible Fiend*. Most of the folks there were authors, and a bunch had gathered in his office, with me there to fetch drinks. I was thirteen, I think. While they shared anecdotes about the arcane workings of the publishing industry I wandered around, looking at the editions of de Camp's books that filled the shelves and at all the strange little pieces of art that he'd collected—statues, carvings, a bat skull, awards, and more. I reached up to take down a copy of a foreign edition of one of the Conan collections (*Conan the Buccaneer*, I believe, the 1971 Lancer edition with the cool Frank Frazetta cover), I accidentally knocked down a small metal statue. It fell and clunked me on the head and then landed on the carpet.

De Camp picked up the figure and when the others saw what it was, they all laughed and told me that I must be a hero because I survived an attack by one of the Great Old Ones.

My response was, "Who?"

The whole group of them stared at me as if I'd just asked what air was. Or what the color blue looked like. It was a reaction that spoke to an inability on their part to comprehend that anyone at that gathering, no matter how young, could possibly *not* know who Cthulhu was.

They gaped at me. First time I'd ever seen people genuinely gape.

So, I said, "Well, who *is* Cthulhu?"

They told me. The explanation of who and, more importantly, *what* Cthulhu was took some telling. And that naturally rolled over into a discussion of its creator, Howard Phillips Lovecraft—his life and work, his stories, his general strangeness, his willingness to let other writers craft stories using his characters and themes, and so on. This was not a short conversation. This was a conversation that spilled over into a general decamping to the living room, it chased us through buffet food and dessert, and I don't think it really reached an ending but was rather terminated by the end of the party.

One immediate effect of that first conversation, though, was that when I left de Camp's house that night I was weighed down with a double-armful of books related in some way to the Cthulhu Mythos. That stack included some valuable reprints of *Weird Tales* in which Lovecraft's first stories appeared. And a great number of collections and anthologies that contained Cthulhu stories by Robert Bloch, Richard F. Searight, Hazel Heald, Clark Ashton Smith, Duane W. Rimel, Robert H. Barlow, Henry Kuttner, Henry Hasse, Manly Wade Wellman, William Lumley, Zealia B. Bishop, August W. Derleth, Will Garth, Charles R. Tanner, Wilfred Owen Morley, Carol Grey, C. Hall Thompson, Vol Molesworth, and Robert E. Howard.

That was the first batch.

Over the years de Camp would frequently suggest tales by other writers. For some of these I was required to read them at de Camp's house in the original magazines—*Weird Tales, Stirring Science Stories, Scorpio, The Unique Magazine, Future Fantasy and Science Fiction, Polaris, Strange Stories, Fanciful Tales, Astounding Stories, The Californian, Unusual Stories,* and others. Then he directed me to libraries and bookstores to find new stories and reliable collections.

But I became fascinated by *Weird Tales.* First off, the name was damn cool. And the premise was compelling. It existed to publish stories that did not fit into any other magazine. "Weird" became its own subgenre, and that overlapped with larger genres like science fiction, various kinds of fantasy, mystery, occultism, and so on. Take any of those genres and stir in an X-factor and you have weird sci-fi, weird horror, and weird, well, anything.

Also, *Weird Tales* debuted three years before the book most pulp experts gush over—*Amazing Stories.* And, no slight to AS, but it was more conventional in storytelling content and structure. I liked reading them, but I was not as emotionally moved by them. Or, perhaps, it was that those more upbeat stories resonated less with a poor kid from a bad neighborhood and an abusive household who knew firsthand that there was darkness in the world. A negative darkness, like poverty and my abusive father, but also a comforting darkness that allowed me to hide in the shadows. And in that stygian darkness find acceptance.

Although de Camp let me read his precious copies of *Weird Tales* because of Cthulhu and Conan, I think he had an evil masterplan of introducing me to the wider world of weird.

Now, let's jump forward to when I met the woman who would become my wife, Sara West. One day we were going through my photo albums and she gasped and said, "Why are you in a photo with Uncle Sprague?"

No, he wasn't her actual uncle, but rather her grandfather's best friend. Her grandpa was the noted pulp fiction writer, editor, anthologist, and literary agent Oscar J. Friend (aka Ford Smith, Owen Fox Jerome, etc.).

Friend had been the junior partner of the Otis Kline Literary

Agency, and they represented writers like Manly Wade Wellman, Ray Bradbury, Isaac Asimov, and—holy crap—Robert E. Howard's estate. When Kline died, Friend bought the agency and ran it with his daughter, my wife's mother.

There's a tall tale about how Glenn Lord supposedly gave Howard's unfinished manuscripts to de Camp, kicking off the Conan revival of the 1950s and '60s. The truth was that it was Friend who offered those manuscripts to de Camp. I believe Lord physically *drove* them from New York to Villanova.

Anyway, here I was, married to someone who was directly connected to de Camp, as well as a slew of writers who wrote for *Weird Tales*. Yes, life really is that weird.

Sometime later, after Sara's father died and the family was clearing out his attic, they found boxes of papers from the Kline Agency. They were going to toss them because they looked—god help me—"old and unimportant." But my wife rescued them and thought I might find them amusing. Yeah. Good call.

In those boxes were correspondence of all kinds with Asimov, Bradbury, Wellman, etc. And also lots of old typescript manuscripts of stories written by their clients. Two of these are treasured parts of my personal collections. *People of the Black Circle* by Robert E. Howard and *Cool Air* by H.P. Lovecraft. The Howard story was serialized in three parts in *Weird Tales* magazine—September, October, and November 1934. The Lovecraft story, though not published in *Weird Tales* (it was in the 1928 issue of *Tales of Magic and Mystery*), was in a pulp that tried to copy and capture the dark magic of *Weird Tales*.

Many of Lovecraft's most important works, in fact, published in *Weird Tales*.

Now, the group that resurrected *Weird Tales* only a few years ago did not know this backstory. My guy on the inside was Tony Eldridge, a film producer with whom I was doing business on something entirely unrelated. Tony knew I was a fan of weird fiction in general, and the pulps, and this was reflected in the kinds of things I write. Yes, most of my novels, comic books, short stories, and even some of my nonfiction is decidedly weird.

They first asked me to write a story for the magazine, which I did. A nod to both Howard and Lovecraft called *The Shadow Beneath the Stone*. Then they upped the stakes and asked me if I'd like to help edit the magazine. I agreed. Of course, I did. Literally a dream come true. I came on board as "editorial director," but as the old editor was ill, I curated the whole first issue of this new incarnation. Issue #363, published in 2019.

By the next issue, I was promoted to full-time editor, and that's where I am now. I wish Sprague de Camp was alive to see it. He'd be delighted.

This anthology is another dream come true.

It collects some of the landmark stories on which *Weird Tales'* reputation was built. There are stories by H.P. Lovecraft, including a personal favorite because it was the second Lovecraft tale I ever read. And, yes, it was in one of de Camp's precious original copies of the magazine, published in January 1925.

Also herein are two stories by my grandfather-in-law's business partner, Otis Adelbert Kline; a creepy lycanthropic tale, *The Werewolf of St. Bonnot* by Seabury Quinn, featuring his relentless occult detective Jules de Grandin; the notorious short story, *Imprisoned with the Pharaohs*—ostensibly written by Harry Houdini but actually ghostwritten by Lovecraft; and wonderfully unusual tales by Frank Belknap Long Jr., Mary S. Brown, Lyllian Huntley Harris, Hasan Vokine, Arthur J. Burks, Greye La Spina, and the notable *The Werewolf of Ponkert* by H. Warner Munn, which was written because of a suggestion by Lovecraft that he'd like to see a story told from the werewolf's point of view.

These stories are fascinating mile markers in the evolution of this kind of storytelling. It is fair to say that, without *Weird Tales*, writers like Clive Barker, Stephen King, Anne Rice, Peter Straub, Guillermo del Toro, and so many others, including myself, would have had vastly different careers. We might not have had *The X-Files, Supernatural, Kolchak: The Night Stalker,* and so many others.

I'm not sure it's possible to overstate the influence this weird little pulp magazine has had on the evolution of pop culture's darker and more imaginative side.

This anthology, and its companion, collect some of the landmark stories from the first decade of *Weird Tales*. Justin Criado and Kaye Lynne Booth, Western Colorado University MA in Publishing students, under the guidance of fellow weird writer, Kevin J. Anderson, have gone into dark territory indeed to resurrect these stories. If you enjoy your science fiction, mystery, fantasy, and horror with a big dose of that X-factor of overt and unapologetic weirdness, then you are in for a treat.

Read on. Enjoy.

And always ... be weird.

—Jonathan Maberry
Editor of *Weird Tales* magazine
San Diego, 2022

IMPRISONED WITH THE PHARAOHS

HOUDINI

ystery attracts mystery. Ever since the wide appearance of my name as a performer of unexplained feats, I have encountered strange narratives and events which my calling has led people to link with my interests and activities. Some of these have been trivial and irrelevant, some deeply dramatic and absorbing, some productive of weird and perilous experiences, and some involving me in extensive scientific and historical research. Many of these matters I have told and shall continue to tell freely; but there is one of which I speak with great reluctance, and which I am now relating only after a session of grilling persuasion from the publishers of this magazine, who had heard vague rumors of it from other members of my family.

The hitherto guarded subject pertains to my non-professional visit to Egypt fourteen years ago, and has been avoided by me for several reasons. For one thing, I am averse to exploiting certain unmistakably actual facts and conditions obviously unknown to the myriad tourists who throng about the pyramids and apparently secreted with much diligence by the authorities at Cairo, who cannot be wholly ignorant of them. For another thing, I dislike to recount an incident in which my own fantastic imagination must have played so great a part. What I saw—or thought I saw—certainly did not take place; but is rather to be viewed as a result of my then recent readings in Egyptology, and of the speculations anent this theme which my environment naturally prompted. These imaginative stimuli, magnified by the excitement of an actual event terrible enough in itself, undoubtedly gave rise to the culminating horror of that grotesque night so long past.

In January 1910, I had finished a professional engagement in England and signed a contract for a tour of Australian theatres. A liberal time being allowed for the trip, I determined to make the most of it in the sort of travel which chiefly interests me; so accompanied by my wife I drifted pleasantly down the Continent and embarked at Marseilles on the P. & O. Steamer *Malwa,* bound for Port Said. From that point I proposed to visit the principal historical localities of lower Egypt before leaving finally for Australia.

The voyage was an agreeable one, and enlivened by many of the amusing incidents which befall a magical performer apart from his work. I had intended, for the sake of quiet travel, to keep my name a secret; but was goaded into betraying myself by a fellow magician whose anxiety to astound the passengers with ordinary tricks tempted me to duplicate and exceed his feats in a manner quite destructive of my incognito. I mention this because of its ultimate effect—an effect I should have foreseen before unmasking to a shipload of tourists about to scatter throughout the Nile Valley. What it did was to herald my identity wherever I subsequently went, and deprive my wife and me of all the placid inconspicuousness we had sought. Travelling to seek curiosities, I was often forced to stand inspection as a sort of curiosity myself!

We had come to Egypt in search of the picturesque and the mystically impressive, but found little enough when the ship edged up to Port Said and discharged its passengers in small boats. Low dunes of sand, bobbing buoys in shallow water, and a drearily European small town with nothing of interest save the great De Lesseps statue, made us anxious to get on to something more worth our while. After some discussion we decided to proceed at once to Cairo and the Pyramids, later going to Alexandria for the Australian boat and for whatever Graeco-Roman sights that ancient metropolis might present.

The railway journey was tolerable enough, and consumed only four hours and a half. We saw much of the Suez Canal, whose route we followed as far as Ismailiya, and later had a taste of Old Egypt in our glimpse of the restored fresh-water canal of the Middle Empire. Then at last we saw Cairo glimmering through the growing dusk; a twinkling constellation which became a blaze as we halted at the great Gare Centrale.

But once more disappointment awaited us, for all that we beheld was European save the costumes and the crowds. A prosaic subway led to a square teeming with carriages, taxicabs, and trolley-cars, and gorgeous with electric lights shining on tall buildings; whilst the very theatre where I was vainly requested to play, and which I later attended as a spectator, had recently been renamed the "American Cosmograph." We stopped at Shepherd's Hotel, reached in a taxi that sped along broad, smartly built-up streets; and amidst the perfect service of its restaurant, elevators, and generally Anglo-American luxuries the mysterious East and immemorial past seemed very far away.

The next day, however, precipitated us delightfully into the heart of the Arabian Nights atmosphere; and in the winding ways and exotic skyline of Cairo, the Bagdad of Haroun-al-Raschid seemed to live again. Guided by our Baedeker, we had struck east past the Ezbekiyeh Gardens along the Mouski in quest of the native quarter, and were soon in the hands of a clamorous cicerone who—notwithstanding later developments—was assuredly a master at his trade. Not until afterward did I see that I should have applied at the hotel for a licensed guide. This man, a shaven, peculiarly hollow-voiced, and relatively cleanly fellow who looked like a Pharaoh and called himself "Abdul Reis el Drogman," appeared to have much power over others of his kind; though subsequently the police professed not to know him, and to suggest that *reis* is merely a name for any person in authority, whilst "Drogman" is obviously no more than a clumsy modification of the word for a leader of tourist parties —*dragoman.*

Abdul led us among such wonders as we had before only read and dreamed of. Old Cairo is itself a story-book and a dream—labyrinths of narrow alleys redolent of aromatic secrets; Arabesque balconies and oriels nearly meeting above the cobbled streets; maelstroms of Oriental traffic with strange cries, cracking whips, rattling carts, jingling money, and braying donkeys; kaleidoscopes of polychrome robes, veils, turbans, and tarbushes; water-carriers and dervishes, dogs and cats, soothsayers and barbers; and over all the whining of blind beggars crouched in alcoves, and the sonorous chanting of muezzins from minarets limned delicately against a sky of deep, unchanging blue.

The roofed, quieter bazaars were hardly less alluring. Spice, perfume, incense, beads, rugs, silks, and brass—old Mahmoud Suleiman squats cross-legged amidst his gummy bottles while chattering youths pulverize mustard in the hollowed-out capital of an ancient classic column—a Roman Corinthian, perhaps from neighboring Heliopolis, where Augustus stationed one of his three Egyptian legions. Antiquity begins to mingle with exoticism. And then the mosques and the museum—we saw them all, and tried not to let our Arabian revel succumb to the darker charm of Pharaonic Egypt which the museum's priceless treasures offered. That was to be our climax, and for the present we concentrated on the mediaeval Saracenic glories of the Caliphs whose magnificent tomb-mosques form a glittering faery necropolis on the edge of the Arabian Desert.

At length Abdul took us along the Sharia Mohammed Ali to the ancient mosque of Sultan Hassan, and the tower-flanked Bab-el-Azab, beyond which climbs the steep-walled pass to the mighty citadel that Saladin himself built with the stones of forgotten pyramids. It was sunset when we scaled that cliff, circled the modern mosque of Mohammed Ali, and looked down from the dizzying parapet over mystic Cairo—mystic Cairo all golden with its carven domes, its ethereal minarets, and its flaming gardens. Far over the city towered the great Roman dome of the new museum; and beyond it—across the cryptic yellow Nile that is the mother of aeons and dynasties—lurked the menacing sands of the Libyan Desert, undulant and iridescent and evil with older arcana. The red sun sank low, bringing the relentless chill of Egyptian dusk; and as it stood poised on the world's rim like that ancient god of Heliopolis—Re-Harakhte, the Horizon-Sun—we saw silhouetted against its vermeil holocaust the black outlines of the Pyramids of Gizeh—the palaeogean tombs there were hoary with a thousand years when Tut-Ankh-Amen mounted his golden throne in distant Thebes. Then we knew that we were done with Saracen Cairo, and that we must taste the deeper mysteries of primal Egypt—the black Khem of Re and Amen, Isis and Osiris.

The next morning we visited the pyramids, riding out in a Victoria across the great Nile bridge with its bronze lions, the island of Ghizereh with its massive lebbakh trees, and the smaller English bridge to the western shore. Down the shore road we drove, between great rows of lebbakhs and past the vast Zoölogical Gardens to the suburb of Gizeh, where a new bridge to Cairo proper has since been built. Then, turning inland along the Sharia-el-Haram, we crossed a region of glassy canals and shabby native villages till before us loomed the objects of our quest, cleaving the mists of dawn and forming inverted replicas in the roadside pools. Forty centuries, as Napoleon had told his campaigners there, indeed looked down upon us.

The road now rose abruptly, till we finally reached our place of transfer between the trolley station and the Mena House Hotel. Abdul Reis, who capably purchased our pyramid tickets, seemed to have an understanding with the crowding, yelling, and offensive

Bedouins who inhabited a squalid mud village some distance away and pestiferously assailed every traveler; for he kept them very decently at bay and secured an excellent pair of camels for us, himself mounting a donkey and assigning the leadership of our animals to a group of men and boys more expensive than useful. The area to be traversed was so small that camels were hardly needed, but we did not regret adding to our experience this troublesome form of desert navigation.

The pyramids stand on a high rock plateau, this group forming next to the northernmost of the series of regal and aristocratic cemeteries built in the neighborhood of the extinct capital Memphis, which lay on the same side of the Nile, somewhat south of Gizeh, and which flourished between 3400 and 2000 B. C. The greatest pyramid, which lies nearest the modern road, was built by King Cheops or Khufu about 2800 B. C., and stands more than 450 feet in perpendicular height. In a line southwest from this are successively the Second Pyramid, built a generation later by King Khephren, and though slightly smaller, looking even larger because set on higher ground, and the radically smaller Third Pyramid of King Mycerinus, built about 2700 B. C. Near the edge of the plateau and due east of the Second Pyramid, with a face probably altered to form a colossal portrait of Khephren, its royal restorer, stands the monstrous Sphinx—mute, sardonic, and wise beyond mankind and memory.

Minor pyramids and the traces of ruined minor pyramids are found in several places, and the whole plateau is pitted with the tombs of dignitaries of less than royal rank. These latter were originally marked by *mastabas,* or stone bench-like structures about the deep burial shafts, as found in other Memphian cemeteries and exemplified by Perneb's Tomb in the Metropolitan Museum of New York. At Gizeh, however, all such visible things have been swept away by time and pillage; and only the rock-hewn shafts, either sand-filled or cleared out by archaeologists, remain to attest their former existence. Connected with each tomb was a chapel in which priests and relatives offered food and prayer to the hovering *ka* or vital principle of the deceased. The small tombs have their chapels contained in their stone *mastabas* or superstructures, but the mortuary chapels of the pyramids, where regal Pharaohs lay, were separate temples, each to the east of its corresponding pyramid, and connected by a causeway to a massive gate-chapel or propylon at the edge of the rock plateau.

The gate-chapel leading to the Second Pyramid, nearly buried in the drifting sands, yawns subterraneously southeast of the Sphinx. Persistent tradition dubs it the "Temple of the Sphinx"; and it may perhaps be rightly called such if the Sphinx indeed represents the Second Pyramid's builder Khephren. There are unpleasant tales of the Sphinx before Khephren—but whatever its elder features were, the monarch replaced them with his own that men might look at the colossus without fear. It was in the great gateway-temple that the life-size diorite statue of Khephren now in the Cairo Museum was found; a statue before which I stood in awe when I beheld it. Whether the whole edifice is now excavated I am not certain, but in 1910 most of it was below ground, with the entrance heavily barred at night. Germans were in charge of the work, and the war or other things may have stopped them. I would give much, in view of my experience and of certain Bedouin whisperings discredited or unknown in Cairo, to know what has developed in connection with a certain well in a transverse gallery where statues of the Pharaoh were found in curious juxtaposition to the statues of baboons.

The road, as we traversed it on our camels that morning, curved sharply past the wooden police quarters, post-office, drug-store, and shops on the left, and plunged south and east in a complete bend that scaled the rock plateau and brought us face to face with the desert under the lee of the Great Pyramid. Past Cyclopean masonry we rode, rounding the eastern face and looking down ahead into a valley of minor pyramids beyond which the eternal Nile glistened to the east, and the eternal desert shimmered to the west. Very close loomed the three major pyramids, the greatest devoid of outer casing and shewing its bulk of great stones, but the others retaining here and there the neatly fitted covering which had made them smooth and finished in their day.

Presently we descended toward the Sphinx, and sat silent beneath the spell of those terrible unseeing eyes. On the vast stone breast we

faintly discerned the emblem of Re-Harakhte, for whose image the
Sphinx was mistaken in a late dynasty; and though sand covered the
tablet between the great paws, we recalled what Thutmosis IV
inscribed thereon, and the dream he had when a prince. It was then
that the smile of the Sphinx vaguely displeased us, and made us
wonder about the legends of subterranean passages beneath the
monstrous creature, leading down, down, to depths none might dare
hint at—depths connected with mysteries older than the dynastic
Egypt we excavate, and having a sinister relation to the persistence of
abnormal, animal-headed gods in the ancient Nilotic pantheon. Then,
too, I asked myself an idle question whose hideous significance was
not to appear for many an hour.

Other tourists now began to overtake us, and we moved on to the
sand-choked Temple of the Sphinx, fifty yards to the southeast, which
I have previously mentioned as the great gate of the causeway to the
Second Pyramid's mortuary chapel on the plateau. Most of it was still
underground, and although we dismounted and descended through a
modern passageway to its alabaster corridor and pillared hall, I felt
that Abdul and the local German attendant had not shown us all
there was to see. After this we made the conventional circuit of the
pyramid plateau, examining the Second Pyramid and the peculiar
ruins of its mortuary chapel to the east, the Third Pyramid and its
miniature southern satellites and ruined eastern chapel, the rock
tombs and the honeycombings of the Fourth and Fifth Dynasties, and
the famous Campell's Tomb whose shadowy shaft sinks precipitously
for 53 feet to a sinister sarcophagus which one of our camel-drivers
divested of the cumbering sand after a vertiginous descent by rope.

Cries now assailed us from the Great Pyramid, where Bedouins
were besieging a party of tourists with offers of guidance to the top, or
of displays of speed in the performance of solitary trips up and down.
Seven minutes is said to be the record for such an ascent and descent,
but many lusty sheiks and sons of sheiks assured us they could cut it
to five if given the requisite impetus of liberal *baksheesh*. They did not
get this impetus, though we did let Abdul take us up, thus obtaining a
view of unprecedented magnificence which included not only remote

and glittering Cairo with its crowned citadel and background of gold-violet hills, but all the pyramids of the Memphian district as well, from Abu Roash on the north to the Dashur on the south. The Sakkara step-pyramid, which marks the evolution of the low *mastaba* into the true pyramid, shewed clearly and alluringly in the sandy distance. It is close to this transition-monument that the famed Tomb of Perneb was found—more than 400 miles north of the Theban rock valley where Tut-Ankh-Amen sleeps. Again I was forced to silence through sheer awe. The prospect of such antiquity, and the secrets each hoary monument seemed to hold and brood over, filled me with a reverence and sense of immensity nothing else ever gave me.

Fatigued by our climb, and disgusted with the importunate Bedouins whose actions seemed to defy every rule of taste, we omitted the arduous detail of entering the cramped interior passages of any of the pyramids, though we saw several of the hardiest tourists preparing for the suffocating crawl through Cheops' mightiest memorial. As we dismissed and overpaid our local bodyguard and drove back to Cairo with Abdul Reis under the afternoon sun, we half regretted the omission we had made. Such fascinating things were whispered about lower pyramid passages not in the guidebooks; passages whose entrances had been hastily blocked up and concealed by certain uncommunicative archaeologists who had found and begun to explore them. Of course, this whispering was largely baseless on the face of it; but it was curious to reflect how persistently visitors were forbidden to enter the pyramids at night, or to visit the lowest burrows and crypt of the Great Pyramid. Perhaps in the latter case it was the psychological effect which was feared—the effect on the visitor of feeling himself huddled down beneath a gigantic world of solid masonry; joined to the life he has known by the merest tube, in which he may only crawl, and which any accident or evil design might block. The whole subject seemed so weird and alluring that we resolved to pay the pyramid plateau another visit at the earliest possible opportunity. For me this opportunity came much earlier than I expected.

That evening, the members of our party feeling somewhat tired after the strenuous programme of the day, I went alone with Abdul Reis for a walk through the picturesque Arab quarter. Though I had seen it by day, I wished to study the alleys and bazaars in the dusk, when rich shadows and mellow gleams of light would add to their glamour and fantastic illusion. The native crowds were thinning, but were still very noisy and numerous when we came upon a knot of reveling Bedouins in the Suken-Nahhasin, or bazaar of the copper-smiths. Their apparent leader, an insolent youth with heavy features and saucily cocked tarbush, took some notice of us; and evidently recognized with no great friendliness my competent but admittedly supercilious and sneeringly disposed guide. Perhaps, I thought, he resented that odd reproduction of the Sphinx's half-smile which I had often remarked with amused irritation; or perhaps he did not like the hollow and sepulchral resonance of Abdul's voice. At any rate, the exchange of ancestrally opprobrious language became very brisk; and before long Ali Ziz, as I heard the stranger called when called by no worse name, began to pull violently at Abdul's robe, an action quickly reciprocated, and leading to a spirited scuffle in which both combat-ants lost their sacredly cherished headgear and would have reached an even direr condition had I not intervened and separated them by main force.

My interference, at first seemingly unwelcome on both sides, succeeded at last in effecting a truce. Sullenly each belligerent composed his wrath and his attire; and with an assumption of dignity as profound as it was sudden, the two formed a curious pact of honor which I soon learned is a custom of great antiquity in Cairo—a pact for the settlement of their difference by means of a nocturnal fist fight atop the Great Pyramid, long after the departure of the last moonlight sightseer. Each duelist was to assemble a party of seconds, and the affair was to begin at midnight, proceeding by rounds in the most civi-lized possible fashion. In all this planning there was much which excited my interest. The fight itself promised to be unique and spec-tacular, while the thought of the scene on that hoary pile overlooking the antediluvian plateau of Gizeh under the wan moon of the pallid small hours appealed to every fiber of imagination in me. A request found Abdul exceedingly willing to admit me to his party of seconds; so that all the rest of the early evening I accompanied him to various dens in the most lawless regions of the town—mostly northeast of the Ezbekiyeh—where he gathered one by one a select and formidable band of congenial cutthroats as his pugilistic background.

Shortly after nine our party, mounted on donkeys bearing such royal or tourist-reminiscent names as "Rameses," "Mark Twain," "J. P. Morgan," and "Minnehaha," edged through street labyrinths both Oriental and Occidental, crossed the muddy and mast-forested Nile by the bridge of the bronze lions, and cantered philosophically between the lebbakhs on the road to Gizeh. Slightly over two hours were consumed by the trip, toward the end of which we passed the last of the returning tourists, saluted the last in-bound trolley-car, and were alone with the night and the past and the spectral moon.

Then we saw the vast pyramids at the end of the avenue, ghoulish with a dim atavistical menace which I had not seemed to notice in the daytime. Even the smallest of them held a hint of the ghastly—for was it not in this that they had buried Queen Nitokris alive in the Sixth Dynasty; subtle Queen Nitokris, who once invited all her enemies to a feast in a temple below the Nile, and drowned them by opening the water-gates? I recalled that the Arabs whisper things about Nitokris, and shun the Third Pyramid at certain phases of the moon. It must have been over her that Thomas Moore was brooding when he wrote a thing muttered about by Memphian boatmen—

> "The subterranean nymph that dwells
> 'Mid sunless gems and glories hid—
> The lady of the Pyramid!"

Early as we were, Ali Ziz and his party were ahead of us; for we saw their donkeys outlined against the desert plateau at Kafr-el-Haram; toward which squalid Arab settlement, close to the Sphinx, we had diverged instead of following the regular road to the Mena House, where some of the sleepy, inefficient police might have observed and halted us. Here, where filthy Bedouins stabled camels and donkeys in

the rock tombs of Khephren's courtiers, we were led up the rocks and
over the sand to the Great Pyramid, up whose time-worn sides the
Arabs swarmed eagerly, Abdul Reis offering me the assistance I did
not need.

As most travelers know, the actual apex of this structure has long
been worn away, leaving a reasonably flat platform twelve yards
square. On this eerie pinnacle a squared circle was formed, and in a
few moments the sardonic desert moon leered down upon a battle
which, but for the quality of the ringside cries, might well have
occurred at some minor athletic club in America. As I watched it, I
felt that some of our less desirable institutions were not lacking; for
every blow, feint, and defense bespoke "stalling" to my not inexperi-
enced eye. It was quickly over, and despite my misgivings as to
methods I felt a sort of proprietary pride when Abdul Reis was
adjudged the winner.

Reconciliation was phenomenally rapid, and amidst the singing,
fraternizing, and drinking which followed, I found it difficult to
realize that a quarrel had ever occurred. Oddly enough, I myself
seemed to be more of a centre of notice than the antagonists; and
from my smattering of Arabic I judged that they were discussing my
professional performances and escapes from every sort of manacle and
confinement, in a manner which indicated not only a surprising
knowledge of me, but a distinct hostility and skepticism concerning
my feats of escape. It gradually dawned on me that the elder magic of
Egypt did not depart without leaving traces, and that fragments of a
strange secret lore and priestly cult-practices have survived surrepti-
tiously amongst the fellaheen to such an extent that the prowess of a
strange "hahwi" or magician is resented and disputed. I thought of
how much my hollow-voiced guide Abdul Reis looked like an old
Egyptian priest or Pharaoh or smiling Sphinx and wondered.

Suddenly something happened which in a flash proved the
correctness of my reflections and made me curse the denseness
whereby I had accepted this night's events as other than the empty
and malicious "frameup" they now shewed themselves to be. Without
warning, and doubtless in answer to some subtle sign from Abdul, the

entire band of Bedouins precipitated itself upon me; and having produced heavy ropes, soon had me bound as securely as I was ever bound in the course of my life, either on the stage or off. I struggled at first, but soon saw that one man could make no headway against a band of over twenty sinewy barbarians. My hands were tied behind my back, my knees bent to their fullest extent, and my wrists and ankles stoutly linked together with unyielding cords. A stifling gag was forced into my mouth, and a blindfold fastened tightly over my eyes. Then, as the Arabs bore me aloft on their shoulders and began a jouncing descent of the pyramid, I heard the taunts of my late guide Abdul, who mocked and jeered delightedly in his hollow voice, and assured me that I was soon to have my "magic powers" put to a supreme test which would quickly remove any egotism I might have gained through triumphing over all the tests offered by America and Europe. Egypt, he reminded me, is very old; and full of inner mysteries and antique powers not even conceivable to the experts of today, whose devices had so uniformly failed to entrap me.

How far or in what direction I was carried, I cannot tell; for the circumstances were all against the formation of any accurate judgment. I know, however, that it could not have been a great distance; since my bearers at no point hastened beyond a walk, yet kept me aloft a surprisingly short time. It is this perplexing brevity which makes me feel almost like shuddering whenever I think of Gizeh and its plateau —for one is oppressed by hints of the closeness to everyday tourist routes of what existed then and must exist still.

The evil abnormality I speak of did not become manifest at first. Setting me down on a surface which I recognized as sand rather than rock, my captors passed a rope around my chest and dragged me a few feet to a ragged opening in the ground, into which they presently lowered me with much rough handling. For apparent aeons I bumped against the stony irregular sides of a narrow hewn well which I took to be one of the numerous burial shafts of the plateau until the prodigious, almost incredible depth of it robbed me of all bases of conjecture.

The horror of the experience deepened with every dragging

second. That any descent through the sheer solid rock could be so vast without reaching the core of the planet itself, or that any rope made by man could be so long as to dangle me in these unholy and seemingly fathomless profundities of nether earth, were beliefs of such grotesqueness that it was easier to doubt my agitated senses than to accept them. Even now I am uncertain, for I know how deceitful the sense of time becomes when one or more of the usual perceptions or conditions of life is removed or distorted. But I am quite sure that I preserved a logical consciousness that far; that at least I did not add any full-grown phantoms of imagination to a picture hideous enough in its reality, and explicable by a type of cerebral illusion vastly short of actual hallucination.

All this was not the cause of my first bit of fainting. The shocking ordeal was cumulative, and the beginning of the later terrors was a very perceptible increase in my rate of descent. They were paying out that infinitely long rope very swiftly now, and I scraped cruelly against the rough and constricted sides of the shaft as I shot madly downward. My clothing was in tatters, and I felt the trickle of blood all over, even above the mounting and excruciating pain. My nostrils, too, were assailed by a scarcely definable menace; a creeping odor of damp and staleness curiously unlike anything I had ever smelt before, and having faint overtones of spice and incense that lent an element of mockery.

Then the mental cataclysm came. It was horrible—hideous beyond all articulate description because it was all of the soul, with nothing of detail to describe. It was the ecstasy of nightmare and the summation of the fiendish. The suddenness of it was apocalyptic and daemoniac—one moment I was plunging agonizingly down that narrow well of million-toothed torture, yet the next moment I was soaring on bat-wings in the gulfs of hell; swinging free and swoopingly through illimitable miles of boundless, musty space; rising dizzily to measureless pinnacles of chilling ether, then diving gaspingly to sucking nadirs of ravenous, nauseous lower vacua. Thank God for the mercy that shut out in oblivion those clawing furies of consciousness which half unhinged my faculties, and tore Harpy-like at my spirit! That one respite, short as it was, gave me the strength and sanity to endure those still greater sublimations of cosmic panic that lurked and gibbered on the road ahead.

It was very gradually that I regained my senses after that eldritch flight through Stygian space. The process was infinitely painful, and colored by fantastic dreams in which my bound and gagged condition found singular embodiment. The precise nature of these dreams was very clear while I was experiencing them, but became blurred in my recollection almost immediately afterward, and was soon reduced to the merest outline by the terrible events—real or imaginary—which followed. I dreamed that I was in the grasp of a great and horrible paw; a yellow, hairy, five-clawed paw which had reached out of the earth to crush and engulf me. And when I stopped to reflect what the paw was, it seemed to me that it was Egypt. In the dream I looked back at the events of the preceding weeks, and saw myself lured and enmeshed little by little, subtly and insidiously, by some hellish ghoul-spirit of the elder Nile sorcery; some spirit that was in Egypt before ever man was, and that will be when man is no more.

I saw the horror and unwholesome antiquity of Egypt, and the grisly alliance it has always had with the tombs and temples of the dead. I saw phantom processions of priests with the heads of bulls, falcons, cats, and ibises; phantom processions marching interminably through subterranean labyrinths and avenues of titanic propylaea beside which a man is as a fly, and offering unnamable sacrifices to indescribable gods. Stone colossi marched in endless night and drove herds of grinning androsphinxes down to the shores of illimitable stagnant rivers of pitch. And behind it all I saw the ineffable malignity of primordial necromancy, black and amorphous, and fumbling greedily after me in the darkness to choke out the spirit that had dared to mock it by emulation. In my sleeping brain there took shape a melodrama of sinister hatred and pursuit, and I saw the black soul of Egypt singling me out and calling me in inaudible whispers; calling and luring me, leading me on with the glitter and glamour of a Saracenic surface, but ever pulling me down to the age-mad catacombs and horrors of its dead and abysmal pharaonic heart.

Then the dream-faces took on human resemblances, and I saw my guide Abdul Reis in the robes of a king, with the sneer of the Sphinx on his features. And I knew that those features were the features of Khephren the Great, who raised the Second Pyramid, carved over the Sphinx's face in the likeness of his own, and built that titanic gateway temple whose myriad corridors the archaeologists think they have dug out of the cryptical sand and the uninformative rock. And I looked at the long, lean, rigid hand of Khephren; the long, lean, rigid hand as I had seen it on the diorite statue in the Cairo Museum—the statue they had found in the terrible gateway temple—and wondered that I had not shrieked when I saw it on Abdul Reis. That hand! It was hideously cold, and it was crushing me; it was the cold and cramping of the sarcophagus ... the chill and constriction of unrememberable Egypt ... It was nighted, necropolitan Egypt itself ... that yellow paw ... and they whisper such things of Khephren.

But at this juncture I began to awake—or at least, to assume a condition less completely that of sleep than the one just preceding. I recalled the fight atop the pyramid, the treacherous Bedouins and their attack, my frightful descent by rope through endless rock depths, and my mad swinging and plunging in a chill void redolent of aromatic putrescence. I perceived that I now lay on a damp rock floor, and that my bonds were still biting into me with unloosened force. It was very cold, and I seemed to detect a faint current of noisome air sweeping across me. The cuts and bruises I had received from the jagged sides of the rock shaft were paining me woefully, their soreness enhanced to a stinging or burning acuteness by some pungent quality in the faint draught, and the mere act of rolling over was enough to set my whole frame throbbing with untold agony. As I turned I felt a tug from above, and concluded that the rope whereby I was lowered still reached to the surface. Whether or not the Arabs still held it, I had no idea; nor had I any idea how far within the earth I was. I knew that the darkness around me was wholly or nearly total, since no ray of moonlight penetrated my blindfold; but I did not trust my senses enough to accept as evidence of extreme depth the sensation of vast duration which had characterized my descent.

Knowing at least that I was in a space of considerable extent reached from the surface directly above by an opening in the rock, I doubtfully conjectured that my prison was perhaps the buried gateway chapel of old Khephren—the Temple of the Sphinx—perhaps some inner corridor which the guides had not shown me during my morning visit, and from which I might easily escape if I could find my way to the barred entrance. It would be a labyrinthine wandering, but no worse than others out of which I had in the past found my way. The first step was to get free of my bonds, gag, and blindfold; and this I knew would be no great task, since subtler experts than these Arabs had tried every known species of fetter upon me during my long and varied career as an exponent of escape, yet had never succeeded in defeating my methods.

Then it occurred to me that the Arabs might be ready to meet and attack me at the entrance upon any evidence of my probable escape from the binding cords, as would be furnished by any decided agitation of the rope which they probably held. This, of course, was taking for granted that my place of confinement was indeed Khephren's Temple of the Sphinx. The direct opening in the roof, wherever it might lurk, could not be beyond easy reach of the ordinary modern entrance near the Sphinx; if in truth it were any great distance at all on the surface, since the total area known to visitors is not at all enormous. I had not noticed any such opening during my daytime pilgrimage, but knew that these things are easily overlooked amidst the drifting sands. Thinking these matters over as I lay bent and bound on the rock floor, I nearly forgot the horrors of the abysmal descent and cavernous swinging which had so lately reduced me to a coma. My present thought was only to outwit the Arabs, and I accordingly determined to work myself free as quickly as possible, avoiding any tug on the descending line which might betray an effective or even problematical attempt at freedom.

This, however, was more easily determined than affected. A few preliminary trials made it clear that little could be accomplished without considerable motion; and it did not surprise me when, after one especially energetic struggle, I began to feel the coils of falling rope as they piled up about me and upon me. Obviously, I thought, the Bedouins had felt my movements and released their end of the rope; hastening no doubt to the temple's true entrance to lie murderously in wait for me. The prospect was not pleasing—but I had faced worse in my time without flinching, and would not flinch now. At present I must first of all free myself of bonds, then trust to ingenuity to escape from the temple unharmed. It is curious how implicitly I had come to believe myself in the old temple of Khephren beside the Sphinx, only a short distance below the ground.

That belief was shattered, and every pristine apprehension of preternatural depth and daemoniac mystery revived, by a circumstance which grew in horror and significance even as I formulated my philosophical plan. I have said that the falling rope was piling up about and upon me. Now I saw that it was *continuing to pile*, as no rope of normal length could possibly do. It gained in momentum and became an avalanche of hemp, accumulating mountainously on the floor, and half burying me beneath its swiftly multiplying coils. Soon I was completely engulfed and gasping for breath as the increasing convolutions submerged and stifled me. My senses tottered again, and I vainly tried to fight off a menace desperate and ineluctable. It was not merely that I was tortured beyond human endurance—not merely that life and breath seemed to be crushed slowly out of me—it was the knowledge of *what those unnatural lengths of rope implied*, and the consciousness of what unknown and incalculable gulfs of inner earth must at this moment be surrounding me. My endless descent and swinging flight through goblin space, then, must have been real; and even now I must be lying helpless in some nameless cavern world toward the core of the planet. Such a sudden confirmation of ultimate horror was insupportable, and a second time I lapsed into merciful oblivion.

When I say oblivion, I do not imply that I was free from dreams. On the contrary, my absence from the conscious world was marked by visions of the most unutterable hideousness. God! If only I had not read so much Egyptology before coming to this land which is the fountain of all darkness and terror! This second spell of fainting filled my sleeping mind anew with shivering realization of the country and its archaic secrets, and through some damnable chance my dreams turned to the ancient notions of the dead and their sojournings in soul *and body* beyond those mysterious tombs which were more houses than graves. I recalled, in dream-shapes which it is well that I do not remember, the peculiar and elaborate construction of Egyptian sepulchres; and the exceedingly singular and terrific doctrines which determined this construction.

All these people thought of was death and the dead. They conceived of a literal resurrection of the body which made them mummify it with desperate care, and preserve all the vital organs in canopic jars near the corpse; whilst besides the body they believed in two other elements, the soul, which after its weighing and approval by Osiris dwelt in the land of the blest, and the obscure and portentous *ka* or life-principle which wandered about the upper and lower worlds in a horrible way, demanding occasional access to the preserved body, consuming the food offerings brought by priests and pious relatives to the mortuary chapel, and sometimes—as men whispered—taking its body or the wooden double always buried beside it and stalking noxiously abroad on errands peculiarly repellent.

For thousands of years those bodies rested gorgeously encased and staring glassily upward when not visited by the *ka,* awaiting the day when Osiris should restore both *ka* and soul, and lead forth the stiff legions of the dead from the sunken houses of sleep. It was to have been a glorious rebirth—but not all souls were approved, nor were all tombs inviolate, so that certain grotesque *mistakes* and fiendish *abnormalities* were to be looked for. Even today the Arabs murmur of unsanctified convocations and unwholesome worship in forgotten nether abysses, which only winged invisible *kas* and soulless mummies may visit and return unscathed.

Perhaps the most leeringly blood-congealing legends are those which relate to certain perverse products of decadent priestcraft —*composite mummies* made by the artificial union of human trunks and limbs with the heads of animals in imitation of the elder gods. At all stages of history the sacred animals were mummified, so that conse-crated bulls, cats, ibises, crocodiles, and the like might return some day to greater glory. But only in the decadence did they mix the human and animal in the same mummy—only in the decadence, when they did not understand the rights and prerogatives of the *ka* and the soul. What happened to those composite mummies is not told of—at least publicly—and it is certain that no Egyptologist ever found one. The whispers of Arabs are very wild, and cannot be relied upon. They even hint that old Khephren—he of the Sphinx, the Second Pyramid, and the yawning gateway temple—lives far underground wedded to the ghoul-queen Nitokris and ruling over the mummies that are neither of man nor of beast.

It was of these—of Khephren and his consort and his strange armies of the hybrid dead—that I dreamed, and that is why I am glad the exact dream-shapes have faded from my memory. My most horrible vision was connected with an idle question I had asked myself the day before when looking at the great carven riddle of the desert and wondering with what unknown depths the temple so close to it might be secretly connected. That question, so innocent and whimsical then, assumed in my dream a meaning of frenetic and hysterical madness. *What huge and loathsome abnormality was the Sphinx originally carven to represent?*

My second awakening—if awakening it was—is a memory of stark hideousness which nothing else in my life—save one thing which came after—can parallel; and that life has been full and adventurous beyond most men's. Remember that I had lost consciousness whilst buried beneath a cascade of falling rope whose immensity revealed the cataclysmic depth of my present position. Now, as perception returned, I felt the entire weight gone; and realized upon rolling over that although I was still tied, gagged, and blindfolded, *some agency had removed completely the suffocating hempen landslide which had overwhelmed me.* The significance of this condition, of course, came to me only gradually; but even so I think it would have brought unconsciousness again had I not by this time reached such a state of emotional exhaustion that no new horror could make much difference. I was alone with *what?*

Before I could torture myself with any new reflection, or make any fresh effort to escape from my bonds, an additional circumstance became manifest. Pains not formerly felt were racking my arms and legs, and I seemed coated with a profusion of dried blood beyond anything my former cuts and abrasions could furnish. My chest, too, seemed pierced by a hundred wounds, as though some malign, titanic ibis had been pecking at it. Assuredly the agency which had removed the rope was a hostile one, and had begun to wreak terrible injuries upon me when somehow impelled to desist. Yet at the time my sensations were distinctly the reverse of what one might expect. Instead of sinking into a bottomless pit of despair, I was stirred to a new courage and action; for now I felt that the evil forces were physical things which a fearless man might encounter on an even basis.

On the strength of this thought I tugged again at my bonds, and used all the art of a lifetime to free myself as I had so often done amidst the glare of lights and the applause of vast crowds. The familiar details of my escaping process commenced to engross me, and now that the long rope was gone I half regained my belief that the supreme horrors were hallucinations after all, and that there had never been any terrible shaft, measureless abyss, or interminable rope. Was I after all in the gateway temple of Khephren beside the Sphinx, and had the sneaking Arabs stolen in to torture me as I lay helpless there? At any rate, I must be free. Let me stand up unbound, ungagged, and with eyes open to catch any glimmer of light which might come trickling from any source, and I could actually delight in the combat against evil and treacherous foes!

How long I took in shaking off my encumbrances I cannot tell. It must have been longer than in my exhibition performances, because I was wounded, exhausted, and enervated by the experiences I had passed through. When I was finally free, and taking deep breaths of a chill, damp, evilly spiced air all the more horrible when encountered without the screen of gag and blindfold edges, I found that I was too cramped and fatigued to move at once. There I lay, trying to stretch a frame bent and mangled, for an indefinite period, and straining my eyes to catch a glimpse of some ray of light which would give a hint as to my position.

By degrees my strength and flexibility returned, but my eyes beheld nothing. As I staggered to my feet I peered diligently in every direction, yet met only an ebony blackness as great as that I had known when blindfolded. I tried my legs, blood-encrusted beneath my shredded trousers, and found that I could walk; yet could not decide in what direction to go. Obviously I ought not to walk at random, and perhaps retreat directly from the entrance I sought; so I paused to note the direction of the cold, foetid, natron-scented air current which I had never ceased to feel. Accepting the point of its source as the possible entrance to the abyss, I strove to keep track of this landmark and to walk consistently toward it.

I had had a matchbox with me, and even a small electric flashlight; but of course the pockets of my tossed and tattered clothing were long since emptied of all heavy articles. As I walked cautiously in the blackness, the draught grew stronger and more offensive, till at length I could regard it as nothing less than a tangible stream of detestable vapor pouring out of some aperture like the smoke of the genie from the fisherman's jar in the Eastern tale. Egypt truly, this dark cradle of civilization was ever the wellspring of horrors and marvels unspeakable! The more I reflected on the nature of this cavern wind, the greater my sense of disquiet became; for although despite its odor I had sought its source as at least an indirect clue to the outer world, I now saw plainly that this foul emanation could have no admixture or connection whatsoever with the clean air of the Libyan Desert, but must be essentially a thing vomited from sinister gulfs still lower down. I had, then, been walking in the wrong direction!

After a moment's reflection I decided not to retrace my steps. Away from the draught I would have no landmarks, for the roughly level rock floor was devoid of distinctive configurations. If, however, I followed up the strange current, I would undoubtedly arrive at an aperture of some sort, from whose gate I could perhaps work round the walls to the opposite side of this Cyclopean and otherwise unnavigable hall. That I might fail, I well realized. I saw that this was no part of Khephren's gateway temple which tourists know, and it struck me that this particular hall might be unknown even to archaeologists, and merely stumbled upon by the inquisitive and malignant Arabs who had imprisoned me. If so, was there any present gate of escape to the known parts or to the outer air?

What evidence, indeed, did I now possess that this was the gateway temple at all? For a moment all my wildest speculations rushed back upon me, and I thought of that vivid mélange of impressions—descent, suspension in space, the rope, my wounds, and the dreams that were frankly dreams. Was this the end of life for me? Or indeed, would it be merciful if this moment *were* the end? I could answer none of my own questions, but merely kept on till fate for a third time reduced me to oblivion. This time there were no dreams, for the suddenness of the incident shocked me out of all thought either conscious or subconscious. Tripping on an unexpected descending step at a point where the offensive draught became strong enough to offer an actual physical resistance, I was precipitated headlong down a black flight of huge stone stairs into a gulf of hideousness unrelieved.

That I ever breathed again is a tribute to the inherent vitality of the healthy human organism. Often I look back to that night and feel a touch of actual *humor* in those repeated lapses of consciousness; lapses whose succession reminded me at the time of nothing more than the crude cinema melodramas of that period. Of course, it is possible that the repeated lapses never occurred; and that all the features of that underground nightmare were merely the dreams of one long coma which began with the shock of my descent into that abyss and ended with the healing balm of the outer air and of the rising sun which found me stretched on the sands of Gizeh before the sardonic and dawn-flushed face of the Great Sphinx.

I prefer to believe this latter explanation as much as I can, hence was glad when the police told me that the barrier to Khephren's gateway temple had been found unfastened, and that a sizeable rift to the surface did actually exist in one corner of the still buried part. I was glad, too, when the doctors pronounced my wounds only those to be expected from my seizure, blindfolding, lowering, struggling with bonds, falling some distance—perhaps into a depression in the temple's inner gallery—dragging myself to the outer barrier and escaping from it, and experiences like that ... a very soothing diagnosis. And yet I know that there must be more than appears on the surface. That extreme descent is too vivid a memory to be dismissed—and it is odd that no one has ever been able to find a man answering the description of my guide Abdul Reis el Drogman—the tomb-throated guide who looked and smiled like King Khephren.

I have digressed from my connected narrative—perhaps in the vain hope of evading the telling of that final incident; that incident which of all is most certainly a hallucination. But I promised to relate it, and do not break promises. When I recovered—or seemed to recover—my senses after that fall down the black stone stairs, I was quite as alone and in darkness as before. The windy stench, bad enough before, was now fiendish; yet I had acquired enough familiarity by this time to bear it stoically. Dazedly I began to crawl away from the place whence the putrid wind came, and with my bleeding hands felt the colossal blocks of a mighty pavement. Once my head struck against a hard object, and when I felt of it I learned that it was the base of a column—a column of unbelievable immensity—whose surface was covered with gigantic chiseled hieroglyphics very perceptible to my touch. Crawling on, I encountered other titan columns at incomprehensible distances apart; when suddenly my attention was captured by the realization of something which must have been impinging on my subconscious hearing long before the conscious sense was aware of it.

From some still lower chasm in earth's bowels were proceeding certain *sounds,* measured and definite, and like nothing I had ever heard before. That they were very ancient and distinctly ceremonial, I felt almost intuitively; and much reading in Egyptology led me to associate them with the flute, the sambuke, the sistrum, and the tympanum. In their rhythmic piping, droning, rattling, and beating I felt an element of terror beyond all the known terrors of earth—a terror peculiarly dissociated from personal fear, and taking the form of a sort of objective pity for our planet, that it should hold within its depths such horrors as must lie beyond these aegipanic cacophonies. The sounds increased in volume, and I felt that they were approaching. Then—and may all the gods of all pantheons unite to keep the like from my ears again—I began to hear, faintly and afar off, *the morbid and millennial tramping of the marching things.*

It was hideous that footfalls so *dissimilar* should move in such perfect rhythm. The training of unhallowed thousands of years must lie behind that march of earth's inmost monstrosities—padding, clicking, walking, stalking, rumbling, lumbering, crawling—and all to the abhorrent discords of those mocking instruments. And then ... God keep the memory of those Arab legends out of my head! The mummies without souls ... the meeting place of the wandering *kas* ... the hordes of the devil-cursed pharaonic dead of forty centuries ... the *composite mummies* led through the uttermost onyx voids by King Khephren and his ghoul-queen Nitokris.

The tramping drew nearer—heaven save me from the sound of those feet and paws and hooves and pads and talons as it commenced to acquire detail! Down limitless reaches of sunless pavement a spark of light flickered in the malodorous wind, and I drew behind the enormous circumference of a Cyclopic column that I might escape for a while the horror that was stalking million-footed toward me through gigantic hypostyles of inhuman dread and phobic antiquity. The flickers increased, and the tramping and dissonant rhythm grew sickeningly loud. In the quivering orange light there stood faintly forth a scene of such stony awe that I gasped from a sheer wonder that conquered even fear and repulsion. Bases of columns whose middles were higher than human sight ... mere bases of things that must each dwarf the Eiffel Tower to insignificance ... hieroglyphics carved by unthinkable hands in caverns where daylight can be only a remote legend.

I *would not* look at the marching things. That I desperately resolved as I heard their creaking joints and nitrous wheezing above the dead music and the dead tramping. It was merciful that they did not speak ... but, God! *Their crazy torches began to cast shadows on the surface of those stupendous columns.* Heaven take it away! *Hippopotami should not have human hands and carry torches ... men should not have the heads of crocodiles.*

I tried to turn away, but the shadows and the sounds and the stench were everywhere. Then I remembered something I used to do in half-conscious nightmares as a boy, and began to repeat to myself, "This is a dream! This is a dream!" But it was of no use, and I could only shut my eyes and pray ... at least, that is what I think I did, for one is never sure in visions—and I know this can have been nothing more. I wondered whether I should ever reach the world again, and at times would furtively open my eyes to see if I could discern any feature of the place other than the wind of spiced putrefaction, the topless columns, and the thaumatropically grotesque shadows of abnormal horror. The sputtering glare of multiplying torches now shone, and unless this hellish place were wholly without walls, I could not fail to see some boundary or fixed landmark soon. But I had to shut my eyes again when I realized *how many* of the things were assembling—and when I glimpsed a certain object walking solemnly and steadily *without any body above the waist.*

A fiendish and ululant corpse-gurgle or death rattle now split the very atmosphere—the charnel atmosphere poisonous with naphtha and bitumen blasts—in one concerted chorus from the ghoulish legion of hybrid blasphemies. My eyes, perversely shaken open, gazed for an instant upon a sight which no human creature could even imagine without panic fear and physical exhaustion. The things had filed ceremonially in one direction, the direction of the noisome wind, where the light of their torches shewed their bended heads ... or the bended heads of such as had heads ... They were worshipping before a great black foetor-belching aperture which reached up almost out of sight, and which I could see was flanked at right angles by two giant staircases whose ends were far away in shadow. One of these was indubitably the staircase I had fallen down.

The dimensions of the hole were fully in proportion with those of the columns—an ordinary house would have been lost in it, and any average public building could easily have been moved in and out. It was so vast a surface that only by moving the eye could one trace its boundaries ... so vast, so hideously black, and so aromatically stinking ... Directly in front of this yawning Polyphemus-door the things were throwing objects—evidently sacrifices or religious offerings, to judge by their gestures. Khephren was their leader; sneering King Khephren *or the guide Abdul Reis,* crowned with a golden pschent and intoning endless formulae with the hollow voice of the dead. By his side knelt beautiful Queen Nitokris, whom I saw in profile for a moment, noting that the right half of her face was eaten away by rats or other ghouls. And I shut my eyes again when I saw *what* objects were being thrown as offerings to the foetid aperture or its possible local deity.

It occurred to me that judging from the elaborateness of this worship, the concealed deity must be one of considerable importance. Was it Osiris or Isis, Horus or Anubis, or some vast unknown God of the Dead still more central and supreme? There is a legend that terrible altars and colossi were reared to an Unknown One before ever the known gods were worshipped.

And now, as I steeled myself to watch the rapt and sepulchral adorations of those nameless things, a thought of escape flashed upon me. The hall was dim, and the columns heavy with shadow. With every creature of that nightmare throng absorbed in shocking raptures, it might be barely possible for me to creep past to the faraway end of one of the staircases and ascend unseen; trusting to Fate and skill to deliver me from the upper reaches. Where I was, I neither knew nor seriously reflected upon—and for a moment it struck me as amusing to plan a serious escape from that which I knew to be a dream. Was I in some hidden and unsuspected lower realm of Khephren's gateway temple—that temple which generations have persistently called the Temple of the Sphinx? I could not conjecture, but I resolved to ascend to life and consciousness if wit and muscle could carry me.

Wriggling flat on my stomach, I began the anxious journey toward the foot of the left-hand staircase, which seemed the more accessible of the two. I cannot describe the incidents and sensations of that crawl, but they may be guessed when one reflects on *what I had to watch steadily in that malign, wind-blown torchlight* in order to avoid detection. The bottom of the staircase was, as I have said, far away in shadow; as it had to be to rise without a bend to the dizzy parapeted landing above the titanic aperture. This placed the last stages of my crawl at some distance from the noisome herd, though the spectacle chilled me even when quite remote at my right.

At length I succeeded in reaching the steps and began to climb; keeping close to the wall, on which I observed decorations of the most hideous sort, and relying for safety on the absorbed, ecstatic interest with which the monstrosities watched the foul-breezed aperture and the impious objects of nourishment they had flung on the pavement before it. Though the staircase was huge and steep, fashioned of vast porphyry blocks as if for the feet of a giant, the ascent seemed virtually interminable. Dread of discovery and the pain which renewed exercise had brought to my wounds combined to make that upward crawl a thing of agonizing memory. I had intended, on reaching the landing, to climb immediately onward along whatever upper staircase might mount from there; stopping for no last look at the carrion abominations that pawed and genuflected some seventy or eighty feet below— yet a sudden repetition of that thunderous corpse-gurgle and death-rattle chorus, coming as I had nearly gained the top of the flight and shewing by its ceremonial rhythm that it was not an alarm of my discovery, caused me to pause and peer cautiously over the parapet.

The monstrosities were hailing something which had poked itself out of the nauseous aperture to seize the hellish fare proffered it. It was something quite ponderous, even as seen from my height; something yellowish and hairy, and endowed with a sort of nervous motion. It was as large, perhaps, as a good-sized hippopotamus, but very curiously shaped. It seemed to have no neck, but five separate shaggy heads springing in a row from a roughly cylindrical trunk; the first very small, the second good-sized, the third and fourth equal and largest of all, and the fifth rather small, though not so small as the first. Out of these heads darted curious rigid tentacles which seized ravenously on the *excessively great* quantities of unmentionable food placed before the aperture. Once in a while the thing would leap up, and occasionally it would retreat into its den in a very odd manner. Its locomotion was so inexplicable that I stared in fascination, wishing it would emerge further from the cavernous lair beneath me.

Then it *did* emerge … it *did* emerge, and at the sight I turned and fled into the darkness up the higher staircase that rose behind me; fled unknowingly up incredible steps and ladders and inclined planes to which no human sight or logic guided me, and which I must ever relegate to the world of dreams for want of any confirmation. It must have been dream, or the dawn would never have found me breathing on the sands of Gizeh before the sardonic dawn-flushed face of the Great Sphinx.

The Great Sphinx! God!—that *idle question* I asked myself on that sun-blest morning before. *What huge and loathsome abnormality was the Sphinx originally carven to represent?* Accursed is the sight, be it in dream or not, that revealed to me the supreme horror—the Unknown God of the Dead, which licks its colossal chops in the unsuspected abyss, fed hideous morsels by soulless absurdities that should not exist. The five-headed monster that emerged … that five-headed monster as large as a hippopotamus … the five-headed monster—*and that of which it is the merest fore paw.*

But I survived, and I know it was only a dream.

THE THING OF A
THOUSAND SHAPES

OTIS ADELBERT KLINE

U ncle Jim was dead.

I could scarcely believe it, but the little yellow missive, which had just been handed to me by the Western Union messenger boy, left no room for doubt. It was short and convincing:

> *"Come to Peoria at once. James Braddock dead of heart failure.
> Corbin & His Attorneys."*

I should explain here that Uncle Jim, my mother's brother, was my only living near relative. Having lost both father and mother in the Iroquois Theatre Fire at the age of twelve years, I should have been forced to abandon my plans for a high school and commercial education but for his noble generosity. In his hometown he was believed to be comfortably well off, but I had learned not long since that it had meant a considerable sacrifice for him to furnish the fifteen hundred dollars a year to put me through high school and business college, and I was glad when the time came for me to find employment, and thus become independent of his bounty.

My position as bookkeeper for a commission firm in South Water Street, while not particularly remunerative, at least provided a comfortable living, and I was happy in it—until the message of his death came.

I took the telegram to my employer, obtained a week's leave-of-absence, and was soon on the way to the Union Depot.

All the way to Peoria I thought about Uncle Jim. He was not old —only forty-five—and when I had last seen him he had seemed particularly hale and hearty. This sudden loss of my nearest and dearest friend was, therefore, almost unbelievable. I carried a leaden weight in my heart, and it seemed that the lump in my throat would choke me.

Uncle Jim had lived on a three-hundred-and-twenty acre farm near Peoria. Being a bachelor, he had employed a housekeeper. The farm work was looked after by a family named Severs—man, wife and two sons—who lived in the tenant house, perhaps a thousand feet to the rear of the owner's residence, in convenient proximity to the barn, silos and other farm buildings.

As I have said, my uncle's neighbors believed him to be comfortably well off, but I knew the place was mortgaged to the limit, so that the income from the fertile acres was practically absorbed by overhead expenses and interest.

Had my uncle been a businessman in the true sense of the term, no doubt he could have been wealthy. But he was a scientist and dreamer, inclined to let the farm run itself while he devoted his time to study and research. His hobby was psychic phenomena. His thirst for more facts regarding the human mind was insatiable. In the pursuit of his favorite study, he had attended séances in this country and abroad with the leading spiritualists of the world.

He was a member of the London Society for Psychical Research, as well as the American Society, and corresponded regularly with noted scientists, psychologists and spiritualists. As an authority on psychic phenomena, he had contributed articles to the leading scientific publications from time to time, and was the author of a dozen well-known books on the subject.

Thus, grief-filled though I was, my mind kept presenting to me memory after memory of Uncle Jim's scientific attainments and scholarly life, while the rumbling car wheels left the miles behind; and the thought that such a man had been lost to me and to the world was almost unbearable.

I arrived in Peoria shortly before midnight, and was glad to find Joe Severs, son of my uncle's tenant, waiting for me with a flivver. After a five-mile ride in inky darkness over a rough road, we came to the farm.

I was greeted at the door by the housekeeper, Mrs. Rhodes, and one of two men, nearby neighbors, who had kindly volunteered to "set up" with the corpse. The woman's eyes were red with weeping, and her tears flowed afresh as she led me to the room where my uncle's body lay in a gray casket.

A dim kerosene lamp burned in one corner of the room, and after the silent watcher had greeted me with a handclasp and a sad shake of the head, I walked up to view the remains of my dearest friend on earth.

As I looked down on that noble, kindly face, the old lump, which had for a time subsided, came back in my throat. I expected tears, heartrending sobs, but they did not come. I seemed dazed —bewildered.

Suddenly, and apparently against my own reason, I heard myself saying aloud, "He is not dead—only sleeping."

When the watchers looked at me in amazement I repeated, "Uncle Jim is *not dead*! He is only sleeping."

Mrs. Rhodes looked compassionately at me, and by a meaning glance at the others said as plainly as if she had spoken, "His mind is affected."

She and Mr. Newberry, the neighbor whom I had first met, gently led me from the room. I was myself dumfounded at the words I had uttered, nor could I find a reason for them.

My uncle was undoubtedly dead, at least as far as this physical world was concerned. There was nothing about the appearance of the pale, rigid corpse to indicate life, and he had, without doubt, been pronounced dead by a physician. Why, then, had I made this unusual, uncalled for—in fact, ridiculous—statement? I did not know, I concluded that I must have been crazed with grief—beside myself for the moment.

I had announced my intention to keep watch with Mr. Newberry and the other neighbor, Mr. Glitch, but was finally prevailed upon to go to my room, on the ground that my nerves were overwrought and I must have rest. It was decided, therefore, that the housekeeper, who had scarcely slept a wink the night before, and I should retire, while the two neighbors alternately kept two hour watches, one sitting up while the other slept on a davenport near the fireplace.

Mrs. Rhodes conducted me to my room. I quickly undressed, blew out the kerosene light and got into bed. It was some time before I could compose myself for sleep, and I remember that just as I was dozing off I seemed to hear my name pronounced as if someone were calling me from a great distance:

"Billy!" and then, in the same far-away voice: "Save me, Billy!"

I had slept for perhaps fifteen minutes when I awoke with a start. Either I was dreaming, or something about the size and shape of a half-grown conger eel was creeping across my bed.

For the moment I was frozen with horror, as I perceived the white, nameless thing, in the dim light from my window. With a convulsive movement I threw the bedclothes from me, leaped to the floor, struck a match, and quickly lit the lamp. Then, taking my heavy walking stick in hand, I advanced on the bed.

Moving the bed clothing cautiously with the stick and prodding here and there, I at length discovered that the thing was gone. The door was closed, there was no transom, and the window was screened. I therefore concluded that it must still be in the room.

With this thought in mind, I carefully searched every inch of space, looking under and behind the furniture, with the lamp in one hand and stick in the other. I then removed all the bedding and opened the dresser drawers, and found—nothing!

After completely satisfying myself that the animal I had seen, or perhaps seemed to see, could not possibly be in the room I decided that I had been suffering from a nightmare, and again retired. Because of my nervousness from the experience, I did not again blow out the light, but instead turned it low.

After a half hour of restless turning and tossing, I succeeded in going to sleep; this time for possibly twenty minutes, when I was once more aroused. The same feeling of horror came over me, as I distinctly heard a rolling, scraping sound beneath my bed. I kept perfectly still and waited while the sound went on. Something was apparently creeping underneath my bed, and it seemed to be moving toward the foot, slowly and laboriously.

Stealthily I sat up, leaned forward and peered over the footboard. The sounds grew more distinct, and a white, round mass, which looked like a porcupine rolled into a ball with bristles projecting, emerged from under my bed. I uttered a choking cry of fright, and the thing *disappeared before my eyes!*

Without waiting to search the room further, I leaped from the bed to the spot nearest the door, wrenched it open, and started on a run for the living room, attired only in pajamas. As I neared the room, however, part of my lost courage came back to me, and I slowed down to a walk. I reasoned that precipitate entrance into the room would arouse the household, and that possibly, after all, I was only the victim of a second nightmare. I resolved, therefore, to say nothing to the watchers about my experience, but to tell them only that I was unable to sleep and had come down for company.

Newberry met me at the door.

"Why what's the matter?" he asked, "You look pale. Anything wrong?"

"Nothing but a slight attack of indigestion. Couldn't sleep, so I came down for company."

"You should have brought a dressing gown or something. You may take cold."

"Oh, I feel quite comfortable enough," I said. Newberry stirred the logs in the fireplace to a blaze, and we moved our chairs close to the flickering circle of warmth. The dim light was still burning in the corner of the room, and Glitch was snoring on the davenport.

"Funny thing," said Newberry, "the instructions your uncle left."

"Instructions? What instructions?" I asked.

"Why, didn't you know? But of course you didn't. He left written instructions with Mrs. Rhodes that in case of his sudden death his body was not to be embalmed, packed in ice, or preserved in any way, and that it was not to be buried under any consideration, until decomposition had set in. He also ordered that no autopsy should be held until it had been definitely decided that putrefaction had taken place."

"Have these instructions been carried out?" I asked.

"To the letter," he replied.

"And how long will it take for putrefaction to set in?"

"The doctors say it will probably be noticed in twenty-four hours."

I reflected on this strange order of my uncle's. It seemed to me that he must have feared being buried alive, or something of the sort, and I recalled several instances, of which I had heard, where bodies, upon being exhumed, were found turned over in their coffins, while others had apparently torn their hair and clawed the lid in their efforts to escape from a living tomb.

I was beginning to feel sleepy again and had just started to doze, when Newberry grasped my arm.

"Look!" he exclaimed, pointing toward the body.

I looked quickly and seemed to see something white for an instant, near the nostrils.

"Did you see it?" he asked breathlessly.

"See what?" I replied, wishing to learn if he had seen the same thing I had.

"I saw something white, like a thick vapor or filmy veil, come out of his nose. When I spoke to you it seemed to jerk back. Didn't you see it?"

"Thought I saw a white flash there when you spoke, but it must have been imagination."

The time had now arrived for Glitch to watch, so my companion awakened him, and they exchanged places. Newberry was soon asleep, and Glitch, being a stoical German, said little. I presently became drowsy, and was asleep in my chair in a short time.

A cry from Glitch brought me to my feet. "Vake up and help catch der cat!"

"What cat?" demanded Newberry, also awakening.

"Der big vite cat," said Glitch, visibly excited. "Chust now he came der door through and yumped der coffin in."

The three of us rushed to the coffin, but there was no sign of a cat, and everything seemed undisturbed.

"Dot's funny," said Glitch. "Maybe it's hiding someveres in der room."

We searched the room, without result.

"You've been seeing things," said Newberry.

"What did the animal look like?" I asked.

"Vite, und big as a dog. It kommt der door in, so, und galloped across der floor, so, und yumped in der casket chust like dot. It vos a fierce-looking beast."

Glitch was very much in earnest and gesticulated rapidly as he described the appearance and movements of the feline. Perhaps I should have felt inclined to laugh, had it not been for my own experience that night. I noticed, too, that Newberry's expression was anything but jocular.

It was now nearly four o'clock, time for Newberry to watch, but Glitch protested that he could not sleep another wink, so the three of us drew chairs up close to the fire. On each side of the fireplace was a large window. The shades were completely drawn and the windows were draped with heavy lace curtains. Happening to look up at the window to the left, I noticed something of a mouse-gray color hanging near the top of one of the curtains. As I looked, I fancied I saw a slight movement as of a wing being stretched a bit and then folded, and the thing took on the appearance of a large vampire bat, hanging upside down.

I called the attention of my companions to our singular visitor, and both saw it as plainly as I.

"How do you suppose he got in?" asked Newberry.

"Funny ve didn't see him before," said Glitch.

I picked up the fire tongs and Newberry seized the poker.

Creeping softly up to the curtain, I stood on tiptoe and reached up to seize the animal with the tongs. It was too quick for me, however, and fluttered out of my reach. There followed a chase around the room. Which lasted several minutes. Seeing that it would be impossible for us to capture the creature by this method, we gave up the chase, whereupon it calmed down and suspended itself from the picture molding, upside down.

On seeing this, Glitch, who had taken a heavy book from the table, hurled it at our unwelcome visitor. His aim was good, and the thing uttered a *squeak* as it was crushed against the wall.

At this moment I thought I heard a moan from the direction of the casket, but could not be certain.

Newberry and I rushed over to where the book had fallen, intent on dispatching the thing with poker and thongs, but only the book lay on the floor. The creature had *completely disappeared.*

I picked up the book, and noticed, as I did so, a grayish smear on the back cover. Taking this over to the light, we saw that it had a soapy appearance. As we looked the substance apparently became absorbed. Either by the atmosphere or into the cloth cover of the book. There remained, however, a dry, white, faintly defined splotch on the book cover.

"What do you make of it?" I asked them.

"Strange!" said Newberry.

I turned to Glitch, and noticed for the first time that his eyes were wide with fear. He shook his head and cast furtive glances toward the casket.

"What do *you* think it is?" I asked.

"A vampire, maybe. A *real* vampire."

"What do you mean by a real vampire?"

Glitch then described how, in the folklore of his native land, there were stories current of corpses which lived on in the grave. It was believed that the spirits of these corpses assumed the form of huge vampire bats at night, and went about sucking the blood of living persons, with which they would return to the grave from time to time and nourish the corpse. This proceeding was kept up indefinitely, unless the corpse were exhumed and a stake driven through the heart.

He related, in particular, the story of a Hungarian named Arnold Paul, whose body was dug up after it had been buried forty days. It was found that his cheeks were flushed with blood, and that his hair, beard and nails had grown in the grave. When the stake was driven through his heart, he had uttered a frightful shriek and a torrent of blood gushed from his mouth.

The vampire story seized on my imagination in a peculiar way. I thought again of my uncle's strange request regarding the disposition of his body, and of the strange apparitions I had seen. For the moment I was a convert to the vampire theory.

My better judgment, however, soon convinced me that there could not be such a thing as a vampire, and, even if there were, a man whose character had been so noble as that of my deceased uncle would most certainly never resort to such hideous and revolting practices.

We sat together in silence as the first faint streaks of dawn showed in the east. A few minutes later the welcome aroma of coffee and frying bacon greeted our nostrils, and Mrs. Rhodes came into announce that breakfast was ready.

After breakfast, my newly made friends departed for their homes, both assuring me that they would be glad to come and watch with me again that night.

However, I read something in the uneasy manner of Glitch which led me to believe that I could not count on him, and I was, therefore, not greatly surprised when he telephoned me an hour later, stating that his wife was ill, and that he would not be able to come.

I strolled outdoors to enjoy a cigar, comforted by the rays of the morning sun after my night's experience.

It was pleasant, I reflected, to be once more in the realm of the natural, to see the trees attired in the autumn foliage, to feel the rustle of fallen leaves underfoot, to fill my lungs with the spicy, invigorating October air.

A gray squirrel scampered across my pathway, his cheek pouches bulging with acorns. A flock of blackbirds, migrating southward, stopped for a few moments in the trees above my head, chattering vociferously; then resumed their journey with a sudden *whirr* of wings and a few hoarse notes of farewell.

"It is but a step," I reflected, "from the natural to the supernatural."

This observation started a new line of thought. After all, could anything be supernatural—above nature? Nature, according to my belief, was only another name for God, eternal mind, omnipotent, omnipresent, omniscient ruler of the universe. If He were omnipotent, could anything take place contrary to His laws? Obviously not.

The word "supernatural" was, after all, only an expression invented by man in his finite ignorance, to define those things which he did not understand. Telegraphy, telephony, the phonograph, the moving picture—all would have been regarded with superstition by an age less advanced than ours. Man had only to become familiar with the laws governing them, in order to discard the word "supernatural" as applied to their manifestations.

What right, then, had I to term the phenomena, which I had just witnessed, supernatural? I might call them supernormal, but to think of them as supernatural would be to believe the impossible: namely, that that which is all-powerful had been overpowered.

I resolved, then and there, that if further phenomena manifested themselves that night, I would, as far as it were possible, curb my superstition and fear, regard them with the eye of a philosopher, and endeavor to learn their cause, which must necessarily be governed by natural law.

A gray cloud of dust and the whirring of a motor announced the coming of an automobile. The next minute an ancient flivver, with whose bumps of eccentricity I had gained some acquaintance, turned into the driveway and stopped opposite me. Joe Severs, older son of my uncle's tenant, stepped out and came running toward me.

"Glitch's wife died this morning," he panted, "and he swears Mr. Braddock is a vampire and sucked her blood."

"What rot!" I replied. "Nobody believes him, of course?"

"I ain't so sure of that," said Joe. "Some of the farmers are takin' it mighty serious. One of the Langdon boys, first farm north of here, was took sick this mornin'. Doctor don't know what's the matter of him. Folks say it looks mighty queer."

Mrs. Rhodes appeared on the front porch.

"A telephone call for you, sir," she said.

I hastened to the phone. A woman was speaking.

"This is Mrs. Newberry," she said. "My husband is dreadfully ill, and asked me to tell you that he cannot come to sit up with you tonight."

I thanked the lady, offered my condolences, and tendered my sincere wishes for her husband's speedy recovery. This done, I wrote a note of sympathy to Mr. Glitch, and dispatched Joe with it.

Here, indeed, was a pretty situation. Glitch's wife dead, Newberry seriously ill, and the whole countryside frightened by this impossible vampire story! I knew it would be useless to ask any of the other neighbors to keep watch with me. Obviously, I was destined to face the terrors of the coming night alone. Was I equal to the task? Could my nerves, already unstrung by the previous night's experience, withstand the ordeal?

I must confess, and not without a feeling of shame, that at this juncture I felt impelled to flee, anywhere, and leave my deceased uncle's affairs to shape themselves as they would.

With this idea in mind, I repaired to my room and started to pack my grip. Something fell to the floor. It was my uncle's last letter, received only the day before the telegram arrived announcing his death. I hesitated—then picked it up and opened it. The last paragraph held my attention:

"And, Billy, my boy, don't worry any more about the money I advanced you. It was, as you say, a considerable drain of my resources, but I gave it willingly, gladly, for the education of my sister's son. My only regret is that I could not have done more.

Affectionately
Uncle Jim."

A flush of guilt came over me. The reproach of my conscience was keen and painful. I had been about to commit a cowardly, dishonorable deed.

"Thank God, for the accidental intervention of that letter," I said fervently.

My resolution was firmly made now; I would see the thing through at all costs. The noble love, the generous self-sacrifice of my uncle, should not go unrequited.

I quickly unpacked my bag and walked downstairs. The rest of the day was uneventful, but the night—how I dreaded the coming of the night! As I stood on the porch and watched the last faint glow of the sunset slowly fading, I wished that I, liked Joshua, might cause the sun and moon to stand still.

Twilight came on all too quickly, accelerated by a bank of heavy clouds which appeared on the western horizon; and darkness succeeded twilight with unwanted rapidity.

I entered the house and trod the hallway leading to the living room, with much the same feeling, no doubt, that a convict experiences when entering the death cell.

The housekeeper was just placing the lamp, freshly cleaned and filled, in the room. Joe Severs's younger brother, Sam, had placed logs in the fireplace, with kindling and paper beneath them, ready for lighting. Mrs. Rhodes bade me a kindly "Goodnight, sir," and departed noiselessly.

At last the dreaded moment had arrived. I was alone with the nameless powers of darkness.

I shuddered involuntarily. A damp chill pervaded the air, and I ignited the kindling beneath the logs in the fireplace. Then, drawing the shades to shut out the pitch blackness of the night, I lighted my pipe and stood in the warm glow.

Under the genial influence of pipe and warmth, my feeling of fear was temporarily dissipated. Taking a book from the library table, I settled down to read. It was called "The Reality of Materialization Phenomena," and had been written by my uncle. The publishers were Bulwer & Sons, New York and London.

It was apparently a record of the observations made by my uncle at materialization séances in this country and Europe. Contrary to my usual custom on starting a book, I read the author's introduction. He began by expressing the wish that those who might read the work should first lay aside all prejudice and all preconceived ideas regarding the subject, which were not based on positive knowledge, then weigh the facts as he had found them before drawing a definite conclusion.

The following passage, in particular, held my attention:

"While it is to be admitted, with regret, that there are many people calling themselves mediums, who deceive their sitters nightly and whose productions are consequently mere optical illusions, produced my chicanery and legerdemain, the writer has nevertheless gathered, at the sittings recorded in this book, where all possibility of fraud was excluded by rigorous examination and control, undeniable evidence that genuine materialization are, and can be, produced.

"The source and physical composition—if indeed it be physical— of a phantasm materialized by a true medium, remains up to the present time, inexplicable. That such manifestations are not hallucinations, has been proved time and again by taking photographs One would indeed be compelled to strain his credulity to the utmost, were he to believe that a mere hallucination could be photographed.

"As I have stated, the exact nature and source of the phenomena are apparently inscrutable; however, it is a notable fact that the strongest manifestations take place when the medium is in a state of catalepsy, or suspended animation. Her hands are cold—her body becomes rigid—her eyes, if open, appear to be fixed on space—"

A roll of thunder, quickly followed by a rush of wind, rudely interrupted my reading. The housekeeper appeared in the doorway, lamp in hand.

"Would you mind helping me close the windows, sir?" she asked. "There is a big rainstorm coming, and they must be closed quickly, or the furnishings and wall paper will be soaked."

Together we ascended the stairs. I rushed from window to window, while she lighted the way with the dim lamp. This duty attended to, she again bade me "Goodnight," and I returned to the living room.

As I entered, I glanced at the casket, and then looked again while a feeling of horror crept over me. Either I was dreaming, or it had been completely draped with a white sheet during my absence.

I rubbed my eyes, pinched myself, and advanced to confirm the evidence of my eyesight by the sense of touch. As I extended my hand, the center of the sheet rose in a sharp peak, as if lifted by some invisible presence, and the entire fabric traveled upward toward the ceiling. I drew back with a cry of dread, watching it with perhaps the same fascination that is experienced by a doomed bird or animal looking into the eyes of a serpent that is about to devour it.

The point touched the ceiling. There was a crash of thunder, accompanied by a blinding flash of lightning which illuminated the room through the sides of the ill-fitting window shades, and I found myself staring at the bare ceiling.

Walking dazedly to the fireplace, I poked the logs until they blazed, and then sat down to collect my thoughts. Torrents of rain were beating against the windowpanes. Thunder roared and lightning flashed incessantly.

I took up my pipe and was about to light it when a strange sight interrupted me. Something round and flat, about six inches in diameter, and of a grayish color, was moving along the floor from the casket toward the center of the room. I watched it, fascinated, while the blood seemed to congeal in my veins. It did not roll or slide along the floor, but seemed rather to *flow* forward.

It reminded me, more than anything else, of an amoeba, one of those microscopic, unicellular animalcule which I had examined in the study of zoology. An amoeba magnified perhaps, several million diameters. I could plainly see it put forth projections resembling pseudopods, from time to time, and again withdraw them quickly in the body mass.

The lighted match burned my fingers, and I dropped it on the hearth. In the meantime the creature had reached the center of the room and stopped. A metamorphosis was now taking place before my eyes. To my surprise, I beheld, in place of a magnified amoeba, a gigantic trilobite, larger, it is true, than any specimen which has ever been found, but, nevertheless, true to form in every detail.

The trilobite, in turn, changed to a brilliantly hued starfish with active wriggling tentacles. The starfish became a crab, and the crab, a porpoise swimming about in the air as if it had been water. The porpoise then became a huge green lizard that crawled about the floor.

Soon the lizard grew large webbed wings, its tail shortened, its jaws lengthened out with a pelican-like pouch beneath them, and its body seemed partially covered with scales of a rusty black color. I afterward learned that this was a phantasmic representation of a pterodactyl, or prehistoric flying reptile. To me, in my terrified condition, it looked like a creature from hell.

The thing stood erect, stretched its wings and beat the air as if to try them; then rose and circled twice about the room, flapping lazily like a heron, and once more alighted in the middle of the floor.

It folded its wings carefully, and I noticed many new changes taking place. The scales were becoming feathers—the legs lengthened out and were encased in a thick, scaly, skin. The claws thickened into two-toed feet, like those of an ostrich. The head also looked ostrich-like, while the wings were shortened and feathered but not plumed. The bird was much larger than any ostrich or emu I have ever seen, and stalked about majestically, its head nearly touching the ceiling.

Soon it, too, stopped in the center of the room—the neck grew shorter and shorter—the feathers became fur—the wings lengthened into arms which reached below the knees, and I was face to face with a huge, gorilla-like creature. It roared horribly, casting quick glances about the room, its deep-set eyes glowing like coals of fire.

I felt that my end had come, but could make no move to escape. I wanted to get up and leap through the window, but my nerveless limbs would not function. As I looked, the fur on the creature turned to a thin covering of hair, and it began to assume a manlike form. I closed my eyes and shuddered.

When I opened them a moment later, I beheld what might have been the "missing link," half man, half beast. The face, with its receding forehead and beetling brows, was apelike and yet manlike. Wrapped about its loins was a large tiger skin. In its right hand it brandished a huge, knotted club.

Gradually it became more manlike and less ape-like. The club changed to a spear, the spear to a sword, and I beheld a Roman soldier, fully accoutered for battle with helmet, armor, target and sandals.

The Roman soldier became a knight, and the knight a musketeer. The musketeer became a colonial soldier.

At that instant there was a crash of glass, and the branch of a tree projected through the windows on the right of the fireplace. The shade flew up with a snap and the soldier disappeared, as a brilliant flash of lightning illuminated the room.

I rushed to the window, and saw that the overhanging limb of an elm had been broken off by the wind and hurled through the glass. The rain was coming in in torrents.

The housekeeper, who had heard the noise, appeared in the doorway. Seeing the rain blowing in at the window, she left and returned a moment later with a hammer, tacks and a folded sheet. I tacked the sheet to the window frame with difficulty, on account of the strong wind, and again pulled down the shade.

Mrs. Rhodes retired.

I consulted my watch. It lacked just one minute of midnight.

Only half of the night gone! Would I be strong enough to endure the other half?

The storm slowly abated, and finally died down altogether, succeeded by a dead calm.

An hour passed without incident, to my inestimable relief. I believed that the phenomena had passed with the storm. The thought soothed me. I became drowsy, and was soon asleep.

Fitful dreams disturbed my slumber. It seemed that I was walking in a great primeval forest. The trees and vegetation about me were new and strange. Huge ferns, some of them fifty feet in height, grew all about in rank profusion. Under foot was a soft carpet of moss.

Giant fungi, colossal toadstools, and mushrooms of varying shades and forms were everywhere.

In my hand I carried a huge knotted club, and my sole article of clothing seemed to be a tiger skin, girded about my waist and falling half way to my knees.

A queer-looking creature, half rhinoceros, half horse, ran across my pathway. Following closely behind it, in hot pursuit was a huge reptilian monster, in outline something like a kangaroo, in size larger than the largest elephant. Its monstrous serpent-like head towered more than twenty-five feet in the air as it suddenly stopped and stood erect on its hind feet and tail, apparently giving up the chase.

Then it spied me. Quick as a flash, I turned and ran, dodging hither and thither, floundering in the soft moss, stumbling over tangled vines and occasionally overturning a mammoth toadstool. I could hear the horrible beast crashing through the fern brakes, only a short distance behind me.

At last I came to a rocky hillside, and saw an opening about two feet in diameter. Into this I plunged headlong, barely in time to escape the frightful jaws which closed behind me with a terrifying snap. I lay on the ground, panting for breath, in the far corner of the cave and just out of reach of the ferocious monster. It appeared to be trying to widen the opening with its huge front feet.

Someone had laid a hand on my arm and was gently trying to awaken me. The cave and the horrible reptile disappeared, and I was again in my uncle's living room. I turned, expecting to see Mrs. Rhodes, but saw no one.

There was, however, a hand on my arm. It ended at the wrist in a sort of indescribable, filmy mass. I was now fully awake, and somewhat startled, as may be imagined. The hand withdrew and seemed to float through the air to the other side of the room.

I now observed in the room a sort of white vapor, from which other hands were forming. Soon there were hands of all descriptions and sizes. They were constantly in motion, some of them flexing the fingers as if to try the newly formed muscles, others beckoning, and still others clasped in pairs, as if in greeting.

There were large, horny masculine hands, daintily formed womanly hands, and active, chubby little hands like those of children. Some of them were perfectly modeled. Others, apparently in the process of formation, looked like floating bits of chiffon, while still others had the appearance of flat, empty gloves.

Two well-developed hands now emerged from the mass and moved a few feet toward me. They waved as if attempting to attract my attention, and then I could see they were forming letters of the deaf and dumb alphabet. They spelled my name: "B-I-L-L-Y."

Then: "S-A-V-E M-E B-I-L-L-Y."

I managed to ask, "Who are you?"

The hands spelled: "I A-M—"

Then they were withdrawn, with a jerk, into the group.

I could now see a new transformation taking place. The hands were drawn together, dissolving into a white, irregular fluted column, surmounted by a dark, hairy looking mass. A bearded face seemed to be forming at the top of the column, which was now widening out considerably, taking on the semblance of a human form. In a moment a white-robed figure stood there, the eyes turned upward and inward as if in fear and supplication, the arms extended toward me.

The apparition began slowly to advance in my direction. It seemed to glide along as if suspended in the air. There was no movement of walking, just a slow, floating motion.

The phantom, when at the other end of the room, had seemed frightful enough, but to see it coming toward me was unnerving—terrifying. The nearer it approached, the more horrible it seemed, and the more firmly I appeared rooted to the spot.

Soon it was towering above me. The eyes rolled downward and seemed to look through mine into my very brain. The arms were extended to encircle me, when the instinct of self-preservation came to my rescue.

I acted quickly, and apparently without volition. Overturning my chair and rushing from the room, I ran out the front door and down the pathway. I did not dare look back, but rushed blindly forth into the night.

Suddenly there was a brilliant glare of light. Something stuck me with considerable force, and I lost consciousness.

When I regained my senses I was lying in a bedroom, the room I had occupied in my uncle's house.

A beautiful girl was bending over me, bathing my fevered forehead from time to time with cold water. Sunlight was streaming in at the window. Outside, a robin was singing his morning song, his farewell to the Northland, no doubt, as the stinging snow-laden winds of winter must soon drive him southward.

I attempted to sit up, but sank back with a groan, as a sharp pain shot through my right side.

My fair attendant laid a soft hand on my brow.

"You mustn't do that again," she said. "The telephone wires are down, so father has driven to town for the doctor."

Memories of the night returned. The apparition—my rush down the pathway—the blinding light—the sudden shock—and then oblivion.

"Do you mind telling me," I asked, "what it was that knocked me out, and how you came so suddenly to my rescue?"

"It was our car that knocked you out," she replied, "and it was no more than right that I should do what I could to make you comfortable until the doctor arrives."

"Please tell me your name—won't you?—and how it all happened."

"My name is Ruth Randall. My father is Albert Randall, dean of the local college. We had motored to Indianapolis, intending to spend the weekend with friends, when we were notified of your uncle's death. He and my father were bosom friends, and together conducted many experiments in psychical research. Naturally we hurried home at once, in order to attend the funeral.

"We expected to make Peoria by midnight, but the storm came, and the roads soon were almost impassable. It was only by putting on chains and running at low speed most of the time that we were able to make any progress. Just as we were passing this house, you rushed in front of the car.

"Father says it is fortunate that we were compelled to run at low speed, otherwise you would have been instantly killed. We brought you to the door and aroused the housekeeper, who helped us get you to your room. Father tried to phone for a doctor, but it was no use, as the lines were torn down by the storm, so he drove to town for one. I think that is he coming now. I hear a motor in the driveway."

A few moments later two men entered—Professor Randall, tall, thin, slightly stooped, and pale of face, and Doctor Rush of medium height and rather portly. The doctor wore glasses with very thick lenses, through which he seemed almost to glare at me. He lost no time in taking my pulse and temperature, pushing the pocket thermometer into my mouth with one hand, and seizing my wrist with the other.

He removed the thermometer from my mouth, then, holding it up to the light and squinting for a moment said "Humph," and proceeded to paw me over in search of broken bones. When he started manhandling my right side I winced considerably. He presently located a couple of fractured ribs.

After a painful half-hour, during which the injured ribs were set, he left me with instructions to keep as still as possible, and let nature do the rest.

The professor lingered for a moment and I asked him to have Doctor Rush examine my uncle's body for signs of decomposition, as it was now more than three days since his death.

Miss Randall, who had left the room during the examination, came in just as her father was leaving, and said nice, sweet, sympathetic things, and fluffed up my pillow for me and smoothed back my hair; and if the doctor had taken my pulse at that moment he would have sworn my auricles and ventricles were racing each other for the world's championship.

"After all," I thought, "having one's ribs broken is not such an unpleasant experience."

Then her father, entered—and my thoughts were turned into new channels.

"Doctor Rush has made a thorough examination," he said, "and can find absolutely no sign of decomposition on your uncle's body. He frankly admits that he is puzzled by this condition, and that it is a case entirely outside his previous experience. He states that, from the condition of the corpse, he would have been led to believe that death took place only a few hours ago."

"If you can spare the time," I said, "and if it is not asking too much, I should like to have you spend the day with me. I have much to tell you, and many strange things have happened on which I sorely need your advice and assistance. Joe Severs can take the doctor home."

The professor kindly consented to stay, and his daughter went downstairs to locate Joe and his flivver.

"The things of which I am about to tell you," I began, "may seem like the visions of an opium eater, or the hallucinations of a deranged mind. In fact, they have even made me doubt my own sanity. However, I must tell someone, and as you are an old and valued friend of my uncle's, I feel that whether or not you accept my story as a verity you will be a sympathetic listener, and can offer some explanation—if, indeed, it be possible to explain such singular happenings."

I then related in detail everything that had happened since my arrival at the farm up to the moment when I rushed head long in front of his automobile.

He listened attentively, but whether he believed my narrative or not I could not tell. When I had finished, he asked many questions about the various phenomena I had witnessed, and seemed particularly interested when I told him about the disappearance of the bat. He asked me where the book, which had been used to dispatch the creature, might be found, and immediately went downstairs, bringing it up a moment later.

A dry, white smudge was still faintly discernible on the cover. This he examined carefully with a pocket microscope, then said: "I will have to put this substance under a compound microscope, and also test it chemically in my laboratory. It may be the means of explaining all of the phenomena you have witnessed. I will drive home this afternoon and make a thorough examination of this sample."

"I should be very glad indeed," I replied, "to have even some slight explanation of these mysteries."

"You are undoubtedly aware," he said "that there are no vampires or similar bats indigenous to this part of the world. The only true vampire bat is found in South America, although there is a type of frugivorous bat slightly resembling it, which inhabits the southeast coast of Asia and Malayan Archipelago, and is sometimes erroneously called a vampire or spectre bat. You have described in detail a creature greatly resembling the true vampire bat, but it is probable that what you saw was no bat at all. What it really was, I hesitate to say until I have examined the substance on this book cover."

"Well, whatever it was, I am positive it was no real vampire, as Glitch says," I replied.

"I don't like this vampire story that is being circulated by Glitch," said the professor. "It may lead to trouble. It is most surprising to find such crude superstition prevailing in these modern times."

At this juncture there was a rap at my door. I called, "come in," and Joe Severs entered.

"Well, Joe, did you get the doctor home without shaking any of his teeth loose?" I asked.

"Yes, sir, I got him home all right, but that ain't what I come to tell you about," he replied. "There's a heap of trouble brewin' around these parts an' I thought I better let you know. Somebody's sick in nearly every family in the neighborhood, an' they're sayin' Mr. Braddock is the cause of it. They're holdin' an indignation meetin' up to the school house now."

"This is indeed serious," said the professor. "Do you know what they propose to do about it?"

"Can't say as to that, but they're sure some riled up about it," replied Joe.

Mrs. Rhodes came in with my luncheon, and announced to the professor that Miss Ruth awaited him in the dining room below, whereupon he begged to be excused. Joe went out murmuring something about having to feed the horses, and I was left alone to enjoy a very tasty meal.

A half hour later the housekeeper came in to remove the dishes, and Miss Randall brought me a huge bouquet of autumn daisies.

"Father has driven to town to analyze a sample of something or other that he has found," she said, "and in the meantime I will do my best to make the hours pass pleasantly for you. What do you want me to do? Shall I read to you?"

"By all means," I replied. "Read or talk, or do anything you like. I assure you I am not hard to amuse."

"I think I shall read," she decided. "What do you prefer? Fiction, history, mythology, philosophy? Or perhaps," she added, "you prefer poetry."

"I will leave the selection entirely to you," I said. "Read what interests you, and I will be interested."

"Don't be too sure of that," she answered, and went down to my uncle's library.

She returned a few moments later with several volumes. From a book of Scott's poems, she chose "Rokeby" and soon we were conveyed, as if by a magic carpet, to medieval Yorkshire with its moated castles, dense forests, sparkling streams, jutting crags and enchanted dells.

She had finished the poem, and we were chatting gaily, when Mrs. Rhodes entered.

"A small boy brought this note for you, sir," she said, handing me a sealed envelope.

I tore it open carelessly, then read:

"Mr. William Ansley.

Dear Sir:

"Owing to the fact that at least one member of nearly every family in this community has been smitten with peculiar malady, in some instances fatal, since the death of James Braddock, and in view of the undeniable evidence that the corpse of the aforesaid had become a vampire, proven by certain things which you, in company with two respected and veracious neighbors witnessed, an indignation meeting was held today, attended by more than one hundred residents, for the purpose of discussing ways and means of combating this terrible menace to the community.

"Tradition tells us that there are two effective ways for disposing of a vampire. One is by burning the corpse of the offender; the other is by burial with a stake driven through the heart. We have decided on the latter as the simpler and more easily carried out.

"You are therefore directed to convey the corpse to the pine grove which is situated a half mile back from the road on your uncle's farm, where you will find a grave ready dug, and six men who will see that the body is properly interred. You have until eight o'clock this evening to carry out these instructions.

"To refuse to do as directed will avail you nothing. IF YOU DO NOT BRING THE BODY WE WILL COME AND GET IT. If you offer resistance, you do so at your peril, as we are armed, and we mean business.

THE COMMITTEE.

P.S. No use to try to telephone or send a messenger for help. Your wires are out of commission and the house is surrounded by armed sentinels."

As the professor had predicted, this was indeed a most serious turn of events. I turned to Mrs. Rhodes.

"Where is the bearer of this letter?' I asked. "Did he wait for a reply?"

"It was given to me by a small boy," she answered. "He said that if you wished to reply, to put your letter in the mail-box, and it would be given to the right party. There was a closed automobile waiting for him in front of the house, and he ran back to it and was driven away at high speed."

"I must dress and go downstairs at once," I said.

"You must do no such thing," replied Miss. Randall. "The doctor's orders are that you must keep perfectly quiet until your ribs heal."

I heard a swift footfall on the stairs, and a moment later the professor entered the room, very much excited.

"Two farmers," he said, "poked shotguns in my face and searched me on the public highway. That's what just happened to me!"

"What do you suppose they were after?" I asked.

"They did not make themselves clear on that point, and they didn't take anything, so I am at a loss to explain their conduct. They merely stopped me, felt through my pockets and searched the car; then told me to drive on."

"Perhaps this will throw some light on their motive," I said, handing him the letter.

As he read it a look of surprise came over his face.

"Ah! It is quite plain, now. These were the armed guards mentioned in the postscript. It seems incredible that such superstition should prevail in this enlightened age; however, the evidence is quite too plain to be questioned. What is to be done?"

"Frankly, I don't know," I replied. "We are evidently so well watched that it would be impossible for anyone to go for help. Of course, they cannot harm my deceased uncle by driving a stake through the corpse, but to permit these barbarians to carry out their purpose would be to desecrate the memory of the best friend I ever had."

"What are they going to do?" asked Miss Randall in alarm. I handed her the letter. She read it hastily, then ran downstairs to see if the telephone was working.

"What would you say if I were to tell you there is a strong possibility that your uncle's body is not a corpse; or, in other words, that he is not really dead?" asked the professor.

"I would say that if there is the slightest possibility of that, they will make a corpse of me before they stage this vampire funeral," I replied, starting to dress.

"I am with you in that," said he, extending his hand, "and now let us examine the evidence."

"By all means," I answered.

"According to the belief of most modern psychologists," he began, "every human being is endowed with two minds. Ones is usually termed the objective, or conscious mind, the other the subjective, or subconscious mind. Some call it the subliminal consciousness. The former controls our waking hours, the latter is dominant when we are asleep.

"You are, no doubt, familiar with the functions and powers of the objective mind, so we will not discuss them. The powers of the subjective mind, which are not generally known or recognized, are what chiefly concern us in this instance.

"My belief that your uncle is not really dead started when I first heard your story. It was later substantiated by two significant facts. I will take up the various points in their logical order, and you may judge for yourself as to whether or not my hypothesis is fully justified.

"First, upon seeing him lying in the casket, you involuntarily exclaimed, 'He is not dead, only sleeping.' This apparently absurd statement, unsubstantiated by objective evidence, was undoubtedly prompted by your subjective mind. One of the best known powers of the subjective mind is that of telepathy, the communication of thoughts or ideas from mind to mind, without the employment of physical means. This message was apparently impressed so strongly on your subjective mind that you spoke it aloud, automatically, almost without the subjective knowledge that you were talking. Assuming that it was a telepathic message, it must necessarily have been projected by some other mind. May we not, therefore, reasonably suppose that the message came from the subjective mind of you uncle?

"Then the second message. Was it not plainly from someone who knew you intimately, someone in dire need? You will recall that, just before you fell asleep, you seemed to hear the words, 'Billy! Save me, Billy.'

"And now, as to the phenomena: I must confess that I was somewhat in doubt, at first, regarding these. Not that I questioned your veracity in the least, for no man rushed blindly in front of a moving automobile without sufficient cause, but the sights which you witnessed were so striking and unusual that I felt sure they must have been hallucinations. On second thought, however, I decided that it would be quite out of the ordinary for you and two other men to have the same hallucinations. It was therefore, apparent that you had witnessed genuine materialization phenomena.

"The key to the whole situation, however, lay in the seemingly insignificant smudge on the book cover. Two years ago your uncle advanced a theory that materialization phenomena were produced by a substance which he termed 'psychoplasm.' After listening to his argument, I was convinced that he was right. Since then, we have attended numerous materialization séances, with the object of securing a sample of this elusive material for examination. It always disappears instantly when bright light is flashed upon it, or when the medium is startled or alarmed, and our efforts in this direction have always been fruitless.

"Needless to say, when you described the deposit left on the book by the phantasmic bat, I was intensely interested. Microscopic examination and analysis show that this substance is something quite different from anything I have ever encountered. While it is undoubtedly organic, it is nevertheless remarkably different, in structure and composition, from anything heretofore classified, either by biologists or chemists. In short, I am convinced it is that substance which has eluded us for so long, namely, psychoplasm.

"No doubt you will wonder what bearing this has on the question under discussion—that is, whether or not your uncle still lives. As far as we are able to learn, psychoplasm is produced only by, or through, living persons, and in nearly every instance it occurs only when the person acting as medium is in a state of catalepsy, or suspended animation. As most of the manifestations took place in the room where your uncle's body lay, and as he is the only one in the house likely to be in that state, I assume that your uncle's soul still inhabits his body.

"The final point, and by no means the least important is that in spite of the time which has elapsed since his alleged death—in spite of that fact that it lay in a warm room without refrigeration or embalming fluid—your uncle's body shows absolutely no sign of decomposition."

"But how is it possible," I asked, "for a person in a cataleptic state to simulate death so completely as to deceive the most competent physicians?"

"How such a thing is possible, I cannot explain any more than I can tell you how psychoplasm is generated. The wonderful powers of the subjective entity are truly amazing. We can only deal with the facts as we find them. Statistics show that no less that one case a week of suspended animation is discovered in the United States. There are, no doubt, hundreds of other cases which are never brought to light. As a usual thing, nowadays, the doctor no sooner pronounces the patient dead than the undertaker is summoned. Needless to say, when the arteries have been drained and the embalming fluid injected, there is absolutely no chance of the patient coming to life."

Together, we walked downstairs and entered the room where Uncle Jim lay. We looked carefully, minutely, for some sign of life, but none was apparent.

"It is useless," said the professor, "to employ physical means at this time. However, I have an experiment to propose, which, if successful, may prove my theory. As I stated previously, you are, no doubt, subjectively in mental en rapport with your uncle. Your subjective mind constantly communicates with his, but you lack the power to elevate the messages to your objective consciousness. My daughter has cultivated to some extent the power of automatic writing. You can, no doubt, establish rapport with her by touch. I will put the questions."

Miss Randall was called, and upon our explaining to her that we wished to conduct an experiment in automatic writing, she readily consented. Her father seated her at the library table, with pencil and paper near her right hand. He then held a small hand mirror before her, slightly above the level of her eyes, on which she fixed her gaze.

When she had looked steadily at the mirror for a short time he made a few hypnotic passes with his hands, whereupon she closed her eyes and apparently fell into a light sleep. Then, placing the pencil in her right hand, he told me to be seated beside her, and place my right hand over her left. We sat thus for perhaps ten minutes, when she began to write, very slowly at first, then gradually increasing in speed until the pencil fairly flew over the paper. When the bottom of the sheet had been reached a new one was supplied, and this was half covered with writing before she stopped.

The professor and I examined the resulting manuscript. Something about it seemed strangely familiar to me. I remember seeing those words in a book I had picked up in that same room. On making a comparison, we found that she had written, word for word, the introduction to my uncle's book, "The Reality of Materialization Phenomena."

"We will now ask some questions," said the professor.

He took a pencil and paper and made a record of his questions the answers to which were written by his daughter. I have copied them verbatim, and present them below.

Q: "Who are you that writes?"

A: "Ruth."

Q: "By whose direction do you write?"

A: "Billy."

Q: "Who directs Billy to direct you to write as you do?"

A: "Uncle Jim."

Q: "How are we to know that it is Uncle Jim?"

A: "Uncle Jim will give proof."

Q: "If Uncle Jim will tell us something which he knows and we do not know, but which we can find out, he will have furnished sufficient proof. What can Uncle Jim tell us?"

A: "Remove third book from left top shelf of book case. Shake book and pressed maple leaf will fall out."

(The professor removed and shook it as directed, and a pressed maple leaf fell to the floor.)

Q: "What further proof can Uncle Jim give?"

A: "Get key from small urn on mantle. Open desk in corner and take out small ledger. Turn to page sixty and find account of Peoria Grain Company. Account balanced October first by check for one thousand two hundred forty-eight dollars and sixty-three cents."

(Again the professor did as directed, and again the written statement was corroborated.)

Q: "The proof is ample and convincing. Will Uncle Jim tell us where he is at the present time?"

A: "Here in the room."

Q: "What means shall we use to awaken him?"

A: "Uncle Jim is recuperating. Does not wish to be awakened."

Q: "But we want Uncle Jim to waken some time. What shall we do?"

A: "Let Uncle Jim alone, and he will waken naturally when the time comes."

The professor propounded several more queries, to which there were no answers, so we discontinued the sitting. Miss Randall was awakened by suggestion.

"We now have conclusive proof that your uncle is alive, and in a cataleptic state," said the professor.

"Is there no way to arouse him?" I asked.

"The best thing to do is to let him waken himself, as he directed us to do in the telepathic message. He is, as he says, recuperating from his illness and should not be disturbed. You are, perhaps, unaware that catalepsy, although believed by many people to be a disease, is really no disease at all. While it is known as a symptom of certain nervous disorders, it may accompany any form of sickness, or may even be caused by a mental or physical shock of some sort.

"It can also be induced in hypnotization by suggestion. Do not think of it as a form of sickness, but, rather, as a very deep sleep, which permits the patient much needed rest for an overburdened body and mind; for it is a well-known fact that when catalepsy intervenes in any form of sickness, death is usually cheated."

"Would it be dangerous to my uncle's health if we were to remove him to his bedroom?" I asked. "It seems to me that a coffin is rather a gruesome thing for him to convalesce in."

"Agreed," said the professor, "and I can see no particular harm in moving him, provided he is handled very gently. Ruth, will you please have Mrs. Rhodes make the room ready? Mr. Ansley and I will then carry his uncle upstairs."

While Miss Randall was doing her father's bidding we tried to contrive a way to outwit the superstitious farmers, who would arrive in a few minutes if they made good their threat.

My eye fell upon two large oak logs, which young Severs had brought for the fireplace, and I said, "Why not weight the casket with these logs and screw the lid down? No doubt they will carry it out without opening it, and when they are well on their way we can place my uncle in your car and be out of reach before they discover the substitution."

"A capital idea," said the professor. "We will wrap the logs well so they will not rattle, and, as the casket is an especially heavy one, they will be none the wiser until it is opened at the grave."

I ran upstairs and tore two heavy comforters from my bed, and with these we soon had the logs well padded. Miss Randall called that the room was ready. The professor and I carefully lifted my uncle from the casket and were about to take him from the room, when a gruff voice commanded:

"Schtop!"

A dozen masked men, armed indiscriminately with shotguns, rifles and revolvers, were standing in the hall. We could hear the stamping of many more on the porch. I recognized the voice and figure of the leader as those of Glitch.

"Back in der coffin," he said, pointing a double-barreled shotgun at me. "Poot him back, or I blow your tam head off."

Then several other men came in and menaced us with their weapons.

I dropped my uncle's feet and rushed furiously at Glitch, but was quickly seized and overpowered by two stalwart farmers.

The professor, however, was more calm. He laid my uncle gently on the floor and faced the men.

"Gentlemen," he said, "may I ask the reason for this sudden and unwarranted intrusion in a peaceful home?"

"Ve are going to bury dot vampire corpse wit a stake t'rough its heart. Dot's vot," replied Glitch.

"What would you do if I were to tell you that this man is not dead, but alive?" asked the professor.

"Alive or dead, he's gonna be buried tonight," said a burly ruffian, stepping up to my uncle. "One o' you guys help me get this in the coffin."

A tall, lean farmer stepped up and leaned his gun against the casket. Then the two of them roughly lifted my uncle into it and screwed down the lid.

In the meantime, another had discovered the wrapped logs, to which he called the attention of his companions.

"Well, I'll be blowed!" he said. "Thought yuh was pretty slick, didn't yuh? Thought yuh could fool us with a coupla logs? Just for that we'll take yuh along to the part so yuh don't try no more fancy capers."

"Gentlemen," said the professor, "do you realize that you will be committing a murder if you bury this man's body?"

"Murder, Hell!" exclaimed one. "He killed my boy."

"He sucked my daughter's blood," cried another.

"An' my brother is lyin' in his deathbed on account of him," shouted a third.

"Come on, let's go," said the burly ruffian. "Some o' you boys grab hold o' them handles, an' we'll change shifts goin' out."

"Yah. Ve vill proceed," said Glitch. "Vorwarts!"

"If you will permit me, I will go and reassure my daughter before accompanying you," said the professor. "She is very nervous and may be prostrated with fear if I do not calm her."

"Go ahead and be quick about it," said the ruffian. "Don't try no funny stunts, though, or we'll use the stake on you, too"

The professor hurried upstairs and, on his return a moment later, the funeral cortege proceeded.

It was pitch dark outside, and therefore necessary for some of the men to carry lanterns. One of these led the way. Immediately after him walked six men bearing the casket, behind which the professor and I walked with an armed guard on either side of us.

Following, were the remainder of the men, some twenty-five all told. There was no talking, except at intervals when the pallbearers were relieved by others. This occurred a number of times, as the burden was heavy and the way none too smooth.

I walked as one in a trance. It seemed that my feet moved automatically, as if directed by a power outside myself. Sometimes I thought it all a horrible nightmare from which I should presently awaken. Then the realization of the terrible truth would come to me, engendering a grief that seemed unbearable.

I mentally reviewed the many kindnesses of my uncle. I thought of his generous self-sacrifice, that I might be educated to cope with the world; and now that the time had come when I should be of service to him—when his very life was to be taken—I was failing him, failing miserably.

I cudgeled my numb brain for some way of outwitting the superstitious farmers. Once I thought of wrestling the gun from my guard and fighting the mob alone, but I knew this would be useless. I would merely delay, not defeat, the grisly plans of these men, and would be almost sure to lose my own life in the attempt. I was faint and weak, and my broken ribs pained incessantly.

All too soon, we arrived at the pine grove, and moved toward a point from which the rays of a lantern glimmered faintly through the trees. A few moments more, and we were beside a shallow grave at which the six grim sextons, masked like their companions, waited.

The casket was placed in the grave and the lid removed. Then a long, stout stake, sharply pointed with iron, was brought forward, and two men with heavy sledges moved, one to each side of the grave.

Here a discussion arose as to whether it would be better to drive the stake through the body and then replace the lid, or to put the lid on first and then drive the stake through the entire coffin. The latter plan was finally decided upon, and the lid replaced, when we were all startled by a terrible screaming coming from a thicket, perhaps a hundred yards distant. It was the voice of a woman in mortal terror.

"Help! Save me—save me!" she cried. "Oh, my God, will nobody save me?"

In a moment, all was confusion. Stake and mauls were dropped, and everyone rushed toward the thicket. The cries redoubled as we approached. Presently we saw a woman running through the under-brush, and after a chase of several minutes over took her. My heart leaped to my throat as I recognized Ruth Randall.

She was crouching low, as if in deadly fear of something which she seemed to be trying to push away from her—something invisible, imperceptible, to us. Her beautiful hair hung below her waist, and her clothing was bedraggled and torn.

I was first to reach her side.

"Ruth! What is the matter?"

"Oh, that huge bat—that terrible bat with the fiery eyes! Drive him away from me! Don't let him get me! Please! Please!"

I tried to soothe her in my arms. She looked up, her eyes distended with terror.

"There he is—right behind you! Oh, don't let him get me! Please don't let him get me!"

I looked back, but could see nothing resembling a bat. The armed men stood around us in a circle.

"There is no bat behind me." I said. "You are overwrought. Don't be frightened."

"But there is a bat. I can see him. He is flying around us in a circle now. Don't you see him flying there?" and she described an arc with her hand. "You men have guns. Shoot him. Drive him away."

Glitch spoke, "It's der vampire again. Ve'll put a schtop to dis business right now. Come on, men."

We started back to the grove. I was nonplussed—mystified. Perhaps there was such a thing as a vampire, after all. But no, that could not be. She was only the victim of overwrought nerves.

Once more we stood beside the grave. Two men were screwing down the coffin lid. The three with the stake and sledges stood ready. I saw that Miss Randall was trembling with the cold, for she had come out without a wrap, and, removing, my coat, I placed it around her.

The professor stood at the foot of the grave, looking down calmly at the men. He appeared almost unconcerned.

The stake was placed on the spot, calculated to be directly above the left breast of my uncle, and the man nearest me raised his sledge to strike.

I leaped toward him.

"Don't strike! For God's sake, don't strike!" I cried, seizing his arm.

Someone hit me on the back of the head, and strong arms dragged me back. My senses reeled, as I saw first one heavy sledge descend, then another. The stake crashed through the coffin and deep into the ground beneath, driven by the relentless blows.

Suddenly, apparently from the bottom of the grave, came a muffled wailing cry, increasing to a horrible, blood-curdling shriek.

The mob stood for a moment as if paralyzed, then, to a man, fled precipitately, stopping for neither weapons nor tools. I found temporary relief in unconsciousness.

My senses returned to me gradually. I was walking, or, rather, reeling, as one intoxicated, between Miss Randall and her father, who were helping me toward the house. The professor was carrying a lantern which one of the men had dropped and fantastic, swaying, bobbing shadows stretched wherever its rays penetrated.

After what seemed an age of painful travel we reached the house, Miss Randall helped me into the front room, the professor following. Sam and Joe Severs were there, and someone reclined in the large Morris chair facing the fire. Mrs. Rhodes came bustling in with a steaming tea wagon.

I moved toward the fire, for I was chilled through. As I did so, I glanced toward the occupant of the Morris chair, then gave a startled cry.

The man in the chair was Uncle Jim!

"Hello, Billy," he said. "How are you, my boy?"

For a moment I was speechless. "Uncle Jim!" I managed to stammer. "Is it really you, or am I dreaming again?"

Ruth squeezed my arm reassuringly. "Don't be afraid. It is really your uncle."

I knelt by the chair and felt Uncle Jim's arm about my shoulders.

"Yes, it is really I, Billy. A bit weak and shaken, perhaps, but I'll soon be as sound as a new dollar."

"But how—when—how did you get out of that horrible grave?"

"First I will ask Miss Ruth if she will be so kind as to preside over the tea wagon. Then I believe my friend Randall can recount the events of the evening much more clearly and satisfactorily than I."

"Being, perhaps, more familiar with the evening's deep-laid plot than some of those present, I accept the nomination," replied the professor, smiling, "although, in doing so, I do not want to detract one iota from the honor due to my fellow plotters for their most efficient assistance, without which my plan would have been a complete failure."

Tea was served, cigars were lighted, and the professor began.

"In the first place, I am sure you will all be interested in knowing the cause of the epidemic on account of which some of our neighbors have reverted to the superstition of the dark ages. It is explained by an article in The Peoria Times, which I brought with me this afternoon, but did not have time to read until a moment ago, which states that the countryside is being swept by a new and strange malady known as 'sleeping sickness,' and that physicians have not, as yet, found any efficient means of combating the disease.

"Now for this evening's little drama. You will, no doubt, recall, Mr. Ansley, that before we joined the funeral procession, I requested a moment's conversation with my daughter. The events which followed were the result of that conversation.

"In order that the plan might be carried out, it was necessary for her first to gain the help of Joe and Sam here, and then make a quick detour around the procession. I know that there are few men who will not rush to the rescue of a woman in distress and I asked her to call for help in order to divert the mob from the grave. She thought of the bat idea herself, and I must say it worked most excellently.

"While everyone was gone, Joe and Sam, who had stationed themselves nearby, came and helped me remove your uncle from the casket. As we did so, I noticed signs of returning consciousness, brought about in some measure, no doubt, by the rude jolting of the casket.

Then the boys carried him to the house, while I replaced the lid. You are all familiar with what followed."

"But that unearthly shriek from the grave," I said. "It sounded like the cry of a dying man."

"Ventriloquism," said the professor, "nothing more. A simple little trick I learned in my high school days. It was I who shrieked."

Uncle Jim and I convalesced together.

When my ribs were knitted and his strength was restored, it was decided that he should go to Florida for the winter, and that I should have charge of the farm. He said that my education and training should make me a far more capable manager than he, and that the position should be mine as long as I desired it.

He delayed his trip, however, until a certain girl, who had made me a certain promise, exchanged the name of Randall for that of Ansley. Then he left us to our happiness.

THE MAGIC MIRROR

MARY S. BROWN

It was a new house which we had rented for the summer. I was alone in the large living room, watching two kittens frolicking on the floor, when someone near me laughed softly. On one side of the room was a full-length cheval mirror, and diagonally across hung a triplicate mirror.

As I turned to discover who had come in, I saw reflected in the central glass of the three-fold mirror the piquant face of a young girl who was smiling softly at the kittens. She wore a large hat of gauzy material which partly hid dark ringlets of hair that clustered around the clear olive skin, and I noticed how white and perfect were the teeth disclosed by the parted lips. Suddenly two soft dark eyes looked straight into mine. A look came over her face like that of a child caught in some naughty act, and then she disappeared.

I rushed to the door to reassure her; I ran around the house; I vaulted the stonewall at the rear and hurried along the edge of the woods. Not a glimpse of the girl did I catch.

"Hiding behind a tree," I muttered. "I won't gratify her by hunting."

I supposed she must be some neighbor's daughter, but no one in the vicinity seemed to know of any girl that answered my description, and I was beginning to forget the occurrence, when she appeared again.

This time I was playing on the violin when, in turning the music, I noticed how the triplicate mirror was reflected in the long glass near me. I dared not move for fear of frightening this mysterious maiden for whom I had so vainly inquired. So I smiled encouragingly, and said quietly: "Come in! Do not be afraid. Can't we be friends?"

She nodded brightly, but when I turned to welcome her the room was empty. I felt annoyed, and resolved to pay no further attention to so capricious a creature. Yet, when I returned to my seat, the face in the mirror was still gazing at me sadly and appealingly.

"Are you trying to play a joke on me" I asked.

She shook her head.

"Would you not like to be friends with me?"

An emphatic nod was her reply.

"If you will not come in and talk to me, how can we be friends?"

A puzzled look came over her face, and then the mirror was empty.

"Of all the queer girls!" I thought, and this time I went outside, walked to the end of the piazza, and came back as mystified as ever.

"That glass is certainly bewitched," I said, thinking of the enchanted ones in my child-time fairy books. Suddenly fingers appeared, in it, holding a slip of paper.

"Shades of Julius Caesar!" I ejaculated, "This house must be haunted, but, whether fairy or spirit, she doesn't look very formidable. I will see how far I can unravel the mystery."

I went nearer to the glass and read: *"I can come so that you can see me, only in this way."*

Evidently she could hear and comprehend, so I said aloud: "Is it because you won't or can't?"

The paper disappeared, and soon another took its place. It read: *"Because I can't"*

"Can you explain why?"

For answer she herself appeared and sadly shook her head. Now that she was nearer I saw that she was very attractive. Her face was thoughtful, and her eyes, which had been merry as she watched the kittens, now startled me with their sadness. Impulsively, I advanced, desiring her to feel sure of my friendliness, but when I came close to the mirror her face disappeared, and I saw only the reflection of my own.

"I don't believe you really want to be friends," I exclaimed, somewhat angrily, and, turning away, I left the room.

The stonewall behind the house divided our land from that of Professor Dolber, the world-renowned scientist. As he was called a recluse I was much pleased to be invited there a few days later for luncheon.

In the dining room I was at first so engrossed in my host's conversation and in the subtle melancholy of his face that I was oblivious to anything else. At last I noticed two oil paintings on my right, and was much surprised to find in one a portrait of the girl in my mirror.

As the professor followed my gaze, I remarked: "That is a fine likeness, only now she looks older and more thoughtful."

He gave me a curious look, but said nothing.

"How old was she then?" I asked.

"Do you mean my daughter?" he said. "That was painted in Holland four years ago."

"Your daughter? I am glad to discover who she is. I hope we shall meet. I know we both like kittens."

His amazed stare checked me. I bit my lip in vexation. It occurred to me that he would scarcely approve of his daughter's coming alone to see me, so I changed the subject and began discussing a new scientific discovery.

When I reached home the daughter of the Episcopal rector was calling on my sister. This young lady was much interested in my good fortune in finding Mr. Dolber so sociable. Although he had many distinguished visitors from all parts of the world, she said he was a man whom strangers found difficult to approach.

"Do you know his daughter?" I asked.

"His daughter? Was a young lady there? It must have been some visitor. He has no family."

"But the portrait—he told me it was painted from his daughter."

"Yes, wasn't she a beauty? It must have been very hard for him to lose his only child, and his wife died of grief only two months later."

No wonder the man had stared at me! He must have thought me either stupid or crazy! But the mirror—I had supposed that I had found a clue, but now the affair had assumed the proportions of a real mystery. How could I ever solve it?

The next morning the family went off on a week's excursion. I had intended to go with them, but now I changed my mind, hoping that their absence would give me a better chance to see more of my uninvited guest who haunted the mirror.

The next day, when I began my music, I was conscious of her presence even before I saw her face in the glass. There was one curious fact in regard to this. I looked directly at the triplicate mirror and saw nothing. It was only when I saw its reflection in the long cheval mirror that she became visible—just as if it required a four-fold reflection to enable the image to become apparent to my sight. This time the face was partly covered by a paper on which was written:

"Do not come too near. You were angry last time because you thought I had gone, but you came so close that you could not see me, although I had not moved."

"Forgive me, " I said contritely, as the paper disappeared, leaving in full view the pretty face. "I will be careful. My people are away, so we can have a talk and get acquainted. I saw your portrait at your father's and I know who you are, so I stayed at home today because I hoped you would come again. We can talk quite well, for I can ask questions and you can answer by 'yes' or 'no' with your head, or you can write. First: Why do you come here?"

"I go to many places, for I am very lonely, but you are the only person that has seen me for two years. I was frightened at first, but when you offered to be friends I was glad. I have wanted a friend so long."

"You poor child! Can't you find friends anywhere else?"

She shook her head sadly.

"Can you tell me the reason?"

"Because I can neither come back nor go on," she wrote.

At this moment the doorbell rang.

It proved to be a college chum unexpectedly in the neighborhood, and I could do no less than invite him to spend Sunday with me.

Often in the lulls of conversation I pondered on that strange answer: "I can neither come back nor go on." What could she have meant by that? And for the first time since I had known him I was glad when my chum left and I was free to watch for my newfound friend again.

I waited nearly all the afternoon before she came, and then I reproached her for her lateness.

"*I have been here several times,*" she wrote, "*but you were not alone, and today I was very busy.*"

"Busy! What were you doing?"

"*Trimming a hat,*" she replied, to my astonishment, and then I noticed that she did have on a different hat.

My ghostly girl, then, was not above coquetry, so I complimented her on the new creation, and she seemed as pleased as any ordinary girl.

"Tell me why I can see you only in the mirror."

She shook her head slowly as though in doubt, and after a minute's reflection she wrote: "*I can not explain, only that I am higher than you and you can not find the direction.*"

"How, then, can I see your image in the mirror?"

"*I do not understand it well myself, for I am not free from the body, but I think it is because I am permitted to get into the right angle of reflection, because they are sorry for me and they are trying to help me.*"

"What astonishing philosophy is this!" I mused. "What can she mean?"

Aloud I asked, "Who do you mean by they?"

"*The ones higher up that take care of me—and, oh, will you tell my father that they take GOOD care of me?—only I am lonely because I don't belong anywhere.*"

"Why can't your father see you?"

"*I do not know, but perhaps he can explain it all to you; he knows so much more than I do; but will you be sure to tell him for me, because he*

*has grieved so every day, and he is so unhappy. They are calling me now
and I must go. Promise me to tell him."*

I promised, and instantly the mirror was empty. I was left to medi-
tate on what she had said. She was not yet free from her body. How
then could she be a spirit? Was it a dream I was living or was I
becoming insane?

I sat down at once and sent a note to her father, asking if I could
see him on a matter of importance, and received the reply: "Come this
evening at seven thirty."

"When I said I wished to speak of his daughter, Mr. Dolber
answered, 'No, no, I cannot talk about her. You spoke the other day as
if you had met her, but how and where?' "

"Listen to my story, which only you can explain."

Several times as I told of my experiences with the mirror he started
as if most excited, but restrained himself until I had finished, when he
rose and holding on to his chair as if to steady himself said: "Thank
you for coming. The message is a relief and comfort to me, but
tonight"—his voice faltered—"I must, think—this has overcome me.
I will send for you soon and explain what I can."

Early in the morning I received a telephone message from
Hugelschon, asking me to come over at once. I found everything there
in confusion. Professor Dolber had been found dead in the library.
His physician had just come and pronounced it heart failure. As I was
the last person to see him, and as on the table there was a letter
addressed to me, I was sent for.

As soon as the doctor had gone the housekeeper begged me to
come into the library. She told me she had been in the family for thirty
years and that since his wife's death he had taken her into his confidence and had depended upon her in many ways.

"Something entirely upset him last night," she added, "for when I
took in some tea as I often did when he sat up late, his head was
buried in his hands, and when I spoke he did not look up nor answer."

I decided to tell her of my experience and what I had said to the
professor, and to ask her advice. As I told my story she did not seem in
the least surprised.

"I am glad you told me about this, for many things of a strange nature have happened here since Freda disappeared, and Mr. Dolber allowed no one but me to enter her room. All her things were kept just as she had left them, only many of them had to be replaced. That is the strange part of it and what worried my master most of all. In fact, night or day, he had no peace of mind for fear she might need something he couldn't remember. Ah, my poor master—my heart ached for him, and I am glad he is at rest." Here she broke down and sobbed bitterly.

When she was calm I asked: "What do you mean by things being replaced?"

"I mean that her clothes, hats, dresses, and many other things disappear. And we have to buy new ones." She lowered her voice. "We are sure that Freda takes them, for everything is kept locked and no one but ourselves has gone in there since she disappeared. It is all a mystery to me, but I never questioned Mr. Dolber, though he trusted me, and I bought new things as fast as he thought she needed them. But, sir, perhaps he has explained. Here is the letter he left for you."

I walked home sad and troubled. Finding my family away still, I sat down where I was wont to see her face in the mirror. I wondered if she would come again, but first I must read the letter, and I began to unfold it, when suddenly I felt the strange sensation I always experienced when I became conscious of her presence. I raised my eyes involuntarily to the mirror, and there—and I confess for the first time in my life that I was afraid—there, instead of Freda, was Mr. Dolber himself!

He smiled as if to reassure me, a smile so glad that the fear left me, and I was sure he had a message. I was right, for in a moment the writing came:

"Hurry at once to Hugelschon and go to Freda's room."

Then the mirror was empty, nor did I ever see in it anything but the reflection of material objects.

I never thought of disobeying the command, so I hurried to Hugelschon. The housekeeper met me, saying excitedly, "I was just going to send for you. Come with me."

She led me upstairs to Freda's room and unlocked the door. We entered, and she locked it again on the inside—and then, to my wondering amazement and joy, I saw the reason for her caution, and for his message in the mirror. Freda herself lay on the bed apparently fast asleep. The housekeeper bent over her, and in a voice of mingled delight and fear, exclaimed, "Oh, what shall I do?"

She voiced my own feelings. How could we account for Freda's appearance? We must act quickly. Would the letter help us? I drew the envelope from my pocket, and read:

"For years I have been investigating every phenomenon that seemed in any way to suggest the presence of a higher space, adjacent to that in which we live. The record of my experiments and their results fills volumes. It is enough to say that I succeeded so well in my investigations that I became able to place objects, even animals, within this space. These objects were always connected with my experimenting table by tubes containing, powerful magnetic currents, by means of which I could bring back anything within range of my vision again. The idea at last came to me that if I could find an intelligent being, willing in the interest of scientific knowledge to cooperate with me, my discovery would be famous. Such a being, if sent into the invisible space, and reclaimed again into our own, would not only immortalize my fame, but also prove my theories by his testimony."

Here the writing abruptly ended. We could only conjecture the rest. He had undoubtedly used Freda as his "intelligent being." She had trusted him, but he had failed to re-attract her sufficiently for her to become visible again. Possibly a human being required more forceful power than he had calculated. Hence the grief which had caused the mother's death and his own torturing remorse. Death must have shown him the way to release her, and he had used the mirror as a medium of communication. He had believed that I would do my best to help Freda, nor was he wrong.

The only time we spoke of her curious experiences, Freda said: "It is not very clear to me now. I know that my father raised the rate of vibration in my body, so that it became invisible to people on this plane, but his formula for bringing me back refused to work—to his tragic dismay. While I was in this higher, or perhaps more inclusive, space, it became clear to me that nothing is ever really destroyed. It only changes its form, as ice becomes water, water turns into steam, and steam into an invisible gas; the elements vibrate differently, and each varying vibration has its own individual form. That is as much as I can explain in terms that you could understand."

Be that as it may, the mirror still reflects my Freda—and I am content. Who now, however, shall prove Professor Dolber's theory of the fourth dimension? I, for one, dare not try.

THE VOW ON HALLOWEEN

LYLLIAN HUNTLEY HARRIS

It was Halloween, the time of revelry, when mysticism holds full sway and hearts are supposed to be united beneath the magic glow of dim lanterns. It was the time of apple bobbing, fortune telling, and masking in motley raiment, the whole glamoured over by the light of wishing candles.

Amid such scenes one never thinks of tragedy, but it treads apace, sometimes among the gay revelers, and many a domino or cowl covers that which would make the staunchest heart quake and is as different from the gay exterior as darkness is from light.

The lanterns glimmered, the varicolored lights shading and darkening with the winds that soughed through the beautiful old garden where the fete was held.

The pergolas, standing whitely aloof from surrounding density, made wonderful trysting places for the age-old stories of love to be whispered.

"You have made me very happy tonight, Audrey," a deep voice was whispering. "I think that all my after life will be a paean of gratitude for this moment of bliss. When you would vouchsafe no word of hope, not even one of pity, I felt hopeless, broken. Life seemed as senseless as a stupid rhyme! But now dearest, life's cup is filled to over-flowing!"

His lips met hers in a lingering caress.

For a moment the lanterns seemed to flicker and dim. A slight shudder ran over her slender frame. She freed herself gently.

"I cannot expect you to understand, Arthur," Audrey replied, "why you were kept waiting. The silence encompassed the whole of the earth and sky to me. It has been a frightful reality, which my tongue refused to explain until today, and my mental anguish has well nigh swayed my reason. A year ago tonight I experienced a terrible ordeal, more uncanny because it has seemed impossible for me to shake off the pall of it. It has changed the course of my life. For a year I have lived the life of a senseless thing, a piece of clay, merely breathing, eating, sleeping, but with no soul left me—"

Her voice trailed off into nothingness, and for a while both were silent. He was awed by her utterances. His arm tightened about her.

"Poor Audrey," he whispered, "you must have worried yourself needlessly. Is not illusion a sort of night to the mind which we people with dreams?"

"It was no illusion, Arthur, but grim reality. But last night a dream came to me which seemed to awaken my dead sensibilities, cut loose the spell under which I was living. In it I was commanded to tell you all."

Gently he caressed her.

"Tell me what you wish, dear, and nothing more. Remember hope is better than memory. I am listening."

"I shall tell you all. You suffered, so nothing shall be withheld. My troubles began when my father had financial reverses. I gave music lessons to eke out a meager income. About this time Rothschild Manny came into my life. He loved me at sight, as intensely as I loathed him. One glance from his slanting, shifty eyes was sufficient to set me cowering in my chair, and if his hand by chance touched mine, cold chills chased over my body. He was like some demon, waiting his chance to spring upon his prey.

"Imagine my dismay, when my parent immediately began insisting on my marriage with this monster! His fortune would retrieve ours and would regain the position we had lost by financial reverses. The horror of it! After one lengthy argument I felt my brain reel, and I fell upon my knees crying and imploring my father to spare me this ordeal. He was obdurate and insisted upon my consent. Finally he sent for Manny, placed my hand in his, and gave me to him formally. But not once did I encourage him, and he seemed to change into a veritable demon. His eyes would become crafty as he looked at me and his face assumed an expression of sardonic intensity.

"One day, the day that is seared upon my memory, one year ago tonight, he sought me out. I was alone in the house, my father having gone to the lodge. Manny was trembling under some terrible emotion.

"'Your welcome does not shine forth from your eyes, my dear,' he said as he seated himself and took my hand.

"With a gesture of horror I jerked it away. The motion seemed to infuriate him, and deepened the intensity of his eyes.

"'I came to take you driving,' he said, with a quick intake of his breath. 'The night is lovely and my new car is without. It will be yours when you are mine.'

"There was a steely intensity in his gaze directed upon me.

"'I don't care to go,' I said quietly.

"' Pray reconsider. I may be able to persuade you to feel differently if you give me a chance.'

"Here I interrupted.

"'I will do nothing of the sort,' I cried, 'I will go nowhere with you. I want nothing to do with you, and, God willing, I will never be your wife!'

"My words infuriated him. He was under some powerful influence of evil. He seized my wrist and, jerking me out of my chair, shook me violently.

"My senses reeled, and I must have lost consciousness. All I remember was being held up by main force, those horrible evil eyes boring malevolently into mine while he shouted in my ear:

"'Remember—young lady you will drive with me—yet! Maybe not now, but some day! This is not a threat, it is a declaration, and neither stars, moon nor even heaven itself, shall deliver you from it.'

"I was thrown violently upon the floor. Merciful oblivion came to me.

"For days I was ill—not knowing, not caring what happened, craving death, to relieve me from the sinister influence and deliver me from the effect of that horrible vow on Halloween. When I recovered I learned that Manny, driving his car that day madly, had lost control and had come to a horrible end. His evil influence seemed to hold me drugged in its power. I longed to die. But death does not come when one craves it. I lived, a piece of senseless clay, until you came to me; and when I looked into your eyes I felt that heaven had been kind in denying me my desire. My heart, my soul, went out to you, but I couldn't let you know. I could never become your wife with that terrible vow sounding in my ears, that terrible power controlling me.

"Then yesterday, in the dim watches of the night a dream came to me. A voice spoke and said: 'Love beyond price is yours. Take and cherish it, lest this priceless gift be withdrawn!'

"I awoke, happy, myself once more, grateful that life could come to me again."

She nestled close and his hand caressed her hair.

"My darling, how you have suffered. My whole life shall be spent in keeping you free of the mirage of this terrible experience—"

"Beg pardon," a suave voice interrupted, and a cowled figure drew near, "this is my dance, I believe. Is it not too warm to repair to the ballroom? I have my car here. A spin will refresh us both."

The cowled figure bowed low. Audrey glanced at her card, and arose with a little laugh.

"You will excuse me, Arthur, won't you? It seems that this august domino person has prior claim."

With a light hand on the newcomer's arm she was lost in the crowd. The music from the palm-shaded orchestra stirred forth, hummed, throbbed, and sobbed into a soft requiem.

Two days later, some belated wayfarers came upon a young woman, who seemed unable to move from her seat in an automobile. Upright beside her was a skeleton, whose sightless eye- sockets even then bored into the soul from which the light of reason had fled forever more!

Manny had kept his threat.

And in an old moonlit garden, under the white pergola where he had lived his one moment of bliss, a figure fell, turned into sudden clay, as the smoking weapon could testify.

The Werewolf of
St. Bonnot

Seabury Quinn

The long European twilight was dying, and darkness crept stealthily across the fields and pasture lands as three horsemen trotted slowly along the forest road of St. Bonnot. Two of the riders carried lutes slung across their shoulders, which marked them as trouveurs—ballade singers—while the third rode slightly to the rear, balancing a portmanteau on his saddle bow, by which token he was labeled attendant of the other two. All three jangled long swords from their hips, for France was under the reign of the weak and vacillating Charles IX, and he who would bring his life and property safely to his journey's end must needs travel prepared to defend them.

"'S'wounds," swore one of the minstrels, drawing his scarlet cloak more tightly about his shoulders, "but this abominable wood is colder than the tomb of the blessed Louis! With winter a good two moons away, methinks this chill i' the air hath more o' the Devil's flavor than of God's good weather."

His companion grunted a reply and sunk his chin deeper in his tippet. The speaker looked right and left at the pale, new moonlight sifting eerily between the tree trunks, and continued, "A flagon of the Count's wine would like me well enough the now. What with a twenty-mile ride, and no provender for man or beast along the way, I'd sing of Alexander the Greek and Arthur the Briton from now till sunup for a single stoup of wine and a morsel of bread and cheese."

Again an inarticulate reply from his mate.

" 'S'death," the conversationally inclined singer went on, "didst ever see such a lonesome, uncanny place as this accursed *bois*? Methinks *Monsieur Loup-Garou* himself would like no better place for his questing."

He flung back his bearded chin with a ringing laugh and began the opening lines of *Bisclaveret* in a deep baritone. The poem, one of France's oldest, dealt with "the multitudinous herd not yet made fast in hell"—the people of the loup-garou, or werewolf, who had sold their souls to the devil in return for the power of transforming themselves into wolves, to kill and devour their enemies. All Europe trembled at the very name of these men-monsters, but no country was more plagued by them than France.

"Hush, hush, Henri!" the taciturn minstrel suddenly broke his silence as the singer expanded the theme of his terrible song. "*Pour l'amour de le bon Dieu*, cease that singing. Suppose a werewolf were in this twenty-times-damned wood—" he glanced fearfully among the shadows—"we should all be torn to bits!"

"Bah!" the other replied. "The loup-garou would be lucky if I did not eat him, famished as I am.

"*Hola*, Monsieur Werewolf," he cried mockingly, "come out of the forest. Come out and be eaten by the hungriest song-singer who ever kissed a tavern wench or drank a gallon of Burgundy at a draught!"

It was as if his challenge had been waited for. From a low clump of bracken beside the road rose such a marrow-freezing howl as no man had heard before, and a huge, gray, shaggy form, larger than any wolf that ever fought a pack of hounds, launched itself straight at the astonished trouveur's throat.

The horses reared in sudden terror, plunging futilely to beat off his assailant. "*A moi*, Louis; *a moi*, Francois. Quick, for the love o' God, or I perish!"

But the other singer and the servant could give no aid. Encumbered by their cloaks and trappings, their horses plunging and rearing in panic fear, they could but fight desperately to retain their saddles and cry supplications to the Virgin.

"Help, help!" the attacked man called again, then, with a shout of desperation, he fell from his saddle, the great, gray thing's teeth fastened in his shoulder near the base of his neck.

For a moment he thrashed among the underbrush, unable to draw his long sword and powerless to thrust back the creature with his bare hands. In the struggle his hand brushed against the hanger in his girdle. He dragged the short cut-and-thrust blade from its scabbard with frantic haste and struck once, twice, three times at the foul creature snarling at his throat. A cry of rage and pain sounded amid the monster's growling, and with a deep, angry bay it rushed off into the forest depths.

"*Mon Dieu!*" gasped the minstrel as he regained his saddle. "Would that I'd heeded thy warning, Louis. Never again will I challenge one of those tailless hounds from the Devil's kennel. Tomorrow morning, if it please our Lady we see the light of another day, this matter goes before my Lord Duke. Holy Church and the secular government must combine to rid the Province of these changeling wolves."

The three riders set spurs to their mounts, nor did they slacken rein till safe within the fortifications of the city of Dôle.

Next morning the two singers and their lackey appeared before the provincial officials and made formal complaint that they had been set upon, and one of them all but killed, by a *loup-garou*, or werewolf, in the forest of St. Bonnot.

The officials looked grave when they had heard the complainants through. This was not the first account of werewolf depredations to come before them. Farmers living in the territory contiguous to the city had brought in accounts of sheep stolen from the fold at dead of night, of dogs killed as they watched the flocks, even of little children found dead and horribly mangled along the roadside and beneath the hedges. Now came these three wayfarers, all of them veterans of the wars, and two of them men of learning and respect, to tell of being boldly attacked on the royal road as they journeyed through the wood.

This thing must not be. The "power of the country" must be raised, and the werewolf, or werewolves, responsible for the outrages sent forthwith to the fiery hell where their master, the Devil, waited the coming of their forfeited souls.

France of 1573 was in no condition to police her country districts. The long and devastating wars between Huguenots and Catholics had made a sort of no man's land of large districts; Charles IX, the king, was a man of wax, molded now by this favorite, now that, and giving no thought to the welfare of his people. Every available sou that taxation could wring from rich or poor was spent to gratify or further the ambitions of the most corrupt and conscienceless politician who ever debased a government, the Queen Mother, Catherine de Medici.

In these circumstances, the Court of Parliament at Dôle might pass as many enactments as it chose, but, lacking force with which to make its mandates effective, its acts were but mere scraps of unavailing paper. One power still remained to the court. This was a *levee en masse* —a general calling to arms of the countryside.

Tradesmen and residents of the towns of those days stood bare-headed when titled swaggerers rode forth, and the agricultural classes were little more important to the nobility than the earth they tilled. For one not holding a patent of nobility to engage in the gentlemanly sport of hunting was to court immediate and merciless punishment. Game must be preserved for the nobles to hunt, though the peasant's stomach went empty and his flocks and herds were depleted by wolves till poverty crushed him to the ground.

Now was a chance to declare an "open season," give the peasants the thrill of engaging in the noble pastime of the chase, rid the country of the dreaded werewolves and save the sorely needed public funds, all at once. Accordingly, the following proclamation was issued by the Court of Parliament at Dôle:

"According to the advertisement made to the sovereign Court of Parliament at Dôle, that in the territories of Epagny, Salvange, Courchapon and the neighboring villages has often been seen and met, for some time past, a werewolf, who, it is said, has already seized and carried off several little children, so that they have not been seen since, and since he has attacked and done injury to divers horsemen in the country, who kept him off only with great difficulty and danger to their persons and lives, the said Court, desiring to prevent any greater danger, has permitted, and by these presents does hereby permit all those who are now abiding and dwelling in said places and others, notwithstanding all and any edicts concerning the chase, to assemble with pikes, halberts, arquebuses and other weapons, to chase and to pursue the said werewolf in every place where they may find him; to seize him, to tie him, or, if necessary, to kill him without incurring any pains or penalties of any sort, kind or nature whatsoever. Given at the convocation of the said Court on the Thirteenth Day of the month of September, 1573."

Mounted heralds were dispatched throughout the territory adjacent to Dôle, and within a few days the court's proclamation was known to every dweller in the vicinity.

Soon quaint processions were seen issuing from all the villages in the neighborhood. Headed by their parish priests, with sacred statues borne before them, the people sallied forth to hunt down the dreaded *loup-garou*. Solemn high mass had been sung, the weapons of the huntsmen had been formally laid in the chancels of their churches and blessed by the *curés*; and now the hunt commenced.

Separating into parties of two, the peasants ranged the fields and woods, seeking everywhere for their accursed prey. It must be admitted that many of them had no stomach for their task, and would have dropped their weapons and fled incontinently at the first sight of anything resembling a werewolf in the most remote way. Others so far forgot the sacred and official duty with which they were charged as to devote themselves to the hunting of edible game, and many a luckless bunny found its way into the pouches (and later to the kettles) of the werewolf hunters. Still others routed forest wolves from their lairs and killed them, so not a few wolves' scalps were brought before the provincial authorities.

But these were all natural wolves, as incapable of assuming human shape as the peasants were of becoming wolves, and, though their deaths doubtless added greatly to the safety of the neighborhood sheepfolds, they brought the werewolf menace no nearer a termination than when the Court of Parliament first issued its proclamation.

Interest in the hunt began to slacken. The peasants had their farmlets to attend, and the great landed proprietors were heartily sick of having their game preserves raided by those supposedly bent on public service. Except among those who had lost children or sheep, the *loup-garou* became little more than a hazy recollection.

And then suddenly, unexpectedly, he was found. On the eighth of November, 1573, when the fields were all but bare of vegetation and the last leaves were reluctantly parting company with the trees, three laborers, hurrying from their work to their homes at Chastenoy by a woodland short-cut, heard the screams of a little girl issuing from a dense tangle of vines and undergrowth. And with the child's screams mingled the baying of a wolf.

Swinging their stout billhooks, cutting a path for themselves through the tangled wildwood, the laborers hastened toward the sounds. In a little clearing they beheld a terrifying sight. Backed against a tree, defending herself with a shepherd's crook, was a ten-year-old girl, bleeding from a half-dozen wounds, while before her was a monstrous creature which never ceased its infernal baying and howling as it attacked her, tooth and nail.

As the peasants ran forward to the child's rescue the thing fled off into the forest on all fours, disappearing almost instantly in the darkness. The men would have followed, but the child demanded all their attention, for, weakened by loss of blood and exhausted with terror, she fell fainting before they could reach her.

The child was carried home and the workmen reported their adventure to the authorities. Their astonishment had been too great and the night too dark for them to make accurate observations, so there was a conflict in their testimony. Two affirmed the thing possessed the body of a wolf, the third swore positively it was a man, and, what was more to the point, *he recognized him*.

The clerical authorities cast their vote with the peasants, asserting the child's assailant a wolf, and there the matter rested for a time.

On the fourteenth of the month the disappearance of a little boy about eight years old was reported. The child had last been seen within an arrow's flight of the gates of Dôle, yet he had vanished as completely as though swallowed by the earth.

Now the civil authorities decided on action. They were not inclined to discount the werewolf theory entirely, for to deny the existence of such monsters in those days was treading dangerously close to the skirts of heresy. But neither were they minded to overlook any clue which pointed a natural explanation to the mystery. The Frenchman is curiously logical and direct, even in matters of superstition.

Two days after the little boy's disappearance was reported, a *sergeant de ville* set out from Dôle, armed with a writ of attachment and a very businesslike sword, and accompanied by six stalwart arquebusiers. Guided by the peasant who claimed to have recognized the little girl's assailant, the party hastened through the forest of St. Bonnot to the home of one Gilles Garnier, which stood beside the banks of a woodland tarn not far from the village of Arnanges.

Gilles Garnier, the man they sought, was a sombre, ill-favored fellow, surly and taciturn. He walked with a pronounced stoop and a shuffling gait, looking neither to right nor left, and usually muttering half crazily to himself. His pale face, repulsive features and livid complexion repelled all advances from those who met him, and little was known of his personal habits. But because of his long, unkempt beard, his filthy and ragged clothing (uncleanliness was next to godliness in those days) and his solitary life, he was popularly known as the hermit of St. Bonnot.

This title, however, carried with it no implication of sanctity. Quite the reverse. Persons with property to lose were wont to lock it up securely when the hermit was known to be in the vicinity, and many a hen roost owed its depreciated population to his evening visits.

The hermit's hut was as dilapidated as its tenant. Its crude roof was made of squares of sod laid across rickety rafters, and its walls of uncemented stones, irregularly piled one upon another, were encrusted with lichen. The floor was of trodden clay and the rough timber door hung crazily on hinges of rawhide. The windows were unglazed, and stopped against the weather with aprons of untanned skins.

The sergeant deployed four of his half-dozen followers in an enveloping movement about the hut, while, accompanied by the remaining two and his guide, he approached the hut and knocked thunderously on its sagging door with the hilt of his sword.

"Who calls?" Gilles Gamier peered evilly from a window.

"I do," the sergeant answered. "Open in the name of the law!"

"What seek ye here?" the hermit parleyed.

"I seek thee, accursed of God—werewolf, slayer of little children," the officer replied. "Come forth and yield ye, or, by'r Lady, I'll come in for thee."

Gilles Gamier bared his long, yellow teeth in an ugly snarl and hunched his rounded shoulders as if to spring upon the messenger of justice, but a second look at the arquebusiers showed him the futility of resistance.

The arquebus was grandfather to the flintlock musket of Revolutionary days, and great-great-grandfather to the modern rifle. It was nearly as tall as a man, had a bore larger than the modern twelve-gauge shotgun, and was fired by its bearer thrusting a glowing fuse, or gunmatch, into a touchhole at its breech. Even with the inferior gunpowder of those days it had a range twice that of the strongest crossbow, and though it was anything but accurate in aim, it carried a charge of leaden slugs and broken nails which scattered almost over a half-acre lot. If one of the soldiers had opened fire at point-blank range, Gilles Gamier would have been mangled almost beyond human recognition.

Gilles Garnier thought it prudent to come out and surrender.

His arms and legs firmly manacled, an iron chain about his neck binding him fast to the sergeant's stirrup, the werewolf of St. Bonnot was brought to Dôle.

For a time there was a controversy whether state or ecclesiastical courts should take jurisdiction. The clerics maintained that the prisoner had committed his crimes in the form of a wolf, and, since he had sold his soul to the Devil in order to become a werewolf, it was a matter cognizable only in the courts spiritual.

The civil authorities declared it had not yet been proven that the accused had committed any crime, and so, if he had committed any, whether as man or beast, it followed he must be tried before the temporal courts.

The civil lawyers won and the trial commenced.

Witnesses were summoned to prove the deaths of children and the condition in which their bodies were found; shepherds appeared to tell of their missing sheep; the two minstrels and their servant told of the attack made on them the previous September.

The little maid rescued by the peasants identified the prisoner positively as her assailant, and showed the court the scars left by his teeth and nails.

Then came the examination of the prisoner. In anticipation of his claims to innocence, a choice collection of racks, thumbscrews, leg-crushers and branding irons was made ready, and the official torturers looked forward to a busy morning. But the prisoner not only confessed all the crimes charged against him, but volunteered information concerning a number of others unknown to the court.

On the last day of Michaelmas (September 29), near the wood of La Serre, while in the form of a wolf, he had attacked and slain with his teeth and claws a little girl of ten or twelve years, drawn her into a thicket and gnawed the flesh from her arms and legs.

On the fourteenth day after All Saints (November 14), also in the form of a wolf, he had seized a little boy, strangled him, and partially eaten him.

Asked how he could have strangled the child if he were in wolf's form at the time, he was at first vague in his replies, but finally recollected that his hands had not been changed, so he still had the use of his fingers.

On the Friday before St. Bartholomew's Day he had seized a boy of twelve or thirteen near the village of Perrouze and killed him, but was prevented from eating him by the approach of some peasants. These men were found and corroborated the prisoner's statement.

Although the little girl whose rescue was the cause of his arrest declared the prisoner had been in human form when he attacked her, Gilles Gamier stoutly, maintained he had been in wolf's shape at the time. And to prove his power to change into a wolf at will, he suddenly sank to his all-fours on the court room floor, began capering about in grotesque imitation of a wolf, and emitted a series of howls, yelps and growls which perfectly simulated those of a ferocious beast of prey.

The court deliberated over his case, decided he had imitated wolf calls only to terrify his victims, but had never actually assumed wolf's form, and consequently voted him guilty of simple murder, unaccompanied by sorcery. As a murderer, he was punishable only by the civil authorities.

Sentence followed hard upon the verdict. On the tenth day following his arrest, Gilles Gamier, the self-confessed werewolf of St. Bonnot was dragged by ropes attached to his ankles over a rough road for a distance of nearly a mile, bound to a stake and burned to death.

Note: The reader must be aware that Gilles Garnier was the victim of that form of insanity known as zoomania, where the patient believes himself an animal. Zoomania, or that branch of it known as loupomania, where the lunatic imagines himself a wolf, is, fortunately, relatively uncommon today, yet frequent enough to be recognized by medico-legal authorities. If it be remembered that Gilles Garnier was obviously a man, of feeble intellect, and that all France, indeed all Europe of that day reeked with terror tales concerning the loup-garou, *which tales Garnier had heard (and implicitly believed) since earliest infancy, it can readily be seen how, when his poor wits finally broke down, he came to imagine himself a werewolf.*

The fact that he was lucid enough on every subject save this one delusion, stamps his ailment as paranoia, or monomania, one of the commonest forms of insanity among the young and middle aged. The man must have been quite powerless to restrain himself when seized with one of his attacks, and, in any modern court, he would have been committed to an institution without even being brought to trial. It does not appear that he ate the flesh of his victims because of hunger. On the contrary, this shocking act must be regarded purely as a symptom of his derangement. When under the spell of his disease the lunatic frequently resorts to the most unlikely diet. The author was once present at an autopsy performed on a paranoiac's body when no less than half a dozen ten-penny nails were extracted from the unfortunate man's stomach, several of them almost entirely eroded by the natural hydrochloric acid of that organ.

The Sea Thing
by Frank Belknap Long Jr.

July 16—We are caught in one of the great calms. There is water in the well, and our food is nearly gone. Everything is hid from view by the fog. I confess that I am a hopeless coward. The situation appalls me. What an expressive word is *despair*. I shall write it large—DESPAIR. Luckily a flying fish came scudding over the rails this morning.

July 17—The fog has lifted, but there is no relief in sight, and the water in the well has risen several inches. The seven of us worked on the pumps all night. Thompson seemed surly and inclined to rebel. He is a man to be envied. He still retains his egoism and he fancies himself a very shrewd and important person. I hadn't the heart to be angry with him. Poor devil! He doesn't know how near we are to the rocks. I speak figuratively, of course. We are at present in the open sea, a thousand miles from land, and our rudder has gone by the board. We drift aimlessly. A fine situation, truly, for the skipper of the *Octopus!* Three months ago I had a full crew, and full sails, and now ... Cholera isn't pleasant! Damn it all, cholera is *not* pleasant.

July 18—I have given up all hope. By working desperately we are able to keep the water in the well from rising, but our food has given out. We have pumped and cursed on empty stomachs for fifteen hours. Bullen collapsed. He collapsed like *the others*, but thank God, his face didn't turn black. We are done with the cholera now. I'll stake my reputation on that. My prompt disposal of the bodies nipped the cholera in the bud. In the bud, did I say? Ha! When a man loses three-fourths of his crew he can't think straight. The cholera really ran its course. It couldn't have lasted much longer. I wish to heaven that it had taken the rest of us.

July 19—It was funny. Another flying fish came aboard today, and Tommy Wells made a dive for it. He dived after it head first, with arms akimbo like a man just awakened from some crazy dream, and he slid along the planks. But he got the fish. He caught it between his two hands and bit into it, and finally disposed of it, bones and all. "That was a devilish thing to do," said Thompson. Big Johnny Boeltzig cursed horribly. I felt rather light in the head, and I didn't say anything. But I was a bit put out. We could have divided the flying fish up, but as I say, it was funny.

July 20—Our case is desperate. There isn't a breath of air stirring and Boeltzig has joined Bullen. They are both below, unable to move an arm between them, and Bullen is very near death. Curiously enough, though, the five of us are able to keep the water down. But we are tired—tired.

July 21—We have one thing to be thankful for. The water has not risen an inch in twelve hours—and we didn't pump. We are too tired to pump. We lay about on the decks, and cursed and made faces at the sky, and we never mentioned food. But Thompson's tongue stuck out queerly. "Put that rag in your mouth." I shouted. It was a coarse remark to make to a starving man, but I was suffering acutely. Why do I continue to write in this log?

July 22—We are saved! Who could have anticipated such glorious good luck? A boatload of provisions and a jolly companion to cheer us up. He claims that he is the sole survivor of the *Princess Clara*. You have undoubtedly heard of the *Princess*. A finer brig never put out from Frisco. And she's gone. A hurricane and a leak did for her. Six or seven got away in the long boat, but my friend (I call him that, because he has saved us all)—my friend threw them overboard. They died first, of course. Get that straight. They died from fright or from drinking salt water, and my friend didn't like the company of corpses. So he just naturally disposed of them.

That's his story, and I accept it at its face value. I'm not a man to go poking about and asking questions. It's enough that he's brought us provisions, and jolly companionship. We were growing weary of each other—we seven. He calls himself Francis de la Vega.

July 24—De Vegie (we call him that) has been with us now for three days. He has the run of the ship, and I have given him the mate's cabin. The mate has no further need for a cabin, since he spends his nights on the ocean floor. A splendid chap, the mate. He was the first to go. But I mustn't rake up old ashes. De Vegie is tall and amazingly lean, and I never saw a paler man. His face is drawn and haggard, and his eyes large—and they consume you. There is something devastating about his eyes. Sometimes they seem a hundred years old. His forehead is high, and as yellow and dry as parchment, and his nose is curved like a simitar. Strangely enough, he reminds me of Poe's Usher. I say strangely enough, because the man has nothing but his appearance in common with the aristocratic neurotic of Poe's tale. He is boyish, gay and utterly free from gloom. His manner is ingenuous and charming. He is all smiles and assurance. And he tells stories that are almost Rabelaisian in their frank, coarse humor. He possesses a remarkable knowledge of medicine, or perhaps I should say, of healing, since he uses no drugs. But he has completely restored Bullen and big Johnny Boeltzig. The eight of us make a jolly crew. He has given us new life, new confidence. His presence is a delight to us. There is one thing curious about him. His hands are cold and almost lifeless. There is no blood in them. I never before saw such hands on a human being. And the nails are astonishingly long.

July 27—De Vegie has kept more to himself. He remained locked in his cabin this morning, and answered my anxious questions through the keyhole. But I was too busy to show surprise. There was a curious chill in the air, which promised wind, and Thompson, Wells and I worked desperately to get up the topgallants and strengthen the weather leaches. The rest were too tired to work and I did not press them. I have no desire to reassert my authority just yet. The first sign of a breeze will increase the crew's morale, and then I hope to regain my old power of discipline.

July 28—I am worried about De Vegie. This morning he came on deck looking so drawn and haggard that I left the taffrail where I had been standing with one hand grasping the weather vane and crossed the deck to comfort him. His eyes looked appealingly into mine. "Couldn't sleep all night," he said. "The ship tosses so. The great calms certainly make a ship roll."

"They do," I replied. "But you don't notice the roll so much on deck. If you wish, you may carry your bedding up, and sleep with the boys on the planks. But don't be startled if a flying fish flops in your face."

De Vegie smiled. "Thanks," he said. "The idea appeals to me. I'll act on it tonight."

July 29—A breeze is surely coming soon. All of the signs point to it. I have been working frantically on a miserable substitute for a rudder. I think that I shall be able to steer fairly well in a pinch, but I hope the breeze doesn't come until we are better prepared.

De Vegie slept on the planks with the crew last night, and this morning he looks ten years younger. His cheeks are flushed and full, and the greenish hollows have disappeared from under his eyes. But Thompson isn't well. He complains of pains in his chest, and once or twice he spat blood. He is abnormally pale.

July 30—Still no breeze. Thompson is sick unto death. He lies in his cabin and groans, and I can do nothing for him. His pallor is genuinely alarming. Even his lips are bloodless. He complains of noises in his ears. And De Vegie has shown his first gleam of ill nature. "I can do nothing for him," he says, and shrugs his shoulders. His eyes smolder when he speaks, and I discern for the first time a hard cruelty in the man. He is not what he pretends to be!

July 31—Thompson died this morning, and De Vegie actually gloated over his death. What does it mean? Why such a sudden change in a man who owes everything to our generosity? It is true that his coming supplied us with food, but we snatched him from the very maws of the sea. That is ingratitude for you! Human beings are utterly despicable, and I have lost faith in them. De Vegie does not differ from the rest. He gloats over the misfortunes of others. He actually smiled when I read the burial service and dropped poor Thompson into the sea. Imagine it!

August 1—There is still no wind. I should welcome any sort of breeze after what I felt today. There is something unnatural about this ship. Even the cook has noticed it. "It ain't natural," he said, "for a ship to smell like this. And that De Vergie's fellow's cabin. Phew! It not only stunk, but—"

I laid my hand over his mouth. "You're an idiot," I shouted. "De Vegie's all right. I don't know what made him smile yesterday when I shipped off poor Thompson, but he isn't a bad sort." I lowered my voice: "He never complains, and his companionship is jolly stimulating. The boys couldn't get along without him. You have a feeling that he knows more than ten ordinary men whenever he opens his mouth to tell one of his amazing yarns. And that tale of the Spanish Inquisition that he frightened Boeltzig with yesterday morning was so real, so vivid—"

"I allus distrusted him," said the perverse fool. I grimaced, and remarked coolly that nothing could be more absurd than the prejudices of a lazy son of a sea cook. But I must confess that the smell of De Vegie's cabin did horrify me. I had entered it while De Vegie was on deck, and the stench nearly laid me on my back. The place smelt like a hellish charnel house. The odor of decaying shellfish mingled with a peculiarly offensive and acrid smell that in some indefinable way suggested newly shed blood. There was no sign, however, of anything amiss in the cabin. I was so horrified that I left almost immediately, slamming the door with a bang. Tonight I shall drink heavily. Oh, I shall get gloriously drunk! I shall make a fool of myself, but what does it matter?

August 2—De Vegie has grown hard and cynical. He curses my men and refuses to speak to me. This morning little Tommy Wells went below and lay down. He was as white as a squid's belly. Something told me to examine him. I commanded him to strip, and I searched his entire body for signs of discoloration. I thought that possibly the cholera had taken a new form. Like influenza, cholera may manifest itself in curious and amazing ways. I had never read of cholera draining the blood from a man, but I wasn't taking any chances. Well, it wasn't cholera. It was a bite. Something had bitten him in the chest. A round, circular discoloration disfigured the center of his chest, and in the very middle were two sharp incisions, from which blood and pus trickled ominously. I didn't like it. Neither did Tommy. When he saw the wound he sat up very stiff and straight, and asked me if I knew any tropic insects capable of such devilry.

"There are no insects a thousand miles from land," I shouted. "Don't be such an incredible imbecile!"

Tommy looked at me reproachfully. "Flies," he said. "They're often found on board. You know that just as well as I do. This stinking hold would breed 'em as big as whales. It couldn't have been anything else. I didn't feel it at all—didn't even know that I had the bite."

"There's something more than flies in this, Tommy," I said. "The thing that bit you came out of the sea. Ever see a lamprey's wound on a fish, Tommy?"

"Did I ever see a man walking with his legs!" snapped Tommy. "But how could a lamprey get me? I didn't sleep on the bottom of the sea. I slept on deck, and I was covered up. I suppose your lamprey climbed over the rail, and walked about, and finally decided that I would make a good juicy meal. Then I dare say he lifted the blankets, and crawled under my shirt and fed until morning. He would be wise enough, of course, to get away and over the side before daybreak. Is that your theory, captain?"

I was curiously impatient with the boy. His levity had somehow stung me. "It's a better theory than your flies," I responded.

Tommy smiled grimly, and turned over in his bunk.

August 3—Tonight I went down into the pit. Something *walks* at night in this ship. "The pestilence that walketh at nightfall"—I wonder if the Hebrew prophet saw what I *felt*. I awoke from a heavy sleep, and something that does not sleep was standing above my bed. The cabin was wrapped in a velvety blackness, and I could see nothing, not even a shadow. But I heard it gulp. And I smelt—the odor of decay was so strong that it stung my nostrils. And I heard the thing above me gulp. It didn't breathe or whisper or cry out, but it simply *gulped*. I tried to rise, but it laid its hand on my head and forced me back. And its hand was slimy, like the hand of a frog.

August 4—An unaccountable incident occurred on deck today. I am obliged to believe that De Vegie is insane. "Red" Walker was working on the braces, and his hand accidentally slipped. He cut himself badly. The blood ran down his arm, and we all feared that he had severed an artery. His under lip trembled, but he didn't complain or cry out. He simply walked with unsteady steps toward the forecastle, while he sought to stanch the flow of blood with his uninjured hand. De Vegie was standing above the lee scuppers, and the sight somehow startled him. He threw up his arms and ran straight for "Red." "Red" saw him coming, and stopped, puzzled and a little hopeful. He recalled De Vegie's power of healing. In a moment De Vegie had seized upon the injured arm. He gripped it forcefully, and *put it under his shirt*. He held "Red" Walker's wrist against his chest, and he seemed horribly excited. His eyes bulged. His checks turned gray, and balls of sweat accumulated on his forehead. De Vegie was making a tremendous effort to achieve something—but we couldn't guess what. The situation was uncanny. I stepped forward to interfere, but when I reached them they were free of each other, and "Red" was examining his arm with horror and amazement. "There's no blood in it," he groaned. "And, my God, it's as cold as ice!" De Vegie scowled, "I didn't expect gratitude," he said dryly, "but you have no right to complain. I've fixed your wrist for you. It won't bleed again—for some time!"

I could only stare. Is De Vegie mad, or has he mastered some monstrous system of healing?

August 5—"Red" Walker is dead. I disposed of his body this morning. It was white and rigid, and I noticed an extraordinary discoloration above the wound on his wrist. From the elbow down, his arm was bright green. I cannot explain it. Blood-poisoning, perhaps—but

I do not like De Vegie. I no longer trust him. His presence has become obnoxious to me.

Something walked again tonight. It bent above my head, and I heard it gulp.

August 6—I am stunned, frightened. Who could have dreamed, who could have expected? The thing is so incredible, so hideous, so utterly outside human experience!

I found the book in the ship's library. It was one of forty water-soaked volumes. It was a very ancient book, and the leaves were yellow and the cover eaten away at the corners. It was dated 1823. But that is not strange. Books one hundred years old are not uncommon on clipper ships that should have been scuttled before the beginning of this century.

I had poked among the absurd books out of curiosity, incidentally seeking something to read that would lift me above a gruesome world of sea and sky and walking pestilence.

I turned the pages of the little book rapidly, and laughed at the ridiculous lore that graced its soiled yellow pages. It was a miscellany, bearing the title, *A Winter's Evening*, and the incongruity of such a book among such surroundings amused and delighted me. And then I discovered the following passage, and I had no longer any desire to laugh: According to Father Fcyjoo, in the month of June 1674, some young men were walking by the seaside in Bilboa, when one of them, named Francis de la Vega, suddenly leaped into the sea, and disappeared presently.

About five years afterward, some fishermen in the environs of Cadiz perceived the figure of a man swimming and sometimes plunging under the water. It is said that his body was entirely covered with scales. They also added that different parts of his body were as hard as shagreen. Father Fcyjoo adds many philosophic rejections on the existence of this phenomenon, and on the means by which a man may be enabled to live at the bottom of the sea!

August 7—This morning I showed Tommy Wells the miscellany. He read it slowly, and his face actually turned yellow. His small blue eyes narrowed. "We must act at once," he said.

Later—We have made our plans. Tommy and I are to bunk together tonight. We have automatics—and a sharp knife. The knife, we feel, will be necessary. This morning Tommy and I discussed vampirism. "A stake or knife must be driven through the heart," said Tommy. "But a sea-vampire, Tommy," I responded, "is—is different." Tommy shrugged, to conceal the horror and uncertainty in his tired brain. *We are resolved to do everything possible.*

August 8—It is over! Poor Tommy is gone, but De Vegie will trouble us no more. I am dazed, horrified—but I must write it all. It is a duty I owe to Tommy. He would want it on record. Tommy was always methodical, and he insisted on regulations. I must put it in the log to please Tommy.

We were awake in our bunks when the door opened. We heard the door creak on its hinges. Something unutterable had entered the room. We could hear the thing gulp. Tommy gripped my arm, and I got ready to strike a match. I waited until its soft, slimy approach became unbearable. I waited until it stood at the foot of my bunk and until its green, glassy eyes were vaguely discernible in the almost total blackness. It was watching me, and I realized that it could see in the dark. I lit the match. My hand shook frightfully, but I carried the match to the tallow wick and then—it sprang.

But it didn't spring at me. It went higher, and it got Tommy about the neck. I could hear him choke and gasp. In passing me the thing had knocked the match from my fingers, and we were once more in total darkness. I had seen something long and green and slimy going upward, and I had heard Tommy's frightful scream. But I saw and heard nothing else for the space of thirty or forty seconds. I was unable to move or think. I sat on the edge of my bunk, and my heart came up in my throat, and flopped over.

I was conscious of two objects struggling and gasping on the floor. I heard a gulping and a low moaning, and then the night was loud with Tommy's screams. He shrieked, and shrieked, and shrieked. And between the screams there came a torrent of jumbled nouns and adjectives. "Green—eyes! Ugh! Ooze! Mouth! Wet!"

I finally got out another match, and struck it. I kept my eyes averted, and carried the match rapidly to the candlewick. I knew that if my eyes fastened upon the thing on the floor I should drop the match. I waited until the wick flared, and then—I looked!

Something was on top of Tommy. It covered him, and seemed apparently about to absorb him. In its evil, distorted features and long-nailed hands I recognized a caricature of De Vegie. But the evil in the man had sprouted. It had turned him into a jellyish, fishy monstrosity. His legs and arms actually gave. They were like nothing in this world under the sun and moon and stars. They lengthened, and enveloped and choked Tommy. But the worst of all, the body of the thing was covered with greenish scales, and it had pink suckers on its chest. The suckers were lustily at work on poor Tommy.

The suckers were draining Tommy dry. His screams kept getting louder and louder. And he muttered pathetic invocations and shameless blasphemies. And his scared eyes watched me. There was a challenge and a mute appeal in them.

I thought of the revolver in my bunk. I turned, and my fingers sought frantically for the weapon. At length I found it. I gripped the butt, and leveled it. I leveled it at Tommy and the thing on the floor.

I fired at Tommy and the thing. I had no intention of sparing Tommy. I knew that Tommy would not want that. The appeal in Tommy's suffering eyes was unmistakable. After that objects refused to retain their identity in my sight. They coalesced and separated and came together again. The objects on the floor merged with the table and chairs and bunk-ends.

I have a vague recollection of carrying two bodies on deck and dumping them overboard. I remember that one body was long and slimy and strangely heavy. The other was amazingly light. Before I carried the long heavy body on deck I drove a knife through its heart. I think that the blood spurted out and spattered my arms and legs. But the memory of this occurrence is more vague than the shadow of a dream. Did the long green body groan when I stabbed it, and did a look of ineffable happiness and gratitude come into its eyes? Did the small body also speak to me before I carried it on deck? Did I later go into De Vegie's cabin and breathe the fresh, clean air that blew through it? I cannot answer these questions, but I do not think that they require an answer.

August 9—A breeze! A breeze! The great calm is broken, and all hands are busy forward. I thank God that by tonight we shall be headed toward Frisco.

Sleigh Bells

Hasan Vokine

It was cold in the fierce, heartless way of Siberia. A desert of snow stretched on every side beyond a lonely little *muzhik* hut. Within, covered by a sheepskin, lay Andrey Taranof. His son, kneeling at his side, listened anxiously to his heartbeats.

For many days they had endured the cold with no food, and now the father was about to cross the border. Painfully he spoke: "Dmitri —goodbye."

The son was unable to answer. He kissed his father and arose. Moving from the pile of straw he slid aside a block of wood, and exposed a small hole in the door. The moon shone down on a silver carpet, crossed and recrossed by the sinister shadows of wolves. He studied the glistening fur which covered their lithe bodies, beautiful despite the shudder they caused.

They seldom congregated in such numbers around a solitary hut save when a man was dead or dying. What strange thing told them of Andrey's condition? Now a long, restless howl made his hand tremble as he replaced the shutter. Turning, he said in a low voice, "Father, let me open the door. You see that we shall die in the end. It would be better than this long waiting."

There was no answer.

His hand rested on the bolt. It turned!

"Dmitri! Wait."

The careworn eyes of the dying man had opened. He was alert.

"Dmitri, don't I hear bells, *droshky* bells? Yes! They come from the west, nearer and nearer."

The son shrugged his shoulders.

"But it could not be, father. No one would come—for us."

"But listen! Ah, don't you hear them?"

Dmitri put his ear to the door. The snow crunched under a hairy paw. That was all.

Still they waited. Dmitri dreamed, as he leaned against the wall, that the cold which crept slowly up his boots from the dirt floor was a pack of wolves, gnawing, gnawing at him, and he drew his long *cherkeska* more tightly about him.

The sun arose, and each beam chased away another wolf. Soon the whole world was glorious and golden, save for the two within the hut. The squalor of their existence was almost unbelievable. Although only exiles, their lot had been worse than that of some Saghalien prisoners. Forced to live in a miserable, one-room hut, or *izba*, not allowed even so much as an implement with which to eat their coarse food there, life was that of beasts.

"Now we must wait another long day—to die," said Dmitri.

"No, no! I cannot be mistaken," insisted the father, slowly and painfully. "I still hear the bells. They were very far off—and now they are nearer."

Dmitri looked at his father and wondered how much longer he would last—surely not until night. When that time came, when the pack had once more collected without the hut, he would tear open the door. In a minute the room would be surging with their cruel, glossy bodies, and in another minute he would have joined his father.

Again he resolved himself to waiting. Late in the afternoon Andrey motioned for water, and his son fed him from a bowl a dirty mess, half water, half snow, which had filtered through the cracks. Darkness came early, and soon the occasional howls of the wolves were heard. A crunch of the hard upper snow some time later told him that one was just without. He carefully sounded the door. The snow was above his waist, which meant that once the door was opened it would be impossible to shut. He prayed that his father would not last much longer, and again he was startled at the old man's strength. Andrey was sitting up! His lips formed the word, "Listen!"

Another howl sounded. Then faintly, from far away, the tinkling of a speeding sleigh reached them.

Dmitri could not believe. He held his ears. It stopped. He released them, and again the tinkling came. It was steadily becoming louder.

It was just too much. In his exhausted condition such an emotion was more than Dmitri could withstand.

Later, as they were taken into a room where there stood a table with a samovar, a big bowl of steaming *schi* and plenty of vodka, Dmitri told his rescuer of how his father had first heard his sleigh bells.

"But," said the farmer, "it must have been about the time I was starting out, miles from you."

So to this day they wonder how that old man, on the point of death, knew.

This is a superstitious story, typical of the Russian peasant. The son's story was taken as an omen that Andrey had been forgiven by the Great Father as well as by their "Little Father" the tsar. Had he not been allowed to visit the misty world of after death? How else had he heard brother Vasili's sleigh bells?

Efficiunt Daemones, ut quae non sunt, sic tamen
quasi sint, conspicienda hominibus exhibeant
—Lactantius

I was far from home, and the spell of the eastern sea was upon me. In the twilight I heard it pounding on the rocks, and I knew it lay just over the hill where the twisting willows writhed against the clearing sky and the first stars of evening. And because my fathers had called me to the old town beyond, I pushed on through the shallow, new-fallen snow along the road that soared lonely up to where Aldebaran twinkled among the trees; on toward the very ancient town I had never seen but often dreamed of.

It was the Yuletide, that men call Christmas though they know in their hearts it is older than Bethlehem and Babylon, older than Memphis and mankind. It was the Yuletide, and I had come at last to the ancient sea town where my people had dwelt and kept festival in the elder time when festival was forbidden; where also they had commanded their sons to keep festival once every century, that the memory of primal secrets might not be forgotten. Mine were an old people, and were old even when this land was settled three hundred years before. And they were strange, because they had come as dark furtive folk from opiate southern gardens of orchids, and spoken another tongue before they learnt the tongue of the blue-eyed fishers.

And now they were scattered, and shared only the rituals of mysteries that none living could understand. I was the only one who came back that night to the old fishing town as legend bade, for only the poor and the lonely remember.

Then beyond the hill's crest I saw Kingsport outspread frostily in the gloaming; snowy Kingsport with its ancient vanes and steeples, ridgepoles and chimney-pots, wharves and small bridges, willow-trees and graveyards; endless labyrinths of steep, narrow, crooked streets, and dizzy church-crowned central peak that time durst not touch; ceaseless mazes of colonial houses piled and scattered at all angles and levels like a child's disordered blocks; antiquity hovering on grey wings over winter-whitened gables and gambrel roofs; fanlights and small-paned windows one by one gleaming out in the cold dusk to join Orion and the archaic stars. And against the rotting wharves the sea pounded; the secretive, immemorial sea out of which the people had come in the elder time.

Beside the road at its crest a still higher summit rose, bleak and windswept, and I saw that it was a burying-ground where black grave-stones stuck ghoulishly through the snow like the decayed fingernails of a gigantic corpse. The printless road was very lonely, and sometimes I thought I heard a distant horrible creaking as of a gibbet in the wind. They had hanged four kinsmen of mine for witchcraft in 1692, but I did not know just where.

As the road wound down the seaward slope I listened for the merry sounds of a village at evening, but did not hear them. Then I thought of the season, and felt that these old Puritan folk might well have Christmas customs strange to me, and full of silent hearthside prayer. So after that I did not listen for merriment or look for wayfar-ers, but kept on down past the hushed lighted farmhouses and shadowy stone walls to where the signs of ancient shops and sea taverns creaked in the salt breeze, and the grotesque knockers of pillared doorways glistened along deserted, unpaved lanes in the light of little, curtained windows.

I had seen maps of the town, and knew where to find the home of my people. It was told that I should be known and welcomed, for village legend lives long; so I hastened through Back Street to Circle Court, and across the fresh snow on the one full flagstone pavement in the town, to where Green Lane leads off behind the Market house. The old maps still held good, and I had no trouble; though at Arkham they must have lied when they said the trolleys ran to this place, since I saw not a wire overhead. Snow would have hid the rails in any case. I was glad I had chosen to walk, for the white village had seemed very beautiful from the hill; and now I was eager to knock at the door of my people, the seventh house on the left in Green Lane, with an ancient peaked roof and jutting second story, all built before 1650.

There were lights inside the house when I came upon it, and I saw from the diamond windowpanes that it must have been kept very close to its antique state. The upper part overhung the narrow grass-grown street and nearly met the overhanging part of the house opposite, so that I was almost in a tunnel, with the low stone doorstep wholly free from snow. There was no sidewalk, but many houses had high doors reached by double flights of steps with iron railings. It was an odd scene, and because I was strange to New England I had never known its like before. Though it pleased me, I would have relished it better if there had been footprints in the snow, and people in the streets, and a few windows without drawn curtains.

When I sounded the archaic iron knocker I was half afraid. Some fear had been gathering in me, perhaps because of the strangeness of my heritage, and the bleakness of the evening, and the queerness of the silence in that aged town of curious customs. And when my knock was answered I was fully afraid, because I had not heard any footsteps before the door creaked open. But I was not afraid long, for the gowned, slippered old man in the doorway had a bland face that reassured me; and though he made signs that he was dumb, he wrote a quaint and ancient welcome with the stylus and wax tablet he carried.

He beckoned me into a low, candle-lit room with massive exposed rafters and dark, stiff, sparse furniture of the seventeenth century. The past was vivid there, for not an attribute was missing. There was a cavernous fireplace and a spinning wheel at which a bent old woman in loose wrapper and deep poke-bonnet sat back toward me, silently spinning despite the festive season. An indefinite dampness seemed upon the place, and I marveled that no fire should be blazing. The high-backed settle faced the row of curtained windows at the left, and seemed to be occupied, though I was not sure. I did not like everything about what I saw, and felt again the fear I had had. This fear grew stronger from what had before lessened it, for the more I looked at the old man's bland face the more its very blandness terrified me. The eyes never moved, and the skin was too like wax. Finally I was sure it was not a face at all, but a fiendishly cunning mask. But the flabby hands, curiously gloved, wrote genially on the tablet and told me I must wait a while before I could be led to the place of festival.

Pointing to a chair, table, and pile of books, the old man now left the room; and when I sat down to read I saw that the books were hoary and moldy, and that they included old Morryster's wild *Marvells of Science,* the terrible *Saducismus Triumphatus* of Joseph Glanvill, published in 1681, the shocking *Daemonolatreia* of Remigius, printed in 1595 at Lyons, and worst of all, the unmentionable *Necronomicon* of the mad Arab Abdul Alhazred, in Olaus Wormius's forbidden Latin translation; a book which I had never seen, but of which I had heard monstrous things whispered. No one spoke to me, but I could hear the creaking of signs in the wind outside, and the whir of the wheel as the bonneted old woman continued her silent spinning, spinning.

I thought the room and the books and the people very morbid and disquieting, but because an old tradition of my fathers had summoned me to strange feastings, I resolved to expect queer things. So I tried to read, and soon became tremblingly absorbed by something I found in that accursed *Necronomicon;* a thought and a legend too hideous for sanity or consciousness. But I disliked it when I fancied I heard the closing of one of the windows that the settle faced, as if it had been stealthily opened. It had seemed to follow a whirring that was not of the old woman's spinning wheel. This was not much, though, for the old woman was spinning very hard, and the aged clock had been striking. After that I lost the feeling that there were persons on the settle, and was reading intently and shudderingly when the old man came back booted and dressed in a loose antique costume, and sat down on that very bench, so that I could not see him. It was certainly nervous waiting, and the blasphemous book in my hands made it doubly so. When eleven struck, however, the old man stood up, glided to a massive carved chest in a corner, and got two hooded cloaks; one of which he donned, and the other of which he draped round the old woman, who was ceasing her monotonous spinning. Then they both started for the outer door; the woman lamely creeping, and the old man, after picking up the very book I had been reading, beckoning me as he drew his hood over that unmoving face or mask.

We went out into the moonless and tortuous network of that incredibly ancient town; went out as the lights in the curtained windows disappeared one by one, and the Dog Star leered at the throng of cowled, cloaked figures that poured silently from every doorway and formed monstrous processions up this street and that, past the creaking signs and antediluvian gables, the thatched roofs and diamond-paned windows; threading precipitous lanes where decaying houses overlapped and crumbled together, gliding across open courts and churchyards where the bobbing lanthorns made eldritch drunken constellations.

Amid these hushed throngs I followed my voiceless guides; jostled by elbows that seemed preternaturally soft, and pressed by chests and stomachs that seemed abnormally pulpy; but seeing never a face and hearing never a word. Up, up, up the eerie columns slithered, and I saw that all the travelers were converging as they flowed near a sort of focus of crazy alleys at the top of a high hill in the centre of the town, where perched a great white church. I had seen it from the road's crest when I looked at Kingsport in the new dusk, and it had made me shiver because Aldebaran had seemed to balance itself a moment on the ghostly spire.

There was an open space around the church; partly a churchyard with spectral shafts, and partly a half-paved square swept nearly bare of snow by the wind, and lined with unwholesomely archaic houses having peaked roofs and overhanging gables. Death-fires danced over the tombs, revealing gruesome vistas, though queerly failing to cast any shadows. Past the churchyard, where there were no houses, I could see over the hill's summit and watch the glimmer of stars on the harbor, though the town was invisible in the dark. Only once in a while a lanthorn bobbed horribly through serpentine alleys on its way to overtake the throng that was now slipping speechlessly into the church.

I waited till the crowd had oozed into the black doorway, and till all the stragglers had followed. The old man was pulling at my sleeve, but I was determined to be the last. Then I finally went, the sinister man and the old spinning woman before me. Crossing the threshold into that swarming temple of unknown darkness, I turned once to look at the outside world as the churchyard phosphorescence cast a sickly glow on the hilltop pavement. And as I did so I shuddered. For though the wind had not left much snow, a few patches did remain on the path near the door; and in that fleeting backward look it seemed to my troubled eyes that they bore no mark of passing feet, not even mine.

The church was scarce lighted by all the lanthorns that had entered it, for most of the throng had already vanished. They had streamed up the aisle between the high white pews to the trap door of the vaults which yawned loathsomely open just before the pulpit, and were now squirming noiselessly in. I followed dumbly down the foot-worn steps and into the dank, suffocating crypt. The tail of that sinuous line of night-marchers seemed very horrible, and as I saw them wriggling into a venerable tomb they seemed more horrible still. Then I noticed that the tomb's floor had an aperture down which the throng was sliding, and in a moment we were all descending an ominous staircase of rough-hewn stone; a narrow spiral staircase damp and peculiarly odorous, that wound endlessly down into the bowels of the hill past monotonous walls of dripping stone blocks and crumbling mortar. It was a silent, shocking descent, and I observed after a horrible interval that the walls and steps were changing in nature, as if chiseled out of the solid rock. What mainly troubled me was that the myriad footfalls made no sound and set up no echoes.

After more aeons of descent I saw some side passages or burrows leading from unknown recesses of blackness to this shaft of nighted mystery. Soon they became excessively numerous, like impious catacombs of nameless menace; and their pungent odor of decay grew quite unbearable. I knew we must have passed down through the mountain and beneath the earth of Kingsport itself, and I shivered that a town should be so aged and maggoty with subterraneous evil.

Then I saw the lurid shimmering of pale light, and heard the insidious lapping of sunless waters. Again I shivered, for I did not like the things that the night had brought, and wished bitterly that no forefather had summoned me to this primal rite. As the steps and the passage grew broader, I heard another sound, the thin, whining mockery of a feeble flute; and suddenly there spread out before me the boundless vista of an inner world—a vast fungous shore litten by a belching column of sick greenish flame and washed by a wide oily river that flowed from abysses frightful and unsuspected to join the blackest gulfs of immemorial ocean.

Fainting and gasping, I looked at that unhallowed Erebus of titan toadstools, leprous fire, and slimy water, and saw the cloaked throngs forming a semicircle around the blazing pillar. It was the Yule-rite, older than man and fated to survive him; the primal rite of the solstice and of spring's promise beyond the snows; the rite of fire and evergreen, light and music. And in the Stygian grotto I saw them do the rite, and adore the sick pillar of flame, and throw into the water handfuls gouged out of the viscous vegetation which glittered green in the chlorotic glare. I saw this, and I saw something amorphously squatted far away from the light, piping noisomely on a flute; and as the thing piped I thought I heard noxious muffled flutterings in the foetid darkness where I could not see. But what frightened me most was that flaming column; spouting volcanically from depths profound and inconceivable, casting no shadows as healthy flame should, and coating the nitrous stone above with a nasty, venomous verdigris. For in all that seething combustion no warmth lay, but only the clamminess of death and corruption.

The man who had brought me now squirmed to a point directly

beside the hideous flame, and made stiff ceremonial motions to the semicircle he faced. At certain stages of the ritual they did groveling obeisance, especially when he held above his head that abhorrent *Necronomicon* he had taken with him; and I shared all the obeisances because I had been summoned to this festival by the writings of my forefathers. Then the old man made a signal to the half-seen flute player in the darkness, which player thereupon changed its feeble drone to a scarce louder drone in another key; precipitating as it did so a horror unthinkable and unexpected. At this horror I sank nearly to the lichened earth, transfixed with a dread not of this nor any world, but only of the mad spaces between the stars.

Out of the unimaginable blackness beyond the gangrenous glare of that cold flame, out of the Tartarean leagues through which that oily river rolled uncanny, unheard, and unsuspected, there flopped rhythmically a horde of tame, trained, hybrid winged things that no sound eye could ever wholly grasp, or sound brain ever wholly remember. They were not altogether crows, nor moles, nor buzzards, nor ants, nor vampire bats, nor decomposed human beings; but something I cannot and must not recall. They flopped limply along, half with their webbed feet and half with their membraneous wings; and as they reached the throng of celebrants the cowled figures seized and mounted them, and rode off one by one along the reaches of that unlighted river, into pits and galleries of panic where poison springs feed frightful and undiscoverable cataracts.

The old spinning woman had gone with the throng, and the old man remained only because I had refused when he motioned me to seize an animal and ride like the rest. I saw when I staggered to my feet that the amorphous flute player had rolled out of sight, but that two of the beasts were patiently standing by. As I hung back, the old man produced his stylus and tablet and wrote that he was the true deputy of my fathers who had founded the Yule worship in this ancient place; that it had been decreed I should come back, and that the most secret mysteries were yet to be performed. He wrote this in a very ancient hand, and when I still hesitated he pulled from his loose robe a seal ring and a watch, both with my family arms, to prove that he was what he said. But it was a hideous proof, because I knew from old papers that that watch had been buried with my great-great-great-great-grandfather in 1698.

Presently the old man drew back his hood and pointed to the family resemblance in his face, but I only shuddered, because I was sure that the face was merely a devilish waxen mask. The flopping animals were now scratching restlessly at the lichens, and I saw that the old man was nearly as restless himself. When one of the things began to waddle and edge away, he turned quickly to stop it; so that the suddenness of his motion dislodged the waxen mask from what should have been his head. And then, because that nightmare's position barred me from the stone staircase down which we had come, I flung myself into the oily underground river that bubbled somewhere to the caves of the sea; flung myself into that putrescent juice of earth's inner horrors before the madness of my screams could bring down upon me all the charnel legions these pest-gulfs might conceal.

At the hospital they told me I had been found half frozen in Kingsport Harbour at dawn, clinging to the drifting spar that accident sent to save me. They told me I had taken the wrong fork of the hill road the night before, and fallen over the cliffs at Orange Point; a thing they deduced from prints found in the snow. There was nothing I could say, because everything was wrong. Everything was wrong, with the broad window shewing a sea of roofs in which only about one in five was ancient, and the sound of trolleys and motors in the streets below. They insisted that this was Kingsport, and I could not deny it.

When I went delirious at hearing that the hospital stood near the old churchyard on Central Hill, they sent me to St. Mary's Hospital in Arkham, where I could have better care. I liked it there, for the doctors were broad-minded, and even lent me their influence in obtaining the carefully sheltered copy of Alhazred's objectionable *Necronomicon* from the library of Miskatonic University. They said something about a "psychosis," and agreed I had better get any harassing obsessions off my mind.

So I read again that hideous chapter, and shuddered doubly

because it was indeed not new to me. I had seen it before, let footprints tell what they might; and where it was I had seen it were best forgotten. There was no one—in waking hours—who could remind me of it; but my dreams are filled with terror, because of phrases I dare not quote. I dare quote only one paragraph, put into such English as I can make from the awkward Low Latin.

"The nethermost caverns," wrote the mad Arab, "are not for the fathoming of eyes that see; for their marvels are strange and terrific. Cursed the ground where dead thoughts live new and oddly bodied, and evil the mind that is held by no head. Wisely did Ibn Schacabao say, that happy is the tomb where no wizard hath lain, and happy the town at night whose wizards are all ashes. For it is of old rumour that the soul of the devil-bought hastes not from his charnel clay, but fats and instructs *the very worm that gnaws;* till out of corruption horrid life springs, and the dull scavengers of earth wax crafty to vex it and swell monstrous to plague it. Great holes secretly are digged where earth's pores ought to suffice, and things have learnt to walk that ought to crawl."

THE WEREWOLF OF PONKERT

A Complete Novelette · by H. Warner Munn

They are neither brute nor human—
They are neither man nor woman—
They are Ghouls.
—Poe: The Bells.

I n the past, when I toured in France, invariably I made a point of never failing to stop at a certain tavern, about thirty miles from Paris. I will not give you more definite directions for reaching it, for it was a discovery of my own and as such I would share it with no one. The fact that the inn has very pretty serving maids is but incidental, the real reason of my visits being the superlative excellence of the wine.

Many a night have I and the old Pierre sat, smoked and drunk till the wee hours of the morning, and many have been the experiences we have exchanged of wild, eerie adventure in various parts of the globe. Pierre also was a great traveler and seeker after adventure before he drifted into the backwater of this placid village, to finish there the remainder of his days.

One night (or morning, I should say), Pierre grew indiscreet under the influence of his nectar, and let fall a few words so pregnant of possibilities that I scented a mystery at once; and when he was sober I demanded an explanation. And, having said so much, seeing that he could not dissuade me, he brought forth proof of his dark hints in regard to a horrible occurrence in the annals of his family.

The proof was a book, bound in hand-tooled leather and locked by a silver clasp. When open it proved to be written in a crabbed hand in old Latin on what was apparently parchment, which was now yellow with age, but must when new have been remarkably white.

It comprised only four leaves, each a foot square and glued or cemented to a thin wooden backing. They were written on only one side and completely covered with this close, crabbed Latin.

On the back of the book were two iron staples, and hanging from each, several links of heavy rusted chain. Evidently, like most valuable books which were available to the public in the past, it had been chained fast to something immovable to prevent theft.

Unfortunately, I cannot read Latin, or in fact any languages but French and English, although I speak several. So it was necessary for my friend to read it to me, which he did.

After I had recovered from the numbness which the curious narrative had thrown over me, I begged him to read it again—slowly. As he read, I copied; and here is the tale for you to judge and believe as you see fit. Told in Hungarian, transcribed in Latin, translated into modern French and from that into English, it is probably both garbled and improved. No doubt anachronisms abound, but be that as it may, it remains without dispute the only authentic document known of a werewolf's experiences, dictated by himself.

Having but a few hours in which to live, I dictate that which follows, hoping that someone thereby may be warned by my example and profit by it. The priest has told me to tell my story to him and he will write it down. Later it will be written down again, but I do not care to think of that now.

My name is Wladislaw Brenryk. For twenty years I lived in the village where I was born, a small place in the northeastern part of Hungary. My parents were poor and I had to work hard—harder, in fact, than I liked, for I was born of a languid disposition. So I used my wits to save my hands, and I was clever, if I do say it myself. I was born for trading and bargaining, and none of the boys I grew to manhood with could beat me in a trade.

Time went on, and before I had reached manhood my father died in a pestilence. Although my mother was pestilence-salted (for she had the plague when she was a girl and recovered), she soon gave up, grew weaker and weaker, finally joining my father in the skies. The priest of our village said that it was the trouble in her lungs that killed her, but I know better, for they had loved each other much.

Alone and lorn for the first time in my life, I could not bear to remain longer amongst the scenes of my happy boyhood. So on a fine spring morning I set forth carrying on my back those possessions which I could not bring myself to part with, and around my waist a well-stuffed money belt, filled with the results of my trading and the sale of our cottage.

For several years I wandered here and there, horse-trading for a time, then again a peddler of jewelry and small articles. Finally I came to Ponkert, and started a small shop in which I sold beautiful silks, jewels and sword hilts. It was the sword hilts that sold the best. They were highly decorated with golden filigree and encrusted with precious stones. Chiefs and moneyed nobles would come or send messengers for many miles to obtain them. I gained a reputation for honesty and fair dealing, likewise a less enviable notoriety for being a miser. It is true that I was careful and cautious, but I defy anyone to prove that I was parsimonious.

I had closed up the shop for the night and harnessed the horses for the long drive home, when for the first time I wished that I lived in the village instead of being so far away. I had always enjoyed the ride before; a man can think much in a ten mile ride and it gave an opportunity to clean my mind of the day's worries and bickering, so as to come to my dear wife and little daughter with thoughts of only them.

What made me look forward with anxiety to the long ride home was the many broad gold pieces secreted in my wallet. I had never been molested on that road, but others had been found robbed and partly devoured, with tracks of both man and beast about them in the snow.

Obviously, thought I at the time, thieves had beaten them down, leaving them for the wolves.

But there was a disturbing factor in the problem: not only were the bodies horribly mutilated and the beast tracks about them extraordinarily large for wolf tracks, but the feet of the men were unprotected by any covering whatever! Barefooted men roaming through the forests, in the snow, on the dim likelihood of discovering prey which could be forced to yield wealth! The very idea was improbable. If I had only known then what I know now, my entire life might have been changed, but it was not so to be.

To return to my story: It was known that I had a large amount of money in my possession, for that afternoon the chief of a large Tartar caravan, which was passing through, had stopped at my shop and taken six of my best sword hilts with him, leaving their equivalent in gold. So I had cause enough to worry. I looked about for some sort of weapon, and found a short iron bar, which I tucked beneath the robes of the sleigh; then I spoke to the mares, and we were off on the long ride home.

For a long time we went creaking along, the sleigh runners squeaking on the well-packed snow. Frost was in the air, and the stars gleamed down coldly upon the dark forest, hardly lighting the road. As yet the moon had not risen.

I turned from the main traveled highway and took the river road. This left the forest behind, but the traveling was much worse. Exposed to the winds, the light snowfall of the morning had drifted, and the roadway was choked. I thought of leaving the road and taking to the smooth surface of the river which gleamed brightly to the left, but this would have meant a mile or more extra to travel, for the river curved in a great bend opposite our home, and there was an impassable barrier of small trees and brush for some distance.

The moon was now rising over the hill I had just quitted, and as the beams struck upon me, I was suddenly seized by a fit of the most unaccountable terror. This peculiar feeling held me rigid in my seat. It seemed as if a hand of ice had been suddenly laid upon the back of my neck.

The mares, it was evident, had felt this strange thrill also, for they imperceptibly increased their speed without urging of mine. Indeed, I could not have moved a muscle while that spell was upon me.

Soon we dipped down into the hollow at the hill's foot, and the power that had frozen me was removed. A strange feeling of exaltation and happiness swept over me, as if I had escaped from some terrible and unthinkable danger.

"Hai!" I shouted, rising in the sleigh and cracking my whip.

The mares responded nobly and we started to climb the next hill. As we did so, a fiendish howling came down the wind, but faintly, as if it were some distance away. I stopped the mares and stood up in the sleigh, the better to listen.

Faintly and far away sounded the cries, mellowed by distance. Then they grew louder and louder as the brutes came nearer, and over the top of the hill I had just quitted swept the devilish pack! They were on my trail, and it was only too plain that before I could reach home they would be upon me.

There was only one chance, and I took it. I clucked to the horses and turned them on to the ice of the river where lay a straight, smooth roadway. As long as the mares kept their feet, I was safe. But if one should stumble—!

Then that same spell of horror threw its icy mantle over me again; I sagged back; the mares took the bit in their teeth; and we rushed like a thunderbolt down the river.

Little puffs of diamond dust shot from the ice into my lap, as the steel-shod hoofs rang and clicked. On we tore, while I sat in the sleigh like a stone, unable to move a muscle. Faster and faster we rushed between the banks of brush that fringed the icy causeway.

Fainter re-echoed the demoniac ululations behind me, until at last they ceased altogether and the horses gradually slackened their furious pace.

Here the spell left me, nor did it ever come again. Now we traveled at a trot, which slowed until the mares were but walking along, their panting breath paling their dark heaving sides to gray, in the frosty air.

Then we rounded the bend, and I saw black, open water ahead.

Here progress, perforce, ceased. There was no way out, except to turn back and mount the bank where less underbrush grew, then into the smooth plain beyond and homeward.

So I tugged at the rein, and we swerved halfway around. In that moment of unpreparedness, all became confusion.

A gloating chuckle sounded evilly from the farther bank, and five great gray shapes charged at me across the ice.

To think was to act with me. I have always been a creature of impulse, and almost instinctively I turned back, slashing the mares till they reared and we plunged straight forward into the onrushing mass of bodies. This resolute move took the beasts by surprise and halted them. They scattered, and I was through, with a clear road before me. But my escape was not so to be accomplished.

Silently, from the shelter of an overhanging rock, trotted two more of the creatures; a very giant of a beast, gaunt and gray, beside which moved a small black one. Roaring, the gray flung himself at the horses, which reared and plunged in terror; and the rest were upon me from the rear.

Then, turmoil of battle, pandemonium of sound, through which cut like a knife the scream of a horse. One was down! I felt the sleigh lurch to one side; heavy bodies struck at me, sharp teeth tore; but I kept my balance until one, such was his velocity, struck me and laid me flat in the bottom of the sleigh, himself rebounding and shooting over the side.

Something offered itself to my hand, something cold and metallic. I raised my arm, smote, felt steel bite bone, felt bone crunch beneath my stroke. I laid about me like a madman, with the bar, and cleared a space. I stood erect and waited for the attack.

But no instant attack followed. The menace of the bar was apparently too strong, and one by one they sank down on their haunches to rest or to wait. Jaws gaped wide and tongues lolled. Panting, they rested after the long run.

As I stood there in the sleigh, watching them, it seemed as if they were laughing, ghoul-like, at my horrible plight. As I soon found, they were!

I became conscious of a noise behind me, a small noise, such as the wind might make blowing a dead leaf across the bare ice; a sound like dead twigs rustling in the breeze, a faint scraping of claws, a padding of feet; and turning, I looked straight into the red glaring dots which were the eyes of the black wolf!

I shouted hoarsely, swung up the bar and brought it down with every ounce of force that I possessed. Unfortunately for myself, the beast, and Hungary, the great gray creature which ran at his side swerved and took the blow instead, squarely between the eyes.

He grunted, choked; a stream of blood shot from his mouth and nostrils. His eyelids opened and closed convulsively. Then lie collapsed. The bar had crashed halfway through his head.

I whirled, expecting to be overwhelmed by the six that still lived, but to my intense surprise the surge of bodies that I had seen from the tail of my eye, when I struck at the black wolf, had subsided and they were now loping round and round the sleigh.

As they moved, the stricken mare followed them with her pain-filled eyes, while the one that was unharmed struggled constantly to be free. As the black leader passed me in the circling rout, I, likewise, slowly turned to keep him always in sight. Instinct told me that from him would come my greatest danger.

Now I noticed a strange thing—about the necks of each of the five gray beasts there hung upon a thong a leathern pouch, about the size of a large fist. These pouches hung flat and flaccid as if they were empty. The black, examine as closely as I might, wore none.

Then, as with one accord, they stopped in their tracks, and sank on their haunches. That for which they had been waiting had at last occurred. There seemed to be some sort of a silent signal given. Simultaneously they lifted their heads and loosed a long, low wail, in which seemed to hang all the desolation and loneliness of eternity. Thereafter none moved or uttered a sound.

Everything was deathly still. Even the wind, which had been sporting in the undergrowth, had now faded into nothingness and died. Only the labored breathing of the two mares and the hoarse panting of the brutes were to be heard.

Little red eyes, swinish and glittering like hell-sparks, shone malevolently at me by the reflected light of the now fully risen moon.

In this unaccountable pause I had time to see the full beauty of the trap. As I have stated, the river formed a great bow, and while I was traveling on the curve between nock and nock, they quitted the river and waited at the rapids, the line of their pursuit forming the string to the bow.

Also, for the first time, I could examine carefully and note what manner of beasts these were that held me in their power.

Far from being wolves, as my first thought had been, they were great gray animals, the size of a large hound, except the leader, who was black and more the size and shape of a true wolf. All, however, had the same general appearance, and the same characteristics. A high intelligent brow, beneath which gleamed little red pig-like eyes, with a glint of a devil in their glance; long and misshapen hind quarters, which caused them to move with a rabbit-like lope when they ran; and most terrifying of all, they were almost hairless and possessed not the slightest rudiment of a tail!

The circle was so arranged that as I stood, wary of possible attack, I could see four of the six. The small black creature was directly in front of me, tongue hanging out, apparently chuckling to himself in anticipation of some ghastly joke to follow.

Two were behind me, in whichever way I turned, but the night was so still that I could have heard them approaching long before they could have rushed me.

As I watched the creatures, I suddenly noticed that they were no longer glaring at me, but at something behind and beyond me and on the ground. I whirled, fearing a charge, but not a move anywhere in the circle had taken place. So I glanced with the tail of my eye for a rush at my back, and set myself to solve the mystery.

There was nothing before me, on the bare ice, but here and there a white line extended across the river, caused by the snow drifting into cracks. Now I noticed that across one of these there lay, inside the circle, the dead body of the thing that I had slain with the bar. The four creatures which I could now see were watching this intently. I did likewise, with senses alert for treachery. I glanced from one end of the warped, twisted and broken thing, to the other. Somehow it seemed more symmetrical than before; longer in a way, and of a more human cast of feature.

Then—God! Shall I never forget that moment?

I looked at its right forepaw, or where its right forepaw should have been and was not. A white hairless hand had taken its place!

I screamed, hoarsely and horribly, grasped my bar firmly, leapt from the sleigh and rushed into the pack, which, risen, was waiting to receive me.

Everything from that moment until my arrival home in the morning is a blur. I remember a black figure, standing erect before me, burning eyes which fixed me like a statue of stone, a command to strip and a sharp stinging pain in the hollow of my elbow, where the great vein lies.

Then more dimly, I seem to recall a moment of intense anguish as if all my bones were being dislocated and reset, a yelping, howling chorus of welcome, a swift rushing over ice on all fours, and a shrill sharp screaming, such as only a horse in mortal fear can give!

Then there is a clear spot of recollection in which I was eating raw flesh and blood of my own mare, with snarling creatures like myself gorging all around me.

How I reached home, I have not the slightest idea, but the next that I remember is a warm room and my dear wife's face bending over mine. All after that, for nearly a week, was delirium, in which I raved incessantly, so they told me, of wolves which were not wolves, and a black fiend with eyes like embers.

When I was well again I went to the scene of my adventure, but the ice had broken up in an early thaw, and only the swollen river rolled where I had been captured. At first, I thought that my half-remembered fancies were freakish memories, born of delirium, but one night in the early spring, as I lay in bed, only half asleep, something occurred which robbed me of this hope. I heard the long, melancholy wail of a wolf! Calling and appealing, it drew me to the window in hopes of seeing the midnight marauder, but nothing was visible as far as I could see, so I turned to go back to bed again. As I moved away from the window it came again, insistently calling. A powerful attraction drew me. I silently opened the window and melted into the darkness outside.

It was a warm spring evening as I padded silently along on bare feet, through the forest, drawn in a direction that led toward the thickest portion of the wood. I must have gone at least for half a mile under the influence of a strange exhilaration that had come over me, like that of a lover who keeps a tryst with his beloved.

Then the wailing cry echoed again, but with a shock I realized that there was no sound in the wood save the usual night noises. I realized the truth! The sound did not exist in reality, but I was hearing with the ears of the spirit rather than my fleshly ones. I suspected danger, but it was too late to turn back.

A figure rose to a standing posture, and I recognized the master, as he called himself, and we also, later. Under a power not my own, I stripped off my night garments, concealed them in a hollow tree which the master showed me, and fell to the ground, a beast! The master had drunk my blood, and the old story that I had never quite believed, to the effect that if a wampyr drinks one's blood, he or she has a power over that person that nothing can break, and eventually he also will be a wampyr, was coming true.

We raced off into the night, were joined later by the other five, and paused for a time in the forest. Here the master transformed himself, and I also. We stood there, and for the first time I heard the master's voice.

"Look well!" it croaked. "Look well! Welcome you to the pack this man?" (From the tone and actions I judged that he was speaking by rote, and using set phrases for the occasion.) Here there arose a howl of assent.

"Look well!" he said to me. "Look well! Do you wish to be one of these?" pointing to the pack. I covered my eyes with my hands and shrank back. "Think well," he spoke again, catching my bare shoulder with one talon, and mouthing into my ear. "Will you join my band of free companions, or furnish them with a meal tonight?" I could imagine that a death's-head grin overspread his features at this, though my eyes were still blinded.

"You have a choice," he said. "We do not harm the poor, only the rich, although now and then we take a cow or horse from them, for that is our due. But the rich we slay, and their jewels and fine gold are ours. I take none myself, all belongs to my companions. What do you say?"

I cried "No!" as loudly as I could, and stared defiantly into his face. Over his shoulder I noted that the pack was gradually moving in, stealthily with eager leering looks.

"Ha!" he cackled, as I paled before that menace; "where now is your bravery? Make your choice. Die here and now, or make a promise to obey me unswervingly, to deviate not a jot from my orders, no matter what they may be, and be my willing slave. I will make you rich beyond your wildest dreams, your people shall wear sables and ermine, and the king himself will be proud to acknowledge you as friend. Come, what say you?" he asked.

I hesitated, temporizing. "Why do you single out me? I have never harmed you, do not even know you. There must be hundreds stronger than I and more willing, within easy reach. Why not use those you have or take someone else?"

"There must be seven in the pack," he answered simply. "You slew one. Therefore must you take his place. It is but justice."

Justice! I laughed in his face. Justice, that a man fighting for his life should also perish if, slaying one of his enemies, he himself still lived!

My laughter infuriated him. "Enough delay!" he cried impatiently. "Come, decide! Go to them, or promise to obey! Death or life. Which? Do you promise?"

What a terrible choice I was offered! A horrible death beneath fangs of beasts which should never have existed, with no one ever to know that I had resisted the temptation of proffered life; or an even more terrible existence as one of these unnatural things, half man, half demoniac beast! But if I chose death, I should have a highly problematical hope of future life in the skies, and my wife and daughter would be left alone.

If I chose life, I should have high adventure to season my prosaic existence; I should have wealth with which I could buy a title. Besides, something might happen to save me from the fate which otherwise would sometime inevitably overtake me. Is it any wonder to you, why I chose as I did? Would you not do the same, in my predicament? Even if I had it all to do over again, knowing what I now know, I think I should say again that which I answered the master: "I promise!"

But God! If I had only chosen death!

The things that I saw, heard, and did that night made a stain on my soul that all eternity will never erase. But finally they were over, and we separated, each returning to his home, and the master where no one knows.

I resumed my form by the tree, and as I did so, I remembered the events that had taken place that night. I fell prone on the grass, screaming, cursing, and sobbing, to think of my fate to come. I was damned forever!

Although I have called myself a wampyr, I was not one in the true sense of the word, at the time of which I speak. Neither were any of the rest of my companions, except the master, for although we ate human flesh, drank blood, and cracked bones to extract the last particle of nourishment therefrom, we did so to assuage our fierce hunger more than because it was necessary for our continued existence. We ate heartily of human food also, in the man form, but more and more we found it unsatisfying and came to possess a cannibalistic appetite, which only flesh and blood would conquer.

Gradually we were leaving even this for a diet consisting solely of blood. This, in my firm belief, was that which the master lived upon. His whole appearance bore this out. He was incredibly aged, and I believe an immortal. (He still may be, for no one has seen him dead, although they tell me that he is.)

His face was like a crinkled, seamed piece of timeworn parchment, coal-black with age. His eyes glittered with youth, seeming to have almost a separate existence of their own. Gradually, very gradually, the expressions of our faces were changing also, and we were turning into true wampyrs when self-brought catastrophe overtook us.

I will not dwell long upon the year or so in which I was the master's slave, for our dark and bloody deeds are too numerous to mention in detail. Some nights we wandered about in fruitless search and returned empty-handed, but usually we left death and destruction behind us. Most times, however, we would be summoned on some definite foray, which culminated in each of us being, the next day, somewhat richer.

We delighted in killing horses and cattle. We went blood-mad on these occasions, sometimes even leaving our original trail to take up an attractive scent of ox or cow. For these, I do not condemn myself, in so far as no human souls were destroyed in these slaughters, to become wampyrs after death. But as I think of those who are ruined forever because of me, I shudder at the thought!

On one occasion when we dragged down humans, my conscience has always rested easily. We had set out on the track of a sleigh, loaded with wealthy travelers from foreign parts; an old man and his two grandsons about three to five years of age. We followed for several miles to find the sleigh bung on its side, the horses gone, and the three travelers, stiff and stark on the dark stained snow, which was churned by many footprints of horse and man. Enraged, not by the murder (for we ourselves had intended no less), but by the loss of our anticipated loot, we took up the trail which led away toward the mountains. Five men on horseback made up the party. They spurred their horses to the utmost when we sang the Hunger Song, baying as we ran, but they were too slow for us. One by one, we pulled them down, slew the slayers and despoiled the thieves, which was a grim and ghastly jest.

But not often could I console myself thus. Many were the helpless and harmless that we removed from existence, and more horrible did we become. Day by day we were growing hardened and inured to our lot, and only rarely did my soul sicken as at my first metamorphosis. At one of these times, I crept into the village church. It was late at night, and except for myself the building was empty.

I knelt at the altar and unburdened my soul. I confessed everything to the unhearing ears of the Greathearted One, abased myself and groveled on the floor. For hours it seemed, I prayed and begged that I might be given a sign, some small hope, that I should not be damned forever. No sign!

I cursed, screamed and prayed; for a time I must have been mad.

Finally I left. At the church door I bared my head and looked up at the sky across which dark clouds were scudding, obscuring the stars. I rose on tiptoe, shook my fist at the racing clouds, cursed God Himself and waited for the lightning stroke, but none came. Only a light rain started to fall and I arrived home, drenched to the skin, with a heavier load on my heart than when I left.

Yet even then, so mysterious are the ways of an inscrutable Providence, my salvation was approaching in a horrible guise. For on that night I had the thought which was to result in annihilation for us all.

Sometimes, when I walked the village streets, I had met people who seemed to glance furtively at me with a wild look. These glances were quickly averted, but by them I had begun to decide within myself just who were the other members of the pack. Growing bolder and more certain, I had accosted certain of them, to find myself correct.

One by one, I sounded them out, but found only Simon the smith to be of my own sentiments toward our gruesome business. The rest all exulted in the joyous hunt, and could not, we were certain, be persuaded to revolt against this odious enslavement.

But gradually, as we became more hardened and unprincipled, more calloused to the suffering we caused, we had become yet more greedy and rapacious. Here Simon and I found a loophole to attack.

As I have said before, the master never took any of the money, jewels or other portable valuables which we found on the bodies or amongst the possessions of those whom we slew.

So I dropped a word here, a hint there, a vague half-question to one individual singly and alone, while Simon did the same. The gist of all our arguing was, "What does the master take?"

This was a very pertinent question, for it was obvious to all of them that the master was not leader for nothing. He obtained something from each corpse when he went to it, alone, and we sat in the circle, waiting eagerly for the signal to rush in.

To me it was plain that this was nothing more material than the lifeblood of the slain unfortunates, which kept the master alive! Simon and I said nothing of this, gradually forming the opinions of the others to the effect that the immortal souls were absorbed into the master's being, giving him eternal life.

This staggering thought opened great possibilities in the minds of most, and as we thought, all; later I was to learn to my sorrow that not all were so credulous. But more and more they became dissatisfied, less patiently did they restrain themselves from leaping in ahead of their turn, on our bandit raids. For working in their minds, like worms in carrion, or smoldering sparks in damp cloth, which will presently burst into flame, was this; "Why not be immortal myself?"

So were discord and revolt fomented, and so was I the unwitting cause of my further undoing and, strangely enough, my redemption.

Now, my wife was a good woman, and I am sure that she loved me as much as I loved her, but this very love worked our ruin. All people have a weakness in one way or another, and she was no exception to the rule. She was jealous—insanely jealous!

My frequent absences, which I thought had been unnoticed, since I had been careful not to make the slightest noise in opening the window and quitting the house, had been observed for weeks.

I found later that one had told the master what Simon and I had started, and it was the only female member of our pack. But he had already perceived, with his cunning senses, the almost imperceptible signs of revolt against his absolute power. Determining to crush this at the start, he decided to make an example of someone to bind the rest more closely to him by means of a new fear.

Why he chose me instead of Simon I have not the faintest idea, unless it was that I was more intelligent than the ignorant clods that made up the rest of the pack. But so it was, I was chosen to be the victim, and this is the way he set about to bind me forever to him.

He enlisted the aid of old Mother Molla, who was regarded as a witch that had sold her soul to the devil. How she got into the house I never was able to discover, for the original excuse was either forgotten later, or merely left untold. But to the house she came one day, probably obtaining an entrance on some flimsy pretext of begging for cast-off clothing, or of borrowing some cooking utensil.

Before she left she casually mentioned that she had seen me in the early morning before sunrise, coming past her hut. There were only two houses in that part of the wood, Mother Molla's and the charcoal burner's, whose name was Fiermann. All would have yet been well, but the old hag insinuated that "Fiermann had a young and pretty daughter and that he himself was in town very often over night." And so the seeds of suspicion were planted in my wife's mind.

She said that she ordered the hag out, and helped her across the threshold with a foot in her back, and when the old witch picked herself out of the mud she screamed, "Look for yourself, at half an hour before midnight," and hobbled away cackling to herself.

The mischief was done. At first my wife resolved to think nothing about the matter, but it preyed on her mind and gnawed at her heart. So to ease her suspicions she worked away a knot in the partition; and that night when I had gone to bed she waited and watched.

She saw me fling back the clothes and step out of bed, fully dressed, then walk silently across the floor and open the window slowly and carefully, vanishing into the moonlit night. At first, she told me later, she was horrified and heartbroken to think me unfaithful; then she resolved to go away or kill herself, so she would not be a hindrance to me any longer. But finally her emotions changed and vanished until only hate was left. She resolved to watch and wait to see what might befall. She sat by the knothole until I came back just as the cock crew; then she went to bed herself, to toss about sleeplessly until morning.

Night after night she waited, sometimes fruitlessly, for it was not every night that the silent call summoned us to the rendezvous. But when in a period of three weeks I had stealthily stolen out eight times, and she had satisfied herself that Fiermann had also been away, by artfully questioning his girl, her suspicions were confirmed. He was with the pack, but neither knew that. So she decided to confront me with the facts and tell me to choose between the two, "herself, the mother of my child, or this upstart chimney sweep" (I use her own words).

All this time the master's mind was working upon hers to such effect, that although she thought she was choosing her own course of action, in reality she was following the plans which the master had made for her.

One night I heard the silent howl, which never failed, when I was in the man form, to send a chill down my back. I had been expecting this for several days, and had remained dressed each night until midnight, to be in readiness for the summons.

I stepped carefully to the window and released the catch that held it down, then lifted—. What was this! It stuck! I tugged harder with no better results.

Well, then, I should have to use the door. It was dangerous, but might be done. At all means, anything was preferable to going mid within the house. So I turned and was struck fairly in the eyes by a splinter of yellow light. Someone was on the other side of the partition door with a lighted candle, and the door was slowly opening!

Instantly I knew that I was discovered. I bounded toward the bed, intending to simulate sleep until she had gone away, but the door flew open with a crash, and my wife stood in the doorway with a scornful look on her face, and a candle held high, which cast its rays upon me. It was too late to hope for escape, so I attempted to brazen it out.

"Well, what is it?" I asked gently.

"What were you doing at the window?" she said.

"It is so hot in here that I was going to let some air in," I replied.

"To let air in or yourself out?" came, though spoken in a low tone, as a thunderclap to me.

I was struck dumb, and then she told me the whole story as she knew it. The mass of lies with which old Molla must have started her mind in a ferment poured into my consciousness in a heap of jumbled words.

Again came the howling cry, that only I could hear, and I thought I detected a note of anger in it at my delay.

"At first," she said, "I did not believe, but when I saw with my own eyes—"

"Silence!" I roared with such vehemence that the window rattled.

"I will be heard!" she cried. "I have nailed down the window and you shall not pass through this door tonight!"

She slammed the door, and stood dauntlessly before it! My heart went out to her in this moment. That blessed, bright little figure, standing there so bravely, made me forget why I must go. I took a step toward her—and that long eerie wail, which only re-echoed in my brain, sounded much more wrathfully—and nearer!

Torn between two desires, I stood still. My face must have been a mask of horror and anguish, for she looked at me in amazement, which softened to pity.

"What is it, dear?" she whispered. "Have I wronged you after all? Won't you tell me, darling?"

Then I felt the pangs of change beginning and knew that the transformation would follow quickly. I seized a heavy stool, and flung it through the window, following it as quickly myself. If I was to escape, not a second could be wasted.

With a swiftness I had never dreamed she possessed, she ran to me as I crouched in the window with my hands on the side, and one knee on the sill, drawing myself up and over.

She seized me by the hair and dragged my head back, crying meanwhile. "No! No! No! You shall not go. You are mine and I shall keep you! That slut Stanoska will wait long tonight!"

Then she pulled so mightily that I fell upon my back. All was lost! It was too late, for I no longer had any desire to leave! Although I still maintained the outward appearance of a man, I thought as a beast.

I have often thought that the change first took place in the brain and later in the body. I shrieked demoniacally, and another cry arose outside the house, sounding loud through the broken window.

She paled at the sound and shrank back against the table, terrified at my wild and doubtless uncanny appearance. I sprang to my feet, tearing madly at my clothes, ripping them from my body in pieces. I had all the terror of a wild animal now for encumbering clothing or anything like a trap.

When completely stripped, I howled again loudly and fell upon all fours, a misshapen creature that should never have existed. I had become a wild beast! But it was not I, who slunk, bellying the floor, hair all abristle with hate, toward the horror-stricken figure by the table; it was not I—I swear before the God that soon will judge me— who crouched and sprang, tearing with sharp, white fangs that beautiful white throat I had caressed so often!

At a sound outside, I turned, standing astride my victim, and ready to fight for my kill.

With forepaws on the windowsill, through the broken pane a wolf's head peered. With hellish significance it glanced at the door of the next room wherein lay our little girl, asleep in her cradle, then turned its eyes upon me in a mute command.

It was I, the man spirit, who for a moment ruled the monstrous form into which my body had been transmuted. It was the man, myself, who curled those thin beastly lips into a silent, menacing grin, who stalked forward, stiff-legged, hackles raised and eager for revenge!

As swiftly as the head had appeared it withdrew and suddenly came again, curiously changing in form. Its outlines grew less decided, everything seemed to swim before my eyes. I grew giddy, and there visibly the wolf's head changed into that inscrutable parchment mask of the master. Those youthful eyes glared balefully into mine, with a smoky flame behind them.

I felt weak; again the beast was in the ascendant, and I forgot my human heritage. Lost was all memory of love or revenge, I, the were-wolf, slunk through the door, over to the cradle, gloatingly stood anticipating for a moment while blood dripped from my parted jaws on my little girl's clean shift. Then I clamped down my jaws on her dress, and heedless of her puny struggles, or her cries, I rose with a long clean leap through the broken window bearing my contribution to the ghoulish feast!

Then to my tortured memory comes one of those curious blank spots that sometimes afflicted me. I dimly remember snarls of fighting animals, and more faintly still, sounds of shots, but that must be the delirium of my wounds that speaks, for it could not be possible at that time of night that one might be wandering about armed with such an untrustworthy weapon.

Soon it was over. Over! I, the last of our line, took up the horrible hunt, blithe and rejoicing.

Down the valley roared the hellpack, and at the head the master. Foam from my bloody jaws flecked the snow with pink as we galloped along, and mounted the hill like a wave breaking on the beach. We were racing along at full speed with the master still ahead and the rest of the pack strung out at varying distances behind, when suddenly he turned in mid-leap, and alighting, confronted us.

The one who was directly in front of me, and behind the master, dug his feet into the ground and slid in order to avoid collision. I was going so swiftly I could not stop and piled up on my mate. The next instant we were at the bottom of a struggling, clawing, snapping heap. For a moment we milled and fought, while the master sat on his haunches and lolled his tongue out of gaunt grinning jaws, breath panting out in white, moist puffs.

Then we scattered as if blown apart, and also settled into a resting position, a very sheepish-looking pack of marauders. At that moment I felt taking place within me the tearing, rending sensation that always preceded the transforming of our bodies from one form to another. My bones clicked into slightly different positions; I began to remember that I was human, and stood erect, a man again.

All of my companions had been transformed likewise, and were standing where they had stopped.

What a contrast! Six men, white men, each a giant in strength, bound till death and after (as the undead which walk but do not move with mortal life), bound to a thing which I cannot call a man. A black creature only four feet high, which physically the weakest of us might have crushed with one hand. But six men were slavishly obedient to his every order, and moved in mortal fear of him. The pity of it! Only two of us were still human enough to understand that we were damned forever and had no means of escape. To look at their faces made that plain, for deeply graven there were lines that brutalized them, marking our swift progress toward the beast.

I was changing also. I had been told frequently how bad I looked, and my friends thought I should rest more, for it was plain that I was overtaxing my energies, but I always changed the subject as soon as possible, for I knew the real reason of my appearance.

But now the master was advancing. An irresistible force urged me toward him, and as I moved the others closed in about me, so that he and I stood in the center of a small circle.

Then he raised his hand, paw, or talon (I cannot say which, for it resembled all three), and spoke shrilly in a piping feeble voice, for the second and last time in my acquaintance with him.

"Fellow comrades." He leered at me, and I grew hot with rage but said nothing. "I have gathered you here with me tonight to give you a warning that you may use for your own profit. Leave me to do as I see fit and all will be well, but try for one instant to change my course of action or to attack me and you will curse the day you were born."

Then he lost control of himself.

"Fools!" he shrilled; "cursed ignorant peasant fools, you who thought you could kill me, whom even the elements cannot harm! Idiots, clumsy dolts, who tried to plot against the accumulated intelligence of a thousand years, listen to me speak!"

Thunderstruck at this sudden outburst, we staggered and reeled under the revelation which came next.

"From the very first," he cried, "I saw through your stupid intrigue against me, and I laughed to myself. Every move you made, every word you spoke in the seeming privacy of your hovels, I knew long before you. This is nothing new to me. Eighty-four times has this been tried upon me, and eighty-four times have I met the problem in the same way. I have made an example of one of you to warn the rest, and there he stands?"

He whirled swiftly and thrust an ash-gray claw at my face. For some time I had been realizing now what he was about to say, and at this sudden blow I averted my eyes from his and sprang at his throat.

We went down together, and he would have died there and then, but they tore us apart. Poor, blind fools! Again he stood erect, rubbing his throat where I had clutched it, and again he croaked, never glancing at me, as I was held powerless by three men.

"All of you have children, wives, or parents dependent upon you, and defenseless. I saw to that before I chose you, having this very thing in mind. I can at any time change any one of you to a beast by the power of my will, wherever I may be. Tomorrow, if you still resist me I will change you, or you," darting his paw at each in quick succession.

From the circle rose cries of "No! No! Do not do that! I am your man," and "Master, you are our father; do with us as you like!"

Triumphant he laughed, there in the snow plain beneath the starry sky, then bent his gaze upon me. Seizing my chin, he forced my eyes to meet his, and growled, "And you? What say you now?"

I could not resist those burning eyes.

"Master," I muttered, "I am your willing slave."

"Then get back to your den," he cried, giving me a push that sent me prone in the snow, "and wait there till I summon you again."

The pack changed from men back to brutes again, and raced off toward the forest, and though I tried to follow, I could not move until the sound of their cries had faded away into the distance. Finally I rose and went to my dreary home again.

I will pass over briefly what followed; I do not think I could repeat my thoughts as I stumbled along through the night, nearly freezing from lack of clothing and the exposure that resulted.

Dawn was just arriving when I came in sight of the four walls I had so recently called home. I staggered in, and sank into a chair, too listless to build a fire.

After a while, mechanically, I dressed myself, started a blaze in the fireplace, and bethought myself of hiding the body, which lay in the other room, until I could flee. Plan after plan suggested itself to my mind, but all were soon cast aside as useless. Tired out, I buried my head on my arms, as I sat by the table, and must have dozed away some little time.

Suddenly I was aroused from the dull apathy into which I had fallen by a small timid knock on the door. My first thought was that I was discovered. A fit of trembling overcame me, which quickly passed, but left me too weak to rise.

Again sounded the rap, followed by the rasp of frosty gravel as footsteps haltingly passed down the clean-swept path.

Suddenly a plan had formulated itself in my poor distracted brain. I steeled my will to resolute action, hastened to the door, and threw it wide. No one was in sight.

Bewildered, I looked about, suspicious of more wizardry, and between two of the trees that fringed the road I spied a figure slowly traveling toward the village.

"Hai!" I shouted, cupping my hands at my mouth. "What do you want? Come back!"

As the figure turned and approached me, I recognized the half-witted creature who limpingly traveled from village to village during the summer months, working when compelled by necessity to do so, but more often begging his food and shelter from more fortunate people.

"Why do you knock at my door?" I asked, as kindly as I could, when he had come near to me.

"I came last evening," he said, "and the lady that lives here said that she was alone and would not let me in or give me anything, but if later I would come when her husband had returned, she would let me have some old clothes, and something good to take with me. So I slept with the cows, and now I am come again."

I forced myself to speak composedly.

"You are a good lad, and if you will do something for me I will see that you receive new clothing and much money. Here is proof that I mean well," and I tossed a broad gold piece to his feet.

Wildly did he scramble in the dust of the path, but I had no mood to laugh, ridiculous as his action would have seemed at another time. He whimpered in his eagerness to be off, looked into my face, and cowered as does a dog that expects a blow.

Some of my agony of spirit must have been reflected in my face, for he shrank away, all his joy vanished, and he faltered fearfully, "What would you have me do, master?"

His pitiable aspect, struck to my heart, and the words I had been about to speak died stillborn on the end of my tongue. I shall never reveal to anyone what my intention had been, but something nobler and purer than I had ever known enlivened my soul. I drew myself to my full height, glared defiantly at the quivering wretch and cried, "Go you to Ponkert. Arouse the people and bring the soldier's from the barracks. I am a werewolf and I have just slain my wife!"

His eyes seemed starting from his head, his nerveless and palsied limbs carried him shakily down the path, the while he watched me over his shoulder as if he expected to see me turn into a wolf and ravenously pursue him. At the end of the path he bethought himself of flight, threw the gold piece down and started with a curious reeling run toward the village.

A little wind was now rising, blowing flurries of snow and leaves about, and the round evil eye of yellow metal lay and blinked at the morning sun until a little whirlwind of dust collapsed on it and buried its gleam. But although I could not see it I knew it was there, the thing that all men slave, war, and die for, that all men desire, and obtaining are not satisfied, the struggle for which has maimed and damned more souls than any other one thing that has ever been. I went in, shut the door, and left it outside in the dirt, whence it came and where it belongs.

It might have been a minute or a year that I sat at the table, with my head buried in my arms, for any memory that I have of it, but so I found myself when I was roused by a dull roar of many voices outside. Opening the door, I stepped out and waited, expecting nothing less than instant death.

A crowd of about fifty persons came surging up the road, and seeing me standing there, passively waiting, milled and huddled together, each anxious to be in at the death, but none caring to be in the forefront and first to meet the dreaded werewolf.

Much coaxing and urging was given certain of the crowd to send them to me, but none was eager for fame.

Finally stepped out one tanner, clad only in his leather apron, and carrying a huge fish spear in his right hand.

"Come," he shouted, "who follows if I lead?"

Just then sounded the pounding of hoofs, far down the road.

"He who comes must hasten," thought I, "if he would see the finish."

The tanner harangued the steadily growing mob without avail, none desiring to be the first.

At last I was out of the common rut in which the rest of the village was sunken. What a moment! Even in my hopeless situation I could not help but exult. Seventy-five or one hundred against one, and not a man dare move!

At last the tanner despaired of assistance and slowly moved toward me, now and then casting a glance behind to be assured of an open lane of retreat if such was necessary.

I believe, in that moment, that had I leapt forward at them, the whole flock of sheep would have fled screaming down the road; but I did nothing of the kind. I did not move, or even make any resistance when the tanner seized me by the shoulder, his spear ready for the deadly stroke. Why should I? Life had no longer any interest for me!

Finding that I stood passively, the tanner released my shoulder, grasped the spear in both hands and towered above me, his mighty muscles standing out like ropes on his naked arms and chest. The whole assemblage held its breath, the silence was that of death, and a loud clatter of hoofs twitched every head around as if they all had been worked simultaneously by a single string. Straight into the crowd, which broke and scattered before it, came a huge black horse, ridden by a large man, in the uniform of the king's soldiery. As he came he smote right and left with the flat of his long straight sword.

Down came the spear, and down swept the sword full upon the tanner's head. He fell like a poleaxed steer, while the spear buried itself for half its length in the ground by the door.

"This man is mine!" he shouted. "Mine and the king's! He must go with me for trial and sentence; touch him at your peril."

The crowd murmured angrily, started for us, but disintegrated again before the rush of half a company of soldiers that had followed their captain.

"And so, sirs," I was concluding my narrative in the prison barracks at Ponkert, "you see to what ends have I been brought by the machinations of this creature. I do not ask for life myself, for I shall be glad to die, and it is but just that I should; but give me revenge, and I will burn in hell for eternity most happily."

For a time I thought that the officer would deny me, for he ruminated long before he spoke.

"Can you," he said, "entrap this hideous band, if I and my men will give you help?"

I leapt from my chair and shouted, "Give me a dozen men, armed, and not one of those fiends will be alive tomorrow morning!"

Carried away by my enthusiasm, he cried, "You shall have fifty and I will lead them myself;" but then more gravely, "you realize that we cannot leave one alive? That all must die? All?"

I nodded, and looked him squarely in the eyes.

"I understand," I said. "When we have won, do with me as you will. I shall not resist, for I am very tired, and shall be glad to rest. But until then, I am your man!"

"You are brave," he said simply, "and I wish I need not do that which I must. Will you grip hands with me before we leave?" he asked almost diffidently.

I said nothing, but our hands met in a strong clasp, and as he turned away I thought I saw moisture fleck his cheek. He was a man, and I wish I had known him earlier. We could have been friends, perhaps; but enough of that

Some distance from Ponkert there stands a wood, so dense that even at midday there in the center of the forest, only a dim twilight exists. Here sometimes laired the pack. At night we made it our meeting place, and now and again in the thickest recesses one or more of us would spend the day in seclusion. So, knowing this, I made my plans.

I tore my clothes, and dabbled them in blood, wound a bloody bandage around my head, and the soldiers tied my hands securely behind me, also putting a cord about my neck.

Toward evening we set out, about eighty of us in all, including the rustics who trailed along behind, carrying improvised arms, such as hayforks, clubs, and farm implements which were clumsy, but deadly.

Straight through the heart of the wood we passed, I traveling in the midst, reeling along with head down as if worn out, which indeed I was. Now and then the soldier who held the other end of the cord would jerk fiercely, almost causing me to stumble, and on one of these occasions I heard a sullen, stifled growl from a thicket which we were passing. No one else apparently heard; I cautiously lifted my head, and saw a form slink silently into the darker shadows. I had been observed, and the plan was succeeding!

We then passed from the forest and came into the sunlight once more. Between the wood and the hills flowed the river that before had served me so ill. Overlooking this there frowned a great castle that had once dominated the river and the trade routes which crossed the plain on the other side. But this was long ago, so long that the castle builders had passed away, their sons, and theirs also, if indeed there ever were such, leaving only the castle to prove they had ever lived.

As the years went on, various parties of brigands had held the great stone structure, and wars had been fought around and within. Slowly, time and the elements had worked their will unchecked, until the central tower squatted down one day and carried the rest of the castle with it.

Still there remained a strong stonewall, which had enclosed the castle once, but now formed a great square, thirty feet in height, around a shapeless mountain of masonry in the center. Under this imposing monument lay the last who had ever lived there, and some say that their ghosts still haunt the ruins, but I never saw any, or met one who had. At each side of the square, in the walls there stood an iron gate. These were still well preserved, but very rusty, so rusty indeed, that it was impossible to open them, and we were obliged to find an easier mode of entrance.

Finally we discovered a large tree, which, uprooted by a heavy wind, had fallen with its top against the wall, and so remained, forming a bridge which connected the wall and the ground by a gentle incline.

To gain the courtyard it was necessary to follow the wall around to where it faced the plain. Here a large section had fallen inward, leaving the wall but twenty feet in height at that point. Here we went down, by the rope which had tormented me so, and prepared our trap.

It was very simple; I was the bait and we knew that when the time came for the change, they would follow my trail unless the master was warned, and once inside the walls could not leap out. We could then slay them at our leisure, for we were more than ten to one, although many of the farmers had refused to enter the haunted castle and returned to the village.

At last it became near midnight, and faintly, far away, I heard the cries down below me in the wood.

"The time is near," I whispered to the captain as we stood in the enclosure. "I hear them gathering."

"Be ready," he warned the men. "Hide yourselves in the rocks. They come!"

Eagerly we waited, though none was visible now except the captain and two or three soldiers, standing by the pile of masonry.

As I waited near a large pile of stone blocks, I heard someone cry sharply, "Now!"

Shooting lights danced before my eyes, followed by black oblivion, and I fell forward on my face. I had been clubbed from behind.

When I became conscious again the stars still gleamed brightly overhead, but they no longer interested me. My sole thought was to escape from these two-legged creatures that held me prisoner. Again I was the beast!

For the first time I had not been aware of the transition when it took place. Now I had no recollection of my past, and for all I knew I might never have been anything but a quadruped.

Came swiftly the realization that I was being called insistently. From the tail of my eye I saw a man standing beside me, but a little distance away. Perhaps I might escape!

I drew my legs up, and my muscles tightened for the spring. I would leap the wall, I would flee for my life, I would ... and then a tremendous weight came crashing down on my hindquarters, breaking both my legs.

The pain was excruciating! I gave vent to a scream of curdled agony which was answered by howls of mingled encouragement and rage from beyond the wall. Then down from the wall came leaping, one at a time, five great gray brutes. They had followed my trail and come, as they thought, to save me, not dreaming they were being led into a trap.

The soldiers had been wiser than I, for they had foreseen what I had failed to see: that if my story was true, inevitably when my nature changed I would betray them to my comrades.

Between man and wild beast there can be no compromise, so they stunned me, and then toppled down a heavy stone, pinning me to the ground. Instead of warning the pack as I undoubtedly would have done had I but known earlier that they were present, I screamed for help, for the sudden pain drove any other emotion from my mind.

Now all was confusion. Howl of beast, and shout of man, mingled in chorus with clash of pike and fang. Now and again, but infrequently, a shot punctuated the uproar, but these new weapons are too slow to be of practical use, so it was a hand-to-paw, and cheek-to-jowl conflict.

The five were giving a far better account of themselves than I had dreamed possible. Springing in and out again, with lightning movements they could tear a man's throat out and be gone before he could defend himself. The confusion was so great, the press so thick, that a man might kill his comrade by accident. I saw this happen twice.

Now only four were visible, springing to and fro, fighting for their lives like cornered rats, and gradually forcing their way to the wall whence they had come. One must be down!

But no! I saw the missing one, old Mother Molla, rending with sharp white fangs at something which lay half hidden beneath her. A soldier stole silently behind her, and with a mighty display of strength thrust a pike completely through her body. But other eyes than mine had seen the cowardly stroke. The next instant he went down and was buried from sight in the center of the snarling pack. Now the pack was, for several seconds, in a tight knot of bodies, and while they thus remained the soldiers leapt in, pikes and clubs rising and falling. Before Mother Molla had reached the corner toward which she was slowly crawling, coughing out, meanwhile, her life in bloody bubbles, the remainder of the pack had avenged her and died themselves.

It was at this critical moment that a head peered over the wall and two bright little red eyes took in the scene. Why the master had thus delayed his arrival I cannot explain. But whatever his faults he was at least no coward, for the first inkling the men had of his presence was the sight of the black wolf springing down and landing on the heap of dead bodies which had represented his former vassals.

With a bound he was in the midst of the soldiers, fighting with fang and claw. They scattered like sheep, but returned, forming now a close-packed circle around him, barring all egress. Now his only chance of life lay in motion so swift that it would be unsafe to aim a weapon at him for fear of injuring one of the men.

He saw now clearly that all was lost, and quite obviously perceived that flight was his only hope. He gave me a glance of encouragement as I lay there raving and frothing, snapping at, and breaking my teeth upon, the cold unyielding rock that held me down; and he rushed madly about the inside of the circle, searching for a weak spot in it. So in they pressed, striking now and then as he passed, but harming him not.

With hot red tongue hanging from his slavering jaws, he raced about the encircling cordon of foes. Soon was his plan of action made. He leapt in midstride straight at an ignorant yokel who wielded a hayfork. The poor fool struck clumsily, instead of dodging, which mistake was his last, for he missed. Instantly the master had torn out his throat with a single snap and was streaking toward the castle wall.

Now the way was clear; puffs of snow rose behind, before him, and on either side, but apparently he bore a charmed life, for none of the missiles struck him. As he reached the wall he left the ground in the most magnificent leap I have ever seen, from either man or beast, hung by his forefeet twenty feet above the ground for the space of time in which a man might count ten; then, while bullets bestarred the ancient masonry all about him, he wildly scrambled with his hind feet to draw himself up, and was soon over the wall and gone!

They rushed to the rusted gates, but their very haste defeated their efforts, and by the time they reached the open the plain was bare of life. But over the hill to the eastward floated a derisive mocking howl. The master's farewell! From that day to this he has never been seen in Ponkert. Thus ended the wampyr's rule!

So now is my ordeal ended, the master ousted, and the fear that held sway over the village is finished. I, out of all the pack that ravaged the land for many miles, alone am left alive. Somewhere perhaps the master still roams silently, stealthily, in the cool darkness of our nights, but I am certain that never again will he return to Ponkert, for here is my assurance.

When his power crumbled to dust in the courtyard of that ancient castle, and he was forced to flee for his life, his last look and cry to me intimated that he would return and rescue me from my captors. There must have been some spark of humanity in that savage heart, something that would not allow him to leave those who had sworn allegiance to him; for witness that magnificent leap from the courtyard wall to the very midst of his foes, to save the one surviving member of his band.

He did return!

While I lay in the barrack dungeon, recovering from my broken bones and other injuries (for I must be in good health before I am permitted to expiate my crime), one night about a week after the fight I heard the old familiar silent cry.

I recognized the master's call and responded. I thought of all things I should like to tell him and could not through two feet of stonewall. I went over in my mind the whole series of actions by means of which I had escaped from his horrible enslavement.

Beginning with the involuntary murder of my wife and child, I related without uttering a spoken word that which I had done, and ended with the moment when I saw him leap the gap, a fugitive. I know he understood, for after a few seconds of silence, just outside the wall there arose the blood-chilling howl of a wolf. Higher and higher it rose, a long sobbing wail of hate, an undulating crescendo of sound; it thinned to a thread whose throaty murmur was drowned in the rushing trample of heavy feet overhead and the crash of exploding powder. Flash after flash tore the velvet night, mingling with the shouts of the soldiers who were firing from the windows, and at some time in the tumult the master turned his back on Ponkert for the last time, I trust.

Utterly alone in the world, friendless and forlorn, I quit tomorrow this mortal form that has known such strange changes.

I go with no reluctance whatever, for I have nothing to live for, and the sooner gone, the sooner I shall expiate my sins and at last win through to where I am expected. For I cannot believe that I shall suffer in torment forever.

Yet, I would even forego that bliss for the greater one of being a beast again and the master a man, so that I might feel my fangs sink into his black wrinkled throat, and feel the blood spurt warm into my mouth. Oh, to rip, to tear, to slash at that fiend, and have him utterly in my power! To feel his bones crunch beneath my powerful jaws, and to tear his flesh with them!

Yet—sometimes I think perhaps he was once as I, was tempted, fell, sinking lower and lower. Perhaps he, too, was not wholly to blame, but even as I, was weak and doomed from the beginning. Is it the fault of the pot that it is misshapen in the making?

They tell me that every pang I suffer now will shorten my punishment in the future. What my pains on earth shall be I know not. I may be broken on the wheel or stretched upon the rack, but I am resigned and fortified against my fate.

But there is one thing of which I am positive, for they have told me, to add pang upon pang, that I shall be flayed alive, my hide tanned like a beast's, and my dark and gloomy history written upon it for all to read who can!

I have never heard of these things being done before, but I have no doubt that they will be done to me. However, I care not. So much have I suffered in heart and thought that no bodily discomfort can surpass my other torments. I am resigned. May he who reads take warning. Farewell to all whom I know and have known. Farewell!

When the manuscript was finished I sat thinking for a little time. So this book was written on a human hide, which when occupied had enclosed Pierre's ancestor.

"I thought," said I to the old man, "that you told me that the person described in the narrative was your grandpère many times removed. But here it relates that his only child was murdered by himself. How do you explain that?" I asked.

"You will remember perhaps that he told how, after the flight from the cottage, immediately succeeding the act was a blank, save for a vague remembrance of shots. What is more probable than that someone aroused by the howling in the night should fire blindly at the noise, not once but several times. Granted that, it is probable that, frightened by the unexpected noise, the beasts would leave their prey. Such is the legend that has accompanied the book for centuries. Also it is said that this book has never been out of the possession of the Hungarian's descendants. Therefore, observing that I now possess the book, which was given to me by my father, as it was to him by his parent, I assume that in my veins courses the diluted strain of the werewolf."

"This may all be true," I said. "Surely in the weeks of his imprisonment he must have been informed that his little girl had not been devoured; yet he speaks consistently through the tale, as if he knew nothing about the rescue."

"Ah," he replied, "that puzzled me also when I first heard of this. But it is my sincere belief that this information was kept purposely from him to add mental torture to his physical punishment. Why should they trouble themselves to ease the spirit of a man that was responsible for so many crimes?" And such a cruel glitter lit his eyes that I had nothing more to say.

After I had left I congratulated myself upon being so fortunate as to exist in the prosaic Twentieth Century, and not in the superstition-ridden ones which we have just barely left. For even superstitions must have a beginning, and who knows how much truth may lie, after all, in this weird tale?

I never went back to the inn after that. I often meant to, but other business was more important, and procrastination finally made the journey useless.

Pierre is dead now, leaving no relatives or friends but myself. I now possess the book and it lies before me, as I write the story it contains for the world to read, and to laugh at in scorn.

VALE OF THE CORBIES

by Arthur J. Burks

My fear is an intangible fear; yet to me it is terribly real. Reason tells me that my experiences are but the figments of realistic nightmares, while my inner consciousness tells me that what I have gone through has been something more than disordered imagining. I know, in my mind, that it has all been a dream, or a series of dreams.

Yet how can I explain to myself those strange red dots on my hands, my face, my neck?

These are very real. They are not hallucinations, for such of my friends as still come to see me at intervals have noted the dots and remarked upon their peculiar appearance.

This fact it is that is slowly but surely driving me to the very door of the insane asylum. Damn it, I know they have all been dreams! Yet dream creatures do not leave their marks upon the body of the dreamer.

But I had best go back and tell it all from the beginning.

I believe that from childhood I dreamed at intervals, widely spaced intervals, of a little secluded valley which had no location except in the recesses of my subconscious mind. It has always been a sunless valley, with a dark cloud hiding the sun. Miasmatic mists have hung like airy shrouds in the still air above the valley's floor. There has been no breeze in this valley, nor anything that lived or moved. The air has been good, freighted with a musty kind of perfume that has ever tantalized my sensitive nostrils; but it has always been air with a strange sort of chill to it that has ever caused me to waken shivering from my dream. I have called the place a valley, yet I do not know for sure that it is a valley, since only my imagination has walled the valley in. It is as though somewhere beyond the mists and the black cloud there were a circle of high hills which I cannot see, just beyond the reach of my vision.

Always, in my dream, I enter the valley through a narrow cleft in the walls of stone. I know it is a cleft, though I have never seen the walls, for countless times have I believed that, by putting forth my hands, I could have touched the walls on either hand—and I have always feared to put forth my hands, lest they encounter nothingness, and this knowledge of nothingness where I had expected walls might cause my mind to collapse with thoughts of wide immensities, or caverns, bottomless, on my right hand and on my left. I prefer not to know the truth, or to delude myself with the knowledge that there may be walls when, possibly, there are none at all.

Straight through this cleft I go until my sensitive feelings tell me that I have entered the valley.

Then begin my strange sensations.

First, there is a terrible feeling of loneliness. A feeling of great space all about me. A sense of surrounding desolation which my eye cannot see. And over all a silence that is as heavy as a giant's cloak upon the shoulders of a mere boy.

There is the inevitable chill in the air which causes me to shiver, even though—as is sometimes the case when I have dreamed of entering the valley swiftly, with much exertion—my body is bathed in perspiration.

Quietly, lest I disturb the eery atmosphere of the place, I seat myself, cross-legged, upon the ground.

And almost at once the queer noises begin to be heard! Always, until a few weeks ago, the noises have been the same, never varying from dream to dream—which, during the passing of the years, have occurred so frequently that the dreams seem to blend into one long nightmare that has no end.

What are the noises?

They are the beating, beating in the air about me of silken, invisible wings! Yet, until a few weeks ago, I had never seen the creatures whose wings I had heard. Out of the misty distances they come, those wings that whir in the air, those creatures that always swerve and dart hither and yon, ever just far enough within the mists that I cannot see the creatures themselves. When I remember hearing the wings the first time I am sure there was but one pair of them. Out of the mists they came whirring, and I heard them slap smartly as the creature who traveled upon them, sensing my presence perhaps, stayed its flight and darted back into the fog. Only to return a few seconds later, slapping its wings together smartly ere it darted back and was lost!

When the dream came again—and this second time I was several months older—it was repeated in all its details as I have outlined it above. Except that now there were two creatures instead of one! Distinctly, while I held my breath to listen, came the whirring of two pairs of wings. Still the creatures were invisible, though I knew from the sound that they were probably identical in shape and kind. Out of the fog they would come, whirring, pausing while their wings beat a startled tattoo in the mists as their flight was stayed.

For a number of times whose exact count I have long since forgotten, the dream was repeated at intervals—which, as I grew older, came closer and closer together. The details never varied except in one particular.

The beating of the wings was greater in volume with each succeeding occurrence of the nightmare! First there had been one pair of wings, then two, then four—ever increasing in numbers until the air all about me, ever beyond my vision, was alive with invisible creatures whose wings whipped the air, caused the fog to swirl eerily— creating a medley of noise that became shortly a continual sound of beating wings, as though the creatures were advancing from the mists in companies and battalions, in regiments and brigades. One group would rush upon me and retire, only to give place to another group which charged me, only to retreat. How many minutes, hours or days I remained in the valley with its unseen walls I have no way of computing; but this I know well: after the first time or two the sound as of wings beating never paused, from my entry to the valley until the dream ceased and I awoke in my bed beneath the eaves at home—with a cold perspiration bathing my body clammily.

And here is another weird circumstance. Even though I know in my dream that it is a dream; even though I know as I travel through the cleft what I shall experience when I have reached the valley at last, I am never able to cause myself to waken—nor am I able to cause the dream to change until it has gone through to its usual conclusion. As I traverse the cleft I try to stay my steps, try to face about and return; but find myself powerless to do so. Always I must go on until I have entered the valley and listened to the rustling and beating of the invisible wings!

Is it any wonder that I have come to fear the approach of nightfall? Is it any wonder that I watch the sun with dread as it slopes down the sky into the west? Is it any wonder that I walk the floor of my study until far into the night, fighting sleep until, from very weariness, I cease to struggle and my eyes close of their own accord? Is it any wonder that a fever has entered my blood, crimsoning my cheeks until I appear like a man far gone in consumption, until the flesh has shrunken on my face so that, except for the roses of fever, my facial appearance is that of a cadaver?

Too much worry and fear because of a tiresome nightmare, you say? A nightmare that comes because I fear that it *will* come and, so fearing, bring on the very dream I dread?

If it were only the beating of the wings! But many months have passed now since it was only the wings that frighted me!

Months, did I say? Months it is; yet it seems that whole years have passed!

For one night when I dreamed, straining my eyes to make out the creatures whose wings I heard, I saw a black blotch against the misty wraiths of the valley—a blotch no bigger than a man's head! The blotch was black, I say! Blacker even than "the raven tresses of midnight!" Just a glimpse it was, a glimpse that chilled me even as the dread coldness of the valley had never done. For there was a definite shape to that black blotch—a shape that spelled, to my disordered imagination, but one thing: that of a vampire bat with a death's head! I waited, my heart in my mouth, for the shape to show itself again. Shortly, then, I saw it—and knew that the creature I saw was not the same which I had first glimpsed. The outline was the same, but there was an indefinable, inexplicable difference which told me that this second glimpse was of a different creature, twin, perhaps, of the first.

But why continue? Night after night it was the same, until, mingled with the never-ending whirring of the silken wings, I stared, mute with a nameless fear, at a veritable wall of black, darting creatures—a wall that came toward me like a flood of blackness, like a sea of ebon smoke; a wall that was alive, that swirled and eddied, writhed and twisted, pouring in, over, and down upon itself, like heavy opaque oil in ferment.

Then came the other sound—a raucous croaking which told me what manner of creature it was that showed such interest in me.

These creatures were not bats, but birds of ebon blackness; birds that caused their wings to whir tirelessly, birds that increased with the speed of thought, birds that gave voice to raucous croakings that grated against the eardrums as the rasping of a file grates against an exposed nerve.

The birds were corbies!

The birds were ravens!

But did the knowledge ease the feeling of tension which, night by night, seemed to clasp me the tighter? No! No! No!

Imagine it if you can. Try mentally to experience it but once. Then multiply that experience by all the countless times that I, dreaming my ever-recurring dream, entered the vale of the corbies and listened to the beating of their wings, to their perpetual croaking— and watched them writhe and twist in the air, so many in number that their evolutions made one think of a sea of plastic ebony.

Do this and you know why I fight the descent of sleep as I would fight the temptations of Satan.

Yet it is but a dream, after all! But is it?

It is only two weeks ago now that, for the first time, I found myself unable to listen, undisturbed, to the beating wings of the corbies—for, as they were emboldened no doubt by my motionless attitude, the natural fear of me which the creatures must have felt began to disappear. I knew it certainly when I noted that the black wall of the darting birds had approached closer to me on all sides—had approached so close that I could feel the breeze caused by the wings, could feel the coolness on my cheeks.

Then I knew, with a suddenness which had the force of some eery inspiration, that the chill along my spine which I had always experienced had had a definite cause—and that cause was the antagonism which the corbies felt toward me! Don't ask me why, for I do not know, yet what happened afterward proves to me that I am correct in this surmise.

From the very first the corbies of the hidden valley hated me! Hated me with a hatred which nothing in the world could quell! Why, then, did they not, in all their countless numbers, overpower me like a resistless flood and smother me with the very weight of their numbers?

Something held them back! Was it the antagonism which I instinctively fostered within myself as a weird sort of protection? Perhaps. Then could these creatures have been creatures of flesh and blood? Or is it only creatures of the astral world that can sense these emanations? Have I not insisted that it is nothing but a never-ending dream?

But wait!

Two nights later, when the wall approached quite too closely, I could stand it no longer. With a cry of anger, a cry that was pregnant with fear and a nameless horror, I leaped to my feet and, for the first time, took active steps against the black creatures which were robbing me of what little reason I still possessed. I rushed pell-mell, my eyes closed tightly, into the thick of the wall of flying corbies—striking out on all sides with clenched fists! I felt my fists strike home in soft, feathery bodies; felt the bodies fall away from my hands. I gathered the creatures in armfuls to my breast, crushing out their little lives against my own body—and fiercely gloated in my power to do them injury.

But what were those little stabs of pain which I felt on my exposed hands, my face, and my neck? I felt them, but at the time did not realize their significance!

Finally, exhausted from my battle against these terrific, somehow intangible odds, I fell back from the fight and sank again to the ground.

But, fast between my two palms, I held a single one of the ebon ravens! He was still alive, and his little eyes seemed to stare into my own with an expression of saturnine, undying hatred—as though he dared me to hurt him. For many minutes I looked into the eyes of the weak, defenseless bird. Unblinking he stared back at me—unafraid.

Slowly his mouth opened, as though he sneered at me. Still with his eyes staring into mine, the raven ducked its head suddenly and drove its pointed bill deep into the flesh of my hand! The blood spurted from the wound! Then I knew the meaning of those stabs of pain I had felt when I had fought against the vanguard of the corbies! The other birds, too, had driven their sharp bills into my flesh. I stared wonderingly at my hands, my attention drawn more closely because the bird between my palms had pierced the flesh—and as I saw the countless punctures I knew that what I had thought to be perspiration bathing my cheeks was not perspiration, but blood which the ravens had drawn!

What did I do then?

Deliberately, not knowing why, just as a small boy does not know why he takes pleasure in being cruel to animals, I looked back at the bird and into its challenging eyes; then, holding it fast in one hand, with the other I slowly twisted the ebony head from the creature's shoulders and hurled it into the mists!

The little body in my hand did not quiver; did not move once after I had cast the head free; but when I had hurled the body after the head it suddenly seemed to come to life, jumping here and there as does any bird which has been beheaded. Then, upright on its two feet, it darted into the fog. But before it had entirely disappeared, I saw it take wing and rise into the air!

My God, what ghastly croaking then came from the billow upon billow of corbies which still circled about

I pressed my hands to my ears to prevent my eardrums from bursting. Then, when I could stand no more, I leaped to my feet and started back the way I had come, while the ravens followed behind me, raucously croaking their wordless anger. I felt them on my shoulders and on my head; I felt them about my legs, retarding my retreat. I felt the slapping of their wings against my unprotected cheeks and face; felt the sharp stabs of pain in my flesh as their savage bills were plunged home.

And awoke in my bed at home with perspiration beading my body!

It was perspiration, too, not blood.

But on my hands, face and neck, there were many, many little red dots—dots which might have been tiny wounds that had healed, leaving fiery weals where the open wounds had been.

This then is why I fear sleep. When I sleep I dream, and when I dream I dream of the vale of corbies—and I know that, sooner or later, the ravens will slay me! Yet a man cannot fight sleep forever—though for over a week I have not closed my eyes. I have imbibed strong coffee, fiery hot and black as the wings of the ravens; I have used many kinds of drugs, increasing the doses swiftly until I use more than any confirmed fiend that ever lived; yet I feel myself growing weaker hour by hour, and know that soon I must sleep. And when I do ...

I, Hans Goodman, brother of the man who wrote the above manuscript, must finish the story, for my brother is dead. What he saw beyond the veil of sleep I do not know—assuredly I do not believe all that he has written above, because I know that it was written in a

fevered frenzy, was born of a mind that had been crazed by drugs and loss of sleep. Call it an insane obsession if you like.

But I found my brother dead in a chair in his study, his body literally covered with the blood which oozed from countless little wounds in his flesh—flesh that, between the wounds, was red with the roses of fever, or red because it had been beaten and pounded by something that was still not powerful enough to break the skin! And who shall say that whirring wings did not paint those roses there—whirring wings that beat an endless tattoo?

THE TENANTS OF BROUSSAC

A Complete Novelette
by Seabury Quinn

T he Rue des Batailles was justifying its name. From my table
on the narrow sidewalk before the Café de Liberté I could
view three distinct fights alternately, or simultaneously. Two
cock-sparrows contended noisily for possession of a wisp of straw, a
girl with unbelievably small feet and incredibly thick ankles addressed
a flood of gamin abuse to an oily-haired youth who wore a dirty black-
silk muffler in lieu of a collar. At the curb a spade-bearded patron,
considerably the worse for *vin ordinaire*, haggled volubly with an
unshaven taxi chauffeur over an item of five francs.

I had dropped my cigar end into my empty coffee cup, motioned
the waiter for my addition and shoved back my chair when a light but
commanding tap fell on my shoulder.

"Now for it," I muttered, feeling sure some passing bravo, aching for a fight, had chosen me for his attentions. Turning suddenly, I looked straight into a pair of light-blue eyes, round as a cat's, and just missing a humorous expression because of their challenging directness. Beneath the eyes was a straw-colored mustache, trimly waxed into a horizontal line and bristling so belligerently as to heighten its wearer's resemblance to a truculent tomcat. Below the feline mustache was a grin wider and friendlier than any I'd seen in Paris.

"*Par la barbe d'un bouc vert!*" swore my accoster. "If it is not truly my friend, the good Dr. Trowbridge, then I am first cousin to the Emperor of China."

"Why, de Grandin," I exclaimed, grasping his small sinewy hand, "fancy meeting you this way! I called at the *École de Médecine* the day after I arrived, but they told me you were off on one of your wild goose chases and only heaven knew when you'd be back."

He tweaked the points of his mustache alternately as he answered with another grin. "But of course! Those dull-witted ones would term my researches in the domain of inexact science a wild goose hunt. *Pardieu!* They have no vision beyond their test tubes and retorts, those ones."

"What is it this time?" I asked as we caught step. "A criminal investigation or a ghost-breaking expedition?"

"*Morbleu!*" he answered with a chuckle; "I think, perhaps, it is a little of both. Listen, my friend, do you know the country about Rouen?"

"Not I," I replied. "This is my first trip to France, and I've been here only three days."

"Ah, yes," he returned, "your ignorance of our geography is truly deplorable; but it can be remedied. Have you an inflexible program mapped out?"

"No. This is my first vacation in ten years, and I've made no plans, except to get as far away from medicine as possible."

"Good!" he applauded. "I can promise you a complete change from your American practice, my friend, such a change as will banish all thoughts of patients, pills and prescriptions entirely from your head. Will you join me?'"

"Hm, that depends," I temporized. "What sort of case are you working on?" Discretion was the better part of acceptance when talking with Jules de Grandin, I knew. Educated for the profession of medicine, one of the foremost anatomists and physiologists of his generation, and a shining light in the University of Paris faculty, this restless, energetic little scientist had chosen criminology and occult investigation as a recreation from his vocational work, and had gained almost as much fame in these activities as he had in the medical world. During the war he had been a prominent, though necessarily anonymous, member of the Allied Intelligence Service, since the Armistice he had penetrated nearly every quarter of the globe on special missions for the French Ministry of Justice. It behooved me to move cautiously when he invited me to share an exploit with him; the trail might lead to India, Greenland or Tierra del Fuego before the case was closed.

"*Eh bien,*" he laughed. "You are ever the old cautious one, Friend Trowbridge. Never will you commit yourself until you have seen blueprints and specifications of the enterprise. Very well, then, listen:

"Near Rouen stands the very ancient château of the de Broussac family. Parts of it were built as early as the Eleventh Century; none of it is less than two hundred years old. The family has dwindled steadily in wealth and importance until the last two generations have been reduced to living on the income derived from renting the château to wealthy foreigners.

"A common story, *n'est-ce-pas?* Very well, wait, comes now the uncommon part: Within the past year the Château Broussac has had no less than six tenants; no renter has remained in possession for more than two months, and each tenancy has terminated in a tragedy of some sort.

"Stories of this kind get about; houses acquire unsavory reputations, even as people do, and tenants are becoming hard to find for the château. Monsieur Bergeret, the de Broussac family's *avoué*, has commissioned me to discover the reason for these interrupted tenancies; he desires me to build a dam against the flood of ill fortune which makes tenants scarce at the château and threatens to pauperize one of the oldest and most useless families of France."

"You say the tenancies were terminated by tragedies?" I asked, more to make conversation than from interest.

"But yes," he answered. "The cases, as I have their histories, are like this:

"Monsieur Alvarez, a wealthy Argentine cattle raiser, rented the château last April. He moved in with his family, his servants and entirely too many cases of champagne. He had lived there only about six weeks when, one night, such of the guests as retained enough soberness to walk to bed missed him at the goodnight round of drinks. He was also missing the following morning, and the following night. Next day a search was instituted, and a servant found his body in the chapel of the oldest part of the château. *Morbleu*, all the doctors in France could not reassemble him! Literally, my friend, he was strewn about the sanctuary; his limbs torn off, his head severed most untidily at the neck, every bone in his trunk smashed like crockery in a china store struck by lightning. He was like a doll pulled to pieces by a peevish child. *Voilà*, the Alvarez family decamped the premises and the Van Brandt family moved in.

"That Monsieur Van Brandt had amassed a fortune selling supplies to the *sale Boche* during the war. *Eh bien*, I could not wish him the end he had. Too much food, too much wine, too little care of his body he took. One night he rose from his bed and wandered in the château grounds. In the place where the ancient moat formerly was they found him, his thick body thin at last, and almost twice its natural length—squeezed out like a tube of *crème* from a lady's dressing table trodden under foot by an awkward servant. He was not a pretty sight, my friend.

"The other tenants, too, all left when some member of their families or suites met a terrifying fate. There was Simpson, the Englishman, whose crippled son fell from the battlements to the old courtyard, and Biddle, the American, whose wife now shrieks and drools in a madhouse, and Muset, the banker from Montreal, who woke one night from a doze in his study chair to see Death staring him in the eye.

"Now Monsieur Luke Bixby, from Oklahoma, resides at Broussac with his wife and daughter, and—I wait to hear of a misfortune in their midst.

"You will come with me? You will help me avert peril from a fellow countryman?"

"Oh, I suppose so," I agreed. One part of France appealed to me as strongly as another, and de Grandin was never a dull companion.

"Ah, good," he exclaimed, offering his hand in token of our compact. "Together, *mon vieux*, we shall prove such a team as the curse of Broussac shall find hard to contend with."

—1—

The sun was well down toward the horizon when our funny little train puffed officiously into Rouen the following day. The long European twilight had dissolved into darkness, and oblique shadows slanted from the trees in the nascent moonlight as our hired *moteur* entered the château park.

"Good evening, Monsieur Bixby," de Grandin greeted as we followed the servant into the great hallway. "I have taken the liberty to bring a compatriot of yours, Dr. Trowbridge, with me to aid in my researches." He shot me a meaning glance as he hurried on. "Your kindness in permitting me the facilities of the château library is greatly appreciated, I do assure you."

Bixby, a big, full-fleshed man with ruddy face and drooping mustache, smiled amiably. "Oh, that's all right, Monsoor," he answered. "There must be a couple o' million books stacked up in there, and I can't read a one of 'em. But I've got to pay rent on 'em, just the same, so I'm mighty glad you, or someone who savvies the lingo, can put 'em to use."

"And Madame Bixby, she is well, and the so charming *Mademoiselle*, she, too, is in good health, I trust?"

Our host looked worried. "To tell you the truth, she ain't," he replied. "Mother and I had reckoned a stay in one of these old houses here in France would be just the thing for her, but it seems like she ain't doin' so well as we'd hoped. Maybe we'd better try Switzerland for a spell; they say the mountain air there—"

De Grandin bent forward eagerly. "What is the nature of *Mademoiselle's* indisposition?" he asked. "Dr. Trowbridge is one of your America's most famous physicians, perhaps he—" He paused significantly.

"That so?" Bixby beamed on me. "I'd kind o' figured you was one of them doctors of philosophy we see so many of round here, 'stead of a regular doctor. Now, if you'd be so good as to look at Adrienne, Doc, I'd take it right kindly. Will you come this way? I'll see supper's ready by the time you get through with her."

He led us up a magnificent stairway of ancient carved oak, down a corridor paneled in priceless wainscot, and knocked gently at a high-arched door of age-blackened wood. "Adrienne, darlin'," he called in a huskily tender voice, "here's a doctor to see you—an American doctor, honey. Can you see him?"

"Yes," came the reply from beyond the door, and we entered a bedroom as large as a barrack, furnished with articles of antique design worth their weight in gold to any museum rich enough to buy them.

Fair-haired and violet-eyed, slender to the borderline of emaciation, and with too high a flush on her cheeks, Bixby's daughter lay propped among a heap of real-lace pillows on the great carved bed, the white of her thin throat and arms only a shade warmer than the white of her silk nightdress.

Her father tiptoed from the room with clumsy care and I began my examination, observing her heart and lung action by auscultation and palpation, taking her pulse and estimating her temperature as accurately as possible without my clinical thermometer. Though she appeared suffering from fatigue there was no evidence of functional or organic weakness in any of her organs.

"Hm," I muttered, looking as professionally wise as possible, "just how long have you felt ill, Miss Bixby?"

The girl burst into a storm of tears. "I'm not ill," she denied hotly. "I'm not—oh, why won't you all go away and leave me alone? I don't know what's the matter with me. I—I just want to be let alone!" She buried her face in a pillow and her narrow shoulders shook with sobs.

"Friend Trowbridge," de Grandin whispered, "a tonic—something simple, like a glass of sherry with meals —is indicated, I think. Meantime, let us repair to the so excellent supper which waits below."

We repaired. There was nothing else to do. His advice was sound, I knew, for all the physician's skill is powerless to cheer a young woman who craves the luxury of being miserable.

—2—

"Find anything serious, Doc?" Bixby asked as de Grandin and I seated ourselves in the château's paneled dining hall.

"No," I reassured him. "She seems a little run down, but there's certainly nothing wrong which can't be corrected by a light tonic, some judicious exercise and plenty of rest."

"Uh-huh?" he nodded, brightening. "I've been right smart worried over her, lately.

"You know, we wasn't always rich. Up to a couple o' years ago we was poor as church mice—land poor, in the bargain. Then, when they begun findin' oil all round our place, Mother kept at me till I started some drillin', too, and darned if we didn't bring in a gusher first crack outa the box.

"Adrienne used to teach school when we was ranchin' it—tryin' to, rather—an' she an' a young lawyer, name o' Ray Keefer, had it all fixed up to get married.

"Ray was a good, upstandin' boy, too. Had a considerable practice worked up over Bartleville way, took his own company overseas durin' the war, an' would a' been run for the legislature in a little while, like as not. But when we started takin' royalties on our leases at the rate of about three hundred dollars a week, Mother, she ups and says he warn't no fittin' match for our daughter.

"Then she and Adrienne had it hot an' heavy, with me stayin' outa the fuss an' bein' neutral, as far as possible. Mother was all for breakin' the engagement off short, Adrienne was set on gettin' married right away, an' they finally compromised by agreein' to call a truce for a year while Ray stayed home an' looked after his practice an' Adrienne come over here to Europe with Mother an' me to see the world an' 'have her mind broadened by travel,' as Mother says.

"She's been gettin' a letter from Ray at every stop we made since we left home, an' sendin' back answers just as regular, till we come here. Lately she ain't seemed to care nothin' about Ray, one way or other. Don't answer his letters—half the time don't trouble to open 'em, even, an' goes around the place as if she was sleep-walkin'. Seems kind o' peaked an' run down, like, too. We've been right worried over her. You're sure it ain't consumption, or nothin' like that, Doc?" He looked anxiously at me again.

"Have no fear, *Monsieur*," de Grandin answered for me. "Dr. Trowbridge and I will give the young lady our greatest care; rest assured, we shall effect a complete cure. We—"

Two shots, following each other in quick succession, sounded from the grounds outside, cutting short his words. We rushed to the entrance, meeting a breathless gamekeeper in the corridor. "*Le serpent, le serpent!*" he exclaimed excitedly, rushing up to Bixby. "*Ohé, Monsieur, un serpent monstrueux, dans le jardin!*"

"What is it you say?" de Grandin demanded. "A serpent in the garden? Where, when; how big?"

The fellow spread his arms to their fullest reach, extending his fingers to increase the space compassed. "A great, a tremendous serpent, *Monsieur*," he panted. "Greater than the boa constrictor in the Paris menagerie—ten meters long, at the shortest!"

"*Pardieu*, a snake thirty feet long?" de Grandin breathed incredulously. "Come, *mon enfant*, take us to the spot where you saw this so great zoological wonder."

"Here, 'twas here I saw him, with my own two eyes," the man almost screamed in his excitement, pointing to a small copse of evergreens growing close beside the château wall. "See, it's here the shots I fired at him cut the bushes"—he pointed to several broken limbs where buckshot from his fowling piece had crashed through the shrubs.

"Here? *Mon Dieu!*" muttered de Grandin.

"Huh!" Bixby produced a plug of tobacco and bit off a generous mouthful. "If you don't lay off that brandy they sell down at the village you'll be seein' pink elephants roostin' in the trees pretty soon. A thirty-foot snake! In this country? Why, we don't grow 'em that big in Oklahoma! Come on, gentlemen, let's get to bed; this feller's snake didn't come out o' no hole in the wall, he came outa a bottle!"

—3—

Mrs. Bixby, a buxom woman with pale eyes and tinted hair, had small courtesy to waste on us next morning at breakfast. A physician from America who obviously did not enjoy an ultra fashionable practice at home, and an undersized foreigner with a passion for old books, bulked of small importance in her price-marked world. Bixby was taciturn with the embarrassed silence of a wife-ridden man before strangers, and de Grandin and I went into the library immediately following the meal without any attempt at making table talk.

My work consisted, for the most part, of lugging ancient volumes in scuffed bindings from the high shelves and piling them on the table before my colleague. After one or two attempts I gave over the effort to read them, since those not in archaic French were in monkish Latin, both of which were as unintelligible to me as Choctaw.

The little Frenchman, however, dived into the moldering tomes like a gourmet attacking a feast, making voluminous notes, nodding his head furiously as statement after statement in the books seemed to confirm some theory of his, or muttering an occasional approving *"Morbleu!"* or *"Pardieu!"*

"Friend Trowbridge," he looked up from the dusty book spread before him and fixed me with his unwinking stare, "is it not time you saw our fair patient? Go to her, my friend, and whether she approves or whether she objects, apply the stethoscope to her breast, and, while you do so, examine her torso for bruises."

"Bruises?" I echoed.

"Precisely, exactly, quite so!" he shot back. "Bruises, I have said it. They may be of the significance; they may not, but if they are present I desire to know it. I have an hypothesis."

"Oh, very well," I agreed, and went to find my stethoscope.

Though she had not been present at breakfast, I scarcely expected to find Adrienne Bixby in bed, for it was nearly noon when I rapped at her door.

"*S-s-s-sh, Monsieur le Docteur,*" cautioned the maid who answered my summons, "Mademoiselle is still asleep. She is exhausted, the poor, pretty one."

"Who is it, Roxanne?" Adrienne demanded in a sleepy, querulous voice. "Tell them to go away."

I inserted my foot in the door and spoke softly to the maid. "*Mademoiselle* is more seriously ill than she realizes; it is necessary that I make an examination."

"Oh, good morning, doctor," the girl said as I brushed past the maid and approached the bed. Her eyes widened with concern as she saw the stethoscope dangling from my hand. "Is—is there anything the matter—seriously the matter with me?" she asked. "My heart? My lungs?"

"We don't know yet," I evaded. "Very often, you know, symptoms which seem of no importance prove of the greatest importance; then, again, we often find that signs which seem serious at first mean nothing at all. That's it, just lie back, it will be over in a moment."

I placed the instrument, against her thin chest, and, as I listened to the accelerated beating of her healthy young heart, glanced quickly down along the line of her ribs beneath the low neckband of her nightrobe.

"Oh, oh, doctor, what is it?" the girl cried in alarm, for I had started back so violently that one of the earphones was shaken from my head. Around the young girl's body, over the ribs, was *an ascending livid spiral,* definitely marked, as though a heavy rope had been wound about her, then drawn taut.

"How did you get that bruise?" I demanded, tucking my stethoscope into my pocket.

A quick flush mantled her neck and cheeks, but her eyes were honest as she answered simply, "I don't know, doctor. It's something I can't explain. When we first came here to Broussac I was as well as could be; we'd only been here about three weeks when I began to feel all used up in the morning. I'd go to bed early and sleep late and spend most of the day lying around, but I never seemed to get enough rest. I began to notice these bruises about that time, too. First they were on my arm, about the wrist or above the elbow—several times all the way up. Lately they've been around my waist and body, sometimes on my shoulders, too, and every morning I feel tireder than the day before. Then—then"— she turned her face from me and tears welled in her eyes— "I don't, seem to be interested in th-things the way I used to be. Oh, doctor. I wish I were dead! I'm no earthly good, and—"

"Now, now," I soothed. "I know what you mean when you say you've lost interest in 'things.' There'll be plenty of interest when you get back to Oklahoma again, young lady."

"Oh, doctor, are we going back, really? I asked Mother if we mightn't yesterday and she said Dad had leased this place for a year and we'd have to stay until the lease expired. Do you mean she's changed her mind?"

"M'm, well," I temporized, "perhaps you won't leave Broussac right away; but you remember that old saying about Mohammed and the mountain? Suppose we were to import a little bit of Oklahoma to France, what then?"

"No!" She shook her head vigorously and her eyes filled with tears again. "I don't want Ray to come here. This is an evil place, doctor. It makes people forget all they ever loved and cherished. If he came here he might forget me as—" the sentence dissolved in a fresh flood of tears.

"Well, well," I comforted, "well see if we can't get Mother to listen to medical advice."

"Mother never listened to anybody's advice," she sobbed as I closed the door softly and hurried downstairs to tell de Grandin my discovery.

—4—

"*Cordieu!*" de Grandin swore excitedly as I concluded my recitation. "A bruise? A bruise about her so white body, and before that on her arms? *Non d'un nom!* My friend, this plot, it acquires the thickness. What do you think?"

"M'm." I searched my memory for long-forgotten articles in the *Medical Times*. "I've read of these stigmata appearing on patients' bodies. They were usually connected with the presence of some wasting disease and an abnormal state of mind, such as extreme religious fervor, or—"

"Ah, bah!" he cut in. "Friend Trowbridge, you cannot measure the wind with a yardstick nor weigh a thought on the scales. We deal with something not referable to clinical experiments in this case, or I am much mistaken."

"Why, how do you mean—?" I began, but he turned away with an impatient shrug. "I mean nothing, now," he answered. "The wise judge is he who gives no decision until he has heard all the testimony." Again he commenced reading from the huge volume open before him, making notations on a slip of paper as his eyes traveled rapidly down the lines of faded type.

Mrs. Bixby did not join us at dinner that evening, and, as a consequence, the conversation was much less restrained. Coffee was served in the small corridor connecting the wide entrance hall with the library, and, under the influence of a hearty meal, three kinds of wine and several glasses of liqueur, our host expanded like a flower in the sun.

"They tell me Joan of Arc was burned to death in Rouen," he commented as he bit the end from a cigar and elevated one knee over the arm of his chair. "Queer way to treat a girl who'd done so much for 'em, seems to me. The guide told us she's been made a saint or somethin' since then, though."

"Yes," I assented idly, "having burned her body and anathematized her soul, the ecclesiastical authorities later decided the poor child's spirit was unjustly condemned. Too bad a little of their sense of justice wasn't felt by the court which tried her in Rouen."

De Grandin looked quizzically at me as he pulled his waxed mustaches alternately, for all the world like a tomcat combing his whiskers. "Throw not too many stones, my friend," he cautioned. "Nearly five hundred years have passed since the Maid of Orleans was burned as a heretic. Today your American courts convict high school teachers for heresy far less grave than that charged against our Jeanne. We may yet see the bones of your so estimable Thomas Jefferson and Benjamin Franklin exhumed from their graves and publicly burned by your heretic-baiters of this today. No, no, my friend, it is not for us of today to sneer at the heretic-burners of yesterday. Torquemada's body lies in the tomb these many years, but his spirit still lives. *Mon Dieu!* What is it that I say? 'His spirit still lives?' *Sacré nom d'une souris!* That may be the answer!" And, as if propelled by a spring, he bounded from his seat and rushed madly down the corridor into the library.

"De Grandin, what's the matter?" I asked as I followed him into the book-lined room.

"*Non, non,* go away, take a walk, go to the devil!" he shot back, staring wildly around the room, his eager eyes searching feverishly for a particular volume. "You vex me, you annoy me, you harass me; I would be alone at this time. Get out!"

Puzzled and angered by his bruskness, I turned to leave, but he called over his shoulder as I reached the door: "Friend Trowbridge, please interview Monsieur Bixby's chef and obtain from him a sack of flour. Bring it here to me in not less than an hour, please."

—5—

"Forgive my rudeness, Friend Trowbridge," he apologized when I re-entered the library an hour or so later, a parcel of flour from Bixby's pantry under my arm. "I had a thought which required all my concentration at the time, and any disturbing influence—even your own always welcome presence—would have distracted my attention. I am sorry and ashamed I spoke so."

"Oh, never mind that," I replied. "Did you find what you were looking for?"

He nodded emphatically. *"Mais oui,"* he assured me. "All which I sought—and more. Now let us to work. First I would have you go with me into the garden where that gamekeeper saw the serpent last night."

"But he couldn't have seen such a snake," I protested as we left the library. "We all agreed the fellow was drunk."

"Surely, exactly; of course," he conceded, nodding vigorously. "Undoubtedly the man had drunk brandy. Do you recall, by any chance, the wise old Latin proverb, *'In vino veritas'*?"

"'In wine is truth'?" I translated tentatively. "How could the fact that the man was drunk when he imagined he saw a thirty-foot snake in a French garden make the snake exist when we know perfectly well such a thing could not be?"

"Oh la, la," he chuckled. "What a sober-sided one you are, *cher ami.* It was here the fellow declared *Monsieur le Serpent* emerged, was it not? See, here are the shot-marks on the shrubs."

He bent, parting the bushes carefully, and crawled toward the château's stone foundation. "Observe," he commanded in a whisper, "between these stones the cement has weathered away, the opening is great enough to permit passage of a sixty-foot serpent, did one desire to come this way. No?"

"True enough," I agreed, "but the driveway out there would give room for the great Atlantic sea serpent himself to crawl about. You don't contend he's making use of it, though, do you?"

He tapped his teeth thoughtfully with his forefinger, paying no attention to my sarcasm. "Let us go within," he suggested, brushing the leaf mold carefully from his knees as he rose.

We re-entered the house and he led the way through one winding passage after another, unlocking a succession of nail-studded doors with the bunch of jangling iron keys he obtained from Bixby's butler.

"And here is the chapel," he announced when half an hour's steady walk brought us to a final age-stained door. "It was here they found that so unfortunate Monsieur Alvarez. A gloomy place in which to die, truly."

It was, indeed. The little sanctuary lay dungeon-deep, without windows or, apparently, any means of external ventilation. Its vaulted roof was composed of a series of equilateral arches whose stringers rose a scant six feet above the floor and rested on great blocks of flint carved in hideous designs of dragons' and griffins' heads. The low altar stood against the farther wall, its silver crucifix blackened with age and all but eaten away with corrosion. Row on row, about the low upright walls, were lined the crypts containing the coffins of long dead de Broussacs, each closed with a marble slab engraved with the name and title of its occupant. A pall of cobwebs, almost as heavy as woven fabrics, festooned from vaulted ceiling to floor, intensifying the air of ghostly gloom which hung about the chamber like the acrid odor of ancient incense.

My companion set the flickering candle-lantern upon the floor beside the doorway and broke open the package of flour. "See, Friend Trowbridge, do as I do," he directed, dipping his hand into the flour and sprinkling the white powder lightly over the flagstone pavement of the chapel. "Back away toward the door," he commanded, "and on no account leave a footprint in the meal. We must have a fair, unsoiled page for our records."

Wonderingly, but willingly, I helped him spread a film of flour ever the chapel floor from altar-step to doorway, then turned upon him with a question: "What do you expect to find in this meal, de Grandin? Surely not footprints. No one who did not have to would come to this ghastly place."

He nodded seriously at me as he picked up his lantern and the remains of the package of flour. "Partly right and partly wrong you are, my friend. One may come who must, one may come who wants. Tomorrow, perhaps, we shall know more than we do today."

—6—

I was in the midst of my toilet when he burst into my bedroom next morning, feline mustache bristling, his round eyes fairly snapping with excitement. "Come, *mon vieux,*" he urged, tugging at my arm as a nervous terrier might have urged his master to go for a romp, "come and see; right away, quick, at once, immediately!"

We hastened through the château's modern wing, passed the doors blocking the corridors of the Fifteenth Century buildings and came at last to the Eleventh Century chapel. De Grandin paused before the oak-and-iron door like a showman about to raise the curtain from an exhibit as he lit the candle in his lantern, and I heard his small, even teeth clicking together in a chill of suppressed excitement. "Behold, *mon ami,*" he commanded in a hoarse whisper more expressive of emotion than a shout, "behold what writings are on the page which we did prepare!"

I looked through the arched doorway, then turned to him, dumb with surprise.

Leading from the chapel entrance, and ending at the center of the floor, directly before the altar, was the unmistakable trail of little, naked feet. No woodcraft was needed to trace the walker's course. She had entered the sanctuary, marched straight and unswervingly to a spot about fifteen feet from the altar, but directly before it, then turned about slowly in a tiny circle, no more than two feet in diameter, for at that point the footprints were so superimposed on each other that all individual traces were lost.

But the other track which showed in the strewn flour was less easily explained. Beginning at a point directly opposite the place the footprints ceased, this other trail ran some three or four inches wide in a lazy zigzag, as though a single automobile wheel had been rolled in an uncertain course across the floor by someone staggeringly drunk. But no prints of feet followed the wheel-track. The thing had apparently traversed the floor of its own volition.

"See," de Grandin whispered, "flour prints lead away from the door"—he pointed to a series of white prints, plainly describing bare heels and toes, leading up the passage from the chapel door, diminishing in clearness with each step until they faded out some ten paces toward the modern part of the château. "And see," he repeated, drawing me inside the chapel to the wall where the other, inexplicable, track began, "a trail leads outward here, too."

Following his pointing finger with my eye I saw what I had not noticed before, a cleft in the chapel wall some five inches wide, evidently the result of crumbling cement, and gradually sinking foundation stones. At the entrance of the fissure a tiny pile of flour showed, as though some object previously dusted with the powder had been forced through the crevice.

I blinked stupidly at him. "Wh-what is this track?" I asked in bewilderment.

"Ah, bah!" he exclaimed disgustedly. "The blindest man is he who shuts his own eyes, my friend. Did you never, as a boy, come upon the trail of a serpent in the dusty road?"

"A snake track"—my mind refused the evidence of my eyes—"but how can that be—here?"

"The gamekeeper *thought* he saw a serpent in the garden *exactly outside this chapel,*" de Grandin replied in a low voice, "and it was where that besotted gamekeeper *imagined* he beheld a serpent that the body of Mijnheer Van Brundt was found crushed out of semblance to a human man. Tell me, Friend Trowbridge—you know something of zoology—what creature, besides the constrictor-snake, kills his prey by crushing each bone of his body till nothing but shapeless pulp remains? *Hein?*"

"Bu—but—" I began, when he cut me short:

"Go call on our patient," he commanded. "If she sleeps, do not awaken her, but *observe the drugget on her floor!*"

I hastened to Adrienne Bixby's room, pushed unceremoniously past Roxanne, the maid, and tiptoed to the girl's bedside. She lay on her side, one cheek pillowed on her arm, sleeping the sleep of utter exhaustion. I bent over her a moment, listening to her even breathing, then, nodding to the maid, turned and walked softly from the room, my eyes glued to the dark-red plush carpet which covered the chamber floor.

Five minutes later I met the little Frenchman in the library, my excitement now as high as his own. "De Grandin," I whispered, involuntarily lowering my voice, "I looked at her carpet. The thing's made of red velvet and shows a spot of dust ten feet away. A trail of faint white footprints leads right up to her bed!"

—7—

"*Sacré nom d'un petit bonhomme!*" He reached for his green felt hat and turned toward the door. "The trail becomes clear; even my good, skeptical friend Trowbridge can follow it, I think. Come *cher ami,* let us see what we can see."

He led me through the château park, between the rows of tall, trembling poplar trees, to a spot where black-boughed evergreens cast perpetual shade above a stone-fenced area of a scant half acre. Rose bushes, long deteriorated from their cultivated state, ran riot over the ground, the whole enclosure had the gloomy aspect of a deserted cemetery. "Why," I asked, "what place is this, de Grandin? It's as different from the rest of the park as—"

"As death is from life, *n'est-ce-pas?*" he interjected. "Yes, so it is, truly. Observe." He parted a mass of intertwined brambles and pointed to a slab of stone, once white, but now brown and roughened with centuries of exposure. "Can you read the inscription?" he asked.

The letters, once deeply cut in the stone, were almost obliterated, but I made out:

CI GIT TOUJOURS RAIMOND
SEIGNEUR DE BROUSSAC

"What does it say?" he demanded.

"'Here lies Raimond, Lord of Broussac,'" I replied, translating as well as I could.

"*Non, non,*" he contradicted. "It does not say, '*Ci git,*' here lies; bat

'*Ci git toujours,*'—here lies always, or forever. Eh, my friend, what do you make of that if anything?"

"Dead men usually lie permanently," I countered.

"Ah, so? Have I not heard your countrymen sing:

> *John Brown's body lies a-moldering in the grave,*
> *But his soul goes marching on?*'

"What of the poor Seigneur de Broussac, is he to lie buried here *toujours*, or shall he, too, not rise once again?"

"I'm not familiar with French idioms," I defended. "Perhaps the stonecutter merely intended to say the Seigneur de Broussac lies here for his last long sleep."

"*Cher* Trowbridge," de Grandin replied, speaking with slow impressiveness, "when a man's monument is carved the words are not chosen without due consideration. Who chose Raimond de Broussac's epitaph thought long upon its wording, and when he dictated those words his wish was father to his thought."

He stared thoughtfully at the crumbling stone a moment, repeating softly to himself, "And *Madame l'abbesse* said, 'Snake thou art, and—'" he shook his shoulders in an impatient shrug as though to throw off some oppressive train of thought. "*Eh bien,* but we waste time here, my friend; let us make an experiment." Turning on his heel he led the way to the stables.

"I would have some boards, a hammer and some sharp nails if you please," he informed the hostler who greeted us at the barn door. "My friend, the very learned *Docteur* Trowbridge, from America, and I desire to test an idea."

When the servant brought the desired materials de Grandin sawed the boards into two lengths, one about eighteen inches, the other about three feet, and through these he drove the sharp-pointed horseshoe nails at intervals of about three-quarters of an inch, so that, when he finished, he had what resembled two large combs of which the boards were the backs and the needle-pointed nails the teeth. "Now," he announced, surveying his work critically, "I think we are prepared to give a little surprise party."

Taking up the hammer and two short pieces of boards in addition to his "combs" he led the way to the spot outside the château walls where the tipsy gamekeeper claimed to have seen the great snake. Here he attached the two strips of wood at right angles to the shorter of the pieces of board through which he had driven the nails, then, using the lateral lengths of wood as staked, attached the comb-like contrivance he had made firmly to the earth, its back resting levelly on the ground, its sharp spikes pointing upward before the crevice in the château foundations. Any animal larger than an earthworm desiring to make use of the crack in the wall as a passageway would have to jump or crawl over the sharp, lancelike points of the nails. *"Bien,"* he commented, viewing his work with approval, "now to put your wise American maxim of 'Safety First' into practice."

We found our way to the ancient, gloomy chapel, and he wedged the longer of the nail-filled boards firmly between the jambs at the inner side of the doorway. "And now," he announced, as we turned once more toward the inhabited part of the house, "I have the splendid appetite for dinner, and for sleep, too, when bedtime arrives."

"What on earth does all this child's play mean, de Grandin?" I demanded, my curiosity getting the better of me.

He winked roguishly by way of answer, whistled a snatch of tune, then remarked, irrelevantly, "If you have the desire to gamble, *cher ami*, I will lay you a wager of five francs that our fair patient will be improved tomorrow morning."

—8—

He won the bet. For the first time since we had been at Broussac, Adrienne Bixby was at the breakfast table the following day, and the healthy color in her cheeks and the clear sparkle of her lovely eyes told of a long, restful sleep.

Two more days passed, each seeing a marked improvement in her spirits and appearance. The purple semicircles beneath her eyes faded to a wholesome pink, her laughter rippled like the sound of a purling brook among the shadows of the château's gloomy halls.

"I gotta hand it to you, Doc," Bixby complimented me. "You've sure brought my little girl round in great shape. Name your figger an' I'll pay the bill, an' never paid one with a better heart, neither."

"Dr. Trowbridge," Adrienne accosted me one morning as I was about to join de Grandin in the library, "remember what you said about importing a little bit of Oklahoma to France the other day! Well, I've just received a letter—the dearest letter—from Ray. He's coming over—he'll be here day after tomorrow, I think, and no matter what Mother says or does, we're going to be married, right away. I've been Mrs. Bixby's daughter long enough; now I'm going to be Mr. Keefer's wife. If Mother makes Dad refuse to give us any money, it won't make the least little bit of difference. I taught school before Father got his money, and I know how to live as a poor man's wife. I'm going to have my man—my own man—and no one—*no one at all* —shall keep him away from me one day longer.'"

"Good for you!" I applauded her rebellion. Without knowing young Keefer I was sure he must be a very desirable sort of person to have incurred the enmity of such a character as Bixby's wife.

But next morning Adrienne was not at breakfast, and the downcast expression of her father's face told his disappointment more eloquently than any words he could have summoned. "Reckon the girl's had a little setback, Doc," he muttered, averting his eyes. His wife looked me fairly between the brows, and though she said never a word I felt she considered me a pretty poor specimen of medical practitioner.

"*Mais non, Monsieur le Docteur,*" Roxanne demurred when I knocked at Adrienne's door, "you shall not waken her. The poor lamb is sleeping, she is exhausted this morning, and she shall have her sleep. I, Roxanne, say so."

Nevertheless, I shook Adrienne gently, rousing her from a sleep which seemed more stupor than slumber. "Come, come, my dear," I scolded, "this won't do, you know. You've got to brace up. You don't want Ray to find you in this condition, do you! Remember, he's due at Broussac tomorrow."

"Is he!" she answered indifferently. "I don't care. Oh, doctor, I'm —so—tired." She was asleep again, almost at the last word.

I turned back the covers and lifted the collar of her robe. About her body, purple as the marks of a whiplash, lay the wide, circular bruise, fresher and more extensive than it had been the day I first noticed it.

"Death of my life!" de Grandin swore when I found him in the library and told him what I had seen. "That *sacré* bruise again! Oh, it is too much! Come and see what else I have found this cursed day!" Seizing my hand he half led, half dragged me outdoors, halting at the clump of evergreens where he had fixed his nail-studded board beside the château wall.

Ripped from its place and lying some ten feet away was the board, its nails turned upward in the morning sunlight and reminding me, somehow, of the malicious grin from a fleshless skull.

"Why, how did this happen?" I asked.

He pointed mutely to the moist earth in which the dwarf cedars grew, his hand shaking with excitement and rage. In the soft loam beside the place where the board had been fixed were the prints of two tiny, bare feet.

"What's it mean?" I demanded, exasperated at the way he withheld information from me, but his answer was no more enlightening than any of his former cryptic utterances.

"The battle is joined, my friend," he replied through set teeth. "Amuse yourself as you will—or can—this day. I go to Rouen right away, immediately, at once. There are weapons I must have for this fight besides those we now have. Eh, but it will be a fight to the death! Yes, *par la croix,* and we shall help Death reclaim his own too. *Pardieu!* Am I not Jules de Grandin? Am I to be made a monkey of by one who preys on women? *Morbleu,* we shall see!"

And with that he left me, striding toward the stables in search of a motorcar, his little yellow mustache bristling with fury, his blue eyes snapping, French oaths pouring from him like spray from a garden-sprinkler.

—9—

It was dark before he returned, his green hat set at a rakish angle over his right ear, a long, closely wrapped brown paper parcel under his arm. *"Eh bien,"* he confided to me with an elfish grin, "it required much argument to secure this. That old priest, he is a stubborn one, and unbelieving, almost as skeptical as you, Friend Trowbridge."

"What on earth is it?" I demanded, looking curiously at the package. Except that it was too long, it might have been an umbrella, judging by its shape.

He winked mysteriously as he led the way to his room, where, having glanced about furtively, as though he apprehended some secret watcher, he laid the bundle on the bed and began cutting the strings securing its brown paper swaddling clothes with his pocketknife. Laying back the final layer of paper he uncovered a long sword, such a weapon as I had never beheld outside a museum. The blade was about three and a half feet in length, tapering from almost four inches in width at the base to an inch and a half at the tip, where it terminated in a beveled point. Unlike modern weapons, this one was furnished with two sharpened edges, almost keen enough to do duty for a knife, and, instead of the usual groove found on the sides of sword blades, its center presented a distinct ridge where the steep bevels met at an obtuse angle as they sloped from the edges. The handle, made of ivory or some smoothly polished bone, was long enough to permit a two-handed grip, and the hilt which crossed the blade at a right angle turned downward toward the point, its ends terminating in rather clumsily carved cherubs' heads. Along the blade, apparently carved, rather than etched, marched a procession of miscellaneous angels, demons and men at arms with a mythological monster, such as a griffin or dragon, thrown in for occasional good measure. Between these crudely carved figures I made out the letters of the motto: *Dei Gratia*—by the grace of God.

"Well?" I asked wonderingly as I viewed the ancient weapon.

"Well?" he repeated mockingly, then: "Had you as many blessings on your head as this old bit of carved metal has received, you would be a very holy man, indeed, Friend Trowbridge. This sword, it was once strapped to the thigh of a saint—it matters not which one—who fought the battles of France when France needed all the champions, saintly or otherwise, she could summon. For centuries it has reposed in a very ancient church at Rouen, not, indeed, as a relic, but as a souvenir scarcely less venerated. When I told the curé I purposed borrowing it for a day or more I thought he would die of the apoplexy forthwith, but"—he gave his diminutive mustache a complacent tweak—"such was my power of persuasion that you see before you the very sword."

"But what under heaven will you do with the thing, now you've got it?" I demanded.

"Much—perhaps," he responded, picking up the weapon, which must have weighed at least twenty pounds, and balancing it in both hands as a wood-chopper holds his ax before attacking a log.

"Nom d'un bouc!" he glanced suddenly at his wristwatch and replaced the sword on his bed. "I do forget myself. Run, my friend, fly, fly like the swallow to Mademoiselle Adrienne's room and caution her to remain within—at all hazards. Bid her close her windows, too, for we know not what may be abroad or what can climb a wall this night. See that stubborn, pig-foolish maid of hers has instructions to lock her mistress' door on the inside and, should *Mademoiselle* rise in the night and desire to leave, on no account permit her to pass. You understand?"

"No, I'll be hanged if I do." I replied. "What—?"

"Non, non!" he almost shrieked. "Waste not time nor words, my friend. I desire that you should do as I say. Hurry, I implore; it is of the importance, I do assure you."

I did as he requested, having less difficulty than I had expected concerning the windows, since Adrienne was already sunk in a heavy sleep and Roxanne possessed the French peasant's inborn hatred of fresh air.

"Good, very, very good," de Grandin commended when I rejoined him. "Now we shall wait until the second quarter of the night—then, ah, perhaps I show you something to think about in the after years, Friend Trowbridge."

He paced the floor like a caged animal for a quarter-hour, smoking one cigarette after another, then: "Let us go," he ordered curtly, picking up the giant sword and shouldering it as a soldier does his rifle. "*Aller au feu!*"

We tramped down the corridor toward the stairway, when he turned quickly, almost transfixing me with the sword blade, which projected two feet and more beyond his shoulder. "One more inspection, Friend Trowbridge," he urged. "Let us see how it goes with Mademoiselle Adrienne. *Eh bien*, do we not carry her colors into battle this night?"

"Never mind that monkey business!" we heard a throaty feminine voice command as we approached Adrienne's room. "I've stood about all I intend to from you; tomorrow you pack your clothes, if you've any to pack, and get out of this house."

"Eh, what is this?" de Grandin demanded as we reached the chamber door and beheld Roxanne weeping bitterly, while Mrs. Bixby towered over her like a Cochin hen bullying a half-starved sparrow.

"I'll tell you what it is!" replied the irate mistress of the house. "I came to say goodnight to my daughter a few minutes ago and this—this hussy!—refused to open the door for me. I soon settled her, I can tell you. I told her to open that door and get out. When I went into the room I found every window locked tight—in this weather, too.

"Now I catch her hanging around the door after I'd ordered her to her room. Insubordination; rank insubordination, it is. She leaves this house bright and early tomorrow morning, I can tell you!"

"Oh, Monsieur Trow-breege, Monsieur de Grandin," sobbed the trembling girl, "I did but attempt to obey your orders, and—and she drove me from my duty. Oh, I am so sorree!"

De Grandin's small teeth shut with a snap like a miniature steel trap. "And you forced this girl to unbar the door?" he asked, almost incredulously, gazing sternly at Mrs. Bixby.

"I certainly did," she bridled, "and I'd like to know what business it is of yours. If—"

He brushed by her, leaping into the bedroom with a bound which carried him nearly two yards beyond the doorsill.

We looked past him toward the bed. It was empty. Adrienne Bixby was gone.

"Why—why, where can she *be*?" Mrs. Bixby asked, her domineering manner temporarily stripped from her by surprise.

"I'll tell you where she is!" de Grandin, white to the lips, shouted at her. "She is where you have sent her, you meddling old ignoramus, you, you—oh, *mon Dieu,* if you were a man how I should enjoy cutting your heart out!"

"Say, see here—" she began, her bewilderment sunk in anger, but he cut her short with a roar.

"Silence, you! To your room, foolish, criminally foolish one, and pray *le bon Dieu* on your bare knees that the pig-ignorance of her mother shall not have cost your daughter her life this night! Come, Trowbridge, my friend, come away; the breath of this woman is a contamination, and we must hurry if we are to undo her fool's work. Pray God we are not too late!"

We rushed downstairs, traversed the corridors leading to the older wing of the house, wound our way down and down beneath the level of the ancient moat till we stood before the entrance of the chapel.

"Ah," de Grandin breathed softly, lowering his sword point a moment as he dashed the sweat from his forehead with the back of his hand, "no sound, Friend Trowbridge. Whatever happens, whatever you may see, do not cry out; 'tis death to one we seek to save if you waken her!"

Raising his hand, he signed himself quickly with the cross, muttering an indistinct *in nomine,* while I gaped in amazement to see the cynical, scoffing little man of science shedding his agnosticism and reverting to a simple act of his childhood's faith.

Lifting the sword in both hands, he gave the chapel door a push with his foot, whispering to me, "Hold high the lantern, Friend Trowbridge, we need light for our work."

The rays from my lamp streamed across the dark, vaulted chapel and I nearly let the lantern crash to the floor at what I beheld.

Standing before the ancient, tumbledown altar, her nude, white body gleaming in the semi-dark like a lovely, slender statue of sun-stained marble, was Adrienne Bixby. Her long, rippling hair, which had always reminded me of molten gold in the assayer's crucible, streamed over her shoulders to her waist, one arm was raised in a gesture of absolute abandon while her other hand caressed some object which swayed and undulated before her. Parted in a smile such as Circe, the enchantress, might have worn when she lured men to their ruin, her red lips were drawn back from her gleaming teeth, while she crooned a slow, sensuous melody the like of which I had never heard, nor wish to hear again.

My astounded eyes took this in at first glance, but it was my second look which sent the blood coursing through my arteries like river water in zero weather. About her slender, virginal torso, ascending in a spiral from hips to shoulders, *was the spotted body of a gigantic snake.*

The monster's horrid, wedge-shaped head swung and swayed a scant half-inch before her face, and its darting, lambent tongue licked lightly at her parted lips.

But it was no ordinary serpent which held her, a laughing pris-oner, in its coils. Its body shone with alternate spots of green and gold, almost as if the colors were laid on in luminous paint, its flickering tongue was red and glowing as a flame of fire, and in its head were eyes as large and blue as those of human kind, but set and terrible in their expression as only the eyes of a snake can be.

Scarcely audible, so low his whisper was, de Grandin hissed a chal-lenge as he hurled himself into the chapel with one of his lithe, catlike leaps: *"Snake thou art, Raimond de Broussac, and snake thou shalt became! Garde à vous!"*

With a slow, sliding motion, the great serpent turned its head, gradually released its folds from the leering girl's body and slipped to the floor, coiled its length quickly, like a giant spring, and launched itself like a flash of green-and-gold lightning at de Grandin!

But quick as the monster's attack was, de Grandin was quicker. Like the shadow of a flying hawk, the little Frenchman slipped aside, and the reptile's darting head crashed against the chapel's granite wall with an impact like a wave slapping a ship's bow.

"One!" counted de Grandin in a mocking whisper, and swung his heavy sword, snipping a two-foot length from the serpent's tail as neatly as a sempstress snips a thread with her scissors. *"En garde, fils du diable!"*

Writhing, twisting, turning like a spring from which the tension has been loosed, the serpent gathered itself for another onslaught, its malign, human-seeming eyes glaring implacable hatred at de Grandin.

Not this time did the giant reptile launch a battering-ram blow at its adversary. Instead, it reared itself six feet and more in the air and drove its wicked, scale-armored head downward with a succession of quick shifting jabs, seeking to take de Grandin off his guard and enfold him in its crushing coils.

But like a veritable *chevaux-de-frise* of points, de Grandin's sword was right, left, and in between. Each time the monster's head drove at the little man the blade engraved with the ancient battle cry stood in its path, menacing the hateful blue eyes and flashing, backward-curving fangs with its sharp, tapering end.

"Ha, ha!" de Grandin mocked; "to fight a man is a greater task than to bewitch a woman, *n'est-ce-pas, M'sieur le Serpent?*"

"Ha! You have it!" Like a wheel of living flame the saintly sword circled through the air, there was a sharp, slapping impact, and the steel sheared clean and clear through the reptile's body six inches behind the head.

"Sa, ha; sa, ha!" de Grandin's face was set in a look of incomparable fury, his small mouth was squared beneath his bristling mustache like that of a snarling wildcat, and the sword blade rose and fell in a quick succession of strokes, separating the writhing body of the serpent into a dozen, twenty, half a hundred sections.

"S-s-sh, no noise!" he cautioned as I opened my lips to speak. "First clothe the poor child's nakedness; her gown lies yonder on the floor."

I looked behind me and saw Adrienne's silk nightrobe lying in a crumpled ring against the altar's lowest step. Turning toward the girl, revulsion and curiosity fighting for mastery of my emotions, I saw she still retained the same fixed, carnal smile, her right hand still moved mechanically in the air as though caressing the head of the loathsome thing yet quivering in delayed death at her white feet.

"Why, de Grandin," I exclaimed in wonder, "why, she's *asleep!*"

"*S-s-sh,* no sound!" he cautioned again, laying his finger on his lips. "Slip the robe over her head, my friend, and pick her up gently. She will not know."

I draped the silken garment about the unconscious girl, noticing, as I did so, that a long, spiral bruise was already taking form on her tender flesh.

"Careful, Friend Trowbridge," de Grandin commanded, picking up the lantern and sword and leading the way from the chapel. "Carry her tenderly, the poor, sinned-against one. Do not waken her, I beseech you. *Pardieu,* if that scolding mother of hers does but open her shrewish lips within this poor lamb's hearing this night I shall serve her as I did the serpent. *Mordieu,* may Satan burn me if I do not so!"

— **10** —

"Trowbridge, Trowbridge, my friend, come and see!" de Grandin's voice sounded in my ear.

I sat up, sleepily staring about me. Daylight had just begun, the gray of early morning still mingled with the first faint rose of the new day, and outside my window the blackbirds were singing.

"Eh, what's up?" I demanded, swinging my feet to the floor.

"Plenty, a very plenty, I do assure you," he answered, tugging delightedly first at one end of his mustache, then the other. "Arise, my friend, arise and pack your bags; we must go, immediately, at once, right away."

He fairly pranced about the room while I shaved, washed and made ready for the journey, meeting my bewildered demands for information only with renewed entreaties for haste. At last, as I accompanied him down the great stairway, my kit bags banging against my knees.

"Behold!" he cried, pointing dramatically to the hall below. "Is it not superb?"

On a couch before the great, empty fireplace of the château hall sat Adrienne Bixby, dressed and ready for a trip, her slender white hands securely held in a pair of bronzed ones, her fluffy golden head pillowed on a broad, homespun-clad shoulder.

"Monsieur Trowbridge," de Grandin almost purred in his elation, "permit that I present to you Monsieur Ray Keefer, of Oklahoma, who is to make happy our so dear Mademoiselle Adrienne at once, right away, immediately. Come, *mes enfants,* we must away," he beamed on the pair of lovers. "The American consul at Rouen, he will unite you in the bonds of matrimony, then—away for that joyous wedding trip, and may your happiness never be less than it is this day. I have left a note of explanation for *Monsieur* your father, *Mademoiselle*; let us hope he gives you his blessing. However, be that as it may, you have already the blessing of happiness."

A large motor was waiting outside, Roxanne seated beside the chauffeur, mounting guard over Adrienne's baggage.

"I did meet Monsieur Keefer as he entered the park this morning," de Grandin confided to me as the car gathered speed, "and I did compel him to wait while I rushed within and roused his sweetheart and Roxanne from their sleep. Ha, ha, what was it *Madame* the Scolding One did say to Roxanne last night, that she should pack her clothes and leave the house bright and early this morning? *Eh bien,* she has gone, *n'est-ce-pas?*"

Shepherded by de Grandin and me, the lovers entered the consulate, emerging a few minutes later with a certificate bearing the great seal of the United States of America and the information that they were man and wife.

De Grandin hunted feverishly in the gutters, finally discovered a tattered old boot, and shied it after them as, with the giggling Roxanne, they set out for Switzerland, Oklahoma and happiness.

"Name of a little green man!" he swore, furtively flicking a drop of moisture from his eye. "I am so happy to see her safe in the care of the good young man who loves her that I could almost bring myself to kiss that so atrocious Madame Bixby!"

"Now de Grandin," I threatened, as we seated ourselves in a compartment of the Paris express, "tell me all about it, or I'll choke the truth out of you!"

"*La, la,*" he exclaimed in mock terror, "he is a ferocious one, this *Americain!* Very well, then, *cher ami,* from the beginning:

"You will recall how I told you houses gather evil reputations, even as people do? They do more than that, my friend, they acquire character.

"Broussac is an old place; in it generations of men have been born and have lived and met their deaths, and the record of their personalities—all they have dreamed and thought and loved and hated—is written fair upon the walls of the house for him who cares to read. These thoughts I had when first I went to Broussac to trace down the reason for these deaths which drove tenant after tenant from the château.

"But fortunately for me there was a more tangible record than the atmosphere of the house to read. There was the great library of the de Broussac family, with the records of those of it who were good, those who were not so good, and those who were not good at all written down. Among those records I did find this story:

"In the years before your America was discovered there dwelt at Broussac one Sieur Raimond, a man beside whom the wickedest of the Roman emperors was a mild-mannered gentleman. What he desired he took, this one, and as most of his desires leaned toward his neighbors' women folk, he was busy at robbery, murder and rapine most of the time.

"*Eh bien,* he was a mighty man, this Sieur Raimond, but the Bishop of Rouen and the Pope at Rome were mightier. At last, the wicked gentleman came face to face with the reckoning of his sins, for where the civil authorities were fearful to act the church stepped in and brought him to his trial.

"Listen to this which I found among the chronicles at the

château, my friend. Listen and marvel." He drew a sheaf of papers
from his portmanteau and began reading slowly, translating as he
went along:

Now when the day for the wicked Sieur Raimond's execution was
come, a great procession issued from the church where the company
of faithful people were gone to give thanks that earth was to be ridded
of a monster.

Francois and Henri, the de Broussac's wicked accomplices in
crime, had become reconciled to Mother Church, and so were
accorded the mercy of strangling before burning, but the Sieur
Raimond would have none of repentance, but walked to his place of
execution with the smile of a devil on his false, well-favored face.

And as he marched between the men at arms toward the stake set
up for his burning, behold, the Lady Abbess of the convent of Our
Lady of Mercy, together with the gentlewomen who were her nuns,
earns forth to weep and pray for the souls of the condemned, even the
soul of the unrepentant sinner, Raimond de Broussac.

And when the Sieur Raimond was come over against the place
where the abbess stood with all her company, he halted between his
guards and taunted her, saying, "What now, old hen, dost seek the
chicks of thy brood who are missing?" (For it was a fact that three
novices of the convent of Our Lady had been ravished away from their
vows by this vile man, and great was the scandal thereof everywhere.)

Then did the Lady Abbess pronounce these words to that wicked
man, "Snake thou art, Raimond de Brouasac, snake thou shalt
become and snake thou must remain until some good man and true
shall cleave thy foul body into as many pieces as the year hath weeks."

And I, who beheld and heard all, do declare upon the rood that
when the flames were kindled about that wicked man and his sinful
body had been burned to ashes, a small snake, of the colors of green
and gold, was seen by all to emerge from the fire and, maugre the
efforts of the men at arms to slay it, did escape to the forest of the
château of Broussac.

"Eh! What think you of that, Friend Trowbridge?" he asked as he
laid the papers beside him on the car seat.

"Rather an interesting medieval legend," I answered, "but hardly convincing today."

"Truly," he conceded, "but as your English proverb has it, where there is much smoke there is apt to be a little flame. Other things I found in the records, my friend. For instance:

"The ashes of this Raimond de Broussac could not be buried in the château chapel among his ancestors and descendants, for the chapel is consecrated ground, and he died excommunicate. They buried him in what was then a pine forest hard by the house where he had lived his evil life, and on the stone which they set over him they did declare that there he lay forever.

"But one year from the day of his execution, as the de Broussac chaplain was reciting his office in the chapel, he did see a green-and-gold snake, something thicker than a monk's girdle but not so long as a man's forearm, enter that chapel, and the snake attacked the holy man so fiercely that he was much put to it to defend himself.

"Another year went by, and a servant bearing oil to refill the sanctuary lamp in the chapel did behold a similar snake, but now grown to the length of a man's arm, coiled above one of the tombs, and the snake also attacked that servant, and nearly slew him.

"From year to year the records go on. Often about Broussac was seen a snake, but each succeeding time it appeared larger than before.

"Too, there were strange stories current—stories of women of the locality who wandered off into the woods of Broussac, who displayed strange bruises upon their bodies, and who died eventually in a manner unexplained by any natural cause. One and all, *mon ami*, they were crushed to death.

"One was a member of the de Broussac family, a distant kinswoman of Sieur Raimond himself, who had determined to take the veil. As she knelt at prayer in the chapel one day, a great sleep fell upon her, and after that, for many days, she seemed distrait—her interest in everything, even her religious vocation, seemed to wane to nothing. But it was thought she was very saintly, for those who watched her did observe that she went often to the chapel by night. One morning she was found, like the others, crushed to death, and on her face was the look not of the agony of dying, but the evil smile of an abandoned woman. Even in death she wore it.

"These things I had already read when that gamekeeper brought us news of the great snake he had seen in the garden, and what I had noted down as idle legend appeared possible to me as sober fact—if we could prove it.

"You recall how we spread flour on the chapel floor; you also recall the tracks we read in that flour next day.

"I remembered, too, how that poor Madame Biddle, who went mad in the château Broussac, did so when she wandered one day by chance into the chapel, and I remembered how she does continually cry out of a great snake which seems to *kiss* her. The doctor who first attended her, too, when her reason departed, told me of a bruise, not to be explained, a spiral bruise about the poor lady's arm.

"*Pardieu!* I think I will test these legends some more, and I search and search until I find this wicked Sieur Raimond's grave. It was even as the chronicler wrote, for, to prove it, I made you go with me and read the inscription on the tombstone. *Morbleu!* Against my reason I am convinced, so I make what you called my 'combs' and place them so that their sharp nails would scratch the belly of any snake—if he really were a snake—who tried to crawl over them. Voilà next day Mademoiselle Adrienne, she was better. Then I knew for a certainty that she was under the influence of this Sieur Raimond snake, even as that poor intending-nun lady who met so tragic a death in the days of long ago.

"Something else I learn, too. This demon snake, this relic of the accurst Raimond de Broussac, was like a natural snake. Material iron nails would keep him from the house his wickedness had so long held under a spell. If this was so, then a natural weapon could kill his body if one man was but brave enough to fight him. 'Cordieu, I am that man!' says Jules de Grandin to Jules de Grandin.

"But in the meantime what do I see? *Hélas!* That wicked one has now so great an influence over poor Mademoiselle Adrienne that he can compel her, by his wicked will, to rise from her bed at night and go barefoot to the garden to tear away the barrier I have erected for her protection.

"*Nom d'un coq!* I am angered, I am furious. I decide this snake-devil have already lived too long; I shall do even as the Lady Abbess prescribed and slash his so loathly body into as many parts as the year has weeks.

"*Morbleu!* I go to Rouen and obtain that holy sword, I come back, thinking I shall catch that snake waiting alone in the chapel for his assignation, since I shall bar *Mademoiselle's* way to him. And then her so stupid mother must needs upset all my plans, and I have to fight that snake in almost silence—I cannot shout and curse at him as I would, for if I raise my voice I may waken that poor, unconscious child, and then, perhaps, she goes mad, even as did Madame Biddle.

"*Eh bien*, perhaps it is for the best. Had I said all the foul curses I had in mind as I slew that blue-eyed snake, all the priests, clergymen and rabbis in the world could scarce have shriven my soul of their weight.

"*Voilà tout!* We are in Paris once more, my friend. Come, let us have a drink."

THE PHANTOM WOLFHOUND

OTIS ADELBERT KLINE

Doctor Dorp reluctantly laid aside the manuscript on which he had been working, capped and pocketed his fountain pen, and rose to meet his callers.

He was visibly annoyed by this, the third interruption of the afternoon, but his look of irritation changed to a welcoming smile when he saw the bulky form that was framed in the doorway. He recognized Harry Hoyne of the Hoyne Detective Agency, a heavy-set, florid-faced man whose iron gray hair and moustache proclaimed him well past middle age.

The slender, stoop-shouldered individual who accompanied him was a total stranger. He had pale, hawklike features, small snaky eyes that glittered oddly from cavernous sockets, and long, bony fingers that suggested the claws of a bird.

"Hello, Doc," boomed the detective genially, crushing the hand of his host in his great, muscular paw. "Meet Mr. Ritsky."

The doctor was conscious of a cold, clammy sensation as he took the hand of the stranger and acknowledged the introduction. Was it the contrast between those chill fingers and the strong warm ones of the detective that had caused this feeling? He did not know; but somehow, instinctively, he disliked Mr. Ritsky.

"I've got a queer case for you, Doc," said Hoyne, taking a proffered cigar and inserting it far back in his cheek, unlighted. "Just your specialty—ghosts and all that. I told Mr. Ritsky you'd be the only man to unravel the mystery for him. Was over to his house last night and the thing got me—too unsubstantial—too damned elusively unreal. And yet I'll swear there was something there. I heard it; but it got away and didn't leave a trace. When it comes to fingerprints and things like that you know I ain't exactly a dumb-bell, but I gotta admit this thing, whatever it is, had me hopelessly horn-swoggled."

Ritsky declined a cigar, saying he didn't dare smoke because of heart trouble. The doctor selected one with care, lighted it slowly, puffed it with a relish, and settled back with a look of eager anticipation in his eyes.

"What happened last night?" he asked.

"Maybe we better begin at the beginning," said Hoyne. "You see, there's quite a story goes along with this case, and Mr. Ritsky can tell it better than I. Don't be afraid to give him all the dope, Mr. Ritsky. The doctor knows all about such things—wrote a book about 'em, in fact. Let's see. What was the name of that book, Doc?"

"'Investigations of Materialization Phenomena.'"

"Righto! I never can remember it. Anyhow, Mr. Ritsky, tell him your story and ask him all the questions you want to. He's headquarters on this stuff."

Ritsky studied his claw-like hands for a moment clasping and unclasping the bony fingers. Suddenly he looked up.

"Do animals have immortal souls?" he asked, anxiously.

"I'm afraid you have sadly overrated my ability as a recorder of scientific facts," replied the doctor, smiling slightly. "Frankly, I do not know. I don't believe anyone knows. Most people think they haven't, and I incline toward that belief."

"Then such a thing as a ghost of a—a hound could not be?"

"I would not say that. Nothing is impossible. There are undoubtedly more things in heaven and earth, as Shakespeare said, than we have dreamed of in our philosophy. However, I would consider a materialization of the disembodied spirit of a canine, or any of the other lower animals, as highly improbable."

"But if you saw one with your own eyes—"

"I should probably be inclined to doubt the evidence of my senses. Have you seen one?"

"Have I seen one?" groaned Ritsky. "Good Lord, man, I'd give every cent I own to be rid of that thing! For two years it's turned my nights into hell! From a perfectly healthy, normal human being I've been reduced to a physical wreck. Sometimes I think my reason is slipping. The thing will either kill me or drive me mad if it is not stopped."

He buried his face in his hands.

"This is most strange," said the doctor. "You say the apparition first troubled you two years ago?"

"Not in its present form. But it was there, nevertheless. The first time I saw it was shortly after I killed that cursed dog. A month, to be exact. I shot him on the twenty-first of August, and he, or it, or something, came back to haunt me on the twenty-first of September.

"How vividly I remember the impressions of that first night of terror! How I tried, the next day, to make myself believe it was only a dream—that such a thing could not be. I had retired at eleven o'clock, and was awakened from a sound sleep some time between one and two in the morning by the whining, yapping cry of a dog. As there were no dogs on the premises, you can imagine my surprise.

"I was about to get up when something directly over the foot of my bed riveted my attention. In the dim light it appeared a grayish white in color, and closely resembled the head and pendant ears of a hound. I noticed, with horror, that it was moving slowly toward me, and I was temporarily paralyzed with fright when it emitted a low, cavernous growl.

"Driving my muscles by a supreme effort of will, I leaped from the bed and switched on the light. In the air where I had seen the thing hanging there was nothing. The door was bolted and the windows were screened. There was nothing unusual in the room, as I found after a thorough search. Mystified, I hunted through the entire house from top to bottom, but without finding a trace of the thing, whatever it was, that had made the sounds.

"From that day to this I have never laid my head on a pillow with a feeling of security. At first it visited me at intervals of about a week. These intervals were gradually shortened until it came every night. As its visits became more frequent the apparition seemed to grow. First it sprouted a small body like that of a terrier, all out of proportion to the huge head. Each night that body grew a little larger until it assumed the full proportions of a Russian wolfhound. Recently it has attempted to attack me, but I have always frustrated it by switching on the light."

"Are you positive that you have not been dreaming all this?" asked the doctor.

"Would it be possible for someone else to hear a dream of mine?" countered Ritsky. "We have only been able to retain one servant on account of those noises. All, with the exception of our housekeeper, who is quite deaf, heard the noises and left us as a result."

"Who are the members of your household?"

"Other than the housekeeper and myself, there is only my niece and ward, a girl of twelve."

"Has she heard the noises?"

"She has never mentioned them."

"Why not move to another apartment?"

"That would do no good. We have moved five times in the last two years. When the thing first started we were living on the estate of my niece near Lake Forest. We left the place in charge of caretakers and moved to Evanston. The apparition followed us. We moved to Englewood. The thing moved with us. We have had three different apartments in Chicago since. It came to all of them with equal regularity."

"Would you mind writing for me the various addresses at which you have lived?"

"Not at all, if they will assist in solving this mystery."

The doctor procured a pencil and a sheet of notepaper, and Ritsky put down the addresses.

Doctor Dorp scanned them carefully.

"Villa Rogers," he said. "Then your niece is Olga Rogers, daughter of millionaire James Rogers and his beautiful wife, the former Russian dancer, both of whom were lost with the *Titanic?*"

"Olga's mother was my sister. After the sudden death of her parents, the court appointed me her guardian and trustee of the estate."

"I believe that is all the information we need for the present, Mr. Ritsky. If you have no objection I will call on you after dinner this evening, and if Mr. Hoyne cares to accompany me we will see what we can do toward solving this mystery. Please take care that no one in your home is apprised of the object of our visit. Say, if you wish, that we are going to install some electrical equipment"

"I'll be there with bells," said Hoyne as they rose to go.

Shortly after his guests' departure, Doctor Dorp was speeding out Sheridan Road toward Villa Rogers.

The drive took nearly an hour, and he spent another half-hour in questioning the caretakers, man and wife. He returned home with a well-filled notebook, and on his arrival he began immediately assembling paraphernalia for the evening's work. This consisted of three cameras with specially constructed shutters, several small electrical mechanisms, a coil of insulated wire, a flashgun, and a kit of tools.

After dinner he picked up Hoyne at his home, and they started for the "haunted house."

"You say you investigated this case last night, Hoyne?" asked the doctor.

"I tried to, but there was nothing to it, so far as I could see, except the whining of that dog."

"Where were you when you heard the noises?"

"Ritsky had retired. I slept in a chair in his room. About two o'clock I was awakened by a whining noise, not loud, yet distinctly audible. Then I heard a yell from Ritsky. He switched on the light a moment later, then sat down on the bed, trembling from head to foot, while beads of perspiration stood out on his forehead.

"'Did you see it?' he asked me.

"'See what?' I said.

"'The hound.'

"I told him I hadn't seen a thing, but I heard the noise all right. Between you and me, though, I did think I saw a white flash for a second beside his bed, but I can't swear to it"

"We won't trust our eyes tonight," said the doctor. "I have three eyes in that case that will not be affected by hysteria or register hallucinations."

"Three eyes? What are you talking about?

"Cameras, of course."

"But how—"

"Wait until we get there. I'll show you."

A few moments later they were admitted to the apartment by the housekeeper, a stolid woman of sixty or thereabout. Ritsky presented, them to his niece, a dreamy-eyed, delicately pretty schoolgirl with silky golden curls that glistened against the pale whiteness of her skin.

"If you don't mind," said the doctor, "we will look things over now. It will take some time to install the wiring and make other necessary preparations."

Ritsky showed them through the apartment, which was roomy, furnished in good taste and artistically decorated. The floor plan was quite simple and ordinary. First came the large living room that extended across the front of the house. This opened at the right into the dining room and at the center into a hallway which led through to the back of the building. Behind the dining room was the kitchen, and behind that the servant's room. Ritsky's bedroom was directly across the hall from the dining room. Then came his niece's bedroom, a spare bedroom and a bathroom. Each of the three front bedrooms was equipped with a private bath and large clothes closet.

The doctor began by installing the three cameras in Ritsky's room, fastening them on the wall in such a manner that they faced the bed from three directions. After focusing them properly, he set the flashgun on a collapsible tripod and pointed it toward the bed.

The room was lighted by an alabaster bowl that suspended from the ceiling and could be turned on or off by a switch at the bedside. There were, in addition, two wall lights, one on each side of the dresser, and a small reading lamp on a table in one corner. These last three lights were operated by individual pull cords.

Ritsky procured a stepladder for him, and, after switching off the drop light, he removed one of the bulbs from the cluster and inserted a four-way socket. From this socket he ran wires along the ceiling, and down the wall to the three cameras and the flashgun. By the time these preparations were completed Miss Rogers and the housekeeper had retired.

Hoyne surveyed the finished job with frank admiration.

"If there's anything in this room when Ritsky turns the switch those three mechanical eyes will sure spot it," he said enthusiastically.

"Now, Mr. Ritsky," began the doctor, "I want you to place yourself entirely in our hands for the night. Keep cool, fear nothing, and carry out my instructions to the letter. I suggest that you go to bed now and endeavor to get some sleep. If the apparition troubles you, do just as you have done in the past—turn on the light. Do not, however, touch the light switch unless the thing appears. The photographic plates, when developed, will tell whether you have been suffering from a mere hallucination induced by auto-suggestion or if genuine materialization phenomena have occurred."

After closing and bolting the windows they placed the stepladder in the hallway beside Ritsky's door. Then they obtained a duplicate key from him and asked him to lock himself in, removing his key so they might gain entrance at any time.

When everything was ready they quietly brought two chairs into the hall from the spare bedroom and began their silent vigil.

"Both men sat in silence for nearly three hours. The doctor seemed lost in thought, and Hoyne nervously masticated his inevitable unlighted cigar. The house was quiet, except for the ticking of the hall clock and its hourly chiming announcements of the flight of time.

Shortly after the clock struck two they heard a low, scarcely audible moan.

"What was that?" whispered the detective, hoarsely.

"Wait!" the doctor replied.

Presently it was repeated, followed by prolonged sobbing.

"It's Miss Rogers," said Hoyne, excitedly.

Doctor Dorp rose and softly tiptoed to the door of the child's bedchamber. After listening there for a moment he noiselessly opened the door and entered. Presently he returned, leaving the door ajar. The sobbing and moaning continued.

"Just as I expected," he said. "I want you to go in the child's room, keep quiet, and make a mental note of everything you see and hear. Stay there until I call you, and be prepared for a startling sight."

"Wh—what is it?" asked Hoyne, nervously.

"Nothing that will hurt you. What's the matter? Are you afraid?"

"Afraid, hell!" growled Hoyne. "Can't a man ask you a question—"

"No time to answer questions now. Get in there and do as I say if you want to be of any assistance."

"All right, Doc. It's your party."

The big detective entered the room of the sobbing child and squeezed his great bulk into a dainty rocking chair from which he could view her bed. She tossed from side to side, moaning as if in pain, and Hoyne, pitying her, wondered why the doctor did not awaken her.

Presently she ceased her convulsive movements, clenched her hands, and uttered a low, gurgling cry, as a white, filmy mass slowly emerged from between her lips. The amazed detective stared with open mouth, so frightened that he forgot to chew his cigar. The filmy material continued to pour forth for several minutes that seemed like hours to the tense watcher. Then it formed a nebulous, wispy cloud above the bed, completely detached itself from the girl, and floated out through the half-opened door.

Doctor Dorp, standing in the hallway, saw a white, misty thing of indefinite outline emerge from the bedroom. It floated through the hall and paused directly in front of Ritsky's door. He approached it cautiously and noiselessly, and noticed that it grew rapidly smaller. Then he discovered the reason. It was flowing through the keyhole!

In a short time it had totally disappeared. He waited breathlessly.

What was that? The whining cry of a hound broke the stillness! He mounted the stepladder in order to view the interior of the room through the glass transom. He had scarcely placed his foot on the second step when the whining noise changed to a gurgling growl that was followed by a shriek of mortal terror and the dull report of the flashgun.

Leaping down from the ladder, the doctor called Hoyne, and they entered the "haunted" bedchamber. The room was brilliantly lighted by the alabaster bowl and filled with the sickening fumes of flash-powder.

Hoyne opened the windows and returned to where the doctor was thoughtfully viewing

Ritsky, who had apparently fainted. He had fallen half out of bed, and hung there with one bony arm trailing and his emaciated face a picture of abject fear.

"My God!" exclaimed Hoyne. "Look there on his throat and chest The frothy slaver of a hound!"

The doctor took a small porcelain dish from his pocket, removed the lid, and with the blade of his pocketknife, scraped part of the slimy deposit into the receptacle.

"Hadn't we better try to bring him to?" inquired Hoyne.

After they had lifted him back in bed the doctor leaned over and held his ear to the breast of the recumbent man. He took his stetho-scope from his case and listened again; then he straightened gravely.

"No earthly power can bring him to," he said, softly. "Ritsky is dead!"

The detective remained in the house, pending the arrival of the coroner and undertaker, while Doctor Dorp hurried home with his paraphernalia and the sample of slime he had scraped from the corpse. Hoyne was puzzled by the fact that the doctor searched the house and the clothing of the dead man before departing.

The detective was kept busy at the Ritsky apartment until nearly ten o'clock. After stopping at a restaurant for a bit of breakfast and a cup of coffee, he went directly to the doctor's home.

He found the psychologist in his laboratory, engrossed in a

complicated chemical experiment. He shook a test tube, which he had been heating over a small alcohol lamp, held it up to the light, stood it in a small rack in which were a number of others partly filled with liquid, and nodded cordially to his friend.

"Morning, Doc," greeted Hoyne. "Have you doped out what we are going to tell the coroner yet?"

"I knew the direct cause of Ritsky's death long ago. It was fear. The indirect cause, the thing that induced the fear, required careful examination and considerable chemical research."

"And it was—"

"Psychoplasm."

"I don't get you, Doc. What is psychoplasm?"

"No doubt you have heard of the substance called ectoplasm, regarding which Sir Arthur Conan Doyle has delivered numerous lectures, or an identical substance called teleplasm, discovered by Baron Von Schrenck Notzing while attending materialization séances with the medium known as Eva.

"While the baron was observing and photographing this substance in Europe, my friend and colleague, Professor James Braddock, was conducting similar investigations in this country. He named the substance psychoplasm, and I like the name better than either of the other two, as it is undoubtedly created or generated from invisible particles of matter through the power of the subjective mind.

"I have examined and analyzed many samples of this substance in the past. The plate I now have under the compound microscope, and the different chemical determinations I have just completed, show conclusively that this is psychoplasm."

"But how—where did it come from?"

"I learned something of the history of Ritsky and his ward yesterday. Let me enlighten you on that score first:

"The man told the truth when he said he was appointed guardian of his niece, and also when he said that he had shot a dog. The dog, in question, was a Russian wolfhound, a present sent to the girl by her parents while they were touring Russia. He was only half grown when he arrived, and the two soon became boon companions, frolicking and playing about the grounds together or romping through the big house.

"Some time after the death of Olga's parents, Ritsky, then editor of a radical newspaper in New York, took up his abode at Villa Rogers. The dog, by that time full grown, took a violent dislike to him and, on one occasion, bit him quite severely. When he announced his intention of having the animal shot the girl wept violently and swore that she would kill herself if Shag, as she had named him, were killed. It seemed that she regarded him as a token of the love of her parents who had sailed away, never to return."

"Shag! That's the name!" broke in Hoyne, excitedly. "After that white thing floated out of the room she made noises like a dog and then answered them, saying 'Good old Shag,' and patting an imaginary head. She sure gave me the creeps, though, when she let out that growl."

"The vengeful Ritsky," continued the doctor, "was determined that Shag should die, and found an opportunity to shoot him with a pistol when the girl was in the house. Shortly after, the faithful creature dragged himself to the feet of his mistress and died in her arms. He could not tell her who had taken his life, but she must have known subjectively, and as a result entertained a hatred for her uncle of which she objectively knew nothing.

"Most people have potential mediumistic power. How this power is developed in certain individuals and remains practically dormant in others is a question that has never been satisfactorily explained. I personally believe that it is often developed because of intense emotional repressions which, unable to find an outlet in a normal manner through the objective mind, find expression in abnormal psychic manifestations.

"This seemed to be the case with Olga Rogers. She developed the power subjectively without objective knowledge that it existed. One of the most striking of psychic powers is that of creating or assembling the substance called psychoplasm, causing it to assume various forms, and to move as if endowed with a mind of its own.

"Olga developed this peculiar power to a remarkable degree.

Acting under the direction of her subjective intelligence, the substance assumed the form of her beloved animal companion and sought revenge on its slayer. We arrived a day too late to save the object of her unconscious hatred."

"Too bad you were not there the night before," said Hoyne. "The poor devil would be alive today if you had been on hand with me the first night to dope the thing out."

"We might have saved him for a prison term or the gallows," replied the doctor, a bit sardonically. "You haven't, seen this, of course."

He took a small silver pencil from the table and handed it to the detective.

"What's that got to do with—"

"Open it! Unscrew the top. Careful!" Hoyne unscrewed it gingerly and saw that the chamber, which was made to hold extra leads, was filled with a white powder.

"Arsenic," said the doctor, briefly. "Did you notice the sickly pallor of that girl—the dark rings under her eyes? Her loving uncle and guardian was slowly poisoning her, increasing the doses from time to time. In another month or six weeks she would have been dead, and Ritsky, her nearest living relative, would have inherited her immense fortune."

"Well I'll be damned!" exploded Hoyne

Doctor Dorp's laboratory assistant entered and handed a package of prints to his employer.

"Here are the proofs of last night's photographs," said the doctor. "Care to see them?"

Hoyne took them to the window and scrutinized them carefully.

All showed Ritsky leaning out of bed, his hand on the light switch, his face contorted in an expression of intense horror—and, gripping his throat in its ugly jaws, was the while, misshapen phantasm, of a huge Russian wolfhound!

THE GARGOYLE

A TALE OF DEVIL WORSHIP

by Greye La Spina

—1—

Alias Cagliostro

Luke porter had just ordered supper. His waitress, a chatty and pert young countrywoman, hesitated before departing for the kitchen; it was obvious that she had something on her mind. Luke's light gray eyes twinkled at her half confusion; he was enjoying the play of expression over her face and had no intention of helping her out. At his open amusement she took heart.

"There's a party outside who wants to know if he can have his supper with you," she told him finally. "He says you don't know him, but he thinks he has something interesting to tell you."

"He does, eh?" Luke laughed softly. "Why does he think I will be interested in his information?"

The young woman put her hand into her gingham apron pocket and drew out a newspaper clipping which she held toward him. She waited in silence until the young man had read it, and when he looked up, his face alight with interest, she had her turn at laughter.

"Huh! Changed your mind, didn't you, mister? Shall he come in?"

"Tell him if he doesn't come. I'll go out and pull him in," exclaimed Luke, and once more bent his gaze upon the clipping.

It was a rather astonishing advertisement:

OCCULTIST—I want an initiate occultist of mature years, with an assistant youth of fine physique and handsome, to aid in the completion of important occult experiment. For particulars, address Occult Book Concern, 40 Park Row, New York City.

As Luke stared incredulously, something happened to the print; it went blurry, and then cleared up to a few words in an expanse of white. For a moment he could not understand what had happened; then he read the visiting card that had been laid upon the clipping, and lifted his eyes to see the owner of that formidable and mysterious Cagliostro Moderno, Initiate Occultist.

Imagination had conjured up almost instantaneously a tall and slender figure of fearsome dignity, with flashing black eyes. What confronted him as he rose instinctively to his feet was a black-cloaked form of hardly middle height but of heavy build. The individual enveloped in the cloak was so holding it that his face was almost hidden; all that showed was a small, button-like nose, above which peered pale blue eyes squinting involuntarily as if in distaste at the light which flooded the room in true country hostelry fashion. Carrot-colored hair stood in a stiff pompadour above a sallow face.

"Mr. Moderno?" queried Luke uncertainly.

The mysterious stranger bowed with tremendous dignity.

"Will you be seated, sir? And will you mercifully explain this?"

Luke lifted the newspaper clipping and his gray eyes searched the sallow countenance of the stranger, who seated himself opposite and at once became a figure of far more impressiveness, owing to the fact that his body was long, making him seem much taller, when seated, than he really was. He threw back the black mantle, displaying a flame-colored lining covered with symbolic figures embroidered in various shades. But in tossing back the mantle, he also uncovered his face, so that the combination of button nose, Cupid's bow mouth and squinting pale blue eyes made up an ensemble oddly at variance with his air of mystery and importance.

"Call me Cagliostro," he commanded severely. "Young man, are you married?"

Luke parried.

"Well—what if I am?" he asked. "How can it matter to you?"

"It may matter much to me—and to you as well. Do not be flippant. Give me a direct answer. Upon your single status much depends."

Luke's firm lips curled whimsically at the corners.

"Good friend Cagliostro, I am still heart-whole and fancy-free."

The unknown drew what was obviously a deep sigh of relief.

"Then you can serve as my assistant," he exclaimed, pointing at the clipping which Luke still held between thumb and forefinger of one well-formed hand.

"But, my good chap, I don't know anything about magic of any kind," the young man retorted, humoring what certainly appeared to be a harmless madman. "All my magic consists of splashing colors on canvas."

"But you are young—and good looking—and unmarried," the unknown insisted. "And my nephew disappointed me at the last moment," he confided, leaning across the table and unbending sufficiently from his high pose to look pleadingly at the artist.

Luke Porter stared incredulously at his vis-à-vis, the impulse to shout with laughter seizing almost irresistibly upon him. The man was amusing in his gravity.

"Have some of this steak," he offered. "Potatoes? As long as you are here, you'd better help me eat, good Cagliostro. And then, out with the whole story. You can't expect me to be your assistant unless you tell me the situation, you know."

Cagliostro Moderno hesitated, the squinting blue eyes searchingly upon Luke. Then he let himself relax comfortably in his chair, held out the plate the waitress had provided for the unexpected guest, and began to talk incoherently. Luke listened, and began to gather in details of an eery situation, the like of which he had never in his life believed possible.

Somewhere in the Pennsylvania woods near Shakerville, about a mile up Woddy Ridge from the main road between Shakerville and Spinnerton, there was the replica of a medieval castle, called Fanewold by the owners. This castle had been built by the present Madam Fane in her girlhood, as a surprise for her young husband. Madam Fane had had all the money, but the young husband had not remained with her long after the birth of their child, a boy; he had deserted her, eloping with a country girl from a nearby farm. Since that time Madam Fane had shut herself up with her son in the castle, surrounded by faithful servants, rendered blind, deaf and dumb by the large wages they received.

It was the son, Guy Fane, who was a student of the occult, and who had advertised through the book concern for another occultist to aid him in his experiments. At this point in his recital, Cagliostro grew somewhat darker of color, and drew out a smaller business card than the important one he had first given the artist. On it was printed in unobtrusive lettering: Herbert Binney. Rare books. Occult books a specialty.

"That is the name given me at birth," explained he, the pale blue eyes watchfully on Luke's face to detect the slightest tendency to amusement. "Cagliostro is the name I have—ah—earned, by my research along occult lines. You can readily understand, Mr.—Porter —thank you—that 'Binney' is hardly a name to command such respect as an adept magician merits."

"Naturally, Mr. Binney," agreed Luke, the mobile lips twitching.

"Cagliostro, please," corrected the mage pointedly. "Well, by reason of my correspondence with the book concern, it believed me to be the proper person to attend Mr. Fane in his experiments." He lifted his round little chin; his chest swelled perceptibly.

"Astonishing!"

"I therefore selected my sister's son, a young and handsome boy, to be my assistant, although what Mr. Fane wishes a green youth for is beyond my comprehension," puzzled Cagliostro. "But Bobby got cold feet just before I left, because he was invited to a costume ball and didn't want to miss it," with cold disdain.

"So you are in need of a handsome young man who isn't tied to a wife?" laughed Luke, pushing away his plate and leaning back in his chair easily. "How are you to know I'm not lying, when I say I'm single?"

Cagliostro stiffened. The squinty blue eyes narrowed.

"It would not be easy to deceive me, Mr. Porter," he declared impressively. "I asked you, to be sure, but that was to give you a chance to declare yourself. I knew you weren't married."

"You did? May I ask how?"

"By your eagle look."

"My—?" puzzled Luke.

"You look free—wild—ah—" and the mage, at a loss for appropriate words, waved his hands expressively, displaying on one pudgy finger an oddly carved ring with a heavy blood-red stone.

"I see," murmured Luke, smiling.

"You will go with me after dinner," asserted Cagliostro, with the mien of one who has untold resources at his back to enforce his wishes, "to Fanewold. Whatever emolument I receive for my occult services shall be evenly divided with you. But go alone I dare not, after my correspondence with Mr. Fane. The handsome, unmarried assistant is absolutely obligatory," he finished pleadingly.

"My good Cagliostro," Luke retorted with a slight smile, "I am on my way to Bauers Ridge to visit an old college friend who spends his summers on a farm there. I haven't seen him for four years. I certainly do not intend to give up my visit to go on such a wild goose chase as you have outlined. I am an artist, not a magician."

Cagliostro rose from his seat, drawing the black mantle about him again with an impressive air. One arm held it across his face, hiding all but the small blue eyes that now flashed with a suddenly steely light at the imperturbable young artist.

"I shall be on my way," he announced, "in the taxi I ordered. But I warn you, young man, that before the evening is old you will be at my side, acting in the capacity I have outlined. I need you. And when Cagliostro Moderno needs anything, the whole universe swings that thing toward him," he finished majestically, and stalked toward the dining room door.

At the entrance he turned.

"Shall I dismiss the taxi?" he insinuated, the mantle slipping sufficiently to discover the button nose that looked so childish on the small round face. "Then you can take me there directly in your roadster."

Luke got up from the table a trifle impatiently. His gray eyes darkened.

"My good Cagliostro, when I say a thing I mean it," he remarked pointedly. "I am not going to Fanewold. I am going up the pike, down the third road to the right, and then the first road to the left."

"Down the first road to the left?" repeated the occultist. A sudden flash of expression went across his face. He laughed outright. "Goodnight—or rather, auf Wiedersehen," he said mockingly as he went out of the room.

"Now what the devil did he mean by that?" wondered the artist, as he drove his roadster down the pike half an hour later. "Too darn sure of getting what he wants, that fellow. If I weren't afraid old Ralph might go back to the city in another week or ten days, I'd take up with friend Binney's offer. It was mighty intriguing."

The October dusk was gathering swiftly. Luke switched on his headlights and proceeded with caution along the country road, the third to his right. After going about three miles, he met another car, and the two cars had to manage rather carefully to avoid the deep ditches outlining the road on either side. As the other car passed, the driver leaned out and hailed Luke.

"Your name's Porter, ain't it? The old guy says not to forget the first turn to the left," he yelled.

"Much obliged!" the artist shouted, as he got his car back on to the road and drove slowly away.

He was just a little irritated by the reminder from the occultist, who had only too evidently not forgotten the necessity of a young and handsome assistant, and was still hopeful that Luke might change his mind.

The first road to the left proved to be a dirt road with deep ruts, obviously one that did not see much traffic. Luke turned down it, driving cautiously. The road led, winding, into the very heart of a forest. It went more and more deeply. The headlights darted weirdly between serried ranks of crowding trees, until the wood seemed full of awesome shades that slipped behind the shelter of tree trunks as Luke drove on into their midst. It was, somehow, strangely oppressive and ominous to the sensitive perception of the young artist. He told himself that he would not particularly care to pass the night in such a place, alone, among those slinking shadows. And then, in the glare of the headlights, there appeared another shadow, detached from those that slunk back, massing behind him as he drove on.

Black, with flapping ebon wings that waved on either side as it came toward him, like a tremendous bat running on hind legs down the roadway to intercept him, the thing advanced, stumbling, tripping, but ever nearer.

Luke felt his blood chill in his veins. He dared not drive directly upon that black thing in his way. He stopped the car, letting the engine run. What in God's universe could it be?

And then it came into the full glare of the headlights, and it had a white face like a man's. It was a man. The black wings were only the flapping corners of a great mantle. It was a man, and as it ran, it moaned as if in pain.

Luke stared, incredulous. Stopped the engine. Sprang out of the car to meet him. For he saw now who it was. It was the little occultist, staring-eyed, white face drawn into a Greek tragic mask of horror. He was moaning as he ran blindly along the roadway.

The artist stopped him with a hand on his shoulder as the little man would have fled back along the road toward the pike. And at the touch of Luke's hand, Herbert Binney collapsed like a pricked balloon, tumbling all in a heap upon the road, with a quavering screech of unutterable fear and horror pushing between his distorted lips.

—2—
An Appeal For Help

Even in prohibition days a man can, at a pinch, provide himself with brandy or whisky, if he knows where to go for it. And there are moments when such stimulants are grave necessities. The emergency called for Luke's flask, and he had the satisfaction a little later of seeing the occultist's pale blue eyelids flicker, then tighten as if apprehensive of what they might look upon if they opened.

"All right, friend Cagliostro?" queried the artist, giving the fainting man a slight shake.

The squinting eyes opened widely and fell upon Luke's handsome face in the full glare of the headlights. The squared mouth relaxed with obvious relief. Binney reached out convulsively to grasp Luke's hand.

"God be thanked! You are real! Oh! Oh!" And then the thought of something came back to him, for he staggered up from the roadway, looking apprehensively in the direction from which he had been running. "Did you see anything?" he quavered, very little of the impressive initiate left in his manner. "Did—was there anything after me?"

Luke shook his head. He peered down the road, but there was nothing now. The car stood quiet; the shadows which had but a few minutes ago been slinking from trunk to trunk now remained in ominous hiding. The roadway loomed darkly up a steep and stony slope, unlighted by the headlights because of its pitch.

"Can you—can you turn around here?" quavered Herbert Binney, one pudgy hand grasping Luke's firm arm.

"Why should I turn around?" Luke said, disgustedly.

"Because—because—this isn't the right road for you, Mr. Porter."

"I took the first turn to the left," disputed Luke. "This is the way to Bauers Ridge, isn't it?"

Binney let out a squeak of nervous laughter, which he almost as instantly hushed, with that same apprehensive look up the road.

"You took the first turn to the left," he explained, "but this is a private lane, not the first road to the left, which you should have taken about half a mile farther on. This is a private lane leading to Fanewold," he finished.

Luke stared at him, half irritated, half amused.

"And you were careful to confuse me, so that I would take it and appear at Fanewold as your assistant?" he accused. "Well, now that I'm here, do you mind telling me if you were coming to meet me? If not, why were you running away?"

"Good God! I wasn't meeting anybody!" cried the occultist wildly. "I was—well—not running away." He stopped, then went on a little defiantly. "Yes, I was running away! You'd have done it, too, if you'd been in my place. God, if you'd seen what I did!" His voice rose in a shrill tremolo of emotion. "I saw—the devil himself! Yes, I did! Don't dispute me, Mr. Porter, I beg of you. I'm not a lunatic. I'm a sane man. I'm a man who has seen many strange, supernatural phenomena. But—never before—never, I say—did I see the DEVIL in propria persona. Good God! It was horrible! "

"You'd better get into my car," suggested the artist. "I'll go along here and take a look at Beelzebub, friend Cagliostro. When we've found him, you'll probably discover that you're mistaken—"

"No, no, no!" denied the occultist hurriedly. "I couldn't have been mistaken. The taxi driver left me about a hundred yards from the castle draw, because he was superstitious. I walked up to the moat by myself, carrying my bags. And I was standing there, wondering how I could announce my arrival, when the moon came out from behind the clouds, and I saw that the draw was down."

"Well?" Prompted Luke, waiting impatiently, foot over the starter.

"And there was something—something uncanny about it—"

"About what? The draw being open?" with irony.

"No, no, no! There was—somebody—leaning over the side of it, looking down into the moat. I—I went over to speak to him—to it— and it raised its monstrous countenance and looked at me—and—my God, it was the devil himself!"

"Now, friend Cagliostro, you know as well as I that His Satanic

Majesty isn't in the habit of strolling around in flesh and blood, the way you're telling me," reproved Luke, starting the car.

"Oh, don't go back! Don't! Turn around, I beg you! If you drive ahead, you'll meet—it—too!"

"I'm going to drive ahead, friend Binney. If you don't like it, get out now and walk. I have a mind to see your devil for myself. At least, the experience cannot fail to be stimulating," Luke grinned to himself.

"But his terrible eyes! His hideous smile! That bloated, misshapen nose! The purple face, like decomposing flesh! The twisted, frightful mouth! Good God, Mr. Porter, you don't know what a hideous thing you're going to confront! Turn back, while there is yet time! Turn—"

"Shut up!" snapped Luke. "A fine occultist you are, to let a mere ugly demon terrify you to such an extent!"

This dig was too much for the dignity of the occultist, who sank back in his seat in silence, evidently trying hard to regain something of his previous composure and impressiveness.

Luke was obliged to go into low up the slope, which was not only very steep but covered with large rolling stones over which his car slipped and skidded unpleasantly. But when the summit of the rise had been reached, he was rewarded by an astonishing sight.

The moon was bright in an unclouded sky. Her light threw into high relief the battlements of what might have been an ancient medieval castle, while black shadows blocked out the approach to the great pile of massive granite blocks, so that the drawbridge of which the occultist had spoken remained in darkness. The headlights of the car fell upon this spot as Luke maneuvered the roadster for that purpose, disclosing a bridge across a moat at least ten feet wide. The bridge was solitary. No one stood there in the glare of the headlights. But just inside the portal of the draw a man waited, so impassively that he seemed a wax figure, arrayed in the ancient garb of an old-time page, with doublet and hose.

"Is that your devil?" Luke laughed.

Cagliostro drew a long breath of relief.

"No, that isn't the—thing—I saw. That was unutterably horrible. This is just a man, I imagine."

The car went closer. As it approached the draw, the page came out, holding up one hand in warning. His voice fell clearly, in quite good English, on the night air. He, at least, was flesh and blood.

"Don't drive over the bridge, sir, if you please. You will find the garage around at the side of the castle, to your right, sir. If you will be kind enough to put up your car and come back here on foot, I'll send a man to get your bags, sir."

"Evidently we're expected," Luke murmured to his companion. "I've half a mind to go in, friend Cagliostro. "

"He thinks you are my assistant," whispered the occultist. His voice was under control now. "Are you—will you—?"

"Yes, I am, and I will," decided Luke, curiosity getting the better of him. "Send a man for our bags," he called to the servant, who bowed and disappeared within.

At the left of the castle there seemed to be no road, but the roadway at the right had been given a little attention; ruts had been smoothed out, stones removed. Halfway down beside the castle moat, a large granite garage loomed up. Luke drove the roadster into it, and a minute later two men, also arrayed in medieval costume, appeared and picked up his bags. Painting paraphernalia he left in the car.

"Where are your bags, friend Cagliostro?" he inquired.

The occultist shifted the pale blue eyes uneasily from Luke's amused gray orbs.

"I—ah—left them in front of the draw," he admitted.

"When you—oh, excuse me—I understand," grinned Luke, as he followed the servants back to the draw.

The thing that the artist did not like was that as they entered the courtyard within those lofty stonewalls, a creaking sound announced that the drawbridge was being raised. A quick look behind him confirmed this suspicion. He and Cagliostro Moderno were now cut off from the outside world as completely as if they had been immured in a jail, in solitary confinement; those high walls meant no escape; that wide moat might not be deep enough for a plunge from the battlements.

Luke was suddenly glad to remember that in one of his bags was an automatic.

"If you have no objection, sir," one of the men asked Luke, much to the occultist's discomfiture taking the artist for the principal of the two, "the Master would like to have you wait for ten minutes on the roof garden, until your rooms are made ready. He cannot see you tonight, as he is occupied with an important experiment."

"We will await his pleasure," hastily exclaimed the occultist, assuming the lead with dignity.

He had once more swung his mantle about his plump form, and was permitting only the button nose and squinting eyes to appear above one edge of it.

Luke shrugged indifferent shoulders, as he followed the page up a winding staircase in a tower that rose on one side of the courtyard. They emerged upon what seemed to be a kind of roof garden, located on the broad top of one of the sidewalls of the castle, and wide enough to cover not only the wall but part of that portion of the building. Here the servitor paused, hesitated, then turned directly to Luke.

"The Master has directed me, sir, to ask that you pace back and forth along this central path, until I can come for you a little later."

Luke stared, a quirk of amusement twisting his mobile lips.

"Is that a suggestion, or a command?" he inquired pleasantly.

"Oh, sir, the Master always has a good reason back of the most absurd—that is, apparently absurd—requests," the man amended hastily.

"How about me?" bristled the occultist. "Perhaps he means that it is I who am to walk back and forth? It is I who am the—"

"Pardon me, sir, but it is the younger man to whom the Master's request is directed," the page said respectfully.

Cagliostro retired, slightly peevish, to seat himself on a rustic bench at one side of the narrow path. Luke, with much inward curiosity and amusement, strode back and forth along the pebbled way. The page disappeared. Luke, passing the doorway as he walked, suddenly stopped short, his head jerking to instant attention without turning it in the direction of what he heard. It was a voice; a husky, pleading woman's voice, whispering tensely.

"Don't turn your head! Pretend to be looking at the moon! But if you are a gentleman, don't leave this place without seeing Alden first! Alden. For God's sake, don't fail me! Look! The light—from the Master's tower! I must go, or he will see me here. At four in the morning—on this roof garden is the safest place!"

The voice ceased. There was the slightest rustle, as of a woman's garments. And then a blinding ray of light shot across the garden, disclosing everything as brightly as in broad daylight. Startled out of his astonishment at that mysterious and appealing feminine voice, Luke sprang out of the path of the ray, only to find it following him persistently as he walked.

"Lord! What's that?" gasped Cagliostro, jumping to his feet.

"Somebody's turning a searchlight on us," the artist decided, as he stopped to peer past the light. But it was too blinding.

"I think I understand," gabbled the occultist, the pale eyes thrust up into Luke's perplexed face. "It's him. Taking a look at me," proudly. "He asked you to walk, so that he could tell which of us was which." After this reflection, he hurried to seat himself again on the rustic bench, posing importantly.

"Darned impudent of Mr. Fane," Luke decided. "Must be an eccentric of the first water." He deliberately turned his back to the searchlight, which played about the garden, then back to him, almost as if suggesting that he walk again. But he stood deliberately still.

Within five minutes the page appeared in the doorway and indicated that the two were to follow him. Winding passages gave place to steep and narrow staircases, dimly lighted by scattered candles guttering against dark walls; stairways led to corridors across which tiny slits in the stone of the outer walls threw occasional threads of faint moonlight. At last the servant threw open the door of a room, motioned Cagliostro to enter, left him standing there with a vaguely disturbed expression on his face, and led Luke to another room around a turn in the same corridor.

"If there is anything you'd like, sir, just ring for me—the electric button is here. My name is Mason, by the way, sir. It is the Master's desire that you drink a goblet of hot wine, sir, after your cold drive. I will bring it presently." He threw open a door at one side of the great apartment, disclosing a luxuriously appointed private bath. "I think you will be very comfortable, sir."

Luke looked about him, observing the tapestry-hung walls, the thickly carpeted floor, the over-stuffed armchairs, the immense antique bed. He nodded appreciatively.

"I think I shall," he agreed. "Thank your master for the hot wine," he added. "It will be doubly welcome."

Mason bowed and disappeared. Urged by he knew not what motive, but with the feeling that he would like to be secured against intrusion in this strange place, the artist made a hasty examination of the room, lifting tapestries to peer behind them for hidden doors, and pulling up the bigger rugs for trap-doors. He grinned as he did so, feeling his actions absurd. But the absurdity of it did not keep him from making a thorough examination of his surroundings. The conclusion he arrived at was that he was secure from intrusion from the bathroom, but that any of those blocks of granite forming the walls might be in reality secret doors. Anything, he felt, would be possible, plausible, in this strange castle.

His thoughts ran to the voice of that unseen woman, who had asked him to meet her in the roof garden at four that morning. Was it a man or a woman whom he was to meet? A man—Alden?

Luke prepared for the night by slipping on a dressing gown and slippers, to blind Mason. When the man appeared with the steaming goblet of wine, he was told to leave it on the stand by the bed.

"I'll drink it a little later," the artist said casually. "Spiced rather heavily, isn't it?"

"It makes a good nightcap, sir," Mason remarked, a rather odd expression passing over his face. This unguarded look was not lost on Luke, who inwardly decided not to drink the wine, although it smelled enticing.

"I understand from Mr.—ah—Moderno, sir, that you've both

dined? Is there anything else I can do for you, sir? No, sir? Thank you, sir."

Mason retired, closing the heavy door behind him. Luke at once went across the room, found a massive key, and turned it in the great hand-hammered bronze lock. That door, at least, should be impassable.

Then from his bag he took an electric torch and his automatic, slipping them into different pockets of his coat, which he now reassumed. The spicy odor of the steaming wine penetrated to every corner of the room, affecting Luke soporifically. He picked up the goblet, carried it into the bathroom, and emptied it. He could not afford to sleep this first night in Fanewold.

—3—
Behind The Arras

Despite his intention to remain awake, the artist caught himself on the point of dozing more than once as the night wore on. When a light tap sounded on his door, then he was sure for a moment that he had only imagined it, and looked at his watch with the electric torch, not wishing to turn on even the shaded electric night-lamp. It was half-past one o 'clock, and the rap on his door was no dream, for it came again, timidly, yet persistently.

Luke crossed the room and listened. Again the tap. With one hand in his pocket where the automatic lay, he unlocked the door and very quietly swung it ajar. A dark figure stood in the flickering light of the corridor candles, which contrasted oddly with the luxurious appointments, electric and otherwise, of his apartment. As he opened the door cautiously, this figure moved toward him with a slight rustle of starched garments. It was a woman who came in at the door, pushing it shut behind her. Luke touched the electric button; the room was flooded with light.

She stood without shrinking, her eyes narrowed at the sudden blaze of illumination, an elderly woman with faded blue eyes, fine features that must once have been very lovely but were now lined heavily with the wrinkles of secret anxieties and apprehensions. Her dress was simple, dark, nondescript, but her apron and the cap resting on her straightly-drawn gray hair were snowy and starched, modern to the last extreme. Evidently an upper servant.

"You are the unmarried young man?" she whispered, one finger warning him to keep his voice low.

Luke nodded, smooth brow contracted, gray eyes darkening with puzzlement.

"I am Alden," the woman continued, still in that low, half-frightened manner. "Miss Fane's nurse. That is, I was her nurse; I have been her personal maid for some years, since she grew up from the baby I first cared for."

"Who is Miss Fane?"

"She is the adopted daughter of Madam Fane, Mr. Porter. It is about her that I have come to you, risking God only knows how much, to get your help for her sake. If the Master discovers that I have been to you, he will dispose of me—somehow," she said darkly. "At any rate, he would see to it that I could not help my little Sybil in this moment of dire need. Mr. Porter,"—she laid her worn hand on Luke's arm appealingly—"do not trust Guy Fane. He is a monster who will stop at nothing to gain his own ends." She shuddered convincingly.

"Still I do not understand," Luke said gently.

"Guy Fane is planning some monumental crime against Sybil," the woman whispered tensely. "Just what it is I can only surmise, but my barest imaginings of it are so horrible that I dare not put them into words. It is against her immortal soul that he is plotting, Mr. Porter. What use he wishes to make of an innocent girl, I cannot—dare not—think. But she must be saved—she must!"

"If there is anything I can do," Luke began, vaguely—when Alden seized his arm convulsively between her nervous, working fingers.

"Listen!" She remained in apprehensive silence for a long moment. Then she drew Luke toward the inner wall of his room.

"Lock your door. Now please follow me, in absolute silence. I am going to take you through a secret passage into Miss Fane's room, and hide you behind the tapestry so that you can understand something."

Her finger went to her lips again in warning. She took a pocket flash from her apron and turned it on. Lifting one heavy hanging, she motioned Luke to follow. He did so, feeling as if he were in a strange dream. She pushed something somewhere in the wall. A part of what had seemed solid stone swung slowly away on a central pivot. Into the opening thus discovered she stepped, with beckoning finger. The artist walked behind her closely. Through a short passage, and then she once more hunted for and found some secret spring, which swung back a smaller stone like a window. Again that warning for silence. Then she took Luke's hand in hers, pushed it through the window, until he touched a swinging, heavy material, which he realized was a tapestry hanging similar to those in his own room. As he made the discovery, he heard voices again, and strained against the small opening to hear them better, at a gesture from the woman, who then shut off the flashlight.

Through the chinks in the woven stuff came glints of light. Luke was impatient now to see, and as if she had divined his wish, Alden whispered cautiously that if he had a penknife he might be able to cut out a small piece of the tapestry. The artist took the suggestion, and after a minute's awkward attempt, succeeded, and his eye went to the small opening.

He was looking into a charming boudoir, furnished in modern French fashion with pale blues and pinks, and lighted by a brilliant chandelier of crystal drops. On a bed opposite, a girl was sleeping deeply, a girl whose fair blond loveliness stirred the artist's soul and made his fingers itch to depict her on canvas. On either side of the sleeper's bed stood a figure, and either was ominous to a terrifying degree. One was short, squat, ungainly; draped from head to foot in swathing folds of somber black so thick as to conceal effectually what-ever was beneath them. Not even the face of this individual showed under double thicknesses of black chiffon that left only the flashing of dark eyes to be glimpsed occasionally.

"She sleeps!" came from the thick folds of the veil, in a voice singularly rich and melodious. "Yet for a moment I thought she was only feigning sleep. My fearful imagination! But she sleeps soundly; the opiate never fails to do its work."

The second being—a woman, tall, black-garbed—bent over the sleeping girl.

Snow-white hair was piled above a face of singular but repelling pride and much devastated beauty; mingled in that speaking countenance were the traces of battling emotions that must have been going on in her soul for years, to have altered her face so terribly. Now across it writhed in sequence fury and reluctance; hate, and a kind of disdainful pity.

The man had been watching her attentively, for his voice issued now from the swathing folds of black.

"My dear mother, is it possible that you are considering withdrawal at this late moment? Now, when all lies ready to my hand? When the final act of this stupendous drama is ready to be played out? When—He—has promised to grant my prayers? Impossible!"

"I cannot look upon so much innocence and purity without experiencing something of remorse at the part I must play," cried the dark woman. "I am not withdrawing, Guy. But—she is so beautiful—so unsuspecting—so—"

"Oh, yes, I grant you all this, my dear mother. It is very tender and womanlike for you to feel such sympathy for her. But what about me? Do you not owe me some reparation for what you have done to me? I, who am what your deliberate desire for revenge upon a husband's infidelities made me—a thing so utterly horrible that I dare not look at my hideous mockery of a face lest I perish at my own temerity, my flesh creeping at the revolting and grisly monster that would confront me in my mirror?"

"Enough, Guy! Enough!" The mother wrung her attenuated hands.

"Oh, your revenge upon my father was complete, my dear mother! Yet the worst part of it fell upon me, who was innocent of any wrong. My forbidding deformities have served your purpose. Now you must expiate your crime against me. You must pay, mother. You must pay."

She pressed both hands to her wrinkled cheeks.

"I never dreamed what it would mean to you," she pleaded. "Forgive—"

"Forgive you? Perhaps I may find it in my heart, if there is a human heart within this unsightly, monstrous mass of flesh, to forgive you when the final act of the drama has been played out. Oh, when I have gained the grace and comeliness of which your revengeful hate robbed me, perhaps I may forgive you, then!"

She held her outstretched hands toward him pleadingly.

"Have I rebelled, Guy? Have I not put myself utterly in your hands, even to the extent of endangering my immortal soul!" wailed she, as if in agony.

"Your soul endangered, my dear mother?" The man laughed a short, sneering laugh. "You should have considered your soul—and mine, dear mother, mine—long ago, when you prepared Lucifer's chapel, and frequented it during those months before my hateful birth, thinking only of your unspeakable revenge upon my father. You had your wish; you drove him away in horror at the sight of the monstrous prodigy that would be his heir. Now, I must have my wish. It is only to undo what you did, sweet mother," in mocking tones.

"I sometimes wonder if a demon inhabits your frame, Guy—"

The squat individual chuckled horribly.

"Perhaps it is so, dear mother. Who can tell? But my wish is so modest. I only ask that the exquisite loveliness reposing on this couch deliver up to me some of its charm. And with generosity, I am willing —anxious—to give all, all my own ugliness, all my forbidding deformity, in exchange!"

"But you told me you would use the man," hesitated the woman.

The short figure gave a shrug of its shoulders.

"I tried to see him in the searchlight, but I couldn't tell whether or not he had the physique, the features, that would interest me more than these," motioning toward the girl. "It is the more subtle way, to take them from him, and wreck her soul—afterward," he observed thoughtfully. "Well, tomorrow I must see him and decide."

"Guy, spare her soul! Let it be a stranger! Not this poor child! I tell you, I am afraid! She is too pure, too innocent. The very stars in their courses will fight for her."

"And is not her purity, her innocence, what make her more acceptable to Him? Ah," and he lifted black-swathed arms above the sleeping girl in terrible invocation, "Lucifer, Son of the Morning! Only Thou canst understand how great is my impatience at the delay of these last preparations that will make the sacrifice acceptable unto Thee! I tell you, mother, not until this girl sees her purity and loveliness turning into ugliness, her innocence of thought replaced by the lowest, vilest passions that can enter the human mind, not until then will Lucifer exult in the sacrifice."

"There you err, wretched boy!" cried out the mother passionately. "Her beauty may pass, but her soul is in a higher keeping."

"I have made no mistakes, my mother. Her soul will yet be Lucifer's. He who has been instructed by a prince of the fallen hosts of heaven cannot err."

"But don't you see that because He is a prince of darkness He has failed to take into His calculations the power of light? Guy, Guy, beware of putting overmuch trust in Lucifer. He only seeks to draw down to Himself, not to exalt. It is your mother, your wretched mother, who warns you. Your mother, who has paid ten thousand times in agony and tears for her crime against her unborn son!"

The veiled figure made the travesty of a cross by folding its arms and resting its hands upon its own shoulders. Then the head bent upon the folded arms, while a mocking, ironical laugh issued softly from the folds of the veil.

"You don't believe yet, do you, mother? Well, you shall! In spite of what you have already experienced, what you have seen with your own eyes, you remain incredulous? You persist in your skepticism? Oh!" he cried out with strange passion; "do not dare tell me that you do not believe! Your words unnerve me. I almost feel as if there were some powerful influence near this sleeping girl, some influence mutely but strongly battling against me! To the chapel! To the chapel!"

He moved rapidly to the woman's side and urged her toward the door.

"Not tonight, Guy. I cannot bear it again—so soon. I am not a young woman. You are fearless, but I am unutterably afraid! Not tonight, I implore you!"

"To the chapel!" cried the man's mellifluous voice, inexorably. "I will sacrifice a pair of doves—or a young lamb. You must be convinced, or you cannot help me, and—I must not fail. I would rather die than fail! "

The reluctant woman moved slowly toward the door, followed by the squat figure of the strange being in its black wrappings.

The door of Sybil Fane's room swung to behind those ill-omened figures. As it closed, Alden's hand plucked nervously at Luke Porter's sleeve.

"Mr. Porter, we must get back to your room at once. You are supposed to be asleep, and if the Master should happen to visit your room—" she left the sentence unfinished.

"You go ahead. You know the way," whispered Luke, irritated at the inference unspoken.

He wanted to take one last look at the sleeping beauty in the great antique bed, but the light in the room had been extinguished and there only remained to follow Alden back through the narrow winding of the secret passage. Back in his room, Alden let the tapestry drop over the hidden door and turned to the young man, heavy eyes burning in her wrinkled face.

"I cannot tell the whole story now," she said hurriedly. "If you promise you will not leave here without making an attempt to rescue Sybil, I will try to see you before too many days have passed, and then I will tell you the secrets that I have learned, and the secret that I know, I only."

"That girl is certainly in bad hands, judging from the conversation we have just overheard," Luke decided. "Alden, I'm with you. If she needs me, I am at Miss Fane's service."

"She doesn't know, yet, what danger she is in," Alden pointed out. "So far, she has had the kindest treatment, and has been indulged in every way, except that she has been told she cannot leave the castle until after she is married."

"Then she has never been outside these walls?" asked the artist, astonished.

"She has read about the world, in carefully censored books, but she has been taught that a girl does not emerge from such seclusion as this until she marries. And—there is yet another thing."

"Well?" prompted Luke.

"Mr. Porter, she believes that any day her future husband may appear in Fanewold. She is ready to fall in love with the first good-looking man who comes here. Why that should please the Master I do not know, but I am sure that he intends you to be Sybil's suitor."

"It might be worse," murmured Luke, thinking of the flowerlike loveliness of that sleeping beauty. "Well, Alden, cheer up. When I get a better understanding of the situation, you may rely upon me to do my best for Miss Fane. She is too charming a girl to be left to the tender mercies of such a man as this Guy Fane seems to be, judging from what I've heard tonight."

"Sometime you will know how deeply I appreciate your kindness, Mr. Porter. Sometime, when you know my secret," murmured the woman. "Until then, I beg one thing only: Do not trust the Master."

She unlocked the hall door, listened for a moment, then opened it quietly and slipped out into the light of the flickering candles.

—4—

The Master

From the deep slumber into which his vigils finally plunged him, Luke wakened to hear someone rapping loudly at the door. He got up lazily and unlocked it.

"If you please, sir, the Master has ordered breakfast for you and the other gentleman on the roof garden. The morning is mild and warm, sir. Of course," and the voice altered subtly, "if you prefer to breakfast in bed, I am sure the Master will alter his arrangements."

"Let it be the roof garden, Mason," Luke acquiesced. "I'll be out in ten minutes. Is Mr. Binney—that is, the other gentleman—up?"

"He is already out, sir. A light sleeper, sir, I'd say. Didn't touch the spiced wine, sir," irrelevantly.

"You may as well take out my empty goblet," Luke suggested, "now you're here. That's some wine, Mason. But it makes a fellow sleep," he said casually. Under his heavy eyebrows the keen gray eyes watched Mason's face.

"You may well say so, sir. Miss Sybil always sleeps heavily after drinking it. The Master gives it to her whenever she complains of insomnia."

Mason appeared innocent enough, but Luke fancied that the man was studying him curiously behind that impassive gaze.

"May I give you a hand, sir, with your dressing?"

"Thanks, no. Not used to being valeted, Mason. I'll be upstairs in a few minutes," dismissed Luke.

"Wanted to drug me last night," he murmured to himself. "I'll have to watch out for these quieting nightcaps," he told himself as he dressed, but his thoughts were more on the mystifying remarks he had heard the night before, hidden behind the tapestry of Sybil Fane's room.

He was anxious to meet the girl, and wondered if she would appear at breakfast. There was no one in the garden but the occultist, however, and the little man was pacing nervously up and down the path when Luke appeared at the doorway.

"This is a strange place!" was his greeting. "Did—did you sleep last night?"

"Like a top," Luke replied carelessly.

Cagliostro jerked his carroty head from one side to the other and after his squinty eyes had gazed watchfully about him, he said in a low voice:

"Well, I suppose you drank that wine, didn't you?"

Luke laughed.

"No, my good Cagliostro, I didn't. What do you take me for? A babe in arms? I poured it down the lavatory in the bathroom, and sat up for hours to find out why I'd been offered the potion."

"Then you knew about it?" babbled the occultist, marveling. "How did you know?"

"How did you?" parried Luke, smiling. "By the way, I see our breakfast is ready, and it looks mighty appetizing."

He drew up a chair and would have seated himself so that he was facing the forest, but Mason hastily interfered, pulling out a chair that seated him facing the interior towers of the castle. Slightly puzzled, Luke took the place. As he helped himself to crisp bacon and golden marmalade, his watchful eyes went over the towers that he faced. Within the castle walls there rose a great roof of corrugated glass, admitting sunlight but shutting out all intrusive glances. This translucent roof was built in a series of terraces culminating in a central tower at one end, which style of architecture permitted the insertion of ventilators in the shape of metal blinds set with the openings downward, again with the very obvious end of shielding the courtyard from curious eyes while at the same time affording free access of fresh air.

"That's an odd sort of thing," he started to say to his companion, when he was suddenly half blinded by a brilliant flash of light from the tower above the glass roof, a flash so sharp and sudden that he flung up one hand to protect his eyes. It was as if some mischievous urchin had manipulated a mirror to deflect the sun's rays into his face. When he looked to see what had occasioned the flash, his curiosity was piqued, and at the same time he was slightly irritated. It was a repetition of last night's occurrence with the searchlight. The flash had been occasioned by the reflection of sunlight from glass, but the glass had not been a mirror; it was from the barrels of a field glass in the act of being once more leveled in his direction. Some curious individual was looking him over in this manner.

"Darned impertinence," Luke said aloud. "Cagliostro, what would you take that to be?" He pointed out the two barrels of the field glass which he could observe distinctly between the shutters of a window in the central tower.

The occultist looked back across his shoulders without much interest, obviously preoccupied with his own thoughts.

"Somebody is looking us over, my friend. He didn't get a very good look at us last night, so he's trying it in daylight. And I know who it is," Luke added in a low voice.

The pale blue eyes shifted to look into Luke's. Somewhere in their depths flickered a keener perception than the artist had supposed the little Binney capable of.

"It's—he," whispered the occultist.

"How do you know?"

"I feel it, Mr. Porter."

"Well, I know, because—" and then Luke broke off, remembering that the information he had gained by listening behind the hangings in Sybil Fane's room was not to be imparted in this fashion.

"Did you feel it, too?"

"Why, yes, that is about what I'd think," Luke stumbled awkwardly.

"We are supposed to meet Mr. Fane this morning," the occultist volunteered, as he finished his second cup of coffee with gusto.

"Mr. Fane wishes Mr. Porter to go up to his study first," said Mason's suave voice over Luke's shoulder.

Cagliostro bristled with indignation. His pouting mouth stuck its lips out in protest.

"There's some mistake," he scolded, peevishly. "This young man is merely my—my assistant. I am the occultist, not he."

The major-domo did not smile. He spoke seriously and respectfully.

"Quite so, sir. But Mr. Fane undoubtedly wishes to see if your assistant is satisfactory, before bothering you with an interview. He would not care to take up your time needlessly, I'm sure, sir."

The occultist was satisfied. He seated himself, wrapped in his dark mantle, upon the rustic bench, with immense dignity.

"I will wait here, until you return, Mr. Porter," he announced.

"Will you kindly come with me, sir?" Mason requested. "The Master has asked me to tell you that he hopes you will make allowance for him, if you find him irritable. He is tired and nervous from a sleepless night."

Without giving the artist time to reply, Mason led the way down long corridors and staircases, that led, Luke surmised by the general direction, into the very heart of Fanewold Castle. At last they paused before a door; Mason opened it noiselessly, stepping to one side and motioning the artist to enter. No announcement was made; indeed, as the room was in complete darkness, Luke could hardly believe that anyone was waiting there.

He stepped across the threshold of the room slowly and paused, hardly knowing whether to stop where he was or to feel his way forward through the Stygian darkness. The outer corridor had been dimly illuminated by occasional tall and narrow windows, shadowed by climbing ivy, but this room apparently had no windows, and the only light was that of a single candle standing so far back in the depths of the apartment that it served but to make the darkness visible.

Luke took another step forward. He stood stock-still and waited. He had no intention of breaking a rib by a fall over unseen pieces of antique furniture. He had half a mind to step back out of that uncanny blackness that seemed to be closing in like innumerable invisible presences, alive with inconceivable and strange malevolence. As he stood, half exasperated and half unnerved by the oddity of his bizarre reception, a voice sounded on his ear, so unexpectedly near at hand that the startled young man went back several paces.

The soft and musical notes of that plaintive voice did not move Luke from his quick indignation, and although the first words spoken were in apology, the artist gulped hard to swallow his resentment at those tricks of darkness and an unseen speaker. Memory of the previous night's revelations also angered him.

"Pardon me, my dear sir, I beg of you, for what must seem a strange and inhospitable reception," said the voice. "I am, alas, inflicted with a malady which precludes your reception in other than the dim light of this room. My eyes," went on that melancholy and touching voice plaintively, "cannot bear more than the pale light of a single candle at a distance."

"Such a reception is hardly reassuring," Luke remarked coldly, his nerves yet throbbing. "But since you have been so kind as to explain that it is due to a misfortune, I cannot of course do other than extend sympathy for a malady which shuts you away from the glorious light of day. I am speaking, I presume, to Mr. Guy Fane?"

"I am Guy Fane. Your name, I am informed, is Luke Porter? If you will step forward, Mr. Porter, your hand will find a chair already placed. I would like to ask a few questions of you, if you do not object."

Luke found the indicated chair and sat down uncomfortably. This conversation with an unseen person in the dark was not just to his taste; he loved sunshine and space, not this black, crowding darkness.

"I understand that you have come with—ah—Cagliostro Moderno, as his assistant? Have you ever studied—ah—magic?"

Luke consulted himself hastily. He dared not deny knowledge of the subject entirely, for this might result in his being shut out completely from the strange experiments he was now burning to witness. Moreover, he did not wish to leave Fanewold without first meeting Sybil Fane, and seeing how he could be of service to her if she really needed, as Alden had declared, his help.

"I have not gone very deeply into the subject, Mr. Fane," he admitted with apparent frankness. "But you must know that it is too tremendous in scope for anyone to say that he has done more than—studied—it."

"Then it is our Cagliostro who is the real adept, the initiate?"

A laugh followed the words; a laugh so eery that Luke had much ado to keep his nerves from throbbing uncomfortably again. The cachinnation broke off as suddenly as it had burst forth, leaving in its wake a silence yet more uncanny. Luke felt that through the gloom the unseen Master was gazing at him with keen eyes that pierced the darkness and was cynically enjoying his manifest discomfort. He took himself in hand firmly.

Guy Fane spoke suddenly then, taking up the current of his thought as if he had not broken it off by his uncanny laughter.

"He really doesn't look the part, do you think, Mr. Porter?"

"One doesn't have to look the part, does he, to accomplish what he sets out to do? I don't wear flowing ties and long hair, but I've managed to achieve a small success at painting, and I don't look the part, I've been told often," Luke retorted.

"You are not slow at a parry, Mr. Porter," complimented the invisible host. "What I wish to know is: do you feel skeptical about magic, or have you reason to believe that it exists?"

"I've seen black magic worked in Haiti," Luke said slowly. "After that, can I deny it?"

"Right to the point, aren't you? What does it represent to you?"

The reply came slowly, for Luke felt that Guy Fane laid much stress upon it. The whole affair savored so much of the outré that he felt extreme dislike to discuss such a subject under such conditions. Yet the very silence appeared to wait upon his answer.

"In its final analysis, magic is no more than the power of the imagination, utilized along lines with which the masses are not conversant. The imagination possesses potentialities fraught with more far-reaching influence and potent force than is realized by the average man," he said at last.

"Ah! Your opinion interests me immensely. It coincides with mine. You would concede, then, that under conditions where the human mind has been wrought up to a high tension, incidents ordinarily termed miraculous might take place?"

"Admittedly."

"What would you consider the conditions most favorable for the working of so-called miracles?" asked the Master, eagerness discernible in his mellow voice.

"The Bible states plainly that the first condition is that of ardent demand. The second is that of earnest belief that the demand not only will be fulfilled, but is already fulfilled."

"Then you think results will be quicker and more powerful in proportion to the strength of the faith involved?"

"Assuredly, Mr. Fane."

"I am much gratified to find that we are so deeply in accord on such an interesting subject, Mr. Porter. I am conducting an experiment along magical lines, and shall later on expect some very important assistance from you. My good mother cannot assist me as much as she used to; growing ill-health makes it impossible for her to concentrate mentally."

Luke remained silent. There was a short pause.

"In the meantime, may I ask you to do what you can to make the hours pass agreeably for my cousin? I shall consider as a personal favor all that you do for her. In fact, you will be doing me a great service, which you may understand better, later on. Mason!"

The major-domo appeared in the dim entrance.

"Will you kindly take Mr. Porter to Miss Fane? And bring me the —ah—adept, who must have been waiting impatiently for this pleasant little chat with Mr. Porter to end."

Luke followed the servitor into the corridor, as Guy Fane's velvety voice sank musically into the darkness and died away. But after he had taken the few steps which would bring him to comparative light, he paused, with a vivid impression that something stood before him, blocking his way and staring up at him with eyes that mocked subtly.

"How extremely psychic you are, my dear Mr. Porter," murmured Guy's voice, vibrating with gentle amusement. As he spoke, a soft rustle betrayed the movement of someone near at hand. The way was clear.

Luke followed Mason down the corridor, beneath the light of the guttering candles. As he went, he heard that strange laugh again, full now of what seemed to his sensitive ear malicious enjoyment. The sound of it struck an angry chill through him. As he groped along, he continued to feel strange, peering eyes following his slow progress, and the sensation did not serve in any way to retard his steps.

—5—
Sybil

Conducted by Mason, Luke found himself back in the roof garden after the usual traverse of twisting, winding corridors. The impatient Cagliostro arose immediately, anxious for his own interview with the Master, but on his way out stopped to whisper in Luke's ear:

"Well, is he satisfied? What did he ask you? What did you say to him?"

Luke's lips twitched with amusement. His gray eyes danced.

"Friend Cagliostro, I was asked if I believed in magic, and I said I did."

The occultist's pale blue eyes stared incredulously at him.

"Well, you're rather surprising, Mr. Porter. I had no idea that you were far enough along on the road to believe in the tremendous underlying powers and forces which the average individual doesn't even suspect, let alone believe in. Well, well, well!"

Down the corridor behind the retreating Mason, Luke could hear that astonished echo, of "Well, well, well!" as Cagliostro went to his interview.

The breakfast table had been removed. A gaily red vis-à-vis swing had been stood up in its place, as if in preparation for someone. Luke dropped into one side of it and began mulling over his experiences of the past night and that morning, swinging back and forth as he thought.

That Guy Fane was a monomaniac on the subject of black magic he could see readily. What he disliked was the implication that the innocent Sybil Fane was to be involved to her own injury in some of Guy Fane's villainous or criminal practices. Moreover, Luke himself was also being drawn into them, if he was to believe the hints contained in the words of the Master the night before. Just how he could be useful to the black magician, he could not imagine, and he wondered how much of his knowledge on the subject could safely be imparted to Cagliostro Moderno, whose ingenuous nature he had sensed even at their first meeting. Luke did not believe that the little Herbert Binney cared to be drawn into such vile practices as Guy Fane would be guilty of. To a certain extent, then, Herbert Binney might be trusted, and if his knowledge of black magic was more than merely theoretical, perhaps he would understand why Guy Fane imagined he could rob another man of fine physique, handsome features, for his own vicious purposes.

Sunken in his puzzled thoughts, Luke did not see a slender, girlish figure that tripped from the doorway across the garden path toward him and came to a stop before the swing. Then he looked up, startled for a moment. Sybil's blond hair had been cut in a modern bob, but with its fluffy curls it made a soft frame about her face. She lifted her eyes to him, and the artist almost cried out with exultation, so beautiful was their purple-pansy velvetiness. The play of alert and arch intelligence lightened the lovely face that he had seen the night before in soft repose. Only one defect, if defect it was, made Sybil's eyes seem deep with mystery; the eyebrows that outlined them above were much darker than her hair, making her eyes and her crimson lips stand out with startling prominence on her pale skin.

The artist sprang to his feet.

"Miss Fane?"

The girl put out both hands in such friendly fashion that Luke dropped formality at once. Her charm, her poise, her absolute ingenuousness, made their impression upon the man as well as upon the artist. He took the slender hands in his. They stood for a minute in silence, looking at each other with interested eyes. Then Sybil spoke in a soft, repressed little voice with a nervous undertone trembling through it.

"Are you—are you—my lover?"

The artist remained silent for an astonished moment, his mobile lips parting slightly with the shock of her words. Some movement in the doorway drew his eyes; the gray-haired Alden was standing there, duenna-like, one finger ever so slightly uplifted as if in warning. He remembered her words of the previous night.

"May I be your—lover?" he said quickly.

She nodded with sweet simplicity, honest purple eyes still upon him. Her hands clung with a soft pressure that stirred his heart strangely; he swore to himself that no harm should touch this innocent, ingenuous girl, if he could foresee and prevent it.

"Let us sit on the parapet," proposed Sybil, gayly, drawing him to the garden wall, which overhung the black moat. "There are so many things I want to ask you. And I am so glad you are handsome, dear lover. I have always been afraid you wouldn't look the way I wished."

"And I do?" smiled Luke, letting himself fall in with the mood of the girl, as one humors an innocent child.

"Oh, I love your gray eyes!" she said honestly. "And your teeth are so nice when you smile. And you have a kind of air. You see, lover, I've never yet seen any man but the servants here. My cousin Guy never lets anyone see him, because he has weak eyes, poor dear, and cannot come out in the sun. And you are so different from Mason and the other men."

"I should hope so!" was Luke's fervent, though unspoken, comment.

Mrs. Alden advanced from the doorway. Sybil turned toward her old nurse with a welcoming smile.

"Oh, Alden dear, isn't my lover beautiful?"

The ardent admiration in her voice brought color to the artist's tanned cheeks, but he met the unsmiling gaze of Alden with frank sincerity.

"Isn't Sybil the loveliest thing the world has ever seen?" he asked of no one in particular, but his voice vibrated with an emotion that Alden noted, if the girl did not.

The older woman stood near the two as they sat on the parapet; she looked down into the moat below. Luke, still holding the girl's slender hands in his, artist eyes feasting upon her blond loveliness, enhanced by the crude embroideries on the white woolen sports frock, did not realize at first what Alden was saying. Then, when she repeated her words, he gave them alert attention, realizing that she spoke with a hidden meaning.

"Nobody could hope to swim unhurt through that black water," she was saying significantly. "Ten feet wide, and eight feet deep, is that sluggish water, Mr. Porter. And—look!"

She leaned across the parapet, pointing urgently at something whitish that floated in the turbid water. As Luke leaned over to look, there was the movement of some long, slimy thing below, and the whitish article went whirling in the eddies caused by the abrupt movement of that water snake. It was the body of a dove. The poor thing's plumage was soiled with viscid green and darker stains that might have been dried blood.

Luke's eyes went to Alden's in mute inquiry. The woman shook her head, as if she either could not, or would not, explain. Sybil, however, was not so backward.

"You're wondering about that poor dove?" she asked softly. "Oh, that is one thing I don't like! I don't, indeed! I've told my cousin Guy hundreds of times that I just couldn't bear it to have my doves killed for sacrifices, no matter how great the cause." Her voice trembled slightly, and Luke saw that the pansy eyes were moist. "But he is above worrying over the life of a dove, when he is seeking wonderful things that are so much more important."

There was a dreamy look now in the purple eyes. Alden looked at her charge, a tragic impotence on her wrinkled face.

"Now it is a dove," she said, not directly to Luke, but as if she were talking to herself. "The other day it was a young lamb. And it may some day be—another—lamb."

Luke felt cold chills traversing his spinal column. This black magician, then, was actually sacrificing lives to his devilish gods. Could it be possible that Sybil—and he himself—were already devoted to that devil worship? Luke told himself that in future he would not stir without the automatic in his pocket. The tenseness of his gray eyes did not escape Alden's observation; she sighed as if in relief.

"Don't let's talk about it," hastily interpolated Sybil, with a shudder. "I just can not get used to it. I've told cousin Guy many times that I'm sure the High Powers would appreciate fine fruits, or choice flowers, or incense, as well as a poor little dove's life."

"Shall we talk about painting you, Sybil?" suggested Luke, the artist in him gaining the mastery.

She clapped her hands gayly.

"That would be fun, lover."

"Call me Luke, my dear. That is my name."

"Luke? How odd! But I like it. Where are your canvases and brushes and colors, Luke?"

Luke turned to Alden.

"I left the whole business in my car, outside in the garage. Can I manage to get outside the castle?"

A mysterious smile came over Alden's face.

"No, Mr. Porter, you cannot."

"What?" exploded Luke.

Alden's finger went to her lips again.

"It would be better for you to ask Mason to send a man for your painting things," she suggested pointedly.

Reluctantly, Luke assented. He did not like the idea that he was virtually a prisoner in the castle, but in view of more important things he put that thought aside for the time being. Mason sent a page for the artist's paraphernalia; the easel was set up in the garden, and Sybil seated herself on the parapet, little pointed chin on drawn-up knees about which her arms were clasped in childish fashion. Luke, silent, prepared his palette and began to paint. In this manner the morning fled, and when luncheon was announced he hardly cared to leave his work, which was shaping up in a most gratifying manner.

"After luncheon, I'll pose again," Sybil promised, fluttering around the easel in delight at the more than vague promise Luke had given to her portrait. "Come, Luke. Let's hurry with lunch."

The dining room in Fanewold Castle was extraordinarily handsome. Luke betrayed his artist's interest the moment it burst upon him. It was beautifully paneled with solid mahogany, to judge from the massiveness of the carving that decorated the wood. Around the entire room ran a jutting balcony, enclosed in a marvelously carved balustrade. Above this was a latticework screen. For just what purpose this screen had been designed, Luke did not know, but he concluded that it afforded a fine vantage point from which an invisible observer could look down into the room, Sybil waited, standing by her chair at the table. Presently a woman entered the room, a woman of proud dignity, tall, stately, but a wreck of what must once have been magnificent womanhood. Flashing black eyes gleamed under heavy brows still black, making a strange contrast with snowy hair, piled high. Never had the artist seen a more melancholy and interesting countenance than that of Madam Fane. He could the better observe it now, than at a distance as he had the night previous. The simplicity of her coiffure made more pronounced the sophistication of the concealed fires smoldering in the twin volcanoes under her heavy brows; those occasional brilliant flashes betrayed the vivid and powerfully restrained personality.

Rarely, however, did she raise her heavy lids to look anyone directly in the eye; rather did she turn her face slightly, replying in monosyllables which discouraged direct conversation with her. A strange, silent woman, who gave the impression of forces ill spent in coping vainly with something bigger than herself, and hence chary of so little energy or vitality as might escape her in a single word.

Sybil seated herself after Madam Fane, and motioned Luke to pay no attention to her aunt, as the girl called the older woman.

Conversation during luncheon lagged. This might have been Madam Fane's cold abstraction, or Sybil's intimation that Guy Fane lunched on the balcony, hidden behind the lattice. There was something, too, ominous and oppressive in the older woman's heavy glance, which Luke more than once found fixed with strange intensity upon either Sybil or himself.

Nor was this all. He felt as if a thousand mocking, evil eyes were watching his every movement from behind that lattice, although the brilliantly lighted dining room must have been hard on Guy Fane's weak eyes, unless the Master was posing with regard to his mysterious malady. Luke was glad when the meal was over, and Sybil drew him back to the garden to finish her portrait.

An inquiry as to the whereabouts of Herbert Binney led to the response from the girl that he was probably, with her cousin, preparing himself for the greatest experiment of all, the subject of which she was ignorant about, but for which her cousin had prepared her mentally to look forward joyfully. Cagliostro, in effect, did not show up all the afternoon. At dinner, however, he appeared; serious, distant of mien, obviously wrapped up in his thoughts. Luke's attempts to draw him into conversation met with decided rebuff; the occultist took himself seriously. Whether or not the Master had divulged the object of his experiments, Luke could not discover without a private conversation with Cagliostro, and Cagliostro evaded him neatly after dinner.

The autumn evening had grown slightly chill. Sybil therefore led the way to her boudoir, a charming room where she had a piano, a harp, and a violin. Her taste, she told Luke, had run largely to music, because it stirred her emotions so beautifully. Guy had provided teachers (women always) from time to time, but for some reason none of them remained long.

"Just when they were getting interesting," Sybil said regretfully, "and were telling me more about the outside world, they disappeared. But I've learned to amuse myself a lot with music, Luke. Shall I play to you?"

She played. The evening wore on to 11 o'clock. Mason appeared in the doorway with a silver tray on which steamed the spiced wine which Luke suspected of soporific qualities. Sybil sipped hers innocently enough, but Luke managed to avoid drinking the nightcap, except for a few mouthfuls, which he took partly out of sheer curiosity and partly to disarm the waiting and watchful Mason.

That night Luke let himself slip into a half sleep, induced probably by what little wine he had taken, and partly by lack of much sleep the night before. In some subtle manner, strange thoughts entered his unguarded mind—wild dreams through which flitted figures clad in medieval vestures, carrying tall candlesticks with flickering lights atop. As he dozed, he seemed to hear snatches of talk. So much a dream was it, that he did not make the necessary effort to awake and make sure that it was imagination only.

A figure short and ungainly, with veiled face, obtruded itself. To his half-dazed consciousness there seemed to be an atmosphere thick, murky, prescious in the vicinity of this veiled being, an atmosphere weighing so heavily upon his spirits that he felt his throat choking physically. But the sensation was also of a moral east, a shrinking of the higher senses with repugnance. Another figure, tall and thin, impressed him with deep, shuddering pity, such as one might feel for a soul that regards its own deliberate ruin with affright, yet holds to its terrible course as if chained by bonds too powerful to be broken.

"He is a handsome fellow," a voice murmured. "These fine shapely limbs please me well."

A hand touched Luke lightly. At the loathsome contact he shrank with a half moan. There was a grim laugh. The speaker leaned more closely over the sleeper, who began to draw gasping breaths as if oppressed beyond endurance.

"How my very nearness affects this youth! The spells of Lord Lucifer have indeed been powerful. They have made me another and loftier being than mere man."

Awful pride rang in the words.

"Tell me, dear mother," mockingly, "how long it will be for this youth to grow so ardent in his wooing that Sybil's susceptible heart, so carefully prepared, will yield to his lovemaking?"

"If they are not for each other, it will be never," declared Madam Fane.

"Oh, how you love to croak your woful prophecies! Lucifer, Lord Lucifer, grant my prayer soon! I can wait no longer! My monstrous—my execrable—body is poisoning my soul with detestation!"

"You will waken him," warned the other. "He is starting and muttering in his sleep. Come!"

Both figures melted into nothingness. Luke fell into a deep and dreamless sleep.

—6—

Mephistopheles

Mason, appearing at Luke's door in the morning, brought another message from the Master, who sent word that he would like a few words with Mr. Porter, if possible, directly after breakfast.

"He has arranged to receive you in his study, sir. You may find it more agreeable, sir, as it is fairly well lighted. I may say, sir, that this is most unusual on Mr. Fane's part; he rarely receives visitors except in complete darkness," beamed Mason.

"Where is Mr. Moderno this morning?" Luke inquired. He was

anxious to get in touch with Herbert Binney at the earliest occasion, to see how much the little man knew of Guy Fane's plans.

"I believe he is in the chapel, sir, busy with something for the Master."

With this Luke had to content himself, and immediately after breakfast, at which Sybil did not appear, he followed Mason again down winding stairs and through mazes of corridors.

The room into which he was finally ushered was a spacious apartment, fairly well lighted by carefully shaded candles in sconces on the walls. To a height of four feet from the floor, the walls were lined with solidly packed bookcases. Padded armchairs invited. At the farther end of the room, in a niche in the wall, a great crystal globe, hanging on a hardly discernible, silvery chain, caught, reflected, and broke into shimmering rainbow colors the soft radiance of the shaded candles. The light, however, was not the honest golden glow of the average candle, but a sickly reddish light, augmented by the shades, which were dull red. At the side of the room, far back, a delicate lattice extending to eight feet in height, carried with its presence the inference that the Master was there.

"Pray forgive me if I startle you," begged Guy Fane's voice with plaintive intonation. "I know it must seem strange to converse with a man who remains hidden from sight, but alas, my infliction has laid this heavy cross upon me. You will note that I have done my poor best to light the room better, Mr. Porter. Please try to do me the justice of believing that I am not a mummer who attempts to mystify by such cheap methods as darkness and an unseen speaker. My magic is of an entirely different type, I assure you. Won't you draw up a chair near this screen? Thank you so much! Ah, I feel sure that we shall get along famously, and that your presence here will be fraught with much satisfaction to me."

Luke sensed the undertone of something not in accord with the words. Guy Fane was amusing himself by conveying one meaning to the artist, while he laughed inwardly at a significance in his words intelligible only to himself. Instinctively, Luke was on guard. But in settling the chair, he seated himself in such a way that his face was partly in shadow; he did not intend that the unseen watcher should startle him and read that astonishment on his face.

"When you came here as Cagliostro Moderno's assistant, it was understood that you were heart-whole and unmarried. I must reassure myself on this point. It is the basis of a plan that furnishes the reason for Sybil's existence. I cannot explain fully now, but you shall understand all within a comparatively short time, when I have every reason to hope you will be furnished with the key to the mystery. The first important thing you are here for is to become the suitor of my cousin Sybil. And I shall not frown upon your addresses."

Luke sprang from his chair in some heat.

"That is too much! What do you take me for, that you make such a cold-blooded proposal? I am not the man to fall in love at your behest, I assure you—to say nothing of the implied disrespect toward the young lady."

"Calm yourself, my hot-blooded and enthusiastic young friend," soothed the Master's voice, reaching out after him as he paced the floor, with almost tangible forcefulness. "I take you for a gentleman. But consider I know Sybil's prospects. I have her interests at heart. Her own father desired that she be immured within these walls until I considered it wise for her to emerge; he did not wish her to fall victim to some fortune hunter who might rob her of all and leave her broken-hearted. Her private fortune, Mr. Porter, is immense."

"Which doesn't interest me in the slightest," cried Luke angrily.

"Ah, but consider! I have thought long and gravely how to provide a suitable husband for my pretty little innocent cousin. Through my occult relationships, I tried to find a man—young, handsome, healthy, heart-free—who might find it easy to love such a girl as Sybil, and save her from the suffering she might otherwise experience in less worthy hands. Be honest, Mr. Porter. If you could gain the love and respect of Sybil Fane, would you—granted that you grew to love her—feel it a wrong done the girl, to provide her with a good man who loved her first of all for herself?"

Luke stopped him abruptly.

"I cannot deny that your words are couched in a sophistry that carries reluctant conviction to my intellect. But something tells me—"

"Oh, how you weary me, you cautious and particular man! With your 'somethings' that tell you quite nothing! Forgive me if I point out that you are meeting honest frankness on my part with intellectual distrust on yours. Can sincerity be so rare to your experience, that you cannot recognize it when you meet it face to face?"

The speaker's voice was so earnest with deep feeling that Luke almost discredited his own intuitional misgivings and his knowledge of the speaker's nefarious schemes.

"On the surface you may be right in what you propose, Mr. Fane, but there is something despicably small in discussing Miss Fane in such a way."

"There you are again!" the voice reproached him. "You know that the thing is innately right, but you hold that to discuss it is indelicate. What strange reasoning! Perhaps—perhaps you are not the man I thought you to be, sir? Would you like to retire from this indelicate situation?" Fine irony in the intonation. "If so, you have only to ring for Mason; he will get your belongings; you can shake off the dust of Fanewold Castle from your too-delicate person."

Luke sat down abruptly. This would not be what he wanted. Not now. The die was cast. He knew that he could not leave the castle leaving Sybil to the tender mercies of this strange monomaniac. He spoke quickly, abruptly, and with sincerity.

"I admire your cousin heartily, Mr. Fane. She is a most unusual girl for these modern, flapper days. I can hardly say that my admiration will ripen into something warmer—but—I ardently wish to remain."

"Mr. Porter, I cannot find words to thank you for your decision, with all that it implies," significantly. "For it, I believe I shall owe you a lifelong debt. Credit me with not being as lacking in delicacy as you may have been led to believe by this brief conversation. You will, I am sure, entertain other and stronger feelings toward me as our acquaintance progresses to its destined end."

Luke sensed again some subtle significance in the words that as yet he could not understand.

"It is to be hoped I will," he retorted pointedly.

The unseen laughed softly as if to himself, and that thrill of strange distrust shot through Luke's mind again.

"Look, young man, and say if such an innocent and legitimate temptation was ever offered you before in your life?"

The wall above one bookcase seemed to become misty. It faded more and more. In its place there grew the soft light of an autumn morning. And as the picture grew clearer, Luke realized that by some legerdemain or hypnotic trick he was looking directly at Sybil Fane, as she stood among her doves in the roof garden.

"Is it not easy to love such a woman?" whispered the voice of the unseen. "And easy to win her regard? Could you find a fairer woman in the world? Or one more easily molded to your ideal? I warn you, sir, to make haste with your wooing. In two weeks that girl comes of age, with the right to go out into the world she longs to see. Will you let her fall into unscrupulous hands? Save her, if you are a true man, from those unknown perils that otherwise await her!"

Luke replied from his heart:

"Mr. Fane, what you are and what your designs and motives may be, I do not know. But I warn you, if I fall in love with your cousin, nobody, not you yourself, shall ever lay a finger on her to harm or even to startle her."

"Ah! There speaks the kind of man to whom I can gladly give my cousin's hand," applauded Guy Fane approvingly. "I know you will protect her from everyone but yourself," ambiguously. Before Luke could resent the delicate insinuation, the Master continued: "If you do not mind, I shall be excused now, as I have much to do. I hope to see you again within a few days, Mr. Porter, and I hope that then all my warm wishes shall have come to fruition."

—7—
Alden's Secret

A carefree day passed in Sybil's company. The portrait Luke had begun was growing into a vivid likeness of this charming, ingenuous girl, who in no way concealed the interest she felt for him, firmly believing the artist to be her accepted lover and future husband. As the picture came to completion, Luke realized that he was devoted to Sybil Fane's service, body and soul, no matter at what cost.

During the early evening he managed to get a minute's conversation with Herbert Binney. The little man, draped in a black mantle, was just emerging from his room as Luke happened to be passing. The occultist drew back with what seemed real resentment, when Luke almost collared him in his eagerness.

"Do not touch me!" he cried hastily. "I am engaged in work of such a lofty character that I dare not come in contact with souls as immersed in materialism as yours."

"You needn't shout so, my good Cagliostro," the artist protested. "I'm not deaf, really."

Without, however, lowering his voice, the adept continued, as he tried to slip past the young man:

"Purblind fool! Who are you, to accost one who has been favored by the great Lord Lucifer himself? Stand aside and let me pass!"

"Are you crazy?" Luke managed to ask, in astonishment.

"Stand aside!" shouted Cagliostro Moderno fiercely. "The Master waits."

"But I have something important to tell you, my good Binney."

"We shall meet again, Mr. Porter, I assure you," loudly declared the occultist. "Until then, beware how you approach me uninvited."

With that, he slid off down the corridor at a pace that closely resembled flight, leaving the artist staring after him with the conviction that magic, either black or white, had turned the little man's brain.

Thoughtful, Luke returned to Sybil's boudoir.

"Don't know what's come over Cagliostro," he confided, more to

Alden than to the girl. "He's simply fed up to the neck with mystery and refuses even to shake hands with me!"

Alden's wrinkled face grew tense. She moved across the room so that she would pass close to Luke, and as she walked nearer, she murmured in low tones:

"Four o'clock this morning. The roof garden. Don't fail me."

Luke nodded his head casually as if in time to the music Sybil was now bringing out of the harp, but Alden, catching his eyes, understood.

At dinner that evening Luke avoided with suspicion any food that might serve as a conveyance for an opiate, but the only thing that fell under his suspicion was a highly spiced pudding with wine sauce. He noticed that Madam Fane ate no sauce, but Sybil, fond of sweets, called for a second helping of it. His doubts were confirmed later that evening, as Sybil complained of drowziness, and retired early.

Excitement and anxiety served Luke in good stead. Sleep apparently had deserted him; he was wide awake and alert in every fiber of his being. Understanding that no locks could keep him from inspection by visitors, he decided to feign sleep. He therefore threw himself upon the bed as if overcome by drowziness. Under his pillow he slipped his automatic and his electric flash. Well for him that he took this course, instead of going directly to the garden to wait there for his appointment with Alden! In less than half an hour after he had flung himself upon the bed, wholly dressed, the tapestry stirred vaguely in the light, which he had left on by the bedside, and the tall form of Madam Fane emerged and advanced to his side.

She bent over and regarded him keenly; he could feel that fixed gaze penetrating, even with his eyes closed. After a long moment, she sighed involuntarily, said, "Poor fellow!" and her muffled footfalls died away.

It was some time before he dared open his eyes, but when he did so, the room was quiet and he felt that he was alone once more. Evidently she had wished to make sure that he slept soundly. That meant there was something afoot.

Luke lay with relaxed muscles for what seemed ages before he very cautiously consulted his wrist-watch to find it close upon midnight, that mystic hour when tombs open and unhappy spirits leave their moldy beds for a brief space. An uncontrollable presentiment gripped his heart with intolerable foreboding. Luke was intuitive; just now he could have sworn, without knowing precisely what he meant, that Evil was stalking abroad. He could not stand it any longer to lie supinely on the bed—waiting.

He got up, deciding to slip out into the garden before something happened to detain him. If he chanced to be missed, was it likely that he would be sought out there? And if discovered there, what more natural than that the moon, the starry vault, and a sentimental temperament had combined to attract him to enjoy the romantic beauties of the night? Luke, with the electric flash and the pistol, searched his apartment as thoroughly as he could, to satisfy himself that at least his departure would go unnoticed. He then slipped the pistol into his pocket, retaining the torch, which was heavy enough to make a formidable weapon, at a pinch.

He unlocked the door and opened it cautiously. Not a sound did it make; evidently it had been well oiled by some interested person. Up and down the corridor he glanced; the flickering candles guttered in their sockets but disclosed no one in sight. But he was not a dozen paces from his door before he heard the unmistakable rustling of garments—from which direction he could not tell. He sprang back, regained the shelter of his room, and with the door ajar peered out into the corridor.

A figure draped in flowing, trailing garments of white glided into view. As it approached almost noiselessly save for the frou-frou of its robes, Luke's blood congealed with strange surmises. In this strange place, anything was possible. Was he indeed looking with starting eyes upon a visitant from another sphere? His flesh crept at the unearthly suggestion conveyed by the gliding movement of that white-robed creature, whatever it might be. He shrank back into the welcome shelter of his gloomy room, hoping that if this were a manifestation of life from beyond the grave it would pass on its uneasy way without stopping. His blood curdled in his veins. Heartbeats died into sluggish thuds.

Nearer glided the wraith. Breath almost failed the young man, cold sweat standing out in beads on his icy brow. It passed, still with that soft whispering sound of garments, and whipped around a corner of the corridor. Everything was still again.

Luke flung the cold perspiration from his forehead. Reaction set in. With a sudden revulsion of feeling, his blood ran hot in his veins again and he sprang out to make sure just what it was that he had seen. After all, a spirit's robes would not have rustled as did this wraith's. He gained on the gliding specter, which approached the door of the Master's study, entering as the portal opened silently. As it turned, Luke drew back with a half-stifled groan, so severe was the shock which he received. The face that he saw was the face of Sybil Fane. The door closed upon her, the girl whom he now knew he loved, the girl who had stolen to visit her mysterious cousin in secret while the world slept. Ugly suspicions crowded upon him. Was it possible that she loved her cousin and secretly passed the nights in his company, this girl upon whose innate purity and innocence Luke would have staked his life a few minutes before? Why, then, was Guy Fane so anxious to secure for her a husband? To cover up his own derelictions toward this girl whom he had wronged?

The incredible fact remained. Luke had seen, with his own eyes, Sybil Fane creeping at midnight to her cousin's study. He turned back down the corridor, feeling his way along the wall in the half-light almost stupidly. When another figure crept up behind him and laid a hand on his shoulder, he whirled, bringing the pistol out into position with a lithe movement. The wrinkled, sad face of Alden looked pityingly at him in the dim light.

"You saw?" she whispered.

"My God, yes!" he groaned.

He had never been so unutterably wretched in his life. It was a revelation that something outside himself could so stir the depths of his being.

"Just like that, when the moon comes to fullness, for months past," whispered Alden cautiously, "has she walked like a dream woman to that room. I do not know if she walks in her sleep, or if he has hypnotized her by his magical arts and his influence over her."

Luke caught at the woman's arm impulsively.

"Say it again!" he got out hoarsely. "Say it again! She is not mistress of her own actions!"

Alden shook her head mournfully.

"How like a man! Always ready to believe the worst! You imagined that my lamb went, like a bad woman, to meet her cousin? Oh, I could not forgive you for your suspicions, did I not know how one's confidence in everything good and true is shaken after a short residence here. One even comes to doubt the Almighty. It is in the air, this Evil that is supreme here. But to believe my Sybil, the poor innocent lamb, guilty of—oh, you of all men should have believed in her against the entire world! "

Luke listened in shame to Alden's arraignment.

"I'm sorry," he said simply. "But—for a moment I thought how easy it would be for him—. Good heaven! While we stand talking here, who knows what is happening to Sybil?" He whirled around and pulled the woman with him. "I have my pistol. We'll see whether his magic will protect him from that!"

Alden caught at him with her free hand.

"Hush! Don't be rash, Mr. Porter. Trust me that no harm has yet befallen my lamb. Madam Fane is with her, also. And—only a virgin can be of use to the Master in his experiments. She is safe."

"But there must be something we can do?" begged Luke, almost frantic with apprehension, in spite of Alden's attempt at reassurance.

"Yes, there is something we can do. Follow me."

She withdrew her hand and walked noiselessly but swiftly down the corridor. At last she entered what seemed a blind passage, glanced both up and down the corridor to make sure no one else was in sight, then pressed upon a knurl of the rich carving upon one of the wall panels. A portion of the wall moved slowly, disclosing yawning blackness.

Alden stepped inside, motioning the artist to follow. She

touched another button within, and the door closed upon them. In the light of a pocket flash which she took from her apron pocket, she found matches and lighted candles, disclosing a room about ten by ten feet, holding a couch, a table, two chairs, and piled against one wall a quantity of tinned food, as well as two full gallon bottles of water.

"Guy Fane himself does not know about this room. How I found it years ago would make too long a story. I kept the knowledge to myself, not knowing when it might prove useful. Of late I have often thought I would conceal Sybil here if the worst came to the worst. She could stay here for a couple of weeks, while I got into the outside world and procured help. There is a small window up there, covered with ivy. She would be lonesome, but safe."

She motioned him to a chair, and herself sank upon the couch, heaving a deep sigh as she did so.

"I have a long story to tell you, a painful one to me, but only by listening to it can you understand why I am so absolutely devoted to my charge. I only fear what I have to tell you may turn you from her— if you are less a man than I hope you are."

"Why speak in riddles? I have discovered tonight that I love her. That is sufficient, is it not?"

Alden regarded him steadily for a moment. Her blue eyes were moist then, from what she must have read in his face.

"Well, let me tell you the story, as quickly as I can. I have no regrets, Mr. Porter, for myself. But when I think of Sybil, I wonder if God is punishing me, through her. Do you believe that He would deliver my little girl over to the veriest devils of hell for their sport, to punish her wretched mother for having loved not wisely but too well?"

Luke emitted a low whistle.

"You mean that Sybil is your daughter? How can that be?"

"She is my own child," declared Alden stubbornly. "And now tell me, do you find her less desirable because her father and mother loved each other sufficiently to despise the world's conventions?"

"Stop, please! I have already told you that I love Sybil. I hope to make her my wife as soon as we can get her out of this devilish place. That part of it is settled. What I'd like to know is, how you come to be playing maid to your own child? Does Madam Fane know?"

"Nobody knows, Mr. Porter. Not even Sybil. And if Madam Fane knew, she would have me out of the castle—or worse yet, down in some secret dungeon—the next moment. Yet Madam Fane knows who and what Sybil is. That is the reason that I fear Madam, and the Master."

"For heaven's sake, stop riddling!" Luke said impatiently. "Get at the pith of it, can't you?"

"How can I begin? It tears my very soul to go all over it once more. Yet I must—I must!"

The artist's pity rose for the unhappy and mysterious woman.

"I'm sorry if I appeared abrupt or harsh," he said gently. "But it is important that you give me all the information you can, just as quickly as possible. It may throw light on a confusing situation. I can assure you of one thing; I believe that you did nothing from bad motives. Sybil's mother could have been mistaken—but not wicked."

Alden smiled wanly.

"For that I thank you, Mr. Porter. Here is the situation."

She began the story, telling it in short, terse sentences, each word of which was fraught with significance.

"Finding himself in financial straits, Arthur Fane married a wealthy heiress, who tried in vain to win the love of her handsome husband. Madam Fane discovered that her husband had married her for money and that he was intimate with the daughter of a nearby farmer, a girl whom she had never seen but whom she believed to be the commonest of the common. In a fury of insensate rage, the wife planned revenge. She was a woman of strong passions. Within the castle she had happily built for her husband and herself, she had a strange chapel equipped, and there she spent all her time alone. After the birth of his son and heir, Arthur Fane left the castle, renouncing with a kind of horror the young mother, the child, and the money he had married to procure.

"Until that day, Mr. Porter," Alden declared with simple dignity,

"Mr. Fane and I had been friends only. But when I found that Madam Fane had revenged herself upon him in some secret and horrible way that revolted him to such an extent that he would no longer live under the same roof with her, I gave myself to him gladly, proudly, and have never regretted—for myself—having taken that step to lighten a little the burden of his remorse and grief."

She continued: "Only once did he refer to the reason for his desertion of Madam Fane. 'My God,' he said to me, 'I can never banish that sight from before my eyes! She lifted the cover and showed me my child—. It was not mine. Before God, it was not mine! It was the offspring of some devil out of hell, but not my flesh and blood, I swear.'"

Arthur Fane fled with the farmer's daughter. Untrained to any work that fitted him to support a wife, he struggled along with his faithful and devoted companion for several hard years of poverty and suffering. Typhoid fever attacked his enfeebled frame, robbing Alden of the father of her child, then a lovely little girl of two years. Broken in health, unable to care for herself and still less for the child, Alden permitted an appeal to be made to Madam Fane for the offspring of Arthur Fane.

"I was sick, hopeless, miserably unhappy, longing only to die. Madam Fane sent word that she naturally did not care to see me, but that if I would give up the child to her absolutely, she would bring it up as if it were her own, in expiation of some wrong which she admitted she had done her husband. Sybil was sent to her. But as I grew stronger, my longing for my baby grew. I applied to Madam Fane, under an assumed name, for a position as maid in her household. She needed a nurse for Sybil, and God let me stay to watch over my little girl. "

"And then He must have sent me, also," the artist murmured in low tones, "and the sooner we start to get her out of this hellish place, the better."

"We can do nothing tonight, Mr. Porter. Sybil has disappeared in this manner for months now, always at the full of the moon, or near that time. Madam Fane assists the Master, which fact in a measure is a safeguard for my little girl. And I know—how I cannot explain—that for tonight she is guarded."

"Where is this devil's chapel where Guy Fane performs his experiments?" asked Luke grimly. "I'd like to take a look at it."

Alden mused thoughtfully.

"It might be managed, if they are still in the Master's study. But they may have gone into the chapel to perform invocations, and then—"

"I'm not afraid of that silly rot," Luke snorted scornfully.

Alden regarded him with pity.

"That is because you do not know how powerful the Master is," she asserted sadly. "You would be a babe in his hands."

Luke laughed, regarding his strong, capable hands meaningly. She answered quickly.

"Oh, that isn't what I mean, at all. He can look at you, with his face unveiled, and you would be frozen, at his mercy. You don't know—."

"Nonsense! I'll risk it, anyway. It's quite possible that I can outstare him," Luke suggested, with grim humor.

"Perhaps—but I doubt it," she answered quite seriously. "And now I must ask you to restrain your impatience until I tell you it is time to act in safety. Tomorrow you can, if you will, try to get word to anybody you know, outside. Perhaps you may be successful, where I have found the attempt futile," sadly. "One thing you must promise me, Mr. Porter. Sybil must never know the secret of her birth. She must never learn that I am her mother."

Her pale blue eyes pleaded with him. The artist, sensing her fine desire for sacrifice, acquiesced unwillingly.

"We can go, then, and see if the chapel is unoccupied."

She opened the secret panel, showing Luke how the button worked, and the two emerged hastily, closing it behind them.

—8—
Lucifer's Chapel

"Follow me. Make no sound."

Luke followed down dark passages, up and down winding stairways. At last a closed door at the end of a long corridor was reached.

Alden turned with a warning gesture.

"I am now taking you where you can, unseen, look down into the interior of the chapel. I found the place years ago, by accident." She shuddered convulsively. "Good God—it was—horrible! I have not been there since. And I cannot face the Evil that dwells there. You must go in alone."

Luke's hand was turning the knob with caution, but he whispered sternly:

"If I do not return within a half hour, you must open the door and come for me. For Sybil's sake!"

To himself he was thinking resentfully that if Herbert Binney's mind were not so easily unbalanced, the little occultist might have been of assistance. As matters stood, however, Cagliostro Moderno would be a nuisance instead of a help, owing to his blind, mad devotion to occultism.

Luke opened the door. A stream of brilliant ruby radiance shot out through the chink, casting a lurid and ghastly gleam upon the white face of the poor mother, who dropped to her knees with a terrified gasp, and began to pray fervently.

The artist looked within. There was a long, narrow gallery, with apparently no discernible outlet save the door by which he was now entering. A latticework screen rose from the solid stone balustrade, forming a shield for him while permitting at the same time an unobstructed view of the immense room below. Through the lacy interstices of this screen there poured that intolerably brilliant red light.

Luke closed the door quietly and stepped close to the screen. What he saw below filled him with unutterable horror and loathing. He was looking upon one of those unholy places which have been desecrated to mocking ceremonials, by the foul imaginations of perverted men and women, devoted body and soul to the worship of Evil. The room was a large one, and the crimson light illuminated it sufficiently for him to distinguish fairly well the decorations and furnishings, all of a character so bizarre, so vile, as to force upon him the conclusion that they must have been designed and carried out by diseased imaginations. Walls and hangings were black, absorbing the radiance of that ruby illumination, but here and there the artist could distinguish what he felt must have been, in a white light, embroideries of occult symbols upon the hangings.

Against this background stood, at irregular intervals, great white crosses before which were sculptured figures in black, figures that made him shudder with uncontrollable horror at their repulsive and abhorrent ugliness. It seemed as if the human imagination had here attained the climax of revolting, horrific distortion and deformity in sculpture and pictorial art. Not a statue, not a painting, but showed the human face and form in such revolting deformity as to send sickly shudders through the observer's shrinking frame. The purpose of this ghastly place was obvious. The red light shining everywhere now attracted Luke's attention. It originated in a crystal sphere, hung on almost invisible chains in a shrine just back of the altar. The gleam was not a quiet one; it played about the heart of that globe like darting flames of unquiet, unholy fire. And as these tongues of ruby light played in and out and licked the surface of the sphere uncannily, the shadows in the chapel moved and danced, until it seemed to Luke's excited gaze that they actually possessed life and only waited for the right moment to move from their pedestals and go horribly forward to worship at that altar. Evil—unutterable Evil—hovered about that glowing sphere.

A fugitive gleam of golden light came from behind a draped doorway at one side of the altar. The light grew stronger. A short squat figure voluminously veiled in black emerged, carrying a tall candle of black wax that burned with a yellow flame. The figure advanced to the lower steps of the altar, paused, made a deeply reverent genuflection. Then Guy (for Luke surmised that it was he) placed the candle in a ready holder at one end of a long marble slab which formed an altar. Again he bent deeply, then faced about behind the altar as if waiting.

The curtain swung aside again, this time admitting a processional of three persons. In the van strutted with inconceivable pride and dignity the short, stout form of Cagliostro, draped in trailing red robes embroidered with black symbols of mysticism. The occultist bore another candle, which he as solemnly placed at the lower end of the altar, taking his place then beside the Master. The other two worshipers were women. Madam Fane was the first, kneeling upon the steps before the altar with a kind of shrinking dread discernible on her face. She was in black, but the other figure was white-draped. Luke, a choking sensation in his throat, recognized the tranquil, unmoved face of Sybil Fane.

The girl went forward to the steps of the shrine, bowed deeply, then mounted the stairs until she stood above the two adepts, and immediately before the crystal globe, which began to shimmer vaguely with the violent agitation of those red and evil tongues of lurid light. Madam Fane arose; from a great casket at one side she took double handfuls of some powder, casting it upon a tripod censer that up to now had apparently been unlighted. But at once, following her action, that crystal sphere shot out its tongues of flame—longer—longer. One reached—ignited—the incense; tall spirals of smoke poured out, heavy with some Eastern fragrance that rose almost overpoweringly to Luke's nostrils. As he inhaled it reluctantly, it seemed to him that the obscene sculptured figures below began to stir uneasily, coming to life at last.

Madam Fane sank once more upon her knees, her forehead resting on the stair above her. Sybil continued to stand, immovable, before that glowing sphere, from which an occasional tongue of flame shot out toward her, but retracted before coming in contact with the girl. Behind the altar the two magi now raised their arms in frantic invocation toward the shrine of the ruby globe.

"Lucifer! Lucifer!! Lucifer!!!! Son of the Morning, we offer Thee that sacrifice Thou has demanded. Give us a sign! Appear, we implore Thee!

"The hearts of doves and young lambs have I offered Thee, oh Lord of the Fallen Hosts! Tonight I offer the soul of a virgin, a virgin maid, Lord Lucifer! A sign! A sign, that my sacrifice will be acceptable!"

Cagliostro was stirring uneasily, carroty head lifted from between his outstretched arms. Luke could see inexplicable emotions following each other over that Cupid's bow mouth that twisted so oddly. The squinty blue eyes were now upon Sybil as she stood motionless before the great globe.

He leaned toward Guy Fane and whispered something hurriedly. The Master bent a dark gaze upon him through the folds of the veil.

"Hush, fool! Do you not see that Lord Lucifer is showing Himself to His worshipers?"

Cagliostro, offended, shrank back.

From the sphere shot those quivering tongues as of living flame, licking its surface in gracious curves and reaching out on either side of Sybil's quiescent form like the groping tentacles of an octopus. The still air began to stir with murmuring sounds. A soft, whining hum vibrated on the atmosphere as if some unearthly visitant were cleaving the ether with sweeping wings as it passed through space.

Luke's knees suddenly gave way under him. Some potent influence against which he was powerless to resist had pushed him down. He knelt because he could not stand up. But he could still stare through the lattice with starting eyes. Sybil was moving, as if impelled by some irresistible force. She moved slowly backward down the steps of the shrine until she reached the marble slab. Upon this she bent back, until she lay upon it, arms stiff at her sides.

Guy Fane was throwing his hands into the air with wild and triumphant gestures. Then he fumbled under his enveloping garments and drew forth a knife. As the blade flashed upward, Cagliostro Moderno, awaking from his trance, flung himself forward and knocked the knife clanging and whirring, down into the middle of the room. His face, a mingled materialization of stupefaction and horror, writhed into that squared semblance of a Greek tragic mask which he had worn on the night he had fled through the forest from the monster he had seen bending over the bridge.

"I forbid it!" shouted the little occultist frantically.

"Fool! Let me alone! How dare you interrupt? Lord Lucifer, I implore—"

Madam Fane had come to her feet and was watching the two, who swayed back and forth as they struggled on the steps of the altar. The shrouding veils that concealed her son's face were in the hands of the other mage, who tore at them frantically. They parted—. From his vantage point, Luke strained to see, but Guy Fane's back was toward him. Only the tragic mask of Herbert Binney's round face was visible, and that was frozen into a horror so dreadful, so unbearable, so nearly verging upon utter madness, that Luke's blood congealed in his veins. What was the little man seeing, that he should shrink back, letting the veil fall again over Guy Fane's now motionless figure? Could it be true that the Master could blast with a look of his terrible eyes?

There was a frightful wailing cry from the occultist's widened lips. He staggered away from the altar, down the steps, stumbling as if blinded, and plunged out of sight behind the drapery that hung before the door by which the procession had entered. Luke tried to get to his feet. He managed to rise and cling to the screen. How to rescue Sybil was his overmastering thought, but until he could conquer that strange weakness which had overcome him, it was useless to do other than try, if necessary, to shoot from his concealment, in the hope of at least terrifying Guy Fane enough, to stop the present ceremony. With this in mind, he fumbled for the automatic.

Madam Fane, however, had run up the steps of the altar. She bent over the girl. After a moment, she lifted the golden head upon her arm, regarded Sybil's face intently, and then addressed her son, who watched without changing the position he had held as the horrified Cagliostro fled his presence.

"She is coming out of the trance, Guy," said Madam Fane, almost with eagerness. "You can do nothing more tonight. Let me take her back to her room, my son," she almost pleaded.

A hard laugh issued from the Master.

"I would have won tonight—by now—had not that fool—may he be blasted in soul and body forever!—prevented me. I thought him pliable enough to serve my purpose. Now I must get him out of the way, or he may try to balk me in my plans. Fool! To trust any other human being!"

Madam Fane lifted the supine form into her arms, but as she turned to go she spoke again.

"You lied to me, Guy. You told me you would not resort to the knife —with her. The knife I will not suffer, I tell you. You must find some other way to your purpose. Is not Lucifer powerful enough to give you what you seek, if you deliver over this girl's soul, instead of her body?"

"Oh, mother, mother! How often must you stand in my way, just when I see it clear? Yes, it can be done without blood, but the experiment is difficult, and who knows when she will love enough to build the foundation for her own destruction?"

"As to that, my son, all is ready," asserted Madam Fane.

"Mother! Are you sure?"

Madam Fane walked away, carrying the light form carefully. At the door she turned back for a minute.

"Guy, if you do not play me false in this matter, I will serve you to the bitter end. But I will not have the girl's life given to Lucifer, not while I can prevent it. All shall come as you desire, but with her a living sacrifice."

"Do you feel the prophetic spell upon you, my mother?"

"I am not sure ... But, you can consult—her—later. "

Guy Fane, thinking himself alone, leaped up the shrine steps and prostrated himself before the crystal globe. The tongues of ruby flame grew paler. The chapel's dusk increased.

Luke found himself able to walk, and managed to get to the door. Outside knelt Alden, still praying. He touched her gently on the shoulder, and she started, opening her closed eyes to look at him questioningly.

"Madam Fane has taken Sybil back to her room," Luke told the anxious mother. "But tomorrow we must get her out of this devilish place. I have seen her tonight stretched upon the altar, and Guy Fane would have buried a knife in her heart had not Binney been there to prevent the crime."

"Give me your pistol, please," whispered Alden tensely. "If they try to take her from me again, I can at least save her from such a horrible death ... Better she should die innocent at her mother's hand than a bloody sacrifice to the Powers of Evil."

Luke hesitated a moment, then laid the pistol in the mother's hand.

"I can get along without it, I fancy. And now that Binney seems to have come partly to his senses, perhaps we can enlist him on our side. Unless he is sent away," he added, remembering the Master's words. "And between ourselves, I think it would be wise to warn Sybil of the danger that lies ahead. She ought to know. It might be dangerous to spring it all upon her at the last moment. She believes her cousin a kind of god, doesn't she?"

"She shall know the truth about him," promised Alden grimly.

—9—
The Master Consults An Oracle

Luke's first thought now was to see Herbert Binney immediately and make sure of the little man's coming to his senses. He therefore went from the chapel to the occultist's room, while Alden hurried back to look after her charge.

At his first knock, the artist was sure that he heard smothered moans and incoherent exclamations within the occultist's room. He rapped a little louder. A voice behind the door answered, trembling with some strong emotion.

"Off with you, Sathanas! Get thee behind me, accursed one! I will have no more to do with your evil work."

The voice died away in confused babblings.

"Binney! It isn't Fane. It's Porter talking. Let me in! I must see you at once."

"Away with you! You can not deceive me again, Beelzebub!"

"Open this door!" Luke said, low-toned but forceful. "Pull yourself together, you little idiot! This is Luke Porter speaking. I must see you on a matter of life and death. Open up!"

The doorknob rattled feebly. There was a short pause.

"I'm afraid!" whined the occultist from within. "What if you aren't what you claim to be?"

"If I'm a mage, I could slip in through the keyhole, you little jackass!" Luke exploded, thoroughly out of patience. "Open this door, or I'll shoot off the lock!" (A futile threat, when he had given his automatic to Alden!)

The door knob turned slowly, and the door opened, the pallid face of Herbert Binney appearing in the opening, pale blue eyes squinting in shrinking dread at the artist, who jerked the door from the other man's hands, slipped inside, closed and locked it behind him.

"Thank God, Mr. Porter, it's you!" whined Binney in his scared relief. "Oh," and he clutched at the artist's coat-sleeve frantically, "we must get out of here, immediately! Without waiting for anything! This place is a hell, Mr. Porter, with living demons haunting it! I—I've just met—him—face to face again! Oh, my God, shall I ever be able to brush the awful memory of his horrible countenance from my mind? My blood froze in my veins, I tell you! My—"

Luke reached out, took the little man by the shoulders, and shook him so hard that the fellow's teeth actually played the castanets against each other.

"Keep still for a minute, you incredible idiot!" he snapped, in a low voice. "I saw the whole business, just now, in the chapel. What I want to know is: where do you stand?"

The pale blue eyes stared into Luke's flashing gray orbs with astonishment.

"You—you saw—?" stammered Herbert Binney, stupidly. "How —how could you have seen? Then you saw—his—face—?" The voice broke pitifully, and the occultist began to tremble as if seized by an ague. "Good God, Mr. Porter, you must realize how important it is for us to get out of here immediately!"

"Will you shut up?" Luke apostrophized him through clenched

teeth. He looked distastefully at the terrified magician, "You stopped Guy Fane at a critical moment, Binney—"

"I know," assented the other, his breath catching. "But I never dreamed that he would dare do such a thing. To attack that sweet girl with a knife! Why, only the most evil of spirits would ask for, or expect, such a devilish proceeding, and Mr. Fane assured me that he had no intention of injuring her physically. I haven't been quite sure myself just what his intentions toward her were, but he explained that she wasn't—you understand"—he tapped his forehead significantly with one forefinger—"just right. He thought he could, by giving her a severe shock of some kind, bring back her wandering senses."

"He lied to you, you ass! And you're so fed up with your importance that you swallowed everything he told you, of course," Luke grunted disgustedly. "Now that you've seen something of what he's capable, do you intend to go on with that rotten mummery, or will you help me get Sybil Fane out of this devil's den?"

"Oh, I'm only too anxious to get out myself," the occultist assured him hastily. "But—how do you propose to manage it?"

"I don't know, yet. Tomorrow I shall tell him that Sybil is to be my wife, and that I wish to leave, with her and her maid. If he refuses to let me go, I'll have to think up something else."

"I—I could help you, perhaps," offered Cagliostro, trying desperately to regain something of the ground he felt he had lost in the artist's esteem and respect. "I—I'm not as silly and stupid as" (resentfully) "you think I am. I can meet Guy Fane on his own ground—on magical lines—and hold my own. I know I can," he added, more firmly.

"We don't want any magic," Luke negated, rather unkindly. "It's all rot. Guy Fane knows how to utilize natural forces to make an appearance—"

The squinty blue eyes regarded the artist now with assurance. The button nose wrinkled, as Cagliostro asked pointedly:

"You can say that, after seeing that ceremony in the chapel tonight? Mr. Porter, there was much more in it than I care to admit, myself. Guy Fane is a true adept; a Master of supernatural powers and forces, but of a nature to make a Child of Light shudder sickly."

Luke let go of the little man's shoulders and stepped back from him.

"Listen, Binney! Are you going to let yourself go again, the way you did tonight in the chapel? Just because another human being happens to be more than ordinarily ugly?"

"Listen, Porter!" retorted the mage disrespectfully, but with a measure of return to his old proud impressiveness. "When you find yourself face to face, without previous warning, with the Devil himself, you are apt to let your weak flesh gain the mastery. But when you know beforehand what you're up against, you prepare for the ordeal and—and you conquer—or—die," he finished with a plaintive gravity.

"Then you are ready—?"

"You will have to trust me to help you in my own way," stipulated Cagliostro seriously. "But I can assure you that I am ready, even for death—if by dying I can thwart that devil from hell!"

Luke clasped the little fellow's hand and gave it a hearty grip.

"Then I can look upon you as an ally, tomorrow," he said, rather relieved to find the occultist himself once more.

"I shall get to work along my own lines," assured the mage, with earnestness. "I shall have much to do, to prepare myself for a battle of will with that—with—him. But I shall win. Never fear, Mr. Porter, I shall win!"

Luke left him then, and hurried through the corridors to Sybil's boudoir, at the door of which he tapped cautiously. The door was opened by Alden, whose white face met his questioning gray eyes with agony written on it.

"She hasn't come back! Oh, dear God, she is with Guy Fane in his study, and I am afraid—afraid!"

Luke whirled about.

"I'm going there," he announced. "This thing has got me. I can't sit down quietly while Sybil is in that devil's power. I'm going for her. Never fear, I'll bring her back with me, Alden."

He dashed up the hall, leaving her leaning weakly against the doorframe.

The door of the Master's study swung open silently at his approach, in a sinister fashion which the young man disregarded in his anxiety. He rushed into the room, and all at once stopped, midway to the glowing crystal globe that burned threateningly in the shrine at the farther end of the apartment. It was as if some giant hand had been placed against his breast, holding him to the spot against his will. He struggled vainly to advance. Perspiration poured down his face and streamed from every pore in his body.

"Rash man, beware of too much daring! You have seen how easily I can thwart your impotent purposes. Beware, lest I raise my veil and wither you where you stand," intoned the ominous voice of Guy Fane.

Luke restrained himself by an effort, and all at once that force which had held him back was gone. Before he could move, Guy Fane's voice spoke again.

"It is not well to cross swords with me unadvisedly, Mr. Porter. My door opened to you, because I am not afraid of you, or your petty personal desires and intentions. Remain, if you will, but interrupt at your peril! Interruption will only result in terrible evil to Sybil, who is entranced. To arouse her with any shock might put to flight forever that which forms her individual soul, her personality. There would be left a maundering idiot, Mr. Porter. I have warned you."

Luke had learned something of the practice of modern spiritualism and psychic phenomena; he dared not stir for fear, therefore, of wakening Sybil from her trance. Guy Fane had stopped him most effectually by that warning, which Luke knew to be well founded. He stared about the room.

On a couch under the ruby sphere lay the entranced girl, hands crossed upon her girlish bosom, motionless save for the even rise and fall that showed her still alive and breathing. Before her stood the black-veiled form of the Master, with uplifted arms, in invocation.

"Sybil! Answer! Where are you now?" he exclaimed in a voice of dignity and with an air of high authority.

From the girl's lips came a low murmur, seeming another voice than her ordinary one.

"I hover here, Master, above the clay housing of my spirit, awaiting your commands."

"It is well. I have stripped from your eyes" (he made a sweeping gesture over her face with both hands) "the veil that hides the future. Tell me, shall I soon be free from the hideous and loathsome covering of flesh that conceals my shrinking spirit?"

Without hesitation, that mild voice declared:

"Yes! Before another night shall have passed, you shall shed your monstrous husk and step from it into glorious freedom."

"Lucifer! All-powerful Prince!" exclaimed Guy in wild triumph, tossing his hands high in invocation toward the shining ruby globe. "Not in vain have I called upon Thee, Lord and Master. Oh, I shall serve Thee well, when I shall have won to that face, that form, that are to be mine!—Sybil! Tell me if I shall offer your pulsing heart to the Lord and Master of your destiny, as I have long intended?"

A struggle seemed to be going on in the body of the girl. Her face distorted painfully. Luke clenched his hands, to keep from rushing to her side. Then from the tortured lips issued the reply:

"My heart has already gone forth, and is in the safe keeping of the master of my destiny."

"Strange! Strange! Most strange!" muttered Guy Fane, bending to examine her face closely. "Tell me truly, Sybil, plainly. Shall I offer your heart soon to Lucifer? Your beating, pulsing heart? I conjure you, give me the truth!"

Again the girl's face showed that disturbance, that conflict. Then her voice issued, hardly audible, from writhing lips:

"Proud and presumptuous man, you command the truth! It shall be yours. You have attempted by futile magic arts to alter the decrees of destiny. All that has happened is that you have become a tool in the scheme of greater forces than your puny soul can imagine. You believe you have seized upon the prerogatives of the Ruler of the Universe. You have associated with the evil Fallen One. Harken, Master of Evil

Arts! It is your soul that lies at stake, and not your body. Less yet is there danger to the body of this poor girl through whose lips I speak."

"Lucifer! Who is talking now?" gasped Guy Fane.

Luke could plainly see the trembling of that squat body.

"It matters little who I am. But this innocent girl is protected as you can never imagine. Spare her of your own free will, before she is snatched out of your hands! Show that your hideous body conceals but poorly a noble soul! Mortal, this is your last opportunity for your own salvation!"

The voice ceased. Luke, although realizing that something must have gone wrong, and that Guy Fane was gravely disturbed by the upsetting of his calculations, felt no slightest disturbance, but on the contrary a profound conviction seized upon him that all would yet be well.

"By Lucifer and His seven fiends, you unknown speaker, I shall carry out my plans or die in the attempt! I know not who you are that speaks to me unbidden through the lips of this entranced girl, but I dare you to thwart me, mysterious oracle! Sybil Fane is devoted to expiation of that which her father's sin brought upon me. The Almighty and all His angels cannot hold me back now! I know too much to be disregarded!"

"Then Lucifer must receive that for which He has waited patiently these many years! Farewell, wretched worker of ill spells! You have doomed yourself, when you might have worked a noble magic!"

Silence, terrible and oppressive, reigned after these last words. Then the Master called with fierce energy: "Sybil! Return to this clay before that intruder shall have robbed you of it before what is foreordained shall have come to pass! Return, I say!"

He made frantic passes over that blond head. The girl sighed. Then one hand went up sleepily to rub her eyes.

With a contemptuous gesture, Guy Fane beckoned the artist.

"She is normal now. Take her to her maid. I have finished with her —for the present," ominously.

Luke needed no further invitation. He picked Sybil's slender form up and held her close.

"You shall never lay a finger on her again," he said to Guy Fane tensely, his gray eyes like thunder clouds shot with lightning.

The Master paid no more attention to him. He went to the shrine where swung the ruddy globe, and sank on his knees before it, his forehead touching the marble step.

—10—
Shut Out

Luke carried his precious burden directly to Alden, who, after she had carefully brought Sybil back to consciousness, sat beside her, listening to the artist's recital of that strange possession by some unknown entity of the girl's unconscious body.

Sybil herself, enlightened now by her old nurse and by her lover as to her cousin's nefarious designs upon her, lay with wide violet eyes upon Luke's face, her expression that of one who refuses to believe what appears incredible to intelligence.

"I shall see Guy Fane tomorrow," declared Luke firmly. "I intend to make a formal demand for Sybil's hand, and as he has already given me his permission to marry her, I don't see how he can refuse to let me take her away, especially if we go right down into town and get a license, and hunt up a minister immediately."

Alden shook her head, a bitter smile curling her kindly mouth.

"Don't you think cousin Guy will let us go?" demanded Sybil. "Why, Alden, I'll be of age in another ten days, and then he must let me go. He's told me as much himself, often."

"There is something mysterious about it all, my lamb. But I feel sure he will let none of us go until he has carried out his own plans."

"Then I shall appeal to Madam Fane. She is a woman, with a woman's heart," began Luke, when Alden interrupted him.

"First of all, she is Guy Fane's mother, and she owes him a terrible debt, too horrible for me to put into words," the older woman said unwillingly. "She will think first of her son's plans, Mr. Porter. The rest of us are pawns, to be moved by him as he pleases."

"He makes a mistake, I'm afraid," Luke murmured.

"Perhaps Mr. Binney can suggest something," Sybil offered. "He's a magician, isn't he?"

Luke couldn't help smiling at Sybil's ingenuous conclusion.

"For some reason your cousin has terrified Cagliostro Moderno almost into spasms," he told the girl. "But for all that, he's promised to do what he can. In his own way," he amended.

"But his own way may be the best way," the girl declared.

"Mr. Porter, I think my lamb ought to get a little sleep while she can," Alden suggested darkly. "Do you mind—?"

"Luke, don't go away!" begged Sybil, violet eyes suddenly wide with fright. "Oh, Alden, don't send him away! Let him sleep on the chaise lounge in my boudoir. Then he'll be here, if—if anything should happen." Luke and the older woman exchanged glances.

"Perhaps that isn't such a bad idea, Mr. Porter," conceded Alden. "But I'd hate to have Mr. Fane know."

"There can be no possible harm," Luke decided. "Certainly, the man who is as devoted to Sybil's interests as her future husband must be, can watch over her welfare. Especially after such an experience as she has had tonight," he finished grimly. "Sybil, my darling, sleep. Alden and I will both be here to see that no harm comes to you."

Sybil pouted her crimson lips, and Luke bent, stirred to the depths by her innocent trustfulness, and very tenderly gave her their first kiss.

Luke's resolve to see Guy Fane early that next day was forestalled by the Master himself, in a fashion that made the artist resentful, as it put him in the wrong at once. Mason brought the message, and he brought it to Luke, before the young artist had left Sybil's boudoir. The major-domo wore a certain knowing air for which Luke would have liked to call him to account, except that it was too vague an expression to base such a proceeding upon.

"Mr. Fane asked me to inquire if you didn't think it would be well for you to see him at once, under the circumstances," the man said.

Luke was furious, but there was, after all, nothing upon which he could put his finger. Controlling himself as best he could, he answered shortly:

"Tell your master that after last night's occurrences I feel I have a right to make certain demands of him, and I am only too happy to make them immediately."

Ten minutes afterward, he walked into the open door of Guy Fane's study, his mouth set in a grim line as he advanced toward the protecting screen at the farther end of the room.

"Be seated, Mr. Porter. Pray do not come any farther. As you have had reason to learn, I am—protected."

Luke paused involuntarily. He remembered that giant hand which had stopped his progress the night before.

"That's better, Mr. Porter. Now, if you will be seated, we can get down to business more comfortably. I presume you wish to inquire, with what I must consider characteristic curiosity, my dear sir, into my private affairs?"

"I have come to tell you that I wish to take Sybil away from this— this devil's den," the artist jerked out furiously.

"Ah! How thoughtful of you, dear Mr. Porter! And so you have come to this unwarranted conclusion—"

"Unwarranted?" snapped Luke. "When only by a hair's breadth did that poor girl escape your knife last night?"

A tense pause succeeded upon his words. When Guy Fane spoke now, it was in measured accents.

"I begin to understand. You managed to gain access to the chapel, then?" The troubled note left his voice, and he continued with his wonted imperturbable suavity: "You took the liberty of going where you had no business to enter, and then you jumped to silly conclusions, because you imagined,"—and the voice grew icy with disdain— "I presume, that I was about to take the life of my cousin, a girl who has been brought up under my own eyes, and nurtured as tenderly—. Why, my dear Mr. Porter, I believe you have the instincts of a budding occultist, yourself! I must see to it that you are present at my next experiment," the voice continued with a musing lightness and that hint of double meaning that made Luke writhe.

"If there are any further experiments, you may be sure I shall be present," the artist declared. "But I do not think there will be any more. At least, not with my wife as the subject of them."

"Your wife?"

There was a sudden note of alarm in the Master's voice that did not escape Luke's notice.

"Perhaps I should have said, my promised wife," he amended.

"Oh!"

The exclamation escaped the Master's lips in a gust of breathy relief. And then, as if to cover his momentary lack of restraint, Guy continued smoothly:

"You are certainly what is called, in vulgar vernacular, a quick worker, Mr. Porter. So Sybil is in love with you, and you with her? So quickly!" Admiration in the voice; again Luke writhed.

"Sybil wishes to go with me, and her maid, today, " Luke asserted.

"Why such haste, dear Mr. Porter?" soothed Guy Fane.

He laughed softly.

"But there, young love is always impetuous, isn't it? Have you realized that there must be a license? And that I certainly will not permit my charge to go from here until I see her properly married to you by a regularly ordained clergyman?"

"Are you insinuating—?"

"My dear Mr. Porter, you have acted so like a child that I feel I must take the proper steps to safeguard my innocent cousin. You are afraid that the ceremony—so sadly interrupted by the misunderstanding with the little Cagliostro—was aimed at my cousin's life. No, Mr. Porter, she must live. Live, do you understand? Only a life—but there, you would never understand. I presume you are in a hurry now to rescue the fair lady and make your escape from the roof that has been her safe shelter from childhood?" he pursued plaintively. "So be it, Mr. Porter. Will this afternoon suit your plans?"

Luke's face altered in spite of himself, at this unexpected acquiescence. Guy Fane laughed again.

"You can leave all details to me, impetuous lover. I shall send a couple of servants to impersonate you two at the license bureau, so that you won't have to go down into town until you leave here for

good. I shall have a clergyman sent for. If you don't like him," negligently, with an undertone of mild amusement, "you can get married
again after you leave here. We will have a wedding supper, and tickets
ready for the 10 p.m. New York train. If this suits your plans?"

Bewildered to the last degree, Luke managed to get out:

"I hope I have misjudged you. But—but what did you intend to
do with that knife?"

"My mother, and that foolish magician, have both demanded
explanations on this point," Guy said wearily. "Nothing I tell them
seems clear to their blinded imaginations, which must have run away
with them. I can use the girl living; of what use would she be dead? I
had but started a ceremonial—" and he interrupted himself to cry
with enthusiasm, "Ah, my dear Mr. Porter, one time you shall see such
a ceremonial as I doubt has ever been carried through in its entirety
before in the history of the world! You shall be there, I promise you!"

Something sinister troubled the artist vaguely, but he dared not let
his imagination start working on the Master's veiled insinuations. He
told himself that by evening he and Sybil would be well out of the
purlieus of that strange castle.

"Well, now that we've settled everything," proceeded Guy Fane
gayly, "suppose you tell Sybil that you have my permission, and that
tonight she will see Fanewold Castle for the last time—unless you are
so kind as to bring her back to visit a lonely and afflicted man, some
day. No, do not thank me, Mr. Porter. I am still a little hurt at your
unfounded suspicions of me and my motives. You shall know more of
me before another twenty-four hours," he promised. "And now, if you
will excuse me—"

Luke took the hint and went out, the door shutting behind him,
apparently of its own volition. He lost no time in telling Sybil of
Guy's ready capitulation. Alden's forehead wrinkled more than ever as
she listened.

"I don't know why Sybil's marriage to you should fit in with his
plans," she said in a troubled voice. "And I feel positive that he does
not intend to have her leave Fanewold tonight as your wife."

"Don't be so pessimistic, Alden dear," begged Sybil prettily.

"Come and help me pack. If we're going away tonight," and she turned to Luke gayly, "we must get everything ready. There'll be lots to do. Come, Alden!"

Alden did not follow the girl immediately. She stood looking at Luke irresolutely. At last she said:

"Mr. Porter, if you find it difficult to get away from here with Sybil, don't bother about me. To them I am nothing but a servant who loves her. They won't do anything to me. You can see about me later on."

"Depend upon it, that if I get Sybil safely away from here, my next thought will be for you," Luke said determinedly. "And now, I must pack my bags and painting materials."

It was quite evident to Luke that there was something going on in the place, later that afternoon. Alden whispered to him that all the servants had been sent away. She was white with apprehension, but the artist thought it quite possible that Guy Fane had ordered a lot of marketing done for the wedding supper, and that the castle people had been sent to do these many errands. Going back to his room, he almost collided with Cagliostro Moderno, who was hastening down the corridor.

"Hello, Binney! What are you doing now?" the artist demanded.

"I'm going with Madam Fane to town on an errand," the little occultist replied. He lowered his voice: "Once I get there, I'll get in touch with the authorities and see that some of the police are sent out here, to get you and Miss Fane out. That—devil—tried to explain his stunt with the knife, but I don't trust him. He is sheer fiend."

"Did you tell him that?"

"I'm not the fool you think I am, Mr. Porter," returned the little man with dignity. "I let him think I believed all he said, with the result that I'm now getting the chance to go to town."

"What is he sending you for?" persisted Luke.

With an apprehensive glance up and down the corridor, the occultist whispered:

"He's sent a maid and one of the men to impersonate you and

Miss Fane, to get a license. And I'm supposed to take the license, and then get a minister. Madam Fane is waiting for me," bitterly, "but I shall evade her, if I can. Even if I have to make a scene."

"Don't make a scene," advised Luke, thoughtfully. "Get the clergyman, and when he is here, we'll make him see how the situation is, and that will tie Guy Fane's hands. Besides, we may need you. Never can tell. "

"I'll do my best," promised Herbert Binney, with dignity, pulling his black mantle about him to conceal his insignificant features.

Luke smote him mightily on the shoulders.

"Go to it, old man," he said heartily.

The minutes fled, became hours.

Darkness was falling, now, but Herbert Binney did not return. Moreover, instead of the stir of festive preparations a heavy and oppressive stillness brooded over the castle.

"Come out on the roof garden," Sybil half whispered, the spell of the waiting upon her also. "I think I'd feel better out in the air."

The three went out, just in time to see another part of the mysterious drama played before their eyes.

There was the sound of the drawbridge lowering, and simultaneously the galloping of horses' hoofs. Then a carriage swung into sight, dimly outlined by the carriage lights. It whirled to the draw, and stopped. A woman—"Madam Fane!" cried Alden—sprang out and ran across the draw. The bridge creaked—rose in the air. The driver of the carriage whipped his horses around and back in the direction in which he had come.

And as the three stared with straining eyes, the sound of someone shouting fell upon their ears.

"Help!" cried a masculine voice several times, as a little figure came stumbling and sobbing up the road, only to be brought to a short stop by the sluggish water of the impassable moat.

"Who is it?" shouted Luke through cupped hands.

But he knew only too well who it was.

"It's me—Binney!" wailed the voice, admission of failure in the very use of that hated, commonplace name. "It's me! They've shut me out! They've shut me out!"

Luke recovered from his amazement and wonderment after a moment's astonished exchange of glances with Alden, whose wrinkled face held a deep significance, which he did not like.

"How'd it happen?" he shouted back, abandoning caution, convinced now that matters were not as they should be.

"Minister wasn't at home," wailed the occultist from below. "Madam Fane left word that we'd go there for the ceremony tomorrow. I tried to leave the carriage, but the driver managed to be in my way—and it's cold out and there weren't many people around —and—"

"To make a long story short," Luke told the two women dryly, "our little friend didn't succeed in getting word to anyone of our plight, and now he's been shut outside, so that he can't help us. Hey, Binney, can't you tramp it back to the town? You might bring help, that way."

In the growing darkness the occultist was shaking his head in furious negation.

"No, no, no!" he called up, with more caution. "I must get inside at once. It would take me hours to get back—I'm no walker. And magic must be fought with magic."

"The only way you can get in, Mr. Binney, is by swimming across the moat," began Alden.

"What?" almost screamed the occultist. "Swim among those water snakes and other things? Woman, do you think I'm crazy? "

"Not crazy," coldly called down Alden. "Just a wretched coward, if you will have the truth, Mr. Binney."

She retired from the parapet scornfully, but Luke saw that her face was melancholy with apprehension.

"What made you get out of the carriage?" inquired Luke.

"She dropped her handkerchief outside and asked me to get it for her," confessed the duped magician, mournfully.

"I understand. And the driver whipped up his horses, and they left you in the road, twelve miles out of town! A fine idiot you've shown yourself to be!"

"Oh, Lord! Don't I know it? And now, what am I going to do?"

Alden came back to the parapet, and bent over, speaking with cautiously lowered voice.

"You go to the garage, and when it's dark bring Mr. Porter's car around. Can you drive? All right. Have it near the draw. And then go back to the garage. My room is opposite there, and I may think up some plan to get you into the castle, if I know you will be waiting."

"Whatever you say," agreed the little man submissively. "But get in I must," he added determinedly, "for I am the only one of us who knows how to handle supernatural forces," mysteriously.

Luke felt like saying "Fiddlesticks!" but in grave silence watched the occultist walk off down the side of the moat and disappear into the night.

<h2 style="text-align:center">—11—
The Master Prepares</h2>

"Will Mr. Porter be kind enough to step to Mr. Fane's study for a minute?" asked the suave voice of Madam Fane, as her tall, black-garbed figure appeared in the door.

Luke and Alden, standing close together, exchanged a look of apprehension. Could Madam Fane have heard their conversation with the occultist outside the castle? Whatever she might have realized, Madam Fane's chalky face was impassive with what must have been a deceptive composure, for her smoldering eyes all at once flamed at Luke's momentary indecision.

"Are you aware, Mr. Porter, that my son is awaiting you with considerable eagerness?" she demanded coldly. "The failure of the plans he laid so carefully for you has disturbed him immensely and he wishes to learn your desires in the matter, now that you and my niece cannot be married tonight. You stand in your own light, with your despicable suspicions."

Luke reached out in the dusk to give Sybil's hand a reassuring pressure.

"I'm with you, Madam Fane," he said briefly, and followed her down the corridor, pulling every faculty into alertness for the coming ordeal, be it what it might.

The door of the study was closed, but it opened silently at their approach. The ominous glare of that sickly red light streamed out into the corridor, flickering across Madam Fane's ordinarily pallid face until it appeared transformed, as if writhing with unmentionable emotions.

The black-veiled figure of Guy Fane stood before the crystal globe, facing the door. At the entrance of Luke and Madam Fane, he held up both hands to check their further advance.

"Mr. Porter, I beg of you, no words now on the subject which I know is burning on your tongue. Your marriage must be postponed until tomorrow, and if Sybil then wishes to go on with it"—there was a smooth something in Guy Fane's voice that sent Luke's heart to beating irregularly—"I shall let you both go, with Alden, early in the morning."

"Let us go?" exclaimed Luke hotly.

"Poorly chosen words, my dear Mr. Porter. Believe me, just poorly chosen. Forgive me for my maladroitness with language. I am not as stupid and awkward in other ways, I assure you. And as proof of this, and of the harmlessness of my innocent ceremonials, I am asking you to accompany me to the chapel with my mother as well, and observe one from start to finish. It can not but be instructive to you, who have said that you believe in magic, under certain conditions."

"Supper is being served to Sybil and Alden, in my niece's boudoir," murmured Madam Fane. "Do you mind waiting until later for yours, Mr. Porters?"

"Yes, yes, Mother, that will be best," agreed Guy Fane, eagerly. "First our ceremonial and then the feast to celebrate its success! Ah, Mr. Porter, little do you dream what all this means to me, tonight! To have you present—young, handsome, strong, vital." Guy's voice died away as if in an ecstasy of pleasure; it affected Luke unpleasantly.

"I would like to know, Mr. Fane, why that harmless little Binney has been shut outside the castle by ruse," Luke demanded, his gray eyes dark.

"Harmless? Why, my dear Mr. Porter, that charlatan threatened to ruin one of the most astonishing experiments mortal man has yet made along magical lines. When you have witnessed—and shared—the tremendous thing that is fated to come to pass tonight, you will realize that I could not risk having Herbert Binney"—what infinite scorn over the poor little man's name!—"get excited in his ignorance, and ruin everything! Too risky, my dear young man. But come, let us be on our way to the chapel!"

The squat figure of Guy Fane swept in its rustling black garments ahead of Luke and Madam Fane, who followed in the direction of the chapel. Luke hastened his steps a little and reached the side of the Master.

"I warn you, Mr. Fane, that I have no intention of taking part in any obscene devil worship," he began, when Guy interrupted with an involuntary burst of laughter that to his sensitive ears sounded almost hysterical.

"Devil worship, sir? What the devil do you mean by that? Do you dare insinuate that I would have used an innocent girl in such vile practices? But you shall see for yourself!" And he laughed again as he moved down the long passages.

At last he opened a door, pulled to one side the somber hangings that veiled it from within, and entered, with a backward gesture of his head for Luke to follow. The artist entered warily, to find himself in the body of the chapel upon which he had gazed once before. He looked about him, strange apprehensions creeping into his mind at the sight of the monstrous decorations of the chapel, which made their subtle suggestions to his over-strained nerves, now at their highest tension.

"Look about you, Mr. Porter!" cried the high, mellow voice of the Master genially. "Is it not astonishing that the mind of human beings could have imagined and wrought such bizarre creations as these?"

"Guy, Guy, no more, I beg of you," pleaded Madam Fane, her voice deep with tense emotion. "I—I cannot bear it if you say more!"

"My poor mother, you dislike to have it known that yours was the moving mind? Or is it just modesty?"

Madam Fane's lips emitted a groan. Her son laughed heartily.

"Sit you here, my mother, and when the time is ripe, throw on the incense," he commanded bruskly. "And no more interruptions, when I start to consecrate the holy blade of sacrifice," he added, sharply.

"I didn't understand before, my son," the dark woman murmured as she knelt with bowed head near the tall censer that swung on its tripod at one side of the altar steps.

"Come up here, Mr. Porter, and see if the mechanism of this globe is not interesting," invited Guy Fane. "See how lightly it hangs on its network of fine platinum chains—oh, yes, they must be of platinum, for occult reasons—and then tell me, if you can, why it should start swinging of itself in response to the fragrance of burning incense and the chanting of strange incantations. Tell me, too, why those lapping tongues of flame should shoot from its vibrating surface. Why it should hum and sing its unearthly music."

Accepting the Master's invitation, Luke advanced up the steps of the altar, conscious all the time of an inward arming against some unexpected wile on the part of Guy Fane, whom the artist could not trust. He looked at the crystal globe gingerly; simple enough in appearance, without observable mechanism to produce the sound, the movement, the lifelike flames, it was an interesting thing in itself.

"Remain near it, if you choose, Mr. Porter, and watch it. See if you can detect chicanery in my simple methods of bringing it into startling life. But I would advise, my dear young man, that when you see it spring into glorious ruby life, you step back out of the reach of those tongues of flame. They are very real, I assure you, and I do not care to have you tell me that I did not warn you."

Once again, Luke Porter had the experience of watching the Master at his incantations. But this time it was close at hand, standing behind the very altar itself, close to the crystal ball, watching it closely. Madam Fane tossed great handfuls of incense upon the smoking tripod censer; volumes of faintly acrid haze began to rise and float in fitful currents of air through the gloomy chapel.

"Lucifer! Lord Lucifer! Grant a sign!" implored Guy Fane, bending low with imploring arms outstretched before him.

The still air began to crowd with murmurings, soft, whining sounds that vibrated through the air. The great globe in the shrine began to move, even as Luke watched it; to swing slowly at first, but with increasing rapidity, in a circle within the shrine. As it swung, the humming grew louder. Ruby flames leaped from the crystal's heart, seeming every moment to stretch farther, until the artist hastily stepped back and down the stairs to be out of their way.

From an undertone that merely stirred the atmosphere, vibrations grew in resonance until the entire chapel was vibrating with that rhythmic, sonorous cadence. The sibilant hum beat against the unwilling ears of the artist with an intolerable sweetness, as cloying as the sickening sweet odor of ether to the nostrils.

The dim red dusk only half cut the gloom, through the clouds and eddies of whirling, vaporous incense. The ruby glow at the heart of the sphere grew and grew, until it, too, seemed intolerable with its strange crimson brilliancy. Luke went down one more step, but his dazzled gray eyes were on that swinging, humming, ruby thing, which shot out its sweeping, octopus-like feelers of living fire, that elongated and retracted in every direction. The humming sounded louder again, a dire suggestion of vague and intangible, but none the less potent, evil. The vibrations increased in force and volume. At the foot of the altar lay the Master, prostrate; only muttered exorcisms reached Luke's straining ears. The tongues of flame now shot forth fiercely, and the artist, with a muttered exclamation of alarm, went backward another step—came in contact with the great marble top of the altar —reeled slightly—and crumpled back upon it, weakly, horror on his agonized face.

Guy Fane sprang up the altar stairs with a cry of triumph and leaned over the recumbent young man.

"You are mine, now!" he cried wildly. "Your youth shall fill my veins anew with vitality! Your handsome features shall bring me pleasure where my gruesome mask of horror has brought me only loathing. Your fine limbs—ah, Lucifer! Lucifer! Here lies the youth from whom I am tonight to recruit that for which I have so long yearned!"

Struggling with the despair into which his impotent and unconquerable weakness had plunged him, Luke stirred ever so little. The flashing eyes of the Master were upon him through the folds of the chiffon veil. They threatened.

"Lie still, fool, else I lift my veil! He who looks upon my face can never be the same again!" cried the Master terribly. "Ah, that is better!"

The unhappy artist felt weakness creeping inexorably through his limbs—through his very veins, until it seemed that the beating of his heart was stilled. He could hear—see—all about him, but move he could not; it was as if he were chained to that cold marble slab. He strove to keep his senses, but was sick as he realized that he could not now spring to Sybil's aid, should the girl again fall into the hands of the evil mage.

The Master turned to his mother.

"Woman, the hour is close at hand. Fetch the maiden! Her presence is necessary for this last rite."

There was the sound of rustling garments. Luke realized that he and the Master were alone.

The swinging and humming of the ruby sphere had somewhat lessened, but there was a compelling sound to it now that sent a languid feeling of sensuous and delicious emotion through Luke's body. He could not fight this as he might have done a little since; perforce yielding to it, he felt no repugnance when the ungainly hand of the Master began to pass gloatingly up and down his arms, his legs, over his firm young chest, his youthful face. A glow of thrilling eagerness began to rise hotly throughout his being—eagerness for he knew not what.

The Master leaned closer. Through the veiling chiffon he kissed the smooth cheeks of the helpless man, kissed them in a sheer voluptuous passion of delight. Luke's body trembled sickly.

"Ah! How can I wait, even minutes? To possess these fine limbs!

Lucifer, mighty art Thou above all other angels! How can I thank Thee enough for this most splendid gift? I tingle with mad expectations! Already I feel the racing of his youthful blood through my veins!"

The black velvet curtain parted again, interrupting the Master's rhapsodies. Luke, straining eyes in his motionless head, soon saw the source of the interruption. Advancing before Madam Fane, like a lamb before the slaughterer, came the trembling Sybil, widely awake at last to the horror of her situation.

—12—
Cagliostro To The Rescue

"Sybil, the Master needs you!"

Alden whirled to confront the black-clad figure of Madam Fane, whose dark eyes rested with superb disdain upon the wrinkled face of the devoted nurse.

"Sybil—do not go!" whispered Alden tremulously, twitching at the girl's sleeve.

Madam Fane spoke again, imperiously.

"Sybil, your lover lies in the chapel across Lucifer's altar. Will you leave him there, alone?"

"Luke in Lucifer's chapel?" cried the dazed and horrified girl, her pansy purple eyes roving from one woman to the other.

"He lies on the altar, Sybil," repeated Madam Fane grimly. "Do you intend to leave him there?"

The veiled significance of her words pounded into Alden's whirling brain.

"My darling, my lamb, don't believe her! Don't go!" she implored.

Sybil drew her arm away from her nurse with dignity and decision. Her pale face grew whiter, but she stepped to Madam Fane's side.

"Alden, if he isn't there, tell him at once that I have gone to find him," she murmured. "If he is—oh, no! I won't believe that my cousin could be so vile, so wicked!—Aunt, I am coming."

Before the agonized Alden could detain her, the girl had swung down the corridor after the swiftly retreating figure of Madam Fane, and their footsteps died away into silence.

Alden would have run after them, but her thoughts went suddenly to the little occultist waiting outside the castle walls. If only she could devise a way to get him inside, perhaps he might be able to cope with Guy Fane; Alden knew that she alone would be helpless for she stood in horror of what she might see if the Master were once to lift that protecting veil.

She ran to the wall and looked down. The headlights of Luke's car were on, and to judge by their position, the car stood near the draw-bridge. Alden leaned over and called softly.

"Mr. Binney!"

At once she discerned the little man's squat figure as he ran in front of the car so that she could see him, and called back:

"Who is it?"

"Alden, Mr. Binney. Listen!" Her voice cut through the whispering dusk sharply. "Mr. Porter is lying on the altar in the chapel,"—a husky intake of breath from below apprized her that Cagliostro had heard—"and Miss Fane has been called there, too. I can do nothing alone."

The little figure moved away from the car and close to the edge of the moat, the black waters of which were troubled by swirling things that passed across where it gleamed somberly in the car's illumination.

"Mrs. Alden, if you have anything to make a rope of, I can catch one end of it, and you can fasten the other securely up where you are. Then I can manage to swing across the moat."

"Oh, I can fix something with sheets," called back Alden eagerly.

"Get in I must," declared the occultist, ominous grimness in his voice. "There's devil's work going on in that chapel, and we must make haste. If I can get there in time, I may be able to help those poor young things," finished Cagliostro, his voice breaking.

"I'll be back in five minutes!"

Alden rushed down the corridor to the linen closets and secured a number of sheets. It seemed a century before she had torn and knotted them to make a rope of sufficient length to go, she hoped, across the moat. As Madam Fane unlocked supplies of linen only for each day, Alden was unable to get enough, to her dismay, for when she had fastened one end to the parapet and had flung the other out across the moat, the occultist could not reach it. There it hung, barely touching the surface of the murky water that seemed to mock at both would-be rescuers with a thousand twinkling evil eyes.

She hauled in the improvised rope, gathered it into a bunch, and tossed it out again. Cagliostro, springing to catch at it, just as it fell short of his grasp, slipped and almost fell into the moat.

"Oh, what shall we do?" lamented Alden, trembling with sick apprehension as the precious moments slipped by. "You—you wouldn't dare to risk—?"

Cagliostro grasped the thought that she had hardly dared put into words. He could drop into the moat and swim across to where that rope hung dabbling in the black water. His flesh crept shudderingly on his bones as he bent down to inspect the slimy surface of that repulsive viscid liquid. As he leaned over, something shining writhed out of the blackness and across the light from the car headlights; something that glistened with a nasty slipperiness that struck nausea to his stomach. He caught his breath with a quick gasp of repugnance; was there no other way?

His gaze swept the steep and slippery sides of the moat. If it should happen that he could not pull himself out of the water up to that knotted rope of sheets, or if the knots should give way, or if Alden had not fastened the other end securely, he would slip back—and a horrible death inevitably awaited. His body would fester in the deeps of that stagnant slime, and the things that flourished in it, as vile as its waters, would feed upon his shrinking flesh and pick at his bones

"Have you decided?" pleaded Alden. "Oh, every minute is precious! Will you try—?"

"You don't happen to know which switch on the switchboard in the Master's study controls the workings of the draw, do you?" countered the shuddering Herbert Binney. "He explained some of them to me, but I am not sure now that I know which one to tell you—and if you touch the wrong one, you will open trap-doors all over the castle and another one lights a five-minute fuse to a powder cache that would send Fanewold into the air in ruins!"

Alden moaned and wrung her wrinkled hands frantically.

"I've seen it, but I don't know which switch would be right. Oh, can't you—?"

"Good Lord!" ejaculated the little man piously. "Alden, I'm going to swim the moat."

"Don't make any more commotion than you can help," warned the woman, ominously. "The—the things—would surround you at once. I've seen doves, and once a lamb, floating, half devoured—."

Herbert Binney dared not hear more. He took off his shoes and discarded his coat. Then he dropped quietly over the edge of the moat and slipped gently down into the black water. Ugh! How coldly, how hungrily, it closed about him! With an effort he managed to keep his face above the slimy surface. With shrinking strokes he struck out for the castle wall from which dangled the sheet-rope. The water about him seemed alive with evil things, foul things, venomous things. He could feel the stirring of that evil life as he shot through the turbid waters. Once his hand touched something that slithered across it hastily, leaving him with a sickening nausea. Every moment he expected to feel the fangs of some unknown and hideous reptile fasten in throat or arm.

At last, the final stroke—. He caught quickly at the drabbled end of the rope, and for a moment his faint heart sank, for it gave easily in his grasp. Momentarily he thought the knots had given way. Then he realized with relief that the material was only stretching under his weight. He pulled himself up the wall, bracing himself against it, and in a few minutes felt the outstretched hands of Alden helping him over the parapet.

His gaze, turned downward to the water he had just quitted, showed what seemed myriads of tiny shining points. He realized with a shudder of disgust and loathing that those points were the eyes of the horrors that had waited for him to slip, to fall, that they might crowd in upon him, pull him beneath the slimy water, and tear the shrinking flesh from his bones.

"Dry clothes, first of all," the occultist exclaimed, as he felt himself safely on the parapet.

"But—"

"You must trust me, Alden. I know what I have to do. I cannot go before Guy Fane a dripping scarecrow. Where would be my dignity, the lofty impression that must surround me like an aura, if I am to make the right impression upon him? I have another mantle and other clothes in my room; also, I can not go in my stocking feet," the little man declared decidedly.

Alden, who would have run at once to the chapel, was obliged to wait for Cagliostro. While she waited, she remembered the pistol Luke had given her. She put it in her apron pocket, a grim look about her mouth.

When the occultist emerged from his room, he looked the part of the serious magician he wished to appear, until he let the mantle drop from his face, when the absurd button nose and the squinting pale blue eyes somewhat dulled the new dignity that drew the lines of his Cupid's bow mouth into something strange and hard.

"The Master's study," he said tersely, and led the way.

Behind the screen he showed Alden a switchboard with fifteen buttons.

"One of these operates the draw," the little man said. "I think it is the first one."

"If you don't know; why do you touch it?" cried out the alarmed Alden, catching at his hand.

He shook off her restraining touch imperiously. The next moment he had pressed the first button. She strained her ears to hear the creaking of the drawbridge, but there was no sound to break the night's silence. Cagliostro shook his head, his brow scowling at the switchboard. Then he deliberately put his hand over and pressed the second button. Alden's wrinkled face whitened. Then she uttered a soft exclamation.

"The draw! The second button was right! The way is open!"

"The chapel next," commanded Cagliostro bruskly. He strode on ahead of Alden, who could hear him muttering to himself. "Now, what could that first button have been?" the occultist kept asking himself aloud in perplexity. To Alden he addressed one more observation: "Keep close to the edges of the corridor," he said warningly.

She understood, shuddering. Perhaps the first button had opened yawning traps that would let them down into black gulfs when they stepped upon them. Perhaps—perhaps that first button had meant that Fanewold would fly up into the air, carrying them all to sudden death.

As if this thought had gone home to him also, the occultist now exclaimed:

"Let us run! If we can get there in time, perhaps we can—" He let the sentence go unfinished, as the two of them, careless of what that first button might have done in the way of opening trap-doors, began to run through the winding halls.

—13—
Lucifer Takes Toll

Between the heavy black curtains that shielded the entrance to the chapel, Alden stumbled like one suddenly dazed. The loud humming of the ruby globe dominated the atmosphere, and like one bereft of all will power, all strength, the woman sank down behind one of the evil statues near the doorway, helpless to aid in averting the tragedy that now seemed imminent.

The occultist, more wary because he, perhaps, knew what he would have to confront, stood just inside the curtains, out of sight of the Master but in a position to take in everything. On the marble slab lay the supine figure of Luke Porter, motionless. Before it, with hands outstretched against the nearer advance of the Master, stood Sybil, as if frozen stiff by horror and her impotence. Guy Fane, his arms lifted to the swinging, flame-tongued sphere, was wrapped in ecstasy, as he cried his invocations:

"Behold the spotless sacrifice! Today she was supremely happy, and tonight her abandonment to grief is just as keen. Lord Lucifer, is not this broken spirit meet for a sacrifice unto Thee!"

Madam Fane emptied a handful of incense upon the tripod censer. Her garments rustled like wind in the trees as she turned to her son.

"Guy!" trembled her voice imploringly. "Do not forget your promise to me!"

A hard, triumphant laugh issued from the chiffon swathings that hid the Master's face.

"Woman, what are promises to me, the favored one of Lucifer! I am a free man. Promises cannot bind me!"

"But you told me Sybil should live—"

"She shall live, to endure a living death," he pronounced oracularly. "Unless she stands in my way, when Lucifer tells me her lover's youth and beauty are ripe for my taking. Then—" and the voice was ominous with unspoken threats.

He swept aside his mother's entreating hands.

"Stand aside, woman!" he thundered. "This is no time for your silly chatter. This is my hour!"

Again he lifted both hands in invocation.

"Lucifer! Son of the Morning! I have obeyed Thee. I give Thee the soul of Sybil Fane, once a happy, light-hearted girl, now a sad and agonizing woman. Thou hast promised me in return these limbs—these features,"—and he gestured toward the quiet form on the altar.

"No—no—no!" screamed Sybil, finding voice at last. "I do not know what you intend to do, but you shall not harm Luke! Not while I live to prevent it!"

"Perhaps you will not—live to prevent it, Sybil," responded the magician, pausing in his invocation to address her. "But if you will stand out of my way, I will spare his life."

"Oh, I knew you couldn't be so cruel!" the girl gasped. "You won't hurt him, will you, then?"

Again a laugh issued with malevolent hardness from the veil.

"I shall take that shell of his, and give him mine in return, Sybil. If you can love him still—why, perhaps you can be happy with the monster that he will be."

He turned once more to the globe.

The perfumed incense had created clouds of heavy fragrance redolent of the East and its esoteric mysteries. The Master was plainly on the verge of his diabolic experiment. The whimpering hum of the glowing sphere sounded continuously with a drowsy, numbing effect on the senses. The Master cried out.

"Lucifer! Lucifer!! Lucifer!!! I dedicate to Thee the broken heart of this spotless maid! I offer Thee the pulsing heart of this sturdy man whose youth and comeliness are to be mine!"

The humming of the ruby globe grew louder, heavier, sweeter, until it seemed as if the very atmosphere were charged with some foreign, supernatural potency to draw the vitality out of those who had braved the horrors of that eery chapel. The occultist heard a little sigh, and saw Alden crumpling into a tumbled heap at the foot of the sculptured horror; the automatic slipped from her pocket to the floor. Cagliostro salvaged the weapon; he would try material magic on the Master first.

Madam Fane's voice rang out loudly with sudden sharp reproach.

"No, Guy! You shall not, I tell you! Let her alone!" Her voice rose in a shrill treble of excitement, ending in a shriek that pierced the eardrums with poignancy. "No, Guy, no! Her blood must not be on your hands! She is your own half-sister!"

The Master had swung about, the keen blade of a flashing knife in one hand. With the other he held back the struggling form of his mother, who caught vainly at the deadly blade, her face convulsed with horror and dismay. Sybil, pressed backward across her lover's motionless form, had spread her hands behind her for his protection, and it was this thwarting of his intention that had infuriated Guy Fane, who was threatening her with the knife even while he held back his mother's struggling body.

That shrill scream had acted like a powerful tonic to the other mother, lying apparently unconscious at Cagliostro's feet. Alden was up, and had crossed with a bound the space separating her from the altar. The knife swept downward toward Sybil's breast as Guy flung his mother to one side. Alden met it full. As it clove its way into her unresisting flesh she laughed aloud, a terrible laugh that rang out through the atmosphere with ominous import. Then she slipped to the feet of the dazed Sybil, gasping as she fell five pregnant words:

"Fools! I am her mother!"

It was over in a moment. The actors in the tragedy stood as if paralyzed by this swift movement of events. Then Madam Fane broke into a weakly wailing cry.

"Her mother? Oh, now I understand much. Much! I knew Sybil was protected. Her mother!"

Burning eyes through his veil, the Master turned to look upon the dying woman.

"Her mother!" he echoed numbly. "Oh, I knew something, someone, was watching over her, to thwart me. But I shall not be cheated out of my bargain with Lucifer! The offering which purchases my freedom from this horrible and monstrous form shall yet be his. And it shall be a triple one tonight!"

He took the dead woman's shoulder and drew her to one side roughly. Cagliostro took a step forward from the protection of the statue, but Madam Fane had caught again at her son's arm, this time with a purpose and nervous strength that took him by surprize.

"Guy, you shall not! In that Name I dare not utter in this evil place, I swear that I shall perish before you stain your hand with more blood tonight. Another crime on your soul, my son? Let these poor helpless creatures go—"

"Are you mad?" he shouted, brutally pushed her aside, and reached for Sybil's shoulder.

The terrified girl shrank back, but not for an instant did she forget to shield her lover's body with her own, her purple eyes ablaze with fearless purpose.

Crying: "Give me the knife!" Madam Fane caught at Guy's hand and by sheer force of sudden surprise wrested the blade from his fingers. Then she moved away from him—backward—down the altar steps—holding that horridly dripping thing away from contact with her rustling garments as she backed off.

The horrified occultist had been paralyzed by the swift march of events, and unable to do even so little as lift the pistol into shooting position. Alden's astonishing and tragic death had happened so quickly that he knew he could not have saved the unhappy mother. He stood rooted to the spot now, watching this other mother who had snatched the deadly knife from the hands of that worshiper of Lucifer.

Madam Fane backed away, holding the weapon from her in mingled repulsion and dread. For a moment her son followed her with his eyes, and then realization that without the knife he could not go on with the sacrifice came to him. He took a step toward her.

"Give me the knife!" rang out the stern command.

She shook her head slowly from side to side, continuing her retreat toward the corridor door. Cagliostro lifted the pistol and waited for her to pass him. He intended then to cover Guy Fane, make him stand beside her.

Down the altar steps sprang the Master toward his mother. And then that took place which Providence decreed. As Cagliostro peered cautiously around the statue, watching Madam Fane, he drew back involuntarily at her loud cry of consternation and dismay. He leaned out to stare incredulously. She had disappeared from view as if the earth had opened to swallow her.

The Master stopped short. The paving of the chapel had yawned at his very feet, had swallowed up the sins and sorrows of his mother, and had closed relentlessly upon her. The Master turned his head from side to side uneasily; he knew that someone had tampered with the buttons of the private switchboard.

"And I cannot punish her," he murmured in a low voice. "She has gone beyond my reach, that other mother. It was Sybil's mother—oh, if I could bring her back to life, how I would punish those meddling fingers!"

He turned and retraced his footsteps to the altar, testing each stone on the way with his foot to be sure that it would bear his weight. Muttered words fell from his lips as he once more confronted Sybil.

"There are too many mothers here tonight! Too many mothers. And my knife is gone—but it shall not matter. These hands shall tear his pulsing heart from his breast, Sybil, while you watch him change into my ugliness."

He came closer to her, while she leaned away from him, terrified, but without leaving the man she loved. His thoughts went at random then, and Sybil watched him, fascinated, as he sank upon his knees before the altar.

"Unhappy mother! And that other mother! How could I know that the mothers would ruin everything? Lucifer, why didst Thou not warn me that the mothers would ruin all? Must I remain an eternal prisoner in this monstrous shape, because of the mothers?" His voice rose in plaintive melancholy. "And did not the oracle promise me that tonight I should step from this loathsome body into freedom? Oh, Lord and Master, give me a sign!"

Cagliostro had been creeping closer to the altar. As he went, he managed to make some gesture that caught Sybil's eye. As soon as she saw him, his finger at his lips imposed silence upon her. But he glowed at the look of relief that swept across her pallid face.

The heavy, incense-laden atmosphere vibrated. Flickering lights and shadows danced evilly on the pavement as the ruby tongues of flame darted from the swinging, humming globe of fiery crimson in the shrine. Cagliostro did not wish to wait longer. The moment had come for him to act.

"Lucifer! Grant a sign! The sacrificial knife has been wrested from my fingers. I have but these naked hands. Touch the altar with Thy fire, Lord Lucifer, that I may know it is acceptable!"

Into the radiance of that mystic ruby brilliance sprang the short, heavy figure of the little occultist.

"Hands up, Guy Fane! I have you covered!"

The veiled man rose, turning in a dazed manner that betrayed eloquently how far unaware the Master had been of other presences in the chapel. He came down the steps of the shrine with reluctant dignity but without lifting his hands as Herbert Binney had commanded.

"Put up your hands, Mr. Fane!" With contemptuous gesture and scornful laugh, the Master folded his arms on his breast so that the hands rested on opposite shoulders.

"Do you really imagine, silly little mummer, that I—I—am to be constrained like any common man, to comply with your very rude demand? I, who can lift my veil again, and blast you where you stand. Has not one lesson been sufficient? Must I repeat it?"

The little man shivered. His pale blue eyes squinted from Guy to the eager, strained face of Sybil, and back again.

"Shoot, if it pleases you," observed the Master nonchalantly. "The experience may teach you another lesson. Your bullets cannot penetrate my charmed flesh. None but a silver bullet can harm me, and your bullets are of lead, foolish magician; lead. What, afraid? Am I not a broad target?" He sneered.

"You're unarmed, Mr. Fane," retorted the little man with as much calm as his jumping nervous system would allow him to demonstrate. "I can't shoot an unarmed man. But I want you to undo your spells on that young man, and then you can stand aside while both of those young people go out of this hellish place. I'm not afraid of you," stoutly. "I know now what to expect. You—you took me by surprise before."

The Master laughed soft and long.

"I am not an unarmed man, Mr. Binney. There are occult forces at my disposal, as you have witnessed, that would strip you of the power to press the trigger, but I scorn to use them against such a miserable and puny opponent."

The words stung. Cagliostro Moderno, stepping forward with the pistol pointed at the Master's stomach, said bruskly:

"Move to one side."

Instinctively the Master gave way. Cagliostro sprang past him and up to the altar. He drew Sybil gently to one side and leaned over the prostrate young man. He breathed against the closed eyelids. He whispered into the ears. And then he took both hands and drew Luke Porter into a sitting position.

"All right?" he queried briefly.

Luke drew a long breath of relief.

"Knew what was going on, all the time!" he exclaimed. "But just couldn't speak or move. Give me that pistol, Binney."

The occultist shook his head.

"You take the young lady and run as fast as you can to the draw. It's open. Get out quick. Your car is in front. Never mind me. I can take care of myself. Go, while the draw is open!"

"How wise is our great Cagliostro Moderno!" drawled a mellow voice.

Luke and the occultist both turned like a flash. They had, for the time, forgotten Guy Fane, who had slipped quietly to the entry door and—carefully avoiding the pavement which had swallowed up his unfortunate mother—stood there, leaning against the lintel negligently.

"Do go, while the draw is open!" He laughed. "How long do you think it will take me to reach my study? I, who am acquainted with every passage, every stairway, here? Five minutes after I have reached my study, I shall have the pleasure of going on a long journey, and I think you three will go with me, in fire and flame from the altar of Lucifer! No, do not stir! You cannot escape. I shall close the draw first —and the fuse will burn exactly five minutes."

"Stop him!" shouted Luke, reaching for the pistol.

"You have ruined my hope to be as other human beings are. Perhaps, if I had gained what I desired, I might have acquired a heart as well. Who knows? But now I am harder than the very nucleus of the crystal sphere. You shall not live to triumph over me. This castle will make a splendid funeral pyre, will it not?"

The little occultist stood stupidly while Guy Fane turned to go.

"Give me that pistol!" cried Luke again, snatching at it, and firing after the disappearing Master.

The shot echoed and re-echoed along the chapel walls and out through the adjoining corridors. As it died away, they could hear Guy Fane's eery laughter ringing mockingly through the doorway, mingled with his rapidly retreating footfalls. The Master had gone, unharmed, to carry out his threat!

"The draw! Sybil, give me your hand! Binney, I can't forgive you for not giving me that pistol before. If I'd shot the monster, we would be safe now," snapped Luke, drawing Sybil after him along the pavement blocks that had appeared sound when the Master had retreated.

Cagliostro stared mournfully but did not follow them. A sudden white light of determination broke across his face. He spoke quickly:

"I can stop him—hold him—long enough for you to escape. Run! I'll get at him in his study!"

"Don't be a fool!" shouted Luke, pulling Sybil along down the corridor that led to the courtyard giving upon the draw. "You'll be trapped!"

A strangely transfiguring smile rested on the little occultist's face, transforming it into something finer, bigger, than it had ever appeared before.

"Good-bye!" he said simply, and was gone.

There was no time to dissuade him. Luke swept the panting Sybil up into his arms. Twice she had stumbled in their mad flight. He covered the short remaining distance with his precious burden in record time, and as he emerged into the courtyard saw with grateful heart that the draw was still open, lighted by the headlamps of the waiting car. His limbs braced themselves for the final effort. He staggered out upon the drawbridge, holding the girl closely to him.

"If we go, we go together," he told himself grimily.

At the middle of the draw, it began to tremble and jar. The draw was rising slowly! Guy Fane must have reached his study and have closed it. The cables creaked and groaned. For a moment Luke's heart almost stopped beating, as he flung himself face down—Sybil beside him —on the rapidly perilous slope of the draw. They clung together. In another moment they would lose their hold and slip down, back, into the courtyard, to perish by the explosion.

The jarring recommenced. The draw—miracle of miracles!— began to lower again. Sybil got to her feet dazedly. Luke rose, caught at her hand and drew her along. In another minute they had reached the edge. Another, and they were across the moat and Luke was pulling the girl into the seat of the little car.

He slid in behind the wheel, started the engine. Then he turned and honked several times, watching to see the little occultist in the doorway. A fine column of smoke was rising from midway in the building. A loud crackling. The waving hands of Herbert Binney from the window over the draw. "Good-bye! Don't—forget—Cagliostro!" The little man was smiling wanly.

Rumbling, a heavy, thunderous roar that rose in terrible crashing explosion, shaking the earth, rocking the car's occupants from side to side. Blinding light flashed from the castle on all sides. The landscape stood out distinct as in broad daylight.

It was sheer stupidity to linger in the open. Luke, sick at heart for the fate of the little occultist, who had so nobly risen to that great opportunity of his life, drove off down the steep roadway as rapidly as he dared, to get beyond the radius of falling stone and debris.

Guy Fane had been right. The oracle had spoken truly. The Master had left his monstrous body and stepped out into freedom at last.

ORIGINAL PUBLICATION INFORMATION

"Imprisoned with the Pharaohs" by Houdini, originally published in *Weird Tales* May 1924

"The Thing of a Thousand Shapes" by Otis Adelbert Kline, originally published in *Weird Tales* March 1923 and April 1923

"The Magic Mirror" by Mary S. Brown, originally published in *Weird Tales* November 1923

"The Vow on Halloween" by Lyllian Huntley Harris, originally published in *Weird Tales* May 1924

"The Werewolf of St. Bonnot" by Seabury Quinn, originally published in *Weird Tales* May 1924

"The Sea Thing" by Frank Belknap Long Jr., originally published in *Weird Tales* December 1925

"Sleigh Bells" by Hasan Vokine, originally published in *Weird Tales* April 1925

"The Festival" by H.P. Lovecraft, originally published in *Weird Tales* January 1925

"The Werewolf of Ponkert" by H. Warner Munn, originally published in July 1925

"Vale of Corbies" by Arthur J. Burks, originally published in *Weird Tales* November 1925

"The Tenants of Broussac" by Seabury Quinn, originally published in *Weird Tales* December 1925

"The Phantom Wolfhound" by Otis Adelbert Kline, originally published in *Weird Tales* June 1923

"The Gargoyle" by Greye La Spina, originally published in *Weird Tales* September 1925, October 1925 and November 1925

About the Editors

Jonathan Maberry is a New York Times bestselling author, 5-time Bram Stoker Award-winner, 3-time Scribe Award winner, Inkpot Award winner, and comic book writer. His vampire apocalypse books, V-WARS, was a Netflix original series. He writes in multiple genres including suspense, thriller, horror, science fiction, fantasy, and mystery; for adults, teens and middle grade. His novels include the Joe Ledger thriller series, Bewilderness, Ink, Glimpse, the Pine Deep Trilogy, the Rot & Ruin series, the Dead of Night series, Mars One, Ghostwalkers: A Deadlands Novel, and many others, including his first epic fantasy, Kagen the Damned. He is the editor many anthologies including The X-Files, Aliens: Bug Hunt, Don't Turn Out the Lights, Aliens vs Predator: Ultimate Prey, Hardboiled Horror, Aliens vs Predator, Nights of the Living Dead (co-edited with George A. Romero), and others. His comics include Black Panther: DoomWar, Captain America, Pandemica, Highway to Hell, The Punisher, Bad Blood, among others. He is the president of the International Association of Media Tie-in Writers, and the editor of Weird Tales Magazine. Visit him online at www.jonathanmaberry.com

Justin Criado is an award-winning journalist and editor. The Colorado Press Association has recognized his newspaper features as some of the best in the state over the years, as he's been a writer for the past decade in Colorado, his home state of Pennsylvania and beyond.

His work has been featured in the *Denver Post*, *Westword*, *Salt Lake City Weekly*, *Phoenix New Times*, *Pittsburgh Post-Gazette* and

Pittsburgh Tribune-Review. He's currently the editor of the *Telluride Daily Planet* newspaper in Telluride, Colorado.

Most recently, he and *New York Times* best-selling author and *Weird Tales* editor Jonathan Maberry co-edited this brand new collection.

Justin holds a BA in Communications from Robert Morris University and an MA in Publishing from Western Colorado University.

IF YOU LIKED ...

If you liked *Weird Tales Best of the Early Years: 1923–1925,* you might also enjoy:

Weird Tales Best of the Early Years: 1926–1927
Edited by Jonathan Maberry & Kaye Lynne Booth

The Cthulhu Stories of Robert E. Howard
Edited by M. Scott Lee

War of the Worlds: Global Dispatches
Edited by Kevin J. Anderson